BOOK I · ONE LIFE, ONE SOUL, ONE SWORD

PHATE
the Cosmic Fairytale

JASON ALAN

OLORIS
publishing

Phate: The Cosmic Fairytale © 2016 by Jason Alan. All rights reserved. No part of this book may be used or reproduced in any manner whatsoever, including Internet usage, without written permission from Oloris Publishing LLC., except in the case of brief quotations embodied in critical articles and reviews.

Printed in USA
First Edition
First Printing
ISBN-10: 1-940992-66-4
ISBN-13: 978-1-940992-66-2

Cover art © 2016 by Chris Andruskiewicz
Author photograph © Jason Alan

For more information please see: www.olorispublishing.com.

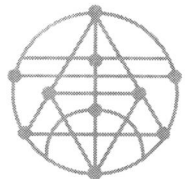

DEDICATION

For being a light when all else was dark, for remaining steadfast in the belief that I was truly creating something extraordinary, for the undying support through all these years, this story is lovingly dedicated to my Mother,
Florene M. Welebny,
The real Morning's Hope.

Thanks Mom, for everything.

CONTENTS

AUTHOR'S NOTE i
PROLOGUE: ALIEN ARRIVAL iii
1 THE THREAT OF DARKNESS RETURNS 1
2 SPIRIT AND STRENGTH 22
3 AN ANGEL'S EMBRACE 38
4 BLACK HOLES 53
5 ENEMIES REVEALED 62
6 THE SON AND SAVIOR OF THE STARS 80
7 THE WALLS RESURRECTED 97
8 UPON THE FACE OF PHATE 102
9 EMANATING EVIL 114
10 ALL THINGS CONSIDERED 119
11 DISTANT VOICES CRY 135
12 WARLOOVE UNLEASHED 149
13 MORNING'S HOPE 165
14 A COSMIC ARRIVAL 179
15 SPECTERS OF A FORGOTTEN SKY 185
16 MARCH OF A MILLION DEAD 201
17 THE MYRIAD FEATURES OF PHATE 207
18 THE DARK EYES OF THE ENEMY 227
19 OCEANS OF ECHOING DARKNESS 232
20 THE CENTURION AND THE STARS 246
21 BATTLEGROUND OF BONES 251
22 FORWARD WITH FATE 262
23 AGAINST THE FALL OF NIGHT 267
24 THE BLOOD OF ANOTHER DIMENSION 288
25 ONE LIFE, ONE SOUL, ONE SWORD 294
26 FACE THE SUN 310

27 SLOWLY, PURPOSEFULLY FORWARD 323
28 BEFORE THE END 327
29 THE DOOM OF PHATE 340
EPILOGUE: ALIEN AWAITING 381
GLOSSARY 385

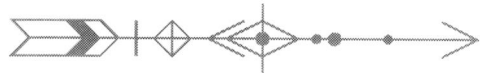

AUTHOR'S NOTE

Hello, oh, adventurous soul! I look forward to the time we'll spend together. I sincerely hope Phate moves you, inspires you, or affects you in the special way that only a fantastical story can. I'm satisfied that it truly is a window into my imagination and, at its best, a window into my heart. Ever since I can remember, I've been completely enchanted by science fiction and fantasy entertainment. *Phate* wasn't written so much as it was transcribed, for it's long existed in my mind's eye. They say an author should strive to write the book they'd want to read. Well, I did that, but I also wrote the movie I'd want to see. As much as I've been influenced by countless books, I've been enthralled by fantastic cinema. As much as I look forward to you reading Phate, I look forward to you **seeing** *Phate*, as I do in my dreams.

What you hold is a pure expression, an indulgence in creativity. I set out not to follow in any footsteps, but to blaze a trail of my own. It was daunting at times, but I followed my heart, trusted my dreams, and set my imagination free.

So thank you again for joining me on this adventure. It's about time we visited Phate's universe, wouldn't you say? Ah, allow me to indulge in one more thing before we go.

I'd like to give a tremendous thank you to the very talented Chris Andruskiewicz of Sparrow Graphics in Fort Myers, Florida. Chris created a book design that far exceeded my expectations and perfectly captured the spirit of the story. And I can't express enough gratitude to Jason R. Jones, author of *The Last Pantheon* series. His talent, inspiration, and determination reinspired me just when I felt my loneliest as a writer. I'd also like to thank my editing empresses. Thank you Julie, Gerda, Lara, Robyn, Stephanie, and everyone at Oloris Publishing. Thank you for giving me this incredible opportunity, and believing in me.

Through all the ups and downs of life, one thing has remained constant—the loyalty and integrity of my friends. I've been incredibly fortunate to be surrounded by so many talented and wonderful people. In a fashion, every one of you is in this book. And if this tale brings any amount of enjoyment, escape, inspiration, or comfort to a single one of you, then my life has been a meaningful one. May the light of hope shine upon you all, may you take a few extra moments to look with wonder at the stars, and may dragons and starships ever fly in your dreams…

To all who dare enter, welcome to PHATE!

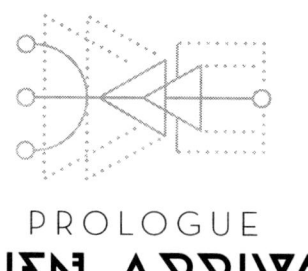

PROLOGUE
ALIEN ARRIVAL

He fell from the stars, a streak of brilliant white fire blasting through the atmosphere and crashing into Corpsewood, my forest dwelling at the bottom of a long-dead volcano. The thundering impact detonated the ground, the explosion blackening trees whose bark was already grey with decay. I was infuriated. No one dares enter my domain unbidden! I swept up to him, my apparitional form swirling like a cyclone, my glowing yellow eyes piercing through it, brightening with disdain. Despite my delight in torturing, I was in no mood to toy with this interloper. Sorcerous songs slipped from my lips like serpentine wraiths, igniting my claws with black fire that was eager to incinerate yet another victim.

But when I came upon him, my fury faded, for he was barely alive.

His skin was burned and smoking like the wreckage of the metal dragon that was strewn in twisted ruin about him. I stayed my sorcery, extinguished my fire. My curiosity was aroused. He was unlike any being I had ever seen, and he bore wounds that are difficult to describe. He was...*slivered*. Entire sections of his limbs were missing. One of his hands had no wrist affixing it to the forearm, but nevertheless, the palm held in place, the fingers clenching with pain I can only imagine would have been excruciating had he been conscious.

And then I saw the tantalizing glimmer of shining green fluid trickle from his lacerated skin...

Blood!

Alien blood, I realized. I had never tasted the blood of an alien and, oh, I was so thirsty! I extended my fangs with euphoric anticipation and knelt over his helpless little grey form to drink.

But before my thirst was sated, I was suddenly compelled to turn away. For even in his seemingly helpless state, the alien exuded a strange aura that stirred fear deep within me. I held my place, though, resisting the urge to flee. I hadn't felt fear in hundreds of years, and I was transfixed, mesmerized, much in the same way I mesmerize my own victims, I would guess.

I wondered—what *was* this being? From what sort of world had he come?

As fascinated as I was frightened, I swirled into solidity, pushed my fear aside and picked him up, reminding myself that this was, after all, *my* domain. I carried him into Castle Krypt, my home amongst the dead trees. There, in its deepest dungeon, I laid him on a slab of stone, my gaze a slave to the blood that stained him. It was so enticing, I *knew* I couldn't resist tasting it! Trembling like a mischievous child, I flicked my forked tongue across his wounds until every drop was gone. It was delectable, savagely sweet...

I could have let him die, you know, could have drunk his body dry, but I didn't. Despite my insatiable thirst, I didn't. I felt a warning inside, an instinct. I don't know, perhaps I was compelled by fear. Regardless, I used what little skill I have in healing to keep him alive. Ah, what can I say, I'm impulsive, prone to whimsy, wherever it leads, and on that night I fancied leaving him alive.

The alien remained unconscious for weeks, months, perhaps; I don't remember, it was so long ago. But, oh, how I remember the night he awoke! Indeed, I'll never forget the first time I looked into his eyes. Those eyes. They were soulless, empty of emotion, and yet, deep, deep within them flowed visions that henceforth haunted my every slumber. In his eyes I saw my own demise, my form consumed in flames; I could actually hear my screams echoing through the night as I flailed and fell into an exploding star... Oh, the visions I saw in his eyes!

Never before had I looked into a soul more wicked than mine.

For a time he remained silent, just staring at me through the misty veil of sorcerous vapors wafting through the chamber. I sensed he could have killed me then, with only his mind had he wished. Instead I was merely startled as his otherworldly words sounded in my head. Though it was a language I had never heard, I somehow understood it. Thus he had displayed yet another facet of his power, and I knew my decision to mend his wounds had been wise. Thereafter I learned of his story…which was destined to run into my own.

I was to be his servant, for in him I saw my salvation.

He calls himself Darkis. It is not his real name, but he said for me, for Phate, this name will suffice. He was the son of a Supreme Galactic Emperor, a being who ruled over billions of worlds. Yes, *billions*. His home planet of Tyranticuss housed cities large enough to cover the entire surface of most other worlds, cities whose light illuminated the planet as if it were itself a star.

He told me of his youth, when he would accompany his father in overseeing his galaxy-sized empire. It was then that he learned of the natural wonders and beauties of the universe: cosmic dungeons orbiting black holes the size of galaxies; war-ridden worlds floundering in the wake of his father's colossal destroyers; godlike beings of ghostly mist swimming in oceans of starlight…

Oh, how I desperately want to see these things for myself!

When he matured, my master succeeded his father as Supreme Galactic Emperor and set out on a new campaign to conquer the galaxy's most fearsome enemy—the Draxiah Meeh. But when Darkis was far from Tyranticuss, traitors loyal to the Draxiah Meeh launched a surprise attack on his home world, and destroyed it.

His father was killed.

Swearing vengeance, Darkis led a massive armada against his enemies, and the largest battle in the history of the universe commenced. To this day, I have difficulty imagining the scale of the confrontations that took place. By the time it ended, thousands of solar systems had been blown into stardust, one hundred trillion beings were dead, and Darkis' own centurion guards had betrayed and captured him. There was no trial, no passing of sentence. He was tortured to the brink of death, then cast onto this doomed world of Phate to die.

That is when I saw him fall from the sky.

And here we are now, my master and I.

He hates it here, oh, how he does hate it!

He yearns to return to the stars, to take revenge upon his enemies, to reclaim rule over his galaxy!

But he is afraid.

Without his world's resources, he is weak, vulnerable... mortal. Oftentimes, I catch him stealing fearful glances at the stars, for he knows his enemies are out there, watching, waiting for him. This both chills and excites me, and when I howl to the midnight sky, I wonder if they can hear me...

I asked Darkis why his enemies do not attack, and he said it is because they do not need to. A great war is coming, a war so terrible, its first moments could annihilate all life on Phate before it goes on to end all time. Indeed, the battle I earlier described would pale in comparison to what lies ahead. Even this fledgling earthling scribe Jason Alan cannot foresee the immensity of the conflict for control over all eternity!

And there is another concern that disturbs me far more than any war. Our ancient sun burns red, for it is weak, weary, and soon to die. When it perishes, it will spew its searing gases across all the solar system, thus immersing Phate in cosmic fire. I tremble to even ponder this. Being consumed in the fiery death throes of an exploded star is a far worse destiny than I can dream up in my most heinous nightmares!

Well, that is not exactly true, is it?

As you know, I've had these nightmares ever since I looked into my master's eyes.

Ah, however, things are not as hopeless as they seem.

Darkis can save us. He can deliver us from this doomed exile, carry us into the far reaches of space, deep into the perpetual night. Remember the metal dragon I spoke of? In actuality, it is not a dragon at all. It is a *starship*, a marvelous creation constructed from alien sorceries. Darkis repaired it after many long years of working in the bowels of my castle. It is functional, *alive* ... but not quite ready to carry us forth into the void.

One thing remains.

Energy.

It needs immeasurable amounts of energy.

Space is so vast, Darkis tells me, it is beyond my comprehension to understand the distances we must travel. He says it would take the greatest of dragons one million lifetimes to reach even the closest star.

The stars are so bright, I have difficulty imagining they are so far away.

This is where my part in the Cosmic Fairytale begins, for my master has commanded me to retrieve the one thing on Phate that contains the energy we need to propel our starship across the cosmos. It is... Ah, I shall not tell you what it is! It must be kept secret. But be patient, for you will learn of it in the chapters to come. And consider yourself warned, for you will also learn of murder and demonic dragons and wicked necromancers taken from other times. You will bear witness to my sorcerous wrath, and journey into the depths of the darkest suns.

There is much to tell.

At last, our time has come.

At last, after long years of suffering, my master and I will leave this cursed world behind. I cannot wait! When I recall the small, savory sips I stole from Darkis, I feel an intense desire to drink from the throat of an alien species. Do you not see? Phate is *nothing* to me, nothing but a cold, lifeless rock all but depleted of fresh blood, a world many thousands of years past its prime. For too long have I done nothing but dream of the eternal dark. For too long have the glittering stars of distant galaxies taunted my waking eyes!

Ah, I am to be forgiven. At times my emotions carry me away.

For now, I have only one more thing to say.

When you turn the page, this *scribe*, this Jason Alan will try to lead you astray, try to tell you that this is someone else's story.

It is a lie.

This story is mine alone!

I am the Vampiric Lord of the Dark Elves, the servant of a Supreme Galactic Emperor who commands my loyalty, and a sorcerer of immense power. I am a dreamer, a cosmic adventurer-in-waiting who gazes with new understanding at the stars. I am these things, and so much more.

I am Warloove.

And whatever world you live on, in whatever time, you would do well to stay out of the shadows of the night. For when my master and I escape, I will be free in time and in space. Be wary. Those eyes you sometimes see gazing at you from the dark? Those eyes might be mine, and I am very thirsty…

CHAPTER ONE
THE THREAT OF DARKNESS RETURNS

Loyalty: above all. Be true to those who are true to you, and you will be victorious.

Drakana
Lord of the Spirit Dragons

In the far distant future, in the darkest region of the universe, a forsaken galaxy of dying stars plunged into a massive cluster of black holes. It was a catastrophe the likes of which the galaxy had never seen. Planets and moons were crushed as their suns sank into the black holes like bodies into a bog. Some stars exploded under the strain. Supernovae bloodied the face of space, and the lights of a trillion precious lives were dimmed before the apathetic eyes of eternity.

And this was only the beginning.

Beyond the event horizons an even greater tragedy awaited. As long foretold, as long feared, Nenockra Rool, the Devil King of the Dark Forever, was returning to conquer the universe and enslave all creation within an everlasting age of torment.

The galaxy lay on the threshold of doom.

More suns were swallowed, more worlds were destroyed, and the black holes swelled as if with joy. With the Gods gone, the gates to the Seven Glories were closed, and the dead had no angels to welcome them. Souls floundered between the planes of existence. For those still alive, hope was fading with the stars.

But all was not lost.

Not yet...

Hidden in the murky fringes of the galaxy's longest arm was the sorcerously constructed world of Phate. It was a barren, battered world. A thousand years before, war with the Dark Forever had laid everything waste. Entire civilizations had been wiped out, the empires of men reduced to dust. The dwarves, minotaurs, and myriad other mystical races had all but disappeared. Of the elven nations, only the most decadent retained some measure of prosperity. Although the world still overflowed with sorcery, what fantastical beauty that sorcery had created was virtually gone. It was a terrible shame, hundreds of thousands of years of crystalline cultivation crumbled and burned beneath the scorching foot of demonic war. Yes, a terrible shame indeed to see those once beautiful and teeming lands crammed with corpses, the once splendid skies haunted and filled with empty kingdoms.

Now Phate's splendor existed only in the bygone dreams of its greater dragons.

Ah, but not all about Phate was so grim and, as I said, all was not lost, for upon this world resided the universe's brightest hope, the one who was destined to defeat Nenockra Rool and ensure the supremacy of light for all time.

This was the Son and Savior of the Stars.

And now I shall tell you his story, the story of Phate....

It all began on Phate's surface, on the western edge of the Continent Isle of Volcar. There, the Cliffs of Moaning Wishes thrust out of the roiling waters of the Raging Sea in mile high slabs of sparkling obsidian. Massive and mighty were the waves that perpetually pounded these cliffs, but ever had the cliffs endured with indomitability. They were loyal guardians, these obsidian walls; for ages untold they had protected the subterranean dark elf realm of Kroon from the mood swings of the sea.

Although the denizens of Kroon rarely stepped from their shadowy realm, on this most unusual night, two dark elves emerged onto a balcony set high up on the cliff face. As expected, they were greeted by sorcerous storms. Rain assailed them like a hail of icy little arrows, and the winds that whipped them were full of wraiths that hissed and howled and moaned. In the distance, ghostly dragons shrieked, multicolored lightning cracked the clouds, and peals of thunder rumbled like a grumbling god.

To the elves' stinging eyes, all the sea and sky appeared as a flashing, greyish-black swirl.

A typical Phatian night.

"Magnificent, is it not, uncle?" said the younger of the two elves.

"Magnificent?" Morigos of the Moom stepped to the stone railing, leaned over it, and spit into the waves. "It is miserable."

"I disagree. It's beautiful. And if you listen closely, you can hear the voices of the Dark Forever on the winds."

"Like you, the winds should be quiet."

Tatoc joined him at the railing. "Why do you look to the sea when you should be looking to the stars?"

Morigos sighed. "Why do you speak when you should be silent?"

They both recoiled then, avoiding the spray from a particularly large wave that had struck the cliffs below.

When the spray dispersed, Morigos placed his elbows back onto the railing, wondering why the sea was so unusually riled. Perhaps this had been arranged by those he looked for. He mulled it over… Yes, he concluded, that was it, the sea's violence was a distraction, a cover for the more subtle forces gathering beneath it. He continued to scan about, his eyes darting back and forth across the waves. Minutes went by, and still nothing. He wondered if anything was going to appear at all, and then…

"Look!" Tatoc thrust a finger into the sky. "There!"

Morigos muttered curses beneath his breath, for he had no interest in the sky on this night. Something flickered out of the corner of his eye, though, so he entertained his annoying nephew and looked up. Through a small break in the clouds he saw a pack of twinkling red stars. They appeared to be enlarging, but he wasn't certain of this, for he only got a momentary glimpse of them before they vanished behind a swift moving column of black clouds.

Tatoc laughed and clapped after they disappeared.

Morigos put his gaze back to the waves and sputtered, "Blasted, blinding surface world. Can't see anything. Sun's dying rays by day, sorcerous storms all night!"

"You saw them!" Tatoc exclaimed. "The Shards of Zyrinthia have come!"

"I couldn't care less."

"It's the foretelling of our conquest!"

Morigos squeezed water from his robes. "It is the foretelling of our doom."

"Doom? We've been given a new beginning, and you do nothing but sulk."

"Beginning?" the elder dark elf scoffed. "Ending is more like it. That you fools actually think the Dark Forever will ally with us is amusing to me."

"If you don't believe, then why are you out here?"

Whatever luster was left in Morigos' eyes dimmed, and his face disappeared into the shadows of his oversized cowl. He whispered, "Because my aims are no longer for evil," but his voice went unheard, overtaken by the whistle of ill winds.

Snorting with derision, Tatoc swiveled on his heels, made for the balcony's arched entranceway. "You can stay out here and drown for all I care, I'm joining my clan."

Morigos pushed himself from the railing, the runes embroidered on his robes glowing a dull green. "You will stay with me!"

"Why?" Tatoc asked from over his shoulder. "We've seen the sign."

"I'll not have the Black Claw rip you to pieces."

"My place is with them, not you."

"To the Dark Forever with the Black Claw!" Morigos growled. "They are nothing when compared to the powers that rule the universe. Stay with me, I command you!"

Tatoc whirled about, pounded his chest. "I'm not yours to command, I'm a warrior!"

"You're a slave!" Morigos lifted his arms, red lightning cracking the sky behind him.

"I'm a dark elf fighter!" Tatoc roared over the ensuing thunder.

Morigos recognized the inflamed expression on Tatoc's face, so he made ready a precautionary spell, his fingertips igniting with green flames.

Although he looked as if he was dressed only in a tight, sleeveless tunic, Tatoc, like all the Fighters of the Black Claw, was a walking arsenal. He was embraced within a suit of invisible steel armor, its hinges magically silenced, its bulk lightened and unnaturally strong. Raindrops dispersed a full two inches from his slender, tightly muscled body. Invisible sickles with extendable shafts crisscrossed his back, and Morigos knew a multitude of other indiscernible weapons attached themselves to his armor.

Tatoc beckoned his uncle with a smile. "Come, old elf."

"You're a fool of a fiend."

Lightning struck again.

And so did Tatoc.

With one, fluid motion, he withdrew his sickles and sprang ten feet into the air. He curled into a ball and flipped over backward, wrists snapping, sickles smacking raindrops into Morigos, further drenching him.

"Damn you!" the mage swore, waving his hands in front of his face in a futile attempt to fend off the offensive droplets.

Tatoc landed, his feet planted exactly where they'd been the instant before he jumped. He leered and hissed, flicking his forked tongue. "Mages. Such a paranoid lot."

Words poured from Morigos' mouth like lava from a newly enraged volcano. "You young fool! I could vaporize you where you stand! You're covered with and dependent upon items that are thick with *my* enchantments!" The fires on his fingers brightened, but he didn't throw them. He knew Tatoc had never intended to actually engage him in combat. It would have been futile. Nevertheless, Morigos had to restrain himself. At any other time, in any other circumstance, he would have destroyed his nephew for daring to even consider challenging his power. He was a Mage of the Moom, a High Councilor of the Cold-Blooded Caves and the right hand of Warloove himself. It was well within his right to separate Tatoc's atoms. But no…not now, not here.

Not yet.

Morigos growled at Tatoc.

Tatoc smiled back.

Morigos shook his head. *Fighters*.

Tatoc relaxed his stance and reached over his shoulders, sheathing his sickles.

The mage dispelled his flames, within and without. "It is wise of you to restrain yourself, Tatoc. I cannot afford to lose you to wrath, be it mine or yours. If you—"

Then something brushed Morigos' mind—a ghost of an impression, a disquieting...presence?

The confident smile fled Tatoc's face. "What's that?"

"Be silent!"

A power cloaked Morigos' conscious, a power much greater than his own. He realized they were being watched, and probably had been all along. He rushed back to the railing and looked down.

Tatoc rejoined him. "What's going on?"

Morigos motioned for him to quiet. He didn't have to, though, for when Tatoc saw what his uncle was looking at, shock robbed the young fighter of words.

They were not alone.

It looked as if the sea was sprouting a thousand bulbous eyes to consider the dark elves with a mild curiosity. Actually, it was row after row of perfectly spaced vessels appearing in the waves. Morigos squinted, struggling to see more detail through the rain. There wasn't much to discern; the vessels appeared as dim, featureless globs, throbbing with a sickly green luminescence. Their most striking characteristic was that they were completely motionless, fixated in their spaces even as the monstrous waves passed over them. They were eerie, disconcerting to look upon.

They were Dreadships.

Morigos pondered the strength of their sorcery. It was considerable. Had these ships been anything other than Dreadships, they would have been dashed to splinters against the stubborn cliffs whose walls had split the hulls of countless vessels through countless ages.

Morigos stepped from the railing, said plainly: "The deep elves are here."

"Deep elves?" Tatoc shrunk back. "Why...why are they here?"

Morigos motioned to the young fighter. "You do not need to know."

"Enough of this!" Tatoc shouted. "Why do you drag me all the way up to this balcony to stare at these unwelcoming eyes of the sea? The celebration commences. I belong below. I am joining the foregathering of my kin!" Then he bolted for the entranceway.

"Stay by my side!" the mage commanded.

Tatoc laughed and said, "Certainly, my uncle," as he disappeared into the shadows inside the cliffs.

Morigos looked to the floor, shook his head and then went after his nephew.

As soon as he was gone, the lead Dreadship quivered ever so slightly. Soon it would break position and head toward the cave port's entrance located in the base of the cliffs. The ship's occupants were uncharacteristically anxious.

There was the dawning of a new age to deliver.

The two elves swept down through a dark that was as deep and impenetrable as a starless night. They were not tentative, for their eyes saw best when not blinded by surface light. They moved swiftly but carefully, deftly avoiding invisible snares that periodically shifted positions all along their path. Morigos floated, his sorcerous song carrying him as smoothly as a specter. Tatoc bounded on all fours, his movements filled with a confident, animal-like grace.

"Your clan," Morigos grunted, "they'd probably be even more delighted to ensnare one of us than to catch an intruder."

Tatoc, who quickly strode out in front of his uncle, called back, "Then use your grating sorcerous tongue to call upon the bats! I do not wish to expend all my energy running, anyway." His voice echoed loudly, the reverberations carrying far into the dark.

Morigos waved off the suggestion, said, "No."

"No? Why do you insist on delaying?"

"Because I want to view this place one last time. *Yes, one last time I want to remember it as it was…*"

In-between strides, Tatoc thrust a hand out to the side. "Ha! Look around, the great cavern is as empty as it has always been. There is nothing here!"

"Nothing?" Morigos called after him. "Once, a thousand years ago, this place was the center of *everything*, before your generation squandered all that was darkly glorious! Once—"

"Stop!" Tatoc interjected. "I've heard your inane ramblings about the past more times than I care!"

When the echoes of their words receded, the place filled with an eerie silence, and Morigos suddenly felt as if he was accompanied by a ghost. *"A ghost indeed."* He exhaled, tilted his head, and shivered as he glanced aside, into the haunting black.

You see, they traversed a rocky shelf that spiraled down the inner rim of the largest space in all the realm, a mile high shaft dug deep into the cliffs. Although it had long been empty, Morigos suddenly couldn't help but to see it as it had once been. Memories filled his eyes like tears, because here, in this place, was Kroon's forsaken past. *His* past. Now his memories flowed forth as words. I'll let him describe what he saw…

"Once, long ago, obsidian fortress towers lined the shaft's sides, gleaming and glinting like black steel swords. Once, long ago, Greater Bat Dragons flew about, waiting for commands to fly to faraway lands and slather enemies with liquid fire that spewed from maws dripping with lava. Oh, yes, I remember! Once upon a time, hundreds of thousands of dark elf fighters strode up and down this shaft; and hundreds, no, *thousands* of Moom hovered all around, conspiring with wizards from faraway moons. And all in the great shaft twinkled and glowed, for the ceiling was encrusted with enchanted slivers of silver, onyx, and gold!"

From somewhere ahead, Tatoc yelled, "*Pleeease*, enough!"

Morigos barely heard him. His eyes glinted for just a moment, perhaps with real tears (well, knowing him as I do, perhaps not), and he whispered, "When did yesterday become so long ago?" The vision of times long past ran dry in his fading eyes. Now all was quiet and dim and dead. Of the great shaft, not a glimmer shone, nor was a shred of life about.

Like much of Phate, for Kroon, history had nearly run out.

"A couple of old fools, you and I," Morigos said to the ancient dark.

"I see only one fool!" Tatoc yelled from afar and below. He was on the other side now, quickly eating up ground with his dark elven claws.

Morigos called after him, "Don't stray too far; wait for me, imbecile!"

Tatoc ignored him, of course, and ran on.

Morigos muttered profanities so vulgar, I'll refrain from scribing them here. He composed himself, sang a string of sorcerous notes, and flew on with a burst of speed. Before too long, he came up right behind his nephew.

They were more than halfway down, and a stink of salt and souls stung their nostrils. The roar of waves pummeling the cliffs outside became apparent. It grew louder the farther down they went. Eventually the sound took on a distinctive voice, as if the waves were a chorus and their crashing was a sloshing song. The sound spurred Tatoc on. He grunted, ran even faster. "Blast this useless giant cavern! How age has slowed you, uncle, come on and hurry!"

Now below could be seen a heaving haze that spread all across the bottom of the great shaft. It looked as if a massive storm cloud had snuck inside. It was a swirling grey vapor, filled with smoke and souls, flickering here and there as molten fires blazed below it. Voices grimly beautiful climbed out of it, mesmerizing notes and languages archaic.

An exhilarated Tatoc raced down around the final curve and into the haze. When he came out from underneath it, the pathway leveled onto a rough, rocky terrain. His uncle soon floated up next to him, then padded to the ground. A waft of smoke crossed before their gaze, then their vision cleared.

Thus they beheld the Cave Port of Kroon.

Tatoc slapped Morigos on the side. "Ah, yes! Look at them!"

The cavern's floor was packed. Ten thousand dark elf fighters swayed like black reeds in an autumn breeze as they chanted in tune with the echoing crash of furious waves that pounded their vile domain. They were a sea unto themselves, these elves. The stench of salt and souls blended with foul sweat, and Morigos felt his heart pound as it had when he was a young killer. While he watched, the elves went wild with ritual celebration, breaking into a frenzied dance of joyous evil. Twenty thousand wickedly enchanted weapons were thrust high into the air and waved about, sometimes even thrown. Dark elves died within their dance, sending souls twisting into the air. Mages of the Moom hovered in the haze like soul vultures, capturing spirits to further feed their sorcerous power.

In an attempt to quell his surge of adrenaline, Morigos took a deep breath. "How quickly the cruel centuries have fled. How sad only a foolish few remain, these decadent fools cavorting at the decaying roots of a once nobler ruin. *Oh, how I have come to hate these people...*"

Tatoc let his euphoria flow. "Yes! Do you feel that? Do you feel it boiling your blood? Our song!" He shook his fists, leaned in close to his uncle. "Do you still deny the strength of the Black Claw?"

Determined to retain the calming demeanor of a mage, Morigos exhaled slowly. "I do not deny its strength, my young nephew, I deny its wisdom."

Tatoc shook his head.

Mages.

Morigos motioned to the side of the cavern, to a path that led around the masses, to the dim, dank regions beyond. "Come with me."

Too late.

Tatoc had already bolted into the midst of the mayhem, his sickles in hand, splitting unwary skulls.

Morigos' lips trembled and quivered with anger and magic. He spat a sorcerous song, and wispy green sorcery poured out of his cowl, tightened about his body, and congealed into a translucent shield. Satisfactorily protected, he chased after his nephew, his arms raised, his fingers swirled with flame. With his magically attuned eyes he soon noticed a familiar pair of sickles. They stuck up from the mob not too far ahead, then maliciously hacked down. A bevy of agonized shrieks ensued.

Morigos groaned. Then he yelled at the top his lungs: "If you should damage or kill yourself, I'll serve your remains to the starving shades of the netherworlds! Tatoc, come back to me!"

That garnered some attention, but not from the one he sought. A dozen growling fighters rushed him, slashed their scimitars across his body. His shield deflected every strike, but his pride was nonetheless pricked. "Insolent bastards," he grumbled. There was a time when no fighter would have dared attack a mage, especially one who served all the Cold-Blooded Caves.

Morigos let some of the adrenaline he had turned aside seep back into his veins, and with astonishing grace and swiftness for one of his advanced age, he whipped his body many times around. His fingers, now bright with green fire, lashed out like daggers. His burning nails slashed through faces, torsos, and limbs. The nails dug deep, their poisonous flames burning flesh and puncturing organs. Half a dozen elves dropped dead, their weapons clanging to the ground. The wounded rest retreated...then snarling they came right back like malicious little shadows sprung from the greater shadow of the crowd. But their weapons, though sharp and true, still could not penetrate the mage's shield.

"Idiot! Idiot! Idiot!" Morigos screamed at each one as he slashed through their necks.

Seconds after the confrontation had begun, only two of the original twelve who had attacked him remained. They turned, made to flee; but in a fit of spiteful rage, Morigos unleashed green fires into each of their backs. The fires punctured their invisible armor and burned all the way through. Black blood gushed from their bellies, and their bodies tumbled into molten pits, their enchanted armor exploding, their limbs blown to bits.

Then something slapped Morigos on the back.

He whirled around, his burning hands ready to slash.

It was his nephew, with eyes open and mouth agape in a wide, crazed smile.

"Uncle!" Tatoc cried, "I am surprised and happy to see you embrace this holy ritual!"

"Fool! You— Oh, curse the Dark Forever, turn around!"

A trio of dark elves was flipping down out of the haze directly toward them. They were singing, their eyes glowing red, their raised black steel swords agleam with glinting flecks of crystallized obsidian.

But before the middle one could even touch the ground, he lost his head, as Tatoc had already leaped into the air and swung his sickles straight through his neck. The head flew off into the throng, and sprays of blood slathered Tatoc as he somersaulted down. The flanking elves flew past Tatoc and slammed to the ground directly in front of Morigos. The mage yelled, "You have such beautiful voices!" as he struck out with crackling flame. The electrified energy raced across his victims' bodies, punctured their invisible chest plates, and stabbed their hearts.

Down to the warm rock they folded, in a heap of burning death.

"Well done!" Tatoc hissed and laughed. "Literally!"

"Enough of this! Come with me, fool!"

Morigos led them forth.

They stomped straight through the melee, the old mage protecting his nephew from any dark elf who got too close. Tatoc whined and complained, for he wished to further bloody his invisible blades. He got a few strikes in, but mostly, Morigos enveloped all who challenged them in a hail of green flame. It was a confusing chaos, to be sure, like navigating through a screaming smoke speckled with flashing violet eyes and silvery glints of elusive swords, all dancing about pools of molten fire. Eventually they fought their way to the edge, pushed their way out of the fray, and came upon the actual cave port.

Before them lay the subterranean lagoon that rimmed the western half of the cavern. A dilapidated dock clung to the lagoon's edge right in front of Morigos, and beneath it lingered a luminous blue mist that reached out over most of the water's surface. Looking at the mist made Morigos shake his head. "*So, bold Herard, soon I surrender all that I was, and forsake all that I remember. We shall see about your alleged hope.*"

"What did you say?" Tatoc asked. "Who's Herard?"

"No one. Nothing. Be quiet."

Morigos winced when he regarded Tatoc, for the young warrior's invisible steel armor was streaked completely over with dirty blood. It was an odd sight. It looked as if Tatoc bore wounds two inches above his body, even though he was virtually unharmed; the gore he wore was the smeared entrails of others. "Wipe the blood off yourself," Morigos demanded, "and straighten up. I won't have you greeting the deep elf ambassador looking like some stricken beast."

"Oh hells, I don't care what some deep elf thinks of me."

"And help me cease the senseless ritual of these rabid fools!"

The request was unnecessary, for at that moment a moan like the sea howling in pain blasted over the lagoon and shot through the whole cavern like a wave of horrifying dragonfear. All the dark elves were stunned. Thousands instantly ceased their celebrating and went silent. Everything did. Even the waves' crashing was muffled. The moan drew out for long seconds, then receded, but its echoes continued to quiver the elves' ears disconcertingly.

Morigos looked across the lagoon, where a huge curtain of enchanted fog draped the cave port's entrance. It was a marvel of dark elven sorcery, that glittering, violet grey membrane, for it had held back the might of the Raging Sea for thousands of years. Morigos mused on how it was about to let in something else, though...

Another moan sounded and the fogwall parted as the prow of the lead Dreadship poked through it like the head of some abyssal beast surfacing from the Raging Sea. All eyes shot to the cave port's entrance. They watched as the ship slipped through and glided across the lagoon, barely disturbing the mist as it moved.

Looking on that ship made even Morigos' jaded soul shiver with icy unease, but outwardly, he managed to maintain his composure.

The Dreadship's hull was shaped like a bloated thorax. It was sickly grey, featureless, and throbbing like a wounded organ. Foul green vapors streamed over it, disorienting its otherwise smooth outline. It was repulsive, yet mysteriously intimidating. Had it not come from the sea, Morigos might have mistaken it for a ship of the stars. There was nothing about it that marked it as a seafaring vessel. It had no deck, no masts and no sails.

Of these things, it had no need.

Tatoc stepped closer to Morigos, his bitterness toward his uncle necessarily vanquished in the face of something that could challenge them all, Moom and Black Claw alike. The mob shuffled closer to the lagoon, some ready to wield wicked weapons, some ready to unleash fiery spells—all stubbornly warring with their fear.

The Dreadship cruised up to the dock. An enchanted chain of metal links extended up from beneath its waterline, snagged a rusty cleat, and pulled the ship tight to the dock's side. Then the ship emitted a strange sort of sigh, and forthwith a dim ray of yellow light appeared and spread out over the warped planks. The wood turned pale and straightened, as if the enfeebling effects of time had suddenly been cast away.

Tatoc stepped to his uncle's side, leaned in and whispered, "So, tell me now, what are they doing here?"

"You want to bring about a new age? Well, here it is."

Tatoc frowned. "I don't understand. If *you* knew they were coming, then why isn't our leader here?"

"Leader?" Morigos shot him a condescending look. "We have no leader."

"How dare you!" Tatoc pushed his words through clenched teeth. "Warloove is our ruler!"

"Rule us he may, but lead us he does not. Now be silent."

The young fighter scoffed at this, but pressed the issue no more.

Morigos felt a familiar presence invade his mind. He recognized it for the feeling he had experienced on the balcony, when they'd first seen the Dreadships. It was unsettling, to say the least. All the elves felt it, and a telepathic message was sent to them. Although there were no decipherable elvish words, they somehow understood: it was a warning to remain still and calm. So, naturally, some of the fighters grumbled and shifted in defiance.

Morigos smacked Tatoc on the chest. "Tell them to calm down! Tell them now!"

Tatoc begrudgingly turned around and shook his head. Some vulgar murmurings continued, but for the most part, the fighters quieted. All seemed under control.

Then another sighing sound came from the ship, and a small part of the hull disappeared, leaving a doorway-sized hole whose bottom sat level with the edge of the newly wrought dock. The dark elves, despite the warning to remain still, inched forward. Morigos hoped they would be disintegrated for their insolence, but, much to his disappointment, they were not. They crammed to the edge of the lagoon in hundreds of tightly packed rows, but left a semicircle of space around Morigos and Tatoc. Members of the Moom flew over the scene, but didn't dare dip too close to the Dreadship.

A shimmering stranger stepped from the inky cabin, and the cavern's silence deepened, as if time itself stood still.

Thousands of fighters clambered for a better view.

Here was a deep elf.

It was like something out of a disturbing dream. It stood on the dock, but its body wasn't quite solid. It wavered, as if its atoms danced between the dimensions.

Morigos shed a magical tear, his vision cleared and, for him alone, the deep elf seemed to solidify.

It was wrapped in a robe that appeared to be made of flowing seawater. Orange eyes peered from a gaunt elvish face with skin the color of rotted seaweed, a green so deep it was bleaker than black. It was slim, not very tall, but exuded a quiet, lethal power. Its arms were overlong and hanging, the skeletal fingers nearly brushing the planks.

Those fingers disturbed Morigos. The magic they held...

Unimpressed, Tatoc snickered. The deep elf looked like a mage, like a thing of sorcery and trickery — a thing not to be trusted. Tatoc's confidence returned, and by the rising sound of blasphemous murmurings, he surmised that many of his brothers in the Black Claw were feeling similarly unimpressed by this stranger from the sea.

He lifted a foot to step forward.

Morigos raised a hand. "Wait." Then he pushed past Tatoc, squeezing the fighter's arm in an effort to encourage his cooperation. Tatoc briefly pondered continuing forward just to spite his uncle, but remained still.

Morigos stepped onto the dock and bowed before the deep elf, his voice sounding with the watery tones of some strange language. The deep elf responded in a similar tone and, after a short exchange, Morigos turned around and faced his people.

"*One more show of words to these fools,*" he whispered to himself. Then he levitated ten feet into the air and spoke to the thousands with a sorcerously enhanced voice, the words echoing loudly throughout all the Cave Port of Kroon.

"The time you've long waited for has come. After a thousand year exile, your god, Nenockra Rool, the Devil King of the Dark Forever, is returning to start another war, and conquer all eternity."

Cheers erupted from the fighters, but they soon died down as Morigos energetically motioned for silence.

He continued.

"Weakened by ghostly black stars, the dimensional walls surrounding our galaxy are again ready to fall and, as always, the walls around our own world are the weakest of all. Hence, the Devil King has once again chosen Phate for his first step into the primary universe. But he cannot ascend until someone tears through the dimensional walls from our side. That is why the deep elves are here. We've agreed to give them a body to house the soul of the one who can break through the dimensions, and in exchange, they've agreed to give us the artifacts that will enable Warloove to steal the Sunsword Surassis, the weapon that could prevent Nenockra Rool's ascension. To put it simply—for those of you too ignorant to understand—*we* will give the deep elves the means to resurrect the deliverer of the Devil King, and *they* will give us the means to ensure that he emerges unchallenged."

Morigos then lowered to the floor, turned to the abyssal ambassador, and said: "My Lord, if you would."

The deep elf lifted its hands over its head, palms facing upward. The skeletal fingers curled open, and a ball of silver fire erupted in the air above them. The flames quickly darkened to black, then separated and solidified into two equal-sized objects, each spinning furiously on a fixed axis.

Morigos turned back to his people.

"The artifacts in question, the Gauntlets of Loathing Light."

The Cave Port of Kroon filled with gasps.

"The gauntlets?" Tatoc lifted an apprehensive eyebrow, then joined his uncle on the dock, all-the-while keeping an eye on the deep elf.

"Yes," Morigos said, "with these gloves, your 'leader' will be protected from the sword's accursed powers of light."

Tatoc motioned to the deep elf. "You said we're to give them a body?"

Morigos nodded.

The young fighter looked around. "Well? Whose?"

The Mage of the Moom couldn't resist a joyfully cruel smile as he gently touched his nephew on the shoulder. "Yours."

"What?" Tatoc reeled back as if the touch had stung him.

Hissing chortles erupted from hundreds of throats. Dozens of warriors broke from the throng, tightening the space around the mage and his nephew. Morigos said, "The deep elves would not sacrifice one of their own, they're too few. So we chose you." He acknowledged everyone in the chamber. "We *all* chose you. Be proud, dear Tatoc. Within your strong, young body, the soul of the one who will free the Dark Forever will reside. You will be immortalized!"

"Wha—?" Tatoc was stupefied into silence.

"Welcome to your new age." Morigos laughed.

Thousands of dark elves cheered.

Tatoc went pale. Chills of terror pushed a cold sweat from his skin. "This is madness!" he screamed as the mass of fighters closed in, cornering him on the dock. His warrior's adrenaline kicked in and he unleashed his sickles. "Come then, I'll fight you all!"

No, my dear reader, as you will see, he most definitely would *not* fight them all.

In fact, his fingers went numb and his beloved sickles fell from his grasp. They went thudding to the planks, as did he, stricken with the paralyzation spell Morigos had just placed upon his shoulder. Straining to even swivel his head, he looked to the lagoon, considered plunging into the water. He tried crawling but it was no use. He could barely breathe, let alone move. Waves of nausea bombarded him, and he was seized by a fit of convulsions. Then he went still.

Tatoc of the Black Claw was completely paralyzed.

The only lively thing about him was the betrayal burning in his eyes.

Morigos bowed to the deep elf ambassador. The abyssal being bowed back, then turned around and strode into the Dreadship, leaving the Gauntlets of Loathing Light floating in the air. The ship's doorway disappeared…and so did Tatoc's body. The paralyzed fighter simply faded from sight, sorcerously stowed away on the ship. The enchanted chain untethered itself, fled below the surface, and the Dreadship departed the dock. It slid across the lagoon and sliced through the fogwall, leaving the Cave Port of Kroon to carry on with its part in the fate of things.

The dock withered back to its shabby state.

The dark elves let out a collective sigh, and so did the Raging Sea; the sound of crashing waves returned.

The Fighters of the Black Claw resumed their ritual. They ran from the lagoon in a mad pack, joyously swinging their swords and throwing their daggers, knowing that on this holiest of nights they had gained the Devil King's favor. And, as an added bonus, the annoying Tatoc was gone. It was all so wonderful! They leaped and danced and thrashed one another. Certainly, more lives had to be sacrificed to properly honor the return of the Dark Forever. The Mages of the Moom were curious about the gauntlets, but forbidden to touch them, so they flew away. They hovered above the fighters, dodging hurled weapons and ensnaring whatever souls they could.

Soon the chamber was the same as it had been when Tatoc and Morigos had first entered it.

The same, except for the Gauntlets of Loathing Light.

The gloves had ceased spinning, but remained hovering in the air, emitting a low, buzzing hum. Morigos stepped directly beneath them to get a better look. They were so gloriously dark, so infinitely black! Their cuffs were inscribed with glowing red runes, words so vile their very utterances would kill anyone who pronounced them incorrectly. Morigos was bewitched, reminded of his younger days, when he had thirsted for murderous magical items. Imagining his hands wrapped with the gauntlets, he reached up to them, stretched his fingers closer, closer...

And then he cried out.

Feeling like his fingertips had been severed by a rusty blade, he wrenched his hands down and slumped to the ground, moaning as the agony spread to fill his whole body with pain. It was awful. It felt like his bones were bending. The runes on his robes dimmed and his hands clenched, fingernails piercing his palms.

"Foolishness!" he sputtered. "Imbecilically stupid!"

He knew he was unable to touch the gauntlets. They were made of otherworldly material, imbued with the freezing cold of space, a forceful cold that far exceeded the power the deep elf had exuded.

There was only one dark elf on Phate who had the power to wear the Gauntlets of Loathing Light.

After a brief time, the pain thankfully set him free, and Morigos stood up, his back turned to the water. Uttering a masterful string of profanities, he flexed his fingers, shook out his hands, and brushed off his black robes.

Behind him, a little bubble broke the surface of the lagoon.

Then another...and another...

Then the lagoon released a gurgling hiss and its surface mist rushed into the center, gathered, and spouted upward like an inverted waterfall. Up and up it went, twenty, thirty, then fifty feet into the air. Its bluish tint brightened to white, and it began to take shape and solidify. Eyes ignited at its peak—blue orbs set in wide, silver slashes. Great wings of mist unfurled from its sides and a snout extended from the developing face. The creature, now close to fully formed, exhaled long and loudly, for it had been holding its breath for a long time.

Morigos heard it.

He slowly turned around...

...and looked into the eyes of a magnificent cloud dragon.

The cloud dragon looked into his.

Morigos cracked a frail smile. In a low voice, he said, "I have done my last task for evil, and my first task for you." He stepped from the dock, away from the Gauntlets of Loathing Light.

Now fully formed, the rearing dragon fell to all fours, its foreclaws splashing in the shallow waters. Morigos could see a saddled rider between the topmost spikes of its serrated spine. The rider was accoutered like an ancient knight, encased in reflective silver armor. One of his hands grasped the reins, the other held high a glinting sword, its blade awash with sparking blue flames.

By now, dozens of dark elves had noticed the huge white beast. At first they couldn't believe their eyes. A cloud dragon, here? They pushed their way through the mob, smacking their brethren's heads, swinging their faces toward the lagoon. Soon, hundreds of fighters and dozens of mages were running and flying for the intruders, ecstatic to have an enemy target for their ritual rage.

The dragon saw the incoming mob, gave Morigos a quick nod and then lunged forward, smashing through the dock and seizing the gauntlets with its foreclaw. Morigos wasn't surprised by its reaction. The dragon shrieked in pain, its grip seared with the freezing burn of the infernal gloves. Nevertheless, it held onto them, turned about, and leaped into the air, toward the cave port's entrance.

Sensing his kin all around him, Morigos threw his arms into the air and screamed, "Kill it! Kill it!"

Fifty fighters in the lead ran up to the lagoon's edge, intent on flinging their glowing obsidian glaives. They brought their arms back, but to no avail, for their heads were lost as the dragon cracked its giant whip of a tail. The elves' bodies crumpled to the ground or plunged with their heads into the lagoon.

Right before it reached the enchanted fogwall, the dragon twisted over, putting itself perpendicular to the water. The maneuver both protected its rider and enabled it to fit through the magical drape, which was much taller than it was wide. But the maneuver also exposed its belly.

For a split second, the dragon was vulnerable.

That was all the time the oncoming horde needed to throw a multitude of swords, spears, and fiery spells into the dragon's exposed hide.

The dragon endured the onslaught and burst through the magical drape, leaving the outraged dark elves screaming by the lagoon. Some of the fighters were enraged enough to dive into the water after it (Morigos couldn't suppress a fit of laughter at that sight). Some scattered for the passageways that led to the balconies. Others held a quick discussion about flying after it, but summarily rejected the idea, for there weren't any among them that could keep pace with a cloud dragon, not even the fighters on their fastest bats.

This was something Warloove himself would have to contend with.

When the initial furor calmed, they all turned to Morigos. Veterans of the Black Claw seized him, shoved him to his knees. The Moom floated down, gathered around him, shaking their heads. Shouts came from all around.

"It's his fault!" "He saw the dragon, why did he not save the gauntlets?" "Will the deep elves return?" "Bring him before our ruler!" "Kill him now!" "Bring him before Warloove!"

Daggers were thrust toward Morigos' face, but the Moom interceded before the mob could slash him apart. The mages warded his sorcery and took him out a side passageway.

"We are all slaves!" Morigos shouted as he was led away. "All of you will die! The Dark Forever will spare no one, and the war will slay us before even the dying sun snuffs our lives!"

Outside, the Raging Sea roared, the sorcerous storms wailed, and more stars disappeared from the sky.

Now our story is in motion.

The race against darkness had begun.

CHAPTER TWO
SPIRIT AND STRENGTH

The passage of time is all the more difficult to endure when one bears the burden of an evil past.

Lord Dark Sorciuss
Wizard, Warlord Ruler of Forn Forlidor

With dozens of venomous blades buried deep in her hide, the cloud dragon let loose an agonizing shriek when she shot out of Kroon's enchanted fogwall. Alas, the night took no pity on her. Hail pelted her head, howling winds battered her wings, and for a moment she mistook the pounding of thunder for the sound of more violent spells. She flinched, then dashed upward, hoping to find more considerate clouds than the ones that now drenched her.

"Yes! Yes!" her rider shouted. "We've done it, Zraz! Fly, fly!"

But Zraz faltered almost immediately.

Poison rapidly spread through her veins, and every movement pulled at her wounds, deepening the penetration of the imbedded blades. The pain was excruciating. And she could feel the dread power of the gauntlets working to bring her down. The vile gloves felt like steel weights in her foreclaw, and their dark aura beset her spirit with despair. It was all too much to bear. After ascending only a few hundred feet, she slowed to a hover.

Her rider called to her. "Zraz?"

She grunted in response.

He reached down, gently patted her. "Stay with me."

She barely managed to say, "Yes...my Lord," for it stung just to speak.

The man glanced to the obscured heavens, whispered, "May the Gods return and help us." Then he looked back to his dragon. "Hope awaits us in the sky. Fly, my beloved, if you possibly can, fly us toward salvation!"

She couldn't, though try as she may. The gauntlets intensified her pain, pushed their nefarious influence into her heart, pulled her down, down toward the sea. She briefly considered putting the black gloves in a saddlebag, but knew they'd only eat right through the material. She was getting desperate, losing altitude. The tip of her tail dangled in the crests of the passing waves.

All went blurry.

Then all went dark...

If the Gauntlets of Loathing Light were a demon, its face would have then been marked with an evil grin. These detestable artifacts delighted in surrounding the dragon's spirit with darkness, rejoiced as she succumbed to despair. And now they just about had her defeated. Her will was shattered, her life force giving out...

But she would not die.

She drew strength from her rider. She had a bond with him, reinforced by traits the gauntlets didn't know how to combat—compassion and trust, loyalty and love. These things empowered the dragon, gave her subconscious the will to persist.

Now the gauntlets weren't so pleased. They fought to sever the bond, to rip it apart, but her rider wouldn't allow it. Apparently, his heart was as stubborn as it was strong.

The gauntlets gave up trying to destroy the bond, but they'd never stop pressing both beings with despair.

"Fly, Zraz! Fly!"

Her rider's incessant screams shook Zraz from her semiconscious state and, mercifully, she felt the weight of the gauntlets lift. But when she blinked through the rain, she saw a monstrous wave coming for her. *No, I belong to the sky. If I am to die, I'll not be taken by the sea.* Her ebbing strength revitalized by a surge of adrenaline, she looked to her sky and said, "Hold fast, my Lord."

Her rider complied. He sheathed his sword, leaned forward, and hung onto the saddlebow for dear life as she flapped her wings hard and darted straight up.

She just made it!

The wave roared in beneath her, tickling her tail with its foamy crest before crashing into the cliff side. Zraz was doused in a spectacular spray, but flew on unhindered. She spun over, faced her belly to the obsidian wall, and soared free of the sea's salty reach.

"Good! Good!" her rider yelled.

The rider was a human named Herard Avari Fang, a man of many stories. But now there was time for only one, and it was unfolding before his rainfilled eyes. It was his guess that they held with them the fate of all stories, for if they failed, there would be no one left to tell them, in any time, in any galaxy. He hoped his dragon had the strength to go on, and he prayed she wasn't as grievously wounded as he suspected. In the cave port, he had heard hundreds of blades cut through the air with whistling malevolence, had felt the rapid fire thudding as many of them imbedded in her hide. Many of them... He winced just thinking about it.

There was no hope, Zraz wasn't going to make it, she—

Herard shook his head, admonished himself. The Gauntlets of Loathing Light—already they made to invade his will with their morbid power! *You will not overtake me.*

"Strength," Herard said to himself as much as to his dragon.

"Strength," Zraz returned, her voice shaky but her resolve firm. She continued skyward, hugging the cliff side, pouring all of her concentration into the beating of her wings. She was so engrossed in her efforts, so focused on reaching the clouds high overhead, she never noticed the dark, spherical distortions enlarging in the air directly above her.

Herard did.

He yelled, "Lookout!" as a trio of black fireballs came streaking down to incinerate them.

Oblivious to what Herard was shouting about, Zraz reacted instinctively, lifting her foreclaws up to shield her face.

The fireballs exploded right on top of her…

…but she did not suffer their burning wrath.

The Gauntlets of Loathing Light's inherent power consumed the explosions as efficiently as the black holes consumed the stars in Phate's galaxy. The fire was stretched out, pulled between Zraz's talons, and sucked right into the gloves' palms. Not a spark escaped. The red runes on the cuffs flared for a moment, then dimmed as the flames disappeared.

Zraz stared at the gauntlets in disbelief. "Such diabolical power…" Then she snapped her wings down hard and flew up as fast as she could, more intent than ever to escape the vile realm of Kroon.

But unfortunately for poor Zraz, escape from Kroon was not yet to be.

Herard lifted his helmeted head and peeked over the saddlebow just in time to see yet another obstruction. "The balcony! The balcony!"

Zraz saw the obstruction this time, but not nearly soon enough to keep from slamming into it.

Three dark elf Mages of the Moom peered over the railing of the balcony that Morigos and Tatoc had earlier been standing on. Assuming the horrific power of their perfectly placed fireballs would have at least slowed the beast, they hadn't contemplated what to do should their sorcery fail. They were completely unprepared as Zraz accelerated toward them. They looked blankly to one another, then scattered.

Too late.

Ten tons of dragon blasted the balcony into serrated shards, crushing the mages and slicing their limbs to pieces. Blood, bones, and shattered stones rained down into the Raging Sea, and Zraz went flailing out from the cliff face, her pain-filled screech echoing through the storm. Disoriented and out of control, it took only a moderate gust of wind to flip her over.

Herard was unseated.

"Argh!"

His legs flung out from underneath him and he lost his embrace on the rain-slicked saddlebow. One of his hands managed to maintain its grip on the reins, though, and he dangled in midair, screaming his dragon's name. Thankfully for him, Zraz recovered almost instantly. She pulled in her wings, let the wind's momentum twist her body all the way around, then looped down beneath him. He thumped back into the saddle, and she called back to him, "My Lord! Are you all right?"

Herard gasped. "May the Gods return! Yes, I'm all right... I think..."

He looked down to his armor. Although dented and punctured, it had absorbed the brunt of the balcony's beating, and he'd survived the collision virtually unscathed. He noticed his chest piece was stained with blue blood, though, Zraz's blood. He was dismayed. The violent collision had undoubtedly inflicted her with more wounds. He looked up to her. She looked back to him. Her eyes fluttered, but did not dim, the fires of conviction smoldering within them. She still clutched the Gauntlets of Loathing Light, her heart ever combating their icy evil.

"Oh, dear Zraz, and what of you?" Herard asked. "Can you carry on?"

She nodded. "I will, my Lord... I must."

And with that, she beat her wings and again challenged the storm. Up, up, up the duo climbed. She fought the elements all the way, but the cold began to numb at least some of her pain. She fell into a rhythm, and eventually scaled the cliffs. She curved over the ledge...

And flew right into a spectral ruin.

"Damn," Herard swore, "as if the gloom of the gauntlets isn't enough!"

He had forgotten—standing on the edge of the cliffs was the ethereal imprint of the Dead Towers of Ulith Urn. It was a fortress compound, a complex of towers and temples that had been raised by the vilest necromancers on Phate to honor the Devil King's first attempt at ascension a thousand years before.

Although the physical structures had long been destroyed, the dark magic that had framed them remained. Now Ulith Urn's towers stood like the guardian ghosts of the sea, flickering between sight and sightlessness. The jagged spires and crenelated fortifications wavered like flags in a lazy breeze, and the temples teetered on the brink of solidity. It was a ruins, but it was also a reminder—the Dark Forever was fated to return.

"Should I turn back?" Zraz asked, the compound's dark blue haze already enclosing all about them.

"No," Herard replied, "just fly through it." They needed to get as far away from Kroon as fast as they could, and it was best not to further strain Zraz by maneuvering about, he mused.

They carried on, straight toward Ulith Urn's center, the oscillating outlines of the towers looming all around them, a paralyzing chill seizing their hearts. "Look at this place," Herard said with a sort of disgusted awe.

"It's…hard to breathe…" Zraz stammered.

Herard nodded in agreement. It *was* hard to breathe. And it was so cold, so quiet. Deathly quiet. There were ghosts here, Herard knew; he could sense their presence, could feel their vaporous fingers slide across his skin.

It was all so dismal.

Herard closed his eyes and reminded himself of all he fought for: Zraz, his home palace, everything and everyone who had come before him, their lives, their sacrifices, their hopes. He thought of those who were yet to walk beneath the warm gaze of a loving sun, of their stories yet unsung.

And he thought of his son.

His beautiful, innocent son.

He smiled.

The simple expression cut through the darkness better than any magical blade ever could. Should he die by the sword, by the spear, or by the incomprehensible muttering of some dark mage's sorcerous song, Herard would accept such and end; but he would not die by the dissolution of his own spirit.

Not on this day, nor any other.

He opened his eyes.

"My dragon," he said.

"My Lord?"

"Remember when you picked me up and carried me from the shores of the Crystalmyst Sea?"

"Yes."

"Do you remember how wounded I was, how frightened?"

"Yes, yes I do." Zraz coughed.

"Do you remember what you said to me?"

She thought for a moment, then shook her head *"no."*

"You said, 'Fear not, for there are no wounds your spirit cannot endure, and there is nowhere you can go, should it even be beyond this life, beyond the Seven Glories itself, where my wings won't be around you.'"

Zraz managed a small smile. "I don't remember saying that, but it's true."

"Zraz, my arms are about *you* now, now and forever. Know that together we will persevere, and remember that the skies were once blue, and for some they will be again."

"I remember, my Lord. I remember. And I'm with you, always."

"For blue skies, my dear friend."

Herard reached down to give her a comforting touch. But when his hand pressed to her back, his fingers moistened with blood, and he could feel her muscles clenching, struggling to hold what remained of her life together. He wouldn't let this undermine his determination, though. *I must remain strong, for her, for everyone!* Spirit and strength had taken them into Ulith Urn's blue chill, and it would take them out.

It did. Zraz cleared the ghostly compound's reach, and they flew into the thicker air of the free sky.

"Well done!" Herard said, his breaths instantly coming easier.

He was compelled to turn around and take a last look at the spectral towers, but dissuaded himself. There was no need, for he knew the night had not yet liberated them from evil.

They had evaded Kroon, but had not yet escaped....

Onward they flew.

They glided low over the Wicked Plains, an expansive plateau that spread back from the cliffs as a tremendous field of ash. Here and there, small patches of yellow reeds struggled to enliven the scorched ground with at least some measure of life, but ever would death dominate the area. Packed with the crumbled corpses of a million unmarked lives, it was essentially a giant cemetery—the perfect back yard for Ulith Urn. You see, it was here the first war with the Dark Forever had pinnacled a thousand years ago, when Ulith Urn's corporeal towers had been felled by the forces of light.

And it was here where war would come again....

As they passed over the plains, Herard uttered a quiet prayer for those who had sacrificed.

They continued inland. The storms intensified. Wild discharges of lightning filled the surrounding clouds with blazing branches of red, yellow, and blue. Herard was wide-eyed. Never had he seen such a chaotic night. "The world itself is restless, my dragon. Pay it no heed! Remember where we go, and why. Remember—we believe the universe is a place of unending light."

"I believe," Zraz murmured, even as she bled a blue streak upon the ground, even as the landscape ever made to remind her of that which now ruled—the death and dark about them.

After a few more miles had passed, the scorched plains ran into a land littered with giant bones. Here, the victims of war had never been laid to rest, for the ground had not the stomach to swallow such gargantuan dead. Here, mile tall titans had grappled enormous demons amidst sorcerous flames as tall as castles. All who had fallen were still entwined, their skeletons locked in deathly embraces. Tens of thousands of remains conjoined for countless miles to either side, and ahead they piled into hills that climbed high into the night.

Thus they had come to the foundation for the Mountains of Might. Herard leaned his head back, squinted his eyes, and glimpsed the grand range's outline far up through the storms. "Stay with me, Zraz, our refuge shouldn't be too far away."

"I'm with you," she returned between increasingly laborious breaths. She toiled upward, flew over the skulls, and soon the mountains appeared in full view.

Ah, now here was a range like no other!

Herard never ceased to be amazed by their sight, for their magnificence was inimitable. Taking up the entire eastern sky, they were the largest mountains in the galaxy. They rose up and up until the storm clouds themselves lingered beneath their peaks like dirtied halos. Long ago, they had existed in tranquility, their bases wrapped with emerald evergreens, their liquid crystal waterfalls nurturing the countryside around them. Now they were burned, black and bleak with the mighty dead at their feet. Over the ages they had turned volcanic. When riled, rivers of lava leaked from their sundered summits, further scalding their stony faces and veining the surrounding lands with glowing tributaries. This led some to refer to the range as the Volcanoes of Volcar.

Herard pointed forward, said, "Do you know what they say about this place?"

Zraz turned her head slightly aside.

"They say the spirits of all the dragons killed in the first war with the Dark Forever are resting beneath those mountains. That even in death their fiery breath ever burns, thus igniting the Volcanoes of Volcar with boundless fury. They say—" Herard cut himself off, rolled his eyes, immediately regretting his rather grim choice of stories. "I'm sorry, I shouldn't have mentioned that."

Zraz shook her head. "No, no, it's good to hear." She coughed, cleared her throat. "I'm comforted by the thought of my ancestors. It will be an honor to join them someday."

"I'm sure it will be," was all Herard gave in reply, for he did not want to dwell on the subject any longer.

They carried on, the winds whirling around them, the rain intensifying, and the howls of a haunted Phatian night echoing through the clouds. When they flew into the shadows of the mountains themselves, it was as if the sky had closed in around them. At first Herard felt comforted by this, but his comfort soon evaporated, for he knew there were no shadows that could hide them from enemy eyes. And then, as if to validate his thought, a growl came from somewhere behind them.

"Zraz," Herard said.

"I heard it."

"They've found us!" Herard swung his head around. He saw only darkness, black clouds. "Damn these endless storms, it's always so difficult to see anything!"

"What course, my Lord?"

"Can you assume cloudform?" Herard grimaced, knowing it was much to ask of his wounded dragon.

"Perhaps, but I do not have the strength to keep us misted for long."

"I know, I know, I'm sorry. Just get us as far up into the mountains as you can. The Fallen Angel should be able to spot us soon." He let his words trail off, for his concentration was focused on searching for something he hoped he wouldn't see. He twisted in his saddle, looked all around, continuously grumbling at the terrible visibility. And then, when a branch of green lightning illuminated the sky directly behind them, he caught a glimpse of something racing through the clouds over the Wicked Plains—something shaped like a diabolically disfigured dragon...only larger.

Much larger.

As if the thing knew it had been spotted, it let loose a high-pitched shriek. The sound was terrible, like the cry of a thousand tortuous deaths crammed into one malicious voice! It was a sound I cringe just to describe, a sound that shook Herard to the very core of his soul. It echoed on for long seconds before finally fading beneath the thunder. As Herard watched, the lightning around the shadowy beast lessened, and it disappeared into the clouds.

No matter, Herard had seen enough.

He knew what pursued them.

Trembling, he turned about. *I must keep my wits.*

"Just keep flying for the mountains," he stammered.

"Yes, my Lord." Zraz was panting now, grunting with every pull of her wings.

Again the horrid shrieking sounded, louder than before.

"They're closing," Herard said, rather unnecessarily.

Zraz pushed through her pain and exhaustion, ascended the foothills of skulls, and finally soared up into the mountains. Herard thought he heard them rumble. *Perhaps they're unnerved by the arrival of the Gauntlets of Loathing Light.* He might have been right, for in some places the ground glowed. The restless lava that lay beneath its rocky hide bubbled, boiled, and began to bleed. Gullies filled with liquid heat. Fissures gasped, and the ground trembled. Rocks jumped and fell in little avalanches down the mountainsides. Zraz darted through the clefts and passes, making her way farther up into the range.

The rumbling intensified.

"Go, go!" Herard urged.

Then, way up over the peaks, a light as bright and red as Phate's sun flashed, and a dozen volcanoes simultaneously spit fire, roaring as the sea could not, shaking the entire Continent Isle of Volcar!

Herard and Zraz were aghast.

They were caught beneath fountains of flame that no storm could extinguish, a sweeping umbrella of hellish geysers that shot thousands of feet into the air...and then rained down. The clouds rimming the mountaintops flickered with a red glow, then exploded. Pyroclastic flows blasted down the mountainsides—wild, boiling rivers of liquid rock melting everything they touched. Stones ruptured and burning boulders bounded into the air as if thrown by enemy catapults.

"Up, up!" Herard screamed. "We must make for the high sky!" He double-wrapped his wrists with the reins and squeezed the saddle with his legs, intent on not being unseated again.

Zraz searched for a break in the firestorm, but there was no way around it.

They would have to fly through.

"My Lord?" she called back.

"I'm with you!" Herard returned. "Go! Go!"

A wall of heat hit their faces, then molten chunks of mountain rained down upon them. Zraz kicked her hind legs out and twisted aside in a desperate maneuver to dodge a showering stream of lava. She managed to avoid it, but thereafter the molten onslaught only intensified. Fiery trails shot down all around her. She shot up, then wrenched hard to her right, flaming rocks streaking by. Then she went left, dodged yet more glowing trails. Up and up she went, shifting back and forth, back and forth, every movement agonizing, every stone that pelted her feeling like a burning brand as she ascended through the storm of fire.

Finally she flew up over the lava plumes, but the pain of all that movement caught up to her and she let out a bitter cry. "Herard! I can't...I can't anymore."

"Hang on just a little bit longer!"

"I can't..." Her adrenaline was spent. She was burned all over, and the debilitating poison from the dark elf blades had all but overcome her. Her head rolled to the side, her wings spread wide, and she glided on the winds, her breathing lapsing into an unremitting moan.

But somehow she still managed to hold onto the gauntlets. "Oh...my Lord..."

"Easy, Zraz, easy," Herard said as his own pain became apparent. What was left of his battered armor was so hot he felt as if he sat in a stove, and a myriad of cuts and burns lined the exposed places on his skin. He shifted in his saddle, grunting with discomfort. At least they still flew; if it hadn't been for the strength of the air currents, his injured dragon might have already plunged them into a mountainside. And that was a most distressing prospect, for when Herard took a quick glance down, he saw the entire range was being swept over by a hurricane of flames.

Oh, if we had lingered any longer beneath those fiery peaks!

And then something happened that disturbed Herard even more than the sight of the flames.

The terrible shrieking returned.

And this time it was from much closer. It was so loud, so piercing, like a great gate with rusted hinges squealing as it slowly closed. Herard shot a look aside, and his heart quickened with fear, for the shadowy dragon beast was coming right at them.

Gods, it was impossibly huge! It was as if the storms had banded together, grown wings, and come alive. It rose up through a great plume of smoke, a shrouded black monstrosity come to tear them from the sky. And as horrid as the creature was, Herard knew the thing that rode it was even more ghastly.

"Zraz!" Herard yelled. "Go to cloudform! Do it now!"

Zraz could only moan in response. The poor dragon was barely conscious, barely aware of the oncoming doom. Her wings folded inward and she plummeted toward the volcanoes. Herard tugged on the torn reins, screaming, "Zraz, listen to me! If ever I could lend you whatever strength I have, it would be now! You must go to cloudform! *You must!*"

Zraz stirred, whispered: "Ever does your heart empower mine, my Lord. I will try."

Her belabored breaths calmed.

Her moans went silent.

And although she had retracted her wings, she no longer fell.

Her wings weren't the only thing that enabled her to fly...

You see, it is the dragons' immortal strength that their spirits are connected to the very fabric of the universe. As much as Zraz was a creature of the sky, she was also a citizen of the stars. At certain times she could disperse some of her atoms into other dimensions, thus softening her solidity and enabling her to soar through the winds of Phate as a cloud. Now she had begun this transformation, but couldn't complete it, for it took a tremendous amount of energy, and the Gauntlets of Loathing Light continued to sap what was left of her strength. They nearly succeeded in severing her connection to the universe and, for a time, Zraz was in danger of losing herself beneath the planes of existence.

But she persevered.

With one last burst of effort, she pushed through the dark power of the gauntlets, and with a quick puff her body diffused into a misty white vapor.

She was in cloudform.

The gauntlets themselves were dragged beneath the surface of physicality, but ever did their determined power try to pull Zraz's body back into Phate's sky. Eventually, inevitably, they would succeed...but not yet.

Herard was also engulfed in Zraz's magic.

His body lightened and he lost consciousness, sank into an immortal sleep. There he experienced immortal dreams. And in those dreams he was given a fleeting glimpse of a blessed universe. He saw alien skies so thick with healthy stars they blazed with solid bands of white light. He saw solar dragons soaring alongside starships, flying for planet-sized cities that encircled artificial suns. He saw lives and love unfold on the shores of nebula seas, he—

Ah, the images faded, and Herard fell deeper into his sleep.

A mortal man given a tiny taste of eternity, he would never remember those dreams. In all his years with Zraz, he had never recollected a single one.

For some, dreams are as elusive as the nights in which they dwell...

Zraz's cloud ascended.

The nightmare beast that pursued her flew in uncertain circles, groping for its prey, but could find nothing. The wounded dragon was gone. All about, the fires were fierce; perhaps its quarry had been taken by the flames.

A great, angered shriek echoed through the mountains while Zraz floated up into a glowing mist that had descended from far above. The mist consumed Zraz, then rose back up into a tremendous, oddly shaped bank of clouds that hid above the storms.

Herard Avari Fang slowly regained consciousness.

He shook his head, rubbed his eyes, and looked around. He was in a world of billowing white. It seemed unreal, as though he still dreamed, or he was in the middle of some optimistic artist's representation of the Seven Glories. Whatever this place was, it was massive, spanning miles above and before him. It was a sky in itself, a great rectangular space surrounded by titanic walls of cloud.

Walls of cloud...

His eyes brightened with realization. They had made it! It was their destination, their refuge, this realm carved out of sorcerously fabricated clouds. "The angel must have found us, must have pulled us into her domain. But where is she?"

The place appeared to be empty, almost as if it had been abandoned. It was eerily calm. There was no rain, no wind, and the only sound came from the crackle of blue lightning that periodically coursed through the cloudy walls. Herard shook his head again, tried to unclutter his thoughts. What had happened?

There were the volcanoes and fire and cloudform and…

His mortally wounded dragon.

Herard flashed a look down.

"May the Gods return! Zraz!"

So engrossed in his surroundings, he hadn't even realized that he still sat in his saddle. He was leaning slightly to the left, with Zraz lying tilted and silent beneath him. He dismounted, slid from her back to land on a floor of polished gemstones. He was horrified when a widening pool of blue blood flowed from beneath her to meet his feet. And he was even more horrified after he ran around and finally saw the terrible damage the dark elves had inflicted upon his dragon.

It was worse than he'd imagined.

Dozens and dozens of blades stuck in her. And the burns…

Oh, it was awful!

He yanked off his helm, tossed it aside, sprinted to her head. Kneeling beside her, he gently said, "Zraz, we've made it. Let the gauntlets fall. Let them go."

Though nearly unconscious, his faithful cloud dragon still clutched the Gauntlets of Loathing Light. She let out a painful sigh, opened her foreclaw, and the gauntlets fell to the floor with a jarring thud.

Herard winced at the sight of her shriveled, decaying palm. He stood, whirled about and cried, "My angel! Are you here? Help us!"

There was no spoken response, but the gemstone floor lengthened into a long pathway in front of him, row after row of smooth crystal stones materializing far across the shifting vapors beyond. The entire realm dimmed for a moment, then came back brighter than before.

Herard's mouth dropped open.

A gigantic palace appeared at the end of the pathway. His eyes tracing it all the way to the top, Herard guessed it to be at least two miles tall. Had it always been there, hidden behind a swirl of clouds, or had it just now materialized from out of nowhere, he wasn't certain. Nevertheless, it was stunning. It held a beauty forgotten on Phate, a beauty of craft and care undiminished by time, a beauty few mortals had ever set eyes upon. Its architecture was smooth and rounded, its many towers twined like braids, their walls glittering with the sparkle of encrusted jewels. Dragons were perched atop the towers and soaring around the spires in wide sweeping circles. Some spread out, sailed high over Herard's head—ice dragons and cloud dragons, soul dragons and lesser translucent dragons, all leaving a glittering wake of sorcery that rained down like a shower of crystal tears.

A sanctuary for dragons, a haven for lost spirits, this was the sky elf palace of Vren Adiri.

Herard lowered his eyes to the set of massive crystal doors set in the base of the central tower. He thought he saw some sort of motion behind them. He squinted, took a tentative step closer. Yes, there was something moving within, some glints of light. He took another step forward, and stumbled. Tears streamed down his face. Shaking, he collapsed to his knees, knelt in Zraz's blood. He did not care. "Please," he said to whoever would listen, "help us, someone, please help us."

Just as the words fled his lips, the glints of light behind the doors flickered, and the doors swung open. Light burst forth from within, radiating outward in a widening array of beams, illuminating all the realm. Music accompanied the doors' opening, the simple, soothing notes of phantom flutes arising from some indiscernible place.

A few seconds later, the beams pulled back and gathered together, condensing into a solid figure of light that stood in front of the doors.

The figure moved forward.

Herard, still on his knees, bowed to the floor.

Here was the Fallen Angel.

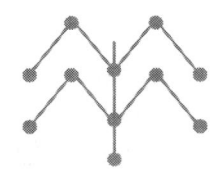

CHAPTER THREE
AN ANGEL'S EMBRACE

All things are enslaved to something. Moons are enslaved to their worlds which are enslaved to their suns which are enslaved to their galaxies which are enslaved to the universe which is enslaved by time. And we? We are slaves to them all.

Zan Zurahn
Necromancer of the New Order of Ill Ill Atheon

Herard was still kneeling in Zraz's blood as the luminous form of the Fallen Angel glided up to him. He thought her as wondrous as the palace behind her. She was a ghost of golden light, an apparition of a sun brighter than the one that now hung dying in Phate's sky. Although she came to him in a humanoid guise, she was unmistakably angelic. Large, folded wings stood tall above her shoulders, imbuing her with a heavenly air of grace and authority. Her slender face had no apparent eyes, no prominent features, and her shining form emitted an aura that glowed like a distant dawn.

When she reached Herard, she spoke, her voice more beautiful than the phantom flutes that accompanied it.

"Welcome, Herard Avari Fang, welcome to Vren Adiri."

Herard pushed an appreciative smile through his tears. He sat up, clapped his hands together. "Bless you, your radiance."

"Bless *you*, Herard, it is an honor to welcome the Emperor of the Sky."

Herard looked aside. "I was never comfortable with that bestowment."

"There is no being worthier. Now, please rise."

His damaged armor creaking, Herard pulled himself from the floor. He motioned to his dying dragon. "Can you help her?"

"I will try."

The Fallen Angel lifted her glittering hands and opened them, releasing a small cloud of sparkling silver flecks that floated onto Zraz's wounded belly. The flecks widened, fused together, then dissolved into a gelatinous liquid, thus forming a Magical Veil of Mending. The angel whispered an ancient song, stirring the sorcerous forces within her soul, and the silvery veil brightened to white, became more and more brilliant...then faded away. Zraz's body heaved, and blood gushed from her wounds, its blue tint turning black as it splashed upon the gemstone floor.

"Zraz!" Herard threw himself to her side.

The Fallen Angel gestured for him to back away.

Thinking Zraz was in serious distress, Herard was reluctant to move. But when he realized she had just been purged of the poisons that soaked her, he obeyed. She gasped, rolled completely to her side, and the dark elf blades slid out of her body and clattered to the floor. All within her was pure again. The angel's song carried on until the pile of weapons sizzled, steamed, and disintegrated.

Zraz's wounds closed. She still looked ill, but no longer did she stand fully in death's door. Her breaths came easier now, the rhythmic rise and fall of her breast as gentle as the swells of a serene sea.

By the grace of the Seven Glories, she was sleeping peacefully.

Herard turned to the angel. "Thank you. Thank you, oh, blessed one."

"Herard, she has lost a lot of blood, and I'm afraid the damage to her organs cannot be fully repaired..." The Fallen Angel paused, dimmed, then with but a whisper said, "I don't want to fill you with false hope. Although she will no longer feel any pain, she will soon die."

The song of the phantom flutes sank to inaudibility.

Herard's eyes glazed over and he turned away. He stood there for some time, just staring into the distance, reminiscing. A thousand images flashed through his mind, a thousand moments and memories spanning decades of adventure, all shared with his loyal companion, his beloved friend.

And now it had all led up to this: to her sacrifice.

Finally, after many minutes, he abruptly exhaled as if he had just surfaced from a long dive. Slowly turning back to the angel, he said, "I understand. I had hoped…but I didn't expect her to live."

"In another time, I may have been able to save her, but not now. Now, my power weakens like the dying sun."

Herard cleared his throat, asked, "And what of the gauntlets?"

The Gauntlets of Loathing Light, their red runes glowing dully through the stains of Zraz's blood, lay sizzling on the floor. They quivered, ever so slightly, then rose into the air as if lifted by invisible hands. They floated over the gemstone floor and disappeared into the palace, the crystal doors closing behind them.

"You've done well to obtain them," the Fallen Angel said, "but they are my responsibility now."

"I can't believe a dark elf conspired with me, with us, I mean, with the side of light. And I cannot believe I entrusted him with… Am I mad?"

The angel lifted a finger. "He is not the only one to step from the shadows. There are others."

"Oh? Who else?"

"It is better if you do not know." She moved past Herard. "Come, let us leave Zraz to rest. Let us walk."

And with that, the two turned from Vren Adiri and made their way to the far end of the floor. Dragons glided overhead. They dipped down, cawing softly, lamenting their fallen kin. Herard was comforted by their presence. He flashed a quick look over his shoulder to Zraz, opened his mouth to speak, but had not the words.

He strode on beside the angel.

They walked to the very edge of the realm, where the floor disappeared into the billowing base of the cloudwall. Herard went right up to the wall, flicked it with his fingers. "Do you believe the gauntlets will be safe here?"

"Why are you—Ah, you were followed."

Herard nodded. He watched the small ripple he had made race up the wall, then he faced the Fallen Angel.

"Tell me," the angel asked, "was it *he* who followed you?"

Herard nodded again. "Aye, it was Warloove. It was unmistakable, his demonic dragon chills me like no other creature on Phate." Thunder echoed in the distance, causing Herard to shift uneasily. "Warloove cannot enter *here*, can he?"

The Fallen Angel looked away. "As I said before, I'm not as powerful as I once was, the light that keeps me no longer has a strong influence on this world." She whirled around, made a wide circle with her glowing arm. "This place's safety is reliant upon a sorcery I cannot forever sustain. Beholden by no god, I am not what I once was…" She hesitated, then looked back to Herard. "Ah, but I digress. Despite my weakening powers, I do not think he can enter here. But regardless, I've made arrangements for the gauntlets to be taken someplace far away…and soon."

The lines on Herard's face compressed into a map of tired anger. "Warloove is a crazed demon."

"Indeed, that he is." There was no melody in the Fallen Angel's voice now.

"That he would steal the sunsword and fight for the Dark Forever!"

The angel tilted her head in contemplation. "Warloove has little to gain from the Dark Forever's conquest of this planet. He would be one demon among billions. No, I've learned he has other plans for the sword."

Herard's face went pale. "Has he found a way to destroy the sword with the gauntlets?"

The Fallen Angel shook her head. "No. No demon, not Nenockra Rool himself, can destroy Surassis! The acquisition of the gauntlets would enable Warloove to wield the sword, not destroy it. And he won't destroy it, he needs its power intact. It is difficult to explain, but he serves an Emperor from an alien world."

"What? Another *world*?"

"His aims are not for conquest, but for survival... But alas, of these things, it is not necessary for you to fully understand."

Herard's head drooped. "Well, whatever his aims, all is happening as foretold. The night brightens with the coming of the Shards of Zyrinthia, and dark things awaken all over the world. What will we—"

"Herard," The Fallen Angel interrupted, "you must let Drinwor go."

The statement struck the man like a blow. He lifted his face, said, "What do you mean?"

"You know what I mean. It's time."

"No," Herard whispered. "How much more must I sacrifice?"

"It's time for the son to fulfill his destiny."

"No. Not Drinwor. He's so innocent, so young..."

"Herard, we both know what's at stake here. It's Drinwor's time. He was created for this. He *is* the Son and Savior of the Stars."

Herard clenched his fists. "He's also my son! *My* son!"

"Only he can wield the Sunsword Surassis," the angel persisted, "and, ultimately, only he can defeat Nenockra Rool."

Herard's face brightened with a desperate idea. "What if... What if I take the sword away? We could hide it from Warloove!"

Although the Fallen Angel had no features, Herard felt her look upon him with a sort of condescending glare. "Herard, you *know* it's no longer a question of hiding it. The Dark Forever is coming. We need the sword empowered and we need the One Life to wield it—it is the only chance for the universe." Then she turned her face skyward, let out something akin to a sigh. "You've known all his life this day would come. Drinwor must set out with the sunsword, while there's still time."

Herard lifted a hand to his weary eyes, filling the palm with tears. Yes, he well knew she was right, but in his heart he had for so long denied this day, the day fate and circumstance would plunge his son into the beginnings of a universal war, the day his son would begin a prophetic quest. He lowered his hand, said, "You know what the sword demands. You're asking my boy to die."

The angel opened her arms. "Herard, it is for the sake of all souls."

"I know, but that's little comfort for this father." He coughed, choked back tears. "First my dragon…and now my son." He turned on his heels, paced back and forth through the mist leaking from the cloudwall onto the edge of the gemstone floor. After a few seconds, he slapped his arms to his sides, said: "I can't believe the Gods have not yet returned! Will they do nothing while the Dark Forever makes to conquer and enslave the universe? To leave the fate of everything in the hands of an untested child is…well, it's unfathomable!"

"We must believe in Drinwor, as the universe does. He's more capable than you can imagine."

Herard stepped close to the angel. "Capable of sacrificing himself?"

The Fallen Angel placed her hand upon Herard's tarnished spaulder. The armor glowed, as did the shoulder beneath it, and Herard felt some strength return to his fatigued body.

"You're wounded." the angel said. "You bleed."

Herard put his hand to his heart. "I've not yet begun to bleed."

Suddenly, the cloudwall erupted with jolts of electricity, startling Herard enough for him to jump backward. Vren Adiri's guardian lightning web was flaring to life. Jagged lines of flickering blue light crisscrossed throughout the entire wall, and within moments the realm was encased in a cage of crackling energy. And then the energy discharged, blasting the storms outside with lightning bolts.

Something inside the storms was struck.

A cry like an enraged banshee's tore through the sky and a giant shadow raced across the cloudwall, darkening all the realm with a wave of dragonfear. The fear was strong enough to rattle the wills of Vren Adiri's own dragons, and even trouble the Fallen Angel herself.

Herard was terror-stricken.

"Warloove is here!" he cried. "Light One, hold onto the gauntlets, hold onto your faith, I will draw him away."

"No, my Lord, you must remain here."

It was not the Fallen Angel's voice.

Herard whirled about.

It was Zraz, who had awakened and crept up behind them unnoticed. "I will lead them away," she said.

"Zraz, no!" Herard ran up to her. "You can't, you're wounded! You—"

"Herard," she said softly, bringing her head down before his, "I'm dying. If not for the strength of the angel, I'd be dead already. Let me die in my sky. Stay here. Be safe. I will lead them away." And then she gently wrapped her battered wing about him.

Herard lifted a hand to her snout. "We've not shared a life of loyalty and trust for me to merely abandon that loyalty now. I'm going with you." He looked deep into her eyes and through a bloodshot glaze saw a blue like the one that had once emblazoned the sky.

Zraz spoke with soft, fluttering words. "Please, stay here, stay alive. And someday, when it is your time, I'll be waiting for you before the gates to the Seven Glories. Of this I swear..."

Herard began to respond, but the lightning web discharged again, louder than before. There was a sizzling bang of bolts followed by the bone-rattling shriek of the heinous beast. Herard then quickly spat his words. "I'm getting awfully tired of hearing that thing's wretched screaming!"

"I've never known Warloove to be so bold as to test the lightning web," the Fallen Angel observed.

Herard stepped back from his dragon's embrace, his expression rigid with resolve. "Zraz, *I'm going with you.* I'll not leave you alone to face *that.*" He pointed to the demonic dragon's passing shadow.

"I beg you to stay," she said, her eyes pleading.

Herard straightened, his tone as firm as his features when he said: "As Emperor, I command you to take me."

Rarely in all their decades together had he given her such a direct order, but it was well within his right. He was the Emperor of the Sky, the Caretaker of Areshria...the father of the Son and Savior of the Stars.

Zraz no longer protested. She simply knelt down and lowered a wing to the floor, thereby allowing Herard to climb atop her. He settled into the dragon saddle's torn seat and looked down to the Fallen Angel. The angel began to speak, but Herard didn't give her the chance. "I know what you will say, but I won't leave her to die alone. Not after all this." Zraz curled her head around to face her Emperor, and a single tear dripped harmoniously from each of their eyes. "And we are not yet defeated, are we Zraz?"

"No, my Lord, never."

The dragonfear waned. The lightning web's energy bolts subsided, but the web itself remained, as if wary of the lingering disquiet that still clung to the air.

"Have they left?" Herard hoped against all reason.

"No," the angel said, "they've backed off, but are still close."

"We must draw that demon and his cursed dragon away from this place!"

While Zraz tested her wings, the Fallen Angel pressed the sky's Emperor with: "Herard, the sunsword, Drinwor. What of them?"

Herard's mouth made a sorry little smile. "Oh, Lord of Light, plans are already in place. Although my heart wishes to deny my son's destiny, my conscience forces me to prepare for it. Despite what I say, I know what Drinwor is, and I know what must be done. Should anything happen to me, Drinwor and the sunsword will be taken from Areshria immediately. Warloove will not find them there. Vu Verian has already agreed to look after this. He will do as you've instructed."

"So," the angel said, "Drinwor *is* ready to face his destiny..."

Herard bowed his head in shame. "No, he is not. Although I've made the arrangements, I have not prepared my son." He hesitated, groaned as if in pain, struggled to loose his next words. "He doesn't know what he is, doesn't know what's going on. I'm sorry, but I just couldn't bring myself to tell him of his fate." He hid his face in his hands, muffling his next words. "He's so pure, so good, and I always thought I'd have more time...time to be a father, a friend... I should have told him."

"At this point, I think it is wise that we *don't* tell him."

Herard dropped his hands to his lap, looked back to the angel with narrowed eyes. "What? With the fates in motion, how can we not tell him what he is?"

"Oh, I will tell him what he is, what must be done, but I will *not* tell him of his ultimate fate, and neither must you, for he will be overburdened as it is. Should he learn of his impending sacrifice now, he would shun his destiny, thus dooming the universe."

Herard looked skyward, moaned, "I understand your reasoning, but may the Gods return, that we deceive my son…"

"When the sword is resurrected, he will learn of his fate, and he will embrace it, for by then he will have become something greater, an entity that will endure for all time. One Life, One Soul, One Sword."

"I feel horrible asking this, but what if someone tells him? What then?"

The angel shook her head. "Besides us, there is no one left who knows the true workings of the sword. What legends linger say nothing of the sacrifice it calls for."

Herard sighed and glanced to the soaring dragons. "The Gods forgive me, my son, I'm so sorry, I should have told you. I have failed you."

The Fallen Angel touched Zraz's wing, then traced her hand across the dragon's wounded side, instilling her with a comforting coolness. "You have failed in nothing, my friend. You gave Drinwor love, and that was far more than you were charged to do. Fear not for him, for once darkness is defeated, his soul will endure for all time, basking in the heavenly light of the Seven Glories, whose gates he himself will open. No, my good friend, you haven't failed. Because of you, hope burns like a newborn star."

Herard smiled weakly. "Hope…we speak of it, but is it just a dream?"

The angel pointed behind her. "Hope is the culmination of dreams."

Herard looked to where she motioned.

Beyond her glittering fingers, the palace of Vren Adiri was swathed in mist, its towers wrapped with rings of dragons. And then the cloudwall behind it disappeared, revealing a scene of deep space. Galaxies twirled in that backdrop, galaxies thick with white stars and life-bearing worlds. It was a vision, a glimpse of lighter times, of hopeful times, when all the universe flourished beneath the loving gaze of the Gods. As Herard lost his stare in that glorious vision, the Fallen Angel's voice arose with beauty again. She said, "Where there are blue skies, there is hope. We fight for blue skies."

"For blue skies," Herard whispered.

The vision dimmed, the scene of space disappearing into the clouds.

Herard wiped tears from his face and tugged on the reins. Zraz lifted her head, made ready to fly. Herard murmured, "My son—"

"Will never be alone," the angel concluded for him, "I give you my solemn promise."

Herard perked up. "Is *she* going to be with him?"

"Morning's Hope? Yes."

"How much does she know?"

"She knows what she must, as far as I can tell. But it is strange, for although she is infinitely wise, she is like your son in many ways."

"What do you mean?"

For the first time since he had known her, the angel's voice evinced a sort of uncertain wonder as she spoke of things unknown. "She is innocent, pure, despite her apparent wisdom. She knows of things long past, and yet, she cannot recall certain events of recent times. Like your son, she came to us as if out of a dream. Of her origin, I cannot tell…though I have my suspicions…" She paused for a moment, then continued. "But worry not, for I have complete faith in her. She is the best of her kind. And most importantly, I know she will be with him always," she motioned to Zraz, "just as your beloved mount will be with you."

A brief moment of silence passed between them, then Herard nodded and patted his dragon. "Let us fly."

Zraz reared.

"Farewell, brave Emperor." The Fallen Angel stepped back. "Your courage emboldens all the universe."

47

"Farewell, Angel of Light," said Herard, "We will keep the demons away from here as long as we can."

And with that, Zraz leaped into the air and flew to the cloud-wall. The lightning before her subsided and she passed through, thus leaving the tranquility of Vren Adiri behind forever...

Herard and Zraz reentered the sorcerous storms.

Cold rain stung their faces and thunder scolded them with its insistent bawl. The winds were wild, the black clouds awhirl. All around them the Mountains of Might stood as blackened heaps of gloom. It was disheartening. Having just come from the soft white of Vren Adiri, the night's darkness seemed all the more sullen.

At least the storms had subdued the outbursts of the volcanoes, Herard thought. The molten tantrum appeared to be over. The glow of the rivers of lava snaking through the rocky lands below was dim. Here and there thin plumes of ash-filled smoke twisted up through the rain, causing Herard's nostrils to twitch.

And Herard's own scent caused the nostrils of something else to twitch.

The predator dragon leaped from a nearby peak, for the hunt had begun anew. Disappointed but not surprised at the swift resurgence of dragonfear, Herard leaned forward, said, "Quickly, to the north, we must draw them away from Vren Adiri, away from Areshria."

Zraz nodded. "Yes, my Lord."

She banked, then angled upward into a thick storm cloud. She knew the demonic dragon would still be able to see her, but hoped the storm would at least hinder its pursuit. With Herard urging her on, she shot through the clouds and wove around the mountaintops, racing away from Vren Adiri as fast as she could. Her streamlined body slid smoothly through the sky, and for a time Herard was reminded of her agility of old.

But she couldn't keep the pace up for long.

When she reached the northernmost peaks of the mountain range, the effects of the Fallen Angel's mending slackened, and she slowed. She could feel the weakening threads of her mortality start to unwind. It was happening quickly.

She was dying.

With her waking eyes she began to see things as if she was in cloudform. The glister of eternity shone through the darkness, beckoning her from beyond. She could hear mystical voices—the ancient call of her progenitors echoing through time and space, encouraging her to let fail her mortal trappings and join them between the stars. After all the pain she had endured, a part of her greatly desired this, but presently she resisted the urge.

Ah, loyal Zraz.

Although her soul was for eternity, whatever was left of her life was for Herard.

The enemy dragon closed the distance between them. They could hear its grunting breaths, its flapping wings, causing the Emperor of the Sky to declare, "We must prepare to fight!"

In a weakened voice, Zraz whispered, "Until the last, my Lord..."

And then the demonic beast glided into the clouds beneath them, prowling like a shark just below the surface of the sea. It matched Zraz's every movement...then launched itself at her.

Dragonfear struck them hard, so hard that Herard jolted in his saddle.

Zraz lost her breath and sank into the clouds.

Herard yelled, "Turn about! Turn about!"

But Zraz had not the strength to maneuver, now. All she could do was curl herself into a ball as the enemy creature rose up to destroy them. Herard looked down, and for a split second whiffed the acrid stench of acidic spittle, felt the heat of infernal fires, and glimpsed a gaping maw large enough to engulf his dragon in one bite.

The maw snapped at them...

... but miraculously missed.

The terrible beast shot up past them like a geyser of satiny shadows. Zraz bumped its side as it brushed by, then unfurled her limbs as she dropped down beneath it. She fought to regain control of herself, but the last grains of the angel's healing magic sifted away, and she was drained. She continued to struggle, anyway, her wings flailing limply. Herard could bear it no longer.

She had struggled enough.

"Ease up Zraz, ease up. We have succeeded. Let go."

The demonic dragon shrieked, angled over, and came diving down.

"But...you, my Lord..."

"Let go, my friend. Let go."

She did.

She lurched, pitched and then gave herself to the winds.

The nightmare creature veered aside right before it would have overtaken her, then flew some distance away. Zraz was barely aware of this. "Herard," she uttered, "I see your son...the stars...and, oh, the light of dragons!"

And then she said no more.

Her blue eyes faded to white and her last breath left her with a discharge of lightning. Her wings crumpled and she folded.

Guardian of Areshria, protector, friend, and companion of Emperor Herard Avari Fang, the ancient cloud dragon known as Zraz died over the volcanoes rimming the Mountains of Might. She fell, another star lost to the cold, dark eternity that awaited all stars on the fringes of the dying galaxy.

The enemy dragon kept its distance, circling her falling body in a wide, descending path. It shrieked threateningly, but didn't move in for the kill. Herard hated the tease of this taunting, found it crueler than if the dragon had engaged him head on. He screamed out a challenge but got no response. He was glad the beast would never sink its talons into Zraz's living flesh, though. Now his enemies could never harm her; they could only defile that which she no longer needed.

Zraz's body began to tumble.

"This is it," Herard whispered.

His world turned over and over and all was a blur. The rush of winds sounded like a tornado and he gulped for air. Throbbing nausea pressed the back of his eyes and he fought to remain conscious—no easy task as the dragonfear itself was stifling even under "normal" circumstances. As the tumbling of Zraz's body became more severe, the fear of a suffocating death seized him. The weight of the ancient beast would be a most unpleasant thing on top of the crushing blow the ground was sure to bring. With great sadness he let go of the reins and floated free of Zraz's carcass. The wildness of his descent stabilized, and she plummeted down beneath him.

And then the world grew even darker.

They had fallen into an enormous burned-out volcano whose mouth was obscured in the storm clouds, its sides shrouded behind walls of mist and rain.

This was not by accident.

Herard and Zraz had been corralled.

But Herard was unaware of this, unaware of what was around him. He was fixated only on what was beneath him, not beside. Peering down, he could see the spindly peaks of some sickly trees reaching up for his dragon's body.

So, he was to meet his end in the arms of some forgotten forest. *So it shall be.*

He watched Zraz's corpse smash into the dead wood. The trees' boughs cracked and splintered, but their intractable trunks held straight, impaling her hide like well forged spears. She was ripped open, her organs exposed, her blue blood splashing the trees.

Herard closed his eyes and plunged in behind her, anticipating the bleak hands of nothingness. He thought of his son, and then he thought of a name: *Vu Ver*—

But before he could finish the thought, he slammed into the interior of his dragon. Her organs ruptured on impact, cushioning his fall, and he was completely submerged in blood. He groped and clawed at the inside walls of her body for a few seconds, fearing the afterlife was like drowning. But when he poked his head up from the surface and opened his eyes, he understood.

"May the Gods return," he gasped, "even in death you save me."

He gave himself a moment to recover his breath, then reached for the trunk of a dead pine and pulled himself from his dragon's bowels. He climbed to the ground, and once there, he peered through the trees, into the blear of mist and shadows that lay beyond. It soon occurred to him that there was no wind, and virtually no rain. Strange. During his fall, he recalled being buffeted by a rather strong—

What was that?

He shot a look over his shoulder. Something…moved?

He looked up to the pines, and was seized by a chill.

Their dead limbs swayed even though the air was bereft of a breeze.

CHAPTER FOUR
BLACK HOLES

Even the stars die, and ever do their selfish ghosts haunt the house of eternity.

Larian
Sky Elf, once Emperor of the Sky, now Lord of the Lost Stars

A century of torture.

That was the price to become a shadow demon.

For one hundred years the being called Drekklor had been chained to an infinitely stretching wall in some unholy dimension and tortured. For one hundred years his body had been ripped, raked, and sheared apart, only to be put back together to be mutilated again…and again…and again.

A century of torture.

That was Drekklor's price.

When the century was over, the place where he was imprisoned went silent. Well, it wasn't the place that had gone silent. *He* had gone silent. The sound of his own screaming had ceased, for he no longer felt any pain. Now he had no flesh to hurt. He had become a thing of shadow, a thing vaporous and sleek as the wind. His mind was as sharp as a blade, for the years of pain had cleared his conscience of compassion. Malice lurked behind the emotionless voids of his eyes, and his hateful heart pounded like an angry fist against the inside of his spectral chest.

He was loosed from the chains that bound him, and the imprisoning wall disappeared. Actually, it was Drekklor himself who had disappeared, but he had no sense of this—some greater power had sifted his spirit into the primary universe.

Now he floated in the infinite sea of space.

He was just beginning to consider his new surroundings when the dark matter before him started to swirl. A vortex-like circle was forming. It expanded rapidly, space rippling from its edge like water from a fast moving hull. It grew and grew to a galactically colossal size! Its interior billowed with crimson clouds of crackling vapor. A great sphere of darkness then appeared in its center.

It was a moon-sized eye of the most morbid black.

Had Drekklor still been mortal, he would have right there burst into flames, for this was the murderous eye of his master and creator, the Supreme Ruler of the Dark Forever, the Devil King, Nenockra Rool.

You see, although the Devil King was unable to tear through the dimensions himself, he had come so very close; and scattered here and there throughout the universe were these inter-dimensional windows, places where the walls between the planes of existence were thin enough so that he could see through them.

Now Nenockra Rool peered at his new creation, and he spoke with a voice that shook the very foundations of existence. It was a guttural, echoing growl, uttering a language Drekklor had never before heard, but somehow understood.

Roughly translated, this is what it said:

"My demon. From the shadows I have shaped you into a thing of silence and speed. With you I will reach into the universe and plant the seeds of my salvation. There is a thing you must do, a place you must go to. It is a place no other can reach. In the deepest pit of the darkest region of the universe, I hid the one who will deliver me from exile, the mortal necromancer, Syndreck the Brooding. You must retrieve this necromancer and bring him back to planet Phate. Give him to the deep elves so that his soul may be secured within the provided body. Then help him, Drekklor, help him raise the Dead Towers of Ulith Urn! Listen to him. Do as he bids, for he is the one who will initiate the Dark Forever's ascension into the primary universe. And then, when all is in motion, I will have another task for you…"

Drekklor wondered how a mortal held any power beyond the infinite might of his master, wondered how something so inherently weak could hold any sway in the foreseeable course of destiny. Tentatively, he asked, "Is this mortal —"

All at once Drekklor was struck with the pain of a million violent deaths, reducing him to a shriveled, screaming thing. The pain lasted only ten seconds, but the agony of those seconds went beyond the entire sum of his hundred years of torture. And then, as quickly as it had come, the pain vanished. He screamed a little while longer, though, for the mere thought of what he had just felt was enough to instill him with lasting terror.

Yes, Drekklor would never forget—though immortalized, he was *not* impervious to Nenockra Rool's ire.

The Devil King bellowed, "Foolish slave! You serve *unquestioningly!* **GO NOW!!**" Then he laughed, the echoes exploding far away worlds whose destruction tipped the cosmic balance closer to evil…

Fearing further wrath, Drekklor immediately shot out into space, leaving the inter-dimensional window to diminish and disappear behind him.

As he pulled his essence through the icy fringes of the universe, Drekklor came to know what it was to be a shadow demon. He could see for thousands of miles in any direction, in any plane of existence. He could push and pull with a strength that far exceeded his pathetic mortal body. And lo, he was fast! Unbelievably fast. He found that he could leap from star to star, instantly race across galaxies, and catch the light of suns long diffused. He had no fear of death, he was already dead. He was of the shadow demons, and he reveled in his new powers.

Eventually, he again heard his master's voice. "Dare not waste my time with your self-indulgence. I said **GO!**" (Apparently, unfortunately, his master kept him under constant surveillance. Pity. It would have been much more enjoyable to be truly free.)

Anyway, Drekklor didn't hesitate; somehow knowing exactly where his master had bidden him to go, he immediately swerved about and shot deeper into space. He sped past many things, a mere blur as he passed the many galaxies that seemed to be fleeing an incomprehensibly huge span of emptiness that lay ahead. He flew into this emptiness. Curious. There was nothing here, not a star, not a—

Wait...

There *was* something here, a lone galaxy tucked into the far corner of this forgotten part of the cosmos. Drekklor flew up to it, raced around its outskirts, viewed its dim, dying stars, its dull, decaying worlds. He couldn't help but wonder why Nenockra Rool so desired to ascend into this dead galaxy, wonder—

No matter.

He suppressed his questioning thoughts, hoping his master hadn't heard them.

When he arced around to the other side of the galaxy, he found a place so thick with darkness it was difficult for even his supernatural eyes to see. "Master," he cried, "There are holes in space, deep, black holes that swallow the stars!"

"Go to them!"

Drekklor didn't particularly want to. They were disturbing, these holes. Nothing that sank into them seemed to survive. Hmm, well, nothing save that single little speck of life Drekklor now spotted in the center of the largest one. He flew in closer to inspect it. Could it be...?

"Yes!" the voice of his master boomed from beyond.

Drekklor had found Syndreck the Brooding. A smirk lined his shadowy face. Nenockra Rool was clever indeed, hiding the necromancer in the center of a super-massive black hole. But how to acquire him? Drekklor sensed even his elusive form might struggle to maneuver in the midst of this collapsed star. He moved forward cautiously, angling around rather than flying straight in. If he could—

He was caught.

The black hole's gravity seized him like the tide of some angry cosmic ocean and pulled. At first he resisted the pull, fearful he'd be torn apart. But soon he realized he had the strength to endure such forces, and he allowed himself to be dragged deep into the black hole's depths, until finally he came right up before the Devil King's prize.

"There he is! Oh, Great One, we have him!"

Curiously, the Devil King's voice did not ring in response, but nevertheless, there was Syndreck, curled up like a fetus inside a transparent grey cocoon. The cocoon rested in a little pocket of space that had been carved into the black hole's central singularity. The body within was hairless and pale, swollen and decrepit, yet somehow alive, throbbing with breath. How this squalid bag of flesh survived where it was, Drekklor thought to be a demonic miracle.

That the Dark Forever's destiny was bound to such a piteous thing...

Drekklor shook off the thought—it was time to release the necromancer. He reached out, his shadowy hands gently curling their vaporous fingers about the cocoon.

Upon being touched, Syndreck's limbs unfolded, rupturing the cocoon's gooey cover and pulling strings of ooze apart. How fragile, how delicate Syndreck appeared to be! His eyes snapped open, revealing bloodshot orbs that shone like the shattered windows to a mind long lost to madness.

And then something unexpected happened.

Syndreck the Brooding began to laugh.

Although he had to have been in agony, though his body was in danger of falling apart, he laughed. And soon his laughing elevated to nefarious cackling. Bluish bile poured from his mouth, and this seemed to amuse him further. Gurgling and choking, he cackled even harder.

Thinking this must be the foulest mortal in existence, Drekklor was beginning to understand his master's interest in him. For although the skin on Syndreck's face was decomposed down to the bone, he could discern an unfailing confidence in the expression, detect a determination swimming behind the insanity of those eyes.

When Syndreck's laughter ceased, he spoke, his lips disintegrating beneath the weight of his words. "Through eons of agony I have waited for this day to come. Finally, I may undo that which has been so wrongly done!" He glared at the shadow demon. "Bring me to Ulith Urn!"

Drekklor's voice emitted like a vicious hiss. "No."

With bile continuing to pour from his mouth, Syndreck said, "What? There is no…no! I am your salvation, demon, I command you!"

"First, Nenockra Rool wishes your soul to be stored in a more durable body, then I may take you to Ulith Urn."

"My soul—"

Syndreck could no longer speak. A sputtering gasp came from his ruined mouth and his chin fell apart. Then he fell unconscious.

Good.

Drekklor hadn't particularly enjoyed bantering with the mortal, and he needed to leave this place before Syndreck decomposed in his arms. The demon stretched some of his own substance about the necromancer, protecting him in his own cocoon of shadow, then moved from the center of the black hole.

It was quite a struggle, squeezing through the inconceivably thick matter, but eventually he managed to break free of the black hole's gravitational influence. Starlight streaked by him and for a second he swore he heard the muffled screams of a billion dying souls. He paid them no mind and soared into the serene nothingness of space, again somehow knowing exactly where he needed to go. With Syndreck in his arms, he flew back to the other side of the galaxy, and came upon the world of Phate.

Now events take us far beneath the tumultuous surface of the Raging Sea, down, down, down to the capital city of the deep elves, which spread some twenty square miles across the abyssal plains.

This was the Kingdom of Krykoss.

The whole realm was essentially a multilevel metropolis of moonstone grottos, coral keeps, and jadestone castles, all interwoven beneath the ruling Emperor's swirling ring of black pearl palaces. Dreadship destroyers patrolled the surrounding waters, and titan crabs crept around the outskirts, for the deep elves were as guarded a race as Phate had ever seen. Steeped in dark history, Krykoss was mighty and mysterious, its further descriptions and tales worthy of many volumes themselves.

But for now, our story concerns itself with a single chamber located deep within the heart of the kingdom, in the sublevels of the sorcerers' Mystic Trident Tower. Until tonight, it had been a thousand years since anyone had occupied this chamber. Now a lone figure stood still and silent in its center. A green glow lamp hanging from the ceiling dimly illuminated the figure's face, whose violet eyes burned with the inner fires of betrayal.

Can you guess to whom these eyes belonged?

I'll give you a hint—the figure was paralyzed. And now he was forced to stare into the recesses of a mirror that was sorcerously suspended before him. It was ornate, this magical mirror, its frame decorated with carved likenesses of demons of the deep, their limbs intertwined, their mouths agape. But the figure saw nothing within, not even his glowing eyes, for the mirror's face was not silvery, but dark, and thus gave no reflection.

Reflection was not its purpose.

The mirror was a portal door.

As the paralyzed figure watched, a shadowy form substantiated in the void that existed within the frame. The form moved closer to the mirror's surface, and behold, it was Drekklor, cradling the broken body of Syndreck the Brooding.

With Drekklor's arrival, six deep elf sorcerers, arranged in a semicircle around the immobile captive, dispelled their invisibility. Scintillating lines of magic coursed down from their heads to their feet, revealing their physical forms. Unbeknownst to the paralyzed figure, they had been there all along.

The most decrepit among them stepped forward and spoke, his words babbling like a brook over the sound of his sloshing seawater robes. "We have done as Nenockra Rool commanded. The Gauntlets of Loathing Light have been delivered to he who will thieve the sunsword. Now give us this mortal."

"Will you do with him as the master bids?" Retrieving the necromancer had been no easy task, and Drekklor was suddenly hesitant to extend Syndreck's bile-lathered body out to these strange sorcerers. "Will you place his soul in a fresh body? That is what our master wishes, is it not?"

The deep elf stepped closer to the mirror, yelled, "Foolish slave! Do as Nenockra Rool commands! Give us the deliverer!"

The sorcerously tinged words helped convince Drekklor to extend his arms out of the mirror. The deep elf took Syndreck from him, careful not to pull off any of the necromancer's extremities. This was a critical time. They needed to keep Syndreck alive, for if he died, his soul could be lost to the Dark Forever, where it would be useless. They needed to act quickly, for Syndreck's body was falling apart.

"Yes, the seed of our ascension," the deep elf hissed as he gently laid the wasted body at the feet of the paralyzed figure. He looked back into the mirror, said, "Go now, dark servant, prepare the Dead Towers of Ulith Urn for his return."

Drekklor disappeared back into the mirror's void.

The elf turned to his brethren, commanded: "Exchange souls."

A single tear dripped from the paralyzed figure's eye, and he struggled to move, to scream, to do anything, for the horror of what was about to happen took residence in his mind. But he was helpless, still afflicted with a certain uncle's ironically cruel spell...

The lead elf retook his place in the semicircle and the six sorcerers of the sea raised their arms. Gurgling chants ensued, and their voices soon deepened and lengthened into a mystical song. Minutes went by. The chamber shuddered. Green smoke arose from the floor, and the light issued by the glow lamp shone through it like the stray ray of some alien sun. An hour went by, and still the sorcerers sang. Both Syndreck and the paralyzed figure trembled. Their eyes rolled to white and they simultaneously loosed a heaving sigh as blue mists seeped from their chests. Syndreck's mist flew into the paralyzed figure, and the figure's mist flew down into Syndreck. They both cried out…then went silent. And so did the elves. Their singing ceased, their arms lowered, and the green smoke subsided.

It was done.

Souls had been exchanged.

Syndreck the Brooding, Dark Mage of the Lost Age, Master of Necromancy and Ripper of Dimensions, now occupied the body of Tatoc of the Black Claw.

Tatoc now occupied the body of Syndreck.

Tatoc, feeling the pain of a wasted body that had endured a thousand year exposure to deep space, let out a horrific wail. The deep elves cringed with annoyance. They teleported him just outside the chamber, where he instantly imploded under the crushing weight of a hundred miles of seawater, thus ridding Tatoc from our tale.

Syndreck was jubilant.

He looked down at his new self, and his brightening eyes were greeted with rippling muscle and smooth, dark skin. "I'm beautiful!" he shouted to the mildly disturbed deep elves. He found himself so beautiful, in fact, he had to contain himself just to keep from tearing off a piece of his own flesh and savoring it between his gleaming new teeth. He threw back his head and belted out with diabolical laughter; laughter that perfectly suited one of his devilish, necromantic kind.

It was glorious.

He would bring the Dark Forever back into the primary universe. He cried out, "To Ulith Urn, yes, bring me to Ulith Urn!"

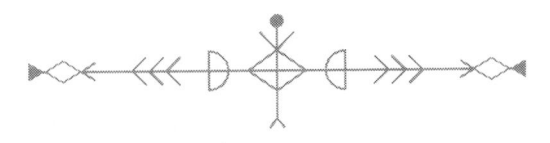

CHAPTER FIVE
ENEMIES REVEALED

No more difficult roads do we tread than the ones we walk alone.

Soviuss
Philosopher Wizard of Inkone Two

Herard was entranced by the dead trees. Their grey trunks were thin, spindly, spotted with sickly white blotches, and yet their leafless branches swayed hypnotically through an air that was as still and stale as a tomb's. Despite the rather unsettling effect the sight was having on his psyche, he just continued to stare at them. He did not understand this, for there was little left in the world that could bewitch him so.

The trees suddenly went still.

Herard flinched, held his breath.

"Are the trees toying with me?"

Never mind, he didn't want to know. He exhaled, slunk back from the nearest tree…and was enfolded in arms of mist.

A damp fog rolled in, refilled the space his dragon had made when she had impacted the ground. As the fog thickened in front of his face, Zraz became obscured, like she was fading away, fading into the cloudy realm of the Seven Glories. Herard reached out, whispered, "Goodbye, my dear friend…I will take your memory into eternity…I will mourn you forever…"

And then he could hold his wellspring of tears no longer.

He bowed his head and let his sorrow flow.

But just moments later he suppressed his tears and composed himself. Now was not the time to mourn Zraz, for his enemies could be upon him at any second. He needed to flee. He looked once more in Zraz's direction, then turned away and blindly plunged into the thickening mist.

He soon discovered he was in no shape for such a frantic flight. His legs were sore with a myriad of cuts and burns, and the fog was thicker than he had first thought. He didn't quite make it fifty feet before stumbling face-first into a tree. The collision caused him to cry out (more in frustration than in pain), and he temporarily halted his haphazard dash through this eerie forest. *Some warrior I am, defeated by some scrawny trees!* Well, maybe not defeated, but a trifle unnerved, certainly.

"Perhaps I should just find somewhere to hide," he mused to the fog.

If the fog held any opinion on the matter, it didn't share it with Herard.

Exasperated, he tilted his head back and sighed.

His gaze now drawn upward, he noticed the layer of mist didn't rise much higher than his head, and above that the sky was nearly indiscernible, a veritable void of blurry black. But then a passing break in the fog revealed a starry circle of space in the center of the darkness high above him.

"What— ? Ah, I see…" The strangeness of his surroundings suddenly made sense.

All his life he'd flown over the Volcanoes of Volcar, but never had he been stranded inside of one. He wasn't particularly fond of the feeling. It was suffocating, like being at the bottom of a great well, and he remembered that many of the old, dead volcanoes were alleged to be haunted. *What a wonderfully timed thought, Herard!*

His heart racing, he patted his chest. "Calm yourself, old man." His head still tilted back, he looked about, tried to see if there was anywhere he could climb—

Suddenly the mouth of the volcano disappeared, and a shadow further darkened a sky that was already black with stormy midnight.

Herard's racing heart skipped a beat. "Perhaps I should have died in the fall…"

The enemies were here.

The demonic beast angled down, flew the perimeter of the forest, and Herard once again felt the dreadful onset of dragonfear. The creature did a full circle, then swept inward, passing directly over him, issuing a stream of hisses that flowed over the treetops like a swarm of invisible snakes. Its whipping wings swirled the fog, exposing Herard.

Heedless of his earlier flight's failure, he launched into a panicked run.

The dragon descended, landing right next to Zraz's body, trees bending and snapping as it crunched to the ground. When it brought its massive wings in, a tremendous rush of air knocked Herard from his feet. He immediately picked himself up and continued running until the tumult of the dragon's landing ceased. Then he ducked behind a tree. He had to snicker at himself, for his trepidation with the trees was instantly vanquished by the more terrifying visage of the demonic dragon. But the brief moment of levity evaporated when the dragon let loose its awful cry. The volcano's interior amplified the shriek, and the echoing sound was so deafening, Herard had to cover his ears. The shriek sustained for many seconds, and then, after it faded, the dragon launched back into the air. Herard poked his head out from behind the tree and watched it fly away. It blotted the mouth of the volcano, then disappeared into the storms.

Had his enemies given up the hunt? Perhaps some more urgent dealings had drawn them away.

Herard exhaled with some modicum of relief.

But then came the voice…

"Herard."

So much for relief.

Herard felt the heat of breath upon the back of his neck and instinctively whirled about.

Nothing. No one. Just the fog, the trees.

The whisper came from behind again. *"Herard…"*

Herard unsheathed his sword and swung it around, the blue-flame blade slashing in a wide arc. But still there was nothing. His sword had sliced through thin air. He knew someone was close by, though, for he felt a chill like a spider creeping up his spine and his instincts screamed of an unwelcome presence.

Warloove...?

His suspicion was confirmed when again came that unmistakable voice.

"Herard!"

This time the voice boomed through the trees, and Herard thought he saw his enemy's dark form slinking toward him...or was that just some stray shadow? He couldn't be certain, for his senses had been dulled by exhaustion, and hopelessness tugged hard at his soul. He knew at least some of his disorientation was brought on by his enemy, for Warloove could press him just as hard from within as he could from without.

He had to make a choice: Would he fold or would he fight?

He decided—if this was to be a game, then he might as well play. The more time the Fallen Angel had to hide the gauntlets, the better. Let him throw aside his fear and lead his enemy on.

Summoning his courage, Herard called through the trees, "Come, Warloove, I have the Gauntlets of Loathing Light! Catch me and I will give them to you!"

"You are already caught," Warloove returned, his voice a distorted, raspy song of oddly intonated syllables.

Herard's courage waned upon hearing those words, and I cannot blame him, for deep down he knew they foretold of an inescapable inevitability.

And then the assault on his senses went from subtle to dramatic.

Suddenly, the dead Forest of Corpsewood came alive.

The sickly trees shed their illusion of ills, darkening and widening to many times their previous size. Thick branches bristling with long black leaves bloomed from their barren trunks and Herard was ensnared as if within some leafy cage. He ducked and sidestepped, tripped over tangles of roots that broke the ground in knobby bunches. An underbrush sprang out of the dirt, its dense vines twining about his legs like coils of thorny rope. He unsheathed his sword and hacked himself free, swearing he heard painful cries as he tore through the bramble. When he looked up from his hacking, slits of yellow eyes ignited in the underbrush like a thousand pairs of candles, and the fog separated into hundreds of spirits whose cloudy fingers reached for his throat. He gasped, chopped through the brush, and scampered away, periodically peeking through the forest for his enemy.

Warloove was nowhere to be seen.

Herard called out, his tone unintentionally meek. "You...you play games, but really you want the gauntlets. Come, I say, take them from me!"

Warloove's gloating voice flitted through the trees. "I have a game for you, it is called, 'Time to Suffer.'"

"I know this game, we've played it before."

"Not this one..." The voice trailed off, then struck from some other indeterminable place. "For so long I have waited, for so long I have thirsted—for freedom, for blood..."

Herard stopped running, looked all about, but still couldn't spot his assailant. He could feel the presence of his enemy closing in on him, though. Warloove emitted a cold fear, an elusive fear that twined sneakily about the soul.

"Come for me, damn you!" Herard challenged. "I have the gauntlets!" His enchanted sword glowed like a wintery blue flame and he snarled like a creature of the night himself. The eyes closest to him shrunk back and the foul foliage receded from his feet.

Good! Let the forest fear him! Here he would stand, here he would fight!

"I *will* have the gauntlets," Warloove swore, "and I will have you."

Herard readied his sword.

But nothing came.

No claws lashed out at him, no fireballs came wailing through the trees to incinerate him, and no wicked weapons came slicing for his head.

No, the attack came quietly.

A sorcerous song arose from somewhere in the trees, and twinkling blue specks of soft light fell from the sky like a storm of tiny stars, blanketing all the forest. It was remarkably…beautiful? Herard was aware of the subtleties of magic enough to know that whatever had just happened was most certainly not as benign as it had appeared. But what was this new devilry?

He awaited the imminent explosion.

It never came, but nonetheless, the attack had begun.

Herard was a victim of the Spell of Time Destruction.

The Forest of Corpsewood was trapped within a moment … and so was Herard.

Seconds stretched into hours.

Hours stretched into days.

But there were no days for the Emperor of the Sky; now he languished in one seemingly endless night…

He was always hungry, but never starving, always thirsty, but never completely parched. He was exhausted, but never slept. He crept all throughout the forest, but somehow could never reach the volcano's walls. Sometimes he'd cry out, "Warloove! Warloove!" but could never garner any response. Always he felt that hot breath upon his neck, the chill of ghostly fingers touching his skin.

Weeks rolled past.

Months went by.

Herard's tender grip on sanity slipped away. The forest sank into his soul, encapsulated his entire existence; he became as much a part of it as the specters whose eyes constantly leered at him from a distance he could never quite close. He became a specter himself, really, a shadow of the man he once was.

For him, time dragged on and on and on…

Then, finally, something came for him. The physical embodiment of the specters, perhaps, or maybe the servants of Warloove himself. They found him resting by the waterside of a small pond where he had sought some long-desired refreshment. Slowly they arose from the water, undead creatures with lava red eyes and bodies of compacted muck. A garbled speech spewed from the sewers of their mouths, and when a surprised Herard noticed them he scrambled back from the pond and leaped to his feet, the warrior part of himself returning with a burst of adrenaline. The ring of unsheathing steel echoed as he screamed, "I'm here! I'm here!"

Finally, a fight! A release!

He put all of his pent up emotions into the edge of his fiery sword as the vile things came at him. They tore at him with pincer-like appendages, slashed at him with cursed weapons. But they were no match for Herard. He was a whirling circle of violence, his blessed sword slicing through their dark substance, vanquishing many into the imperishable night. Those who survived his fury receded back into the pond…but not before they had broken his blade. The curse of some otherworldly axe had been stronger than his sword's blessing. And they had wounded him. Angrily, he freed himself from his shivered armor's jabbing embrace, slamming his chest plate to the ground, flinging his gorget into a tree, tossing his leggings into the water. His noise making became his defiance and he hollered for his enemies to return.

They didn't.

His adrenaline calmed and he quieted. The sting of fresh lacerations settled in his skin and he collapsed to his knees in the shallows, polluting the pond with his pain. His head hanging just over the water's surface, he stared at his reflection, barely recognized the face staring back. The eyes were wide with fear, the expression vague and vacant, and—

Diabolical laughter echoed through the forest.

Herard lifted his head and through blood and spittle screamed, "Betrayer of light! This is not sorcery but sacrilege! You desecrate the very nature of the universe!"

"In Corpsewood," Warloove hissed, "time is mine to manipulate. Did you enjoy your time? It was but a sliver of the centuries I have endured!"

Herard pushed himself up, stepped from the water. He reached for his sword, but of course his sword was broken, discarded, and his hand trembled in the space where the hilt had been. Nevertheless, he took a bold step forward. "Coward! Come and face me yourself!"

"This game is over...another begins..."

The forest brightened, ever so slightly, and all returned to as it was before the Spell of Time Destruction.

Although Herard had perceived the passing of a year, only a few seconds had actually gone by. *Can you imagine that? Enduring such torment for what seemed to be an entire year?* When he realized this he cried out long and loud and in frustration shook his fists at the stars.

But there was no rest nor respite.

The assault continued.

The ground began to tremble, the leaves of the trees rustling together.

"What is this, now?" cried Herard.

All about, the trees were uprooting. Tearing, snapping, crunching, they freed themselves from their soil beds, then slithered backward on their roots, which were curled beneath them like wriggling tentacles. The thorny underbrush pulled away or simply decayed into dust, and before long a prodigious clearing was formed. Then the ground in the clearing exploded. Hundreds of square feet of black dirt blasted into the air, and a ghostly castle shot up as if spewed from the bowels of the world, rocks and dirt tumbling from its sides!

Herard was pelted with grime and knocked back into the pond. He immediately scrambled to stand, and watched as the castle rose to challenge the height of the volcano itself. The structure reminded him of the Dead Towers of Ulith Urn, for its translucent outline shimmered behind a dreary blue haze while its details were shrouded in darkness, and it exuded a bone-soaking cold.

From somewhere beyond, Warloove's voice cut through the clamor. "Welcome to my home. My servants will attend to you now."

The infuriated Emperor of the Sky stepped from the pond, screamed, "Attend to me yourself!"

There was no answer, but the area continued to tremble, for the forest had not yet finished with its expulsion of horrors.

Now in revulsion Herard watched rotted corpses pull themselves from the upturned ground and stagger through the trees, wailing as they came. Spirits of the fog swirled around them, and here and there dark elf sorcerers scampered, their uplifted arms twitching with dark magic. Above, spectral forces flew down from invisible battlements, their shadow-heads topped with golden crowns, their hands wrapped about sentient swords whose blades were crafted from the blackest fires of the blackest souls. They came down before him, twirling and cackling with tortuous threats!

Herard's face looked as if it was covered by an obscene mask of horror. "Madness," was all he could say before he fell unconscious to the ground.

"Welcome, Herard."

Herard opened his eyes.

It was pitch black but for a large ruby chandelier that hung in the darkness above and beyond him. With no apparent chain holding it in place, it spun in a whirlwind, its thousands of facets glinting brilliantly with reflections of dancing red flames. The chandelier was all he could see, but enough for him to know: he was inside the Castle Krypt.

Warloove's castle.

"May the Gods return."

And then he became intensely aware of his pain—the burns, wounds, lacerations...and something else. He felt as if he was being nipped all over by a swarm of nasty little insects. He looked down, saw that his body was tightly wrapped in thorny vines similar to the ones that had earlier hampered his flight through the forest. He was held upright, his arms pinned to his sides and his knees squeezed together, rendering him completely immobile.

Warloove's voice sounded as it usually had since the beginning of this chapter, from somewhere afar. "Welcome, Herard. It has been a long time since I have entertained guests."

"Obviously," Herard muttered, "for I find your hospitality most uninviting."

Echoing laughter, then: "Ah, forgive, I am a rude host. Allow me to make you more comfortable."

"Oh, that won't be necessary; I'm quite comfortable as it is."

More laughter ensued. "But I insist."

And with that, an embroidered carpet of crimson velvet rolled out from beneath Herard's feet. It passed beneath the chandelier and crinkled up into a wide stairway. A banister of bones sprang up from each side of the steps and raced across a balcony of sinew that formed at the top. Furnishings then rose out of the blackness on either side of the carpet. There were demon leather couches and red satin chairs and little tables carved from crimson marble. To Herard's horror, decomposed corpses materialized on the couches and chairs. Though corpses they were, they appeared to be conscious, and I can assure you, they were considerably more comfortable than Herard. They seemed quite content, actually, sipping curdled wine from bone goblets, admiring the animated paintings appearing on the phantom walls—paintings that depicted demons with unspeakable names performing unspeakable acts within frames composed of dried blood.

Although a morbid calmness accompanied the whole scene, the flickering reflections of the spinning chandelier also made it appear as if it was on fire.

After all had settled into place, Herard noticed a distorted cloud of smoke hovering over the top step of the stairs. *Warloove?* Whatever it was floated down the steps, then disappeared.

"Emperor of the Dying Sky," came a whisper, now from close by. Warloove indeed.

"You demon, you murderous demon," Herard growled.

"Demon? No, not exactly."

The smoke reappeared right in front of Herard.

He flinched, closed his eyes...

But he could still see the smoke billowing violently against the black backdrop of the inside of his eyelids.

"You cannot look away," Warloove said, "you cannot hide, I can dance inside your dreams, scamper freely through your mortal mind."

Herard exhaled, and with all courage opened his eyes.

The smoke was gone.

But Warloove's presence was not.

Now Herard's mind was imbued with horrible visions, for you see, Warloove appeared to him not as a physical presence, but as a mere thought, a manifestation of his worst nightmares parading around in his mind's eye. In the span of just a few seconds, Herard envisioned shadows, then smoke, then blood and gore. Then he saw sacrifice, and dismemberment…Herard was repulsed, desperate to escape these visions! But there was no escape; the visions continuously remained in the forefront of his mind.

It was all so ludicrously frightful, he did the only thing he could think to do: he entertained a touch of insanity, and began to laugh. It was his only weapon. If he was to be a prize, a plaything, then he would deny his enemy the pleasure of his fear.

The visions subsided.

But Warloove' physical incarnation reappeared, this time clearer than ever.

Herard watched in horror as he floated toward him.

He was a humanoid-sized apparition of black smoke, swirling like some furious little tornado that emitted a constant clamor of rushing winds, ghostly whispers, and random growls. Although his face peered from behind wisps of smoke, it was clearly visible, leering, penetrating, and practically glowing with deathly white. It was an abomination that face, looking like some wicked elven child's that had been freed from a millennium of mummification to let its fine and angry features fume in a more innocent air. And, oh, his eyes! They weren't seen so much as felt, cavernous slits of black fire burrowing fear deep into the souls of those unfortunate enough to behold them.

To look at Warloove was like being stabbed by darkness, I tell you!

Herard stopped laughing.

"You are no longer amused?" Warloove said with that distorted voice of his. "Pity. I am amused…mildly. Oh, and by the way, thank you for the drink of your dragon. I've been kept so thirsty of late, even a dead cloud dragon's blood is delectable."

Herard spit, and the frothing glob of blood disappeared into Warloove's smoky countenance. "To the Dark Forever with you!"

Warloove swept up to his side. "I have been there," he answered in Herard's right ear. "It is rather stifling for my tastes." Then he curled around to his left ear. "I see you lied. You do not have the Gauntlets of Loathing Light, do you? You left them with the alleged 'angel,' I presume?" The voice shifted again, came from behind. "A futile effort, somewhat inconvenient, but daring nonetheless in your own pathetic little way. This is most unfortunate...for you..."

Herard chortled. "All beings of light will stand against you. The Dark Forever's conquest will *not* go unchallenged."

"The Dark Forever?" Warloove laughed. "I am always amused by the narrow-mindedness of mortals. What makes you think I care for the Dark Forever? I don't. Ah, never mind, you haven't the wit nor the wisdom to understand my desires. Enough. Now I offer you this: retrieve the gauntlets, give me the sunsword, and I swear your son will survive my thirst."

At the mention of his son, Herard gritted his teeth and strained against the thorns, drawing more blood from his already depleted supply.

"Please, please, save some for me," Warloove said.

Herard's rage erupted. "Don't you touch my son! I swear if not by my hand then by someone else's you'll be destroyed, sent back into the crypt you came from!"

"I ask for these items, not for your feeble threats."

"You so desire to lead demons? To take up arms and ally yourself with the Dark Forever? To conquer worlds?" Herard scoffed, "You fool; Nenockra Rool will have no one at his side."

Warloove's smoke suddenly twirled into a scalding whirlwind and he shot around to Herard's face and burned him with words. "No! *You* are the fool! I care nothing for the Dark Forever! Mindless horde!" Then he retreated, lifted up before the ruby chandelier, obscuring its fiery radiance, darkening the chamber. "Have you noticed your sun, lately, Herard? Have you? The witless sky elves! By crafting the sunsword they destroyed the very thing that sustains your fragile life. The sun *bleeds* now! Bleeds with trickles of dying light, poisoning the broken lands you so favor. Soon it will go supernova and this world will be consumed in fire. It is unavoidable. The sky elf traitors have killed us all!"

Herard hung his head, for not all Warloove said was untrue. "It was...a mistake. In crafting the sunsword, they took too much of the sun's light." He lifted his face back up. "But the sword was created to repel you demons from destroying all eternity."

"*Stop speaking as if I am one of them!*" Warloove roared.

"What are you, then?"

Warloove flew back down, and when he spoke again, his voice was surprisingly soft. "A slave of sorts…like you…but no…not like you. You are stranded whereas I will leave this world, leave you to burn as you deserve."

"You're as stranded here as any."

The grit in Warloove's voice continued to smooth out, the volume lessening to a whisper. "Have you ever dreamed of the stars?"

Herard was taken aback by the question. The words were lulling, entrancing; persuading him to let his guard down. His eyes glistened and his thoughts lingered to Zraz. "Yes…yes, I have," he said, though he didn't want to answer.

"I have, too…" Warloove paused, his mind lost in cosmic ruminations. Then, after some moments, he said, "You know there are other sorceries, other powers in the universe. Powers that can create dragons of metal. They can fly beings between the stars, these dragons. There is one such dragon here I will tell you; my master constructed it!"

Herard shook himself from mesmerization. "Then take it. Take it and fly away! Leave my son be, and leave the sword so we can fend off the Dark Forever! I implore you!"

Warloove ignored him, continued. "This metal dragon needs power to fuel it, tremendous power. There is only one thing on Phate that can empower it…one thing."

"The Sunsword Surassis."

"*Yesssss!*" hissed Warloove.

"There must be some other power source you can use," Herard pleaded. "If need be, I'll help you find it."

"There *is* nothing else."

"What if—"

"Shhh…" Now Warloove's swirling smoke calmed, and his face slowly receded into it. "I ask one more time. I give you one more chance. Give me the Gauntlets of Loathing Light, and give me the Sunsword Surassis!"

Herard pondered for but a moment, then whispered, "No."

Warloove whispered back, "Consider your son…"

"*My son…*"

Herard looked aside and noticed the chamber's decor had relented its devilish imagery. The skeletons had been replaced by beautiful women. The paintings now depicted serene vistas of golden fields. The ruby chandelier had diffused its fires and glinted softly with healthy white light.

Herard looked back to his enemy's countenance. There was no horror there now. Trying to lull him into agreement rather than frighten him into acquiescence, Warloove had dwindled into a faceless puff of grey smoke.

Truly, the demon must be desperate for the sword, thought Herard. That Warloove had no desire to conspire with the Dark Forever he couldn't be certain, despite what the Fallen Angel had told him. The vampiric fiend was afraid of dying in the fires of an exploded sun he had no doubt, but alas, it was all irrelevant, for the forces of light needed the sunsword.

Drinwor needed the sunsword.

Herard answered him the only way he could: "In the name of all the universe, in the name of all that still clings to the hope of light…no."

Warloove's frightful face reappeared, and he said, "Then know that all that I do, all the rage I unleash, is because of *you*."

Herard cried out, "Confounded demon! You doom yourself as much as any! Should you even manage to flee this world, Nenockra Rool will find you and kill you!"

"It is almost dawn, and I bored of entertaining you."

Herard was frantic. "Let me confer with the Fallen Angel. Perhaps she can find a way to set you and your master free amongst the stars!"

"Goodnight, Herard Avari Fang, and know that because of you, your son shall be drained of his blood. And know that before the sun again sets, I will claim the sword as my own."

"The sword will be gone from Areshria before the day is through!" Herard shouted in defiance.

Warloove floated closer to him. "Mortals, mortals, mortals... You think me so bound to the night? My reach extends through the darkness and into the day. My pet already makes for your palace—"

"Bastard! Stay away from my son!"

"We are through, be silent now."

Warloove enshrouded Herard within his cloak of smoke. His leering white face came right up to the man's eyes... then fell from sight. "Ah... My master has kept me very thirsty...very thirsty indeed..."

"No, wait..."

Herard's vision went dark.

He was vaguely aware of his remaining vestments being torn away. There was a pressing on his neck, a painful puncturing, and a sound like wind fleeing a hollow tunnel ensued. His body was driven into convulsions, and all the things that encompassed him were sucked into the fangs of the demonic dark elf vampire. Warloove took his memories, feelings, thoughts, passions, fears...and then took his life.

But before Herard Avari Fang's soul stepped into the eternal limbo that existed before the closed gates to the Seven Glories, he thought of a name. He projected that name out into the void, over and over again, until his mind was silenced forever.

Vu Verian...Vu Verian...Vu Verian...

Herard's blood supply was severely depleted, the blood itself with little flavor. What a shame. Such little sustenance, hence, little satisfaction. No matter. This was but a taste of what was to come.

Warloove lifted his blood-soaked face from his feasting, and what remained of Herard crumbled onto the carpet. The vampire then turned about, his smoky form twirling tighter into itself. Soon a head formed behind the white face, and a body materialized beneath the head. He had solidified, returned to his dark elf incarnation. All his physical characteristics were enshrouded, though, for the smoke on his surface continued swirling around him as an all-encompassing robe. Only his eyes peeked through the shroud, now glowing as brilliant yellow slashes.

Warloove called into the shadowy recesses of the chamber. "Slave, come."

"Yes, my Lord."

From beneath the stair, a decrepit being limped into the light of the chandelier. His black robes were tattered, shredded, their embroidered runes ripped and glowing a dull green. He stumbled toward Warloove, relying on a staff that was as crooked as his spine. His breathing was labored and loud. A painful grunt ensued with every step, for many of his bones had been broken, only to be put back together haphazardly. Debilitating diseases saturated his organs and his blood was suffused with poisons. These maladies were not natural. They were a curse.

He had been afflicted with the Ever Dying.

Such was the price for losing the Gauntlets of Loathing Light.

Such was the punishment for Morigos of the Moom!

He stepped up to Warloove and bowed, well, at least insofar as he was able. When he spoke, it sounded more as if he was trying to cough up a stuck piece of meat than he was trying to enunciate words. "What will you have of me, my merciful Lord?"

"What will I have of you? What do you think, fool? The gauntlets! Retrieve what you have lost! They are in that pestiferous palace in the sky, Vren Adiri. You have gained favor with that accursed angel, have you not? So go there and get them!"

"Yes, great one, I am willing...*though thanks to you not quite as able.*"

"What?"

"Nothing, Lord!"

"Go, Morigos, and may the Dark Forever save you if you fail me again."

"Yes, merciful one. Thank you." Morigos turned about and crept back into the darkness beneath the stair.

Warloove called after him, "Remember, if you fail me again, I will see you *burn.*"

Morigos didn't belabor himself by turning about, but paused and nodded. Then he shuffled away, practically rowing himself with his staff, murmuring beneath his breath, "I think not, *merciful* one. It will be me who watches *you* burn…"

"What did you say?"

"I still have so much to *learn*, my Lord!"

"Yes, you do. And always remember, I am more than your master, I am your blood…"

Morigos disappeared into the shadows.

Warloove walked to the center of the chamber and sang sorcery. Thin beams of white light stretched through the air, formed the three dimensional outline of a large pyramid beneath the chandelier. The pyramid emitted a peculiar hum, and the image of a bulbous grey head appeared in the center.

Warloove waited silently, obediently, as the head's oblong eyes stared down at him. They were emptier than a shadow demon's eyes, their depths as hollow as a black hole. The image flickered and the head spoke, its words coldly monotone.

Warloove, you waste precious time toying with these mortals. You share information with them and express to them your desires. Why? I've told you before, do not ever treat them as anything more than slaves.

"I know, I know."

Do you?

Warloove bowed low. "Yes, Darkis."

What am I?

Suddenly, before he could answer, Warloove was washed over with crackling red energy. It was a Robe of Soul Stabbing. Its electric arms shot through his cloak of smoke, dug through his skin, and stabbed down into his dark soul, such was their strength. He struggled through the pain of a thousand jabbing discharges to answer, "You…are my salvation, my master. Please…I beg you!"

As you punish your subjects, know that you, too, will be punished. You're wasting time. Apparently, I have understated how valuable time is. The sun is dying, the Dark Forever is coming, and my enemies search the stars for me. If they find me, I swear the wrath I suffer will be nothing in comparison to what I do to you.

"Yes, master…I understand." Warloove sank to his knees.

The Gauntlets of Loathing Light were handed to your people, and yet you managed to lose them! They must be retrieved! We cannot harness the power of the sunsword without them. Our starship awaits, Warloove.

"We will have both the gauntlets and the sword," Warloove cried. "I swear it!"

The robe's energy intensified.

Warloove fell to his hands. "Please! We have assassinated the Emperor of the Sky. The sword should not be difficult to acquire now."

The robe's energy crackled, Warloove's cloak of smoke sizzled, and his dead skin burned.

"Please, master. The pain!"

Do not fail me, or you will die...again.

Then all went silent.

The Robe of Soul Stabbing disappeared, and the pyramidal image faded.

After a moment's seething, Warloove composed himself, arose, and strode into the bowels of his castle. It was time to conceal himself in the shadows in which he had lived for a thousand years, for soon the sun would arise. But when the stars again dotted the sky, he swore he would unleash his own hell upon those who stood against him.

After the vampire left his entry parlor, Morigos stepped from the darkness beneath the stairway, and smiled.

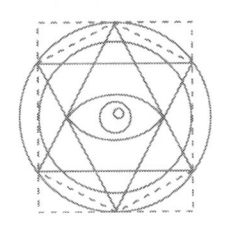

CHAPTER SIX
THE SON AND SAVIOR OF THE STARS

One may bear the ice and rain, the lash of storms, the winds of change;
but can we sanely still remain, within the eyes of hurricanes?

Petroo Chi
Lord Minstrel of the Sleeping Tombs

Vu Verian...

Buffeted by winds of unease, a lone cloud stirred in Phate's sky. It contracted, took shape, its billows smoothing over and unfurling into a pair of silvery-white wings. Talons sprang from the bottom. Tail feathers extended from behind. A large, rounded face pushed forward, revealing sky blue eyes that were wide, sad, and staring. Long ago these eyes had been radiant, but now they were dulled by the weariness of unwanted wisdom. They blinked a few times, and the transformation was complete.

The Great White Owl had awakened.

The elegant creature turned about, then coasted over the Continent Isle of Volcar.

It was dawn.

The sky was a sea of swirling colors that washed the last of the night's black away, and the Shards of Zyrinthia twinkled red over the purple crescents of Rong and the Four Apostles. The owl looked to the moons for a moment, then turned his gaze to the brightening east. There, clouds piled like snowy mountains over the glowing curve of the horizon. Embedded in the clouds' sides, an abandoned city of ivory citadels sparkled in the emerging sun, the spirit dragons soaring above it glittering in the brightening rays.

Dusk was considered magical on many worlds, but on Phate, dawn was miraculous.

The owl soared on, careful to avoid the sorcerous storms that plagued the skyways below him. How careless wizards from previous ages had been! That they'd inflicted the future with the ire of their own age, that multicolored lightning incessantly blasted the lands —

Vu Verian...

"Hello?"

What was that? A voice in his head? Perhaps a lost spirit had just called to him. It was a possibility; Phate's sky was filled with them these days. Or perhaps it was just a lingering effect from his dreams. Yes, that was probably it. His dreams had been troubling of late, haunted by those poor, doomed beings stranded on worlds that lay on the brink of the black holes. Sometimes their voices followed him into the day. There was nothing he could do about this, so he just flew on. A few more minutes went by, and the voice was gone.

Good.

Vu Verian...

"Not again!" Now this was no dream! Something or someone was trying to contact him from beyond the primary universe.

He slowed to a hover and attuned his mystical hearing to all the planes of existence. Moments later, he was able to pinpoint the voice's origin in a dimension typically inhabited by recently deceased souls. Although he couldn't yet tell whose voice it was, he could hear a message coming through. It was difficult to decipher, for the roaring racket of the Dark Forever echoed across the dimensions, thus garbling the words. He concentrated harder. The words began to clarify, but he still didn't recognize—

Vu Verian...

Wait. He *did* recognize the voice.

"May the Gods return, oh, no..."

Now it made sense.

Whatever words were coming through were the last words of his only friend. Although he didn't want to hear them, he knew he must. He sang out, invoking stronger sorcery, lifting the voice above the discordant din of eternity. There was a ripple in the air before him, and the voice spoke out clearly.

This is what it said:

Vu Verian, if you can possibly hear me, know that I have passed into the Forever. I'm sorry, my old friend, I'm afraid the sky needs you once again. You know what must be done. Save the sunsword, and please, help those who will help my son. Tell Drinwor...tell him that I will be watching over him, always.

I have done all I can for this world. I have expended all my hopes. And if there is any hope left, may you find it in the stars, may you see it in the eyes of my son, and may the Gods return your blue sky to you. Farewell, Vu Verian. Someday, when the gates to the Seven Glories reopen, perhaps we shall meet again. Farewell...

And then the voice was gone.

Vu Verian's owl head bowed before his fluttering wings, and he fought back tears. "Yes, Herard," he whispered, "I know what needs to be done." So, the time had come. The universe was now racing headlong into its inescapable fate.

He snapped his wings, and his silvery-white form streaked through the sky like a shooting star.

It was time for the son to be awakened.

Vu Verian passed into the northwestern skies of Volcar, and approached the sky elf palace of Areshria. *"Beautiful Areshria..."* There it stood upon its enchanted cloud bank, gleaming in the morning light, proudly defying the mysterious, magical pull of gravity. It was said the sorcery that held the palace in the sky was so strong it would last forever.

"Forever."

It was an impossibility, Vu Verian mused. Nothing that stood before the face of time lasted forever; not even time itself would endure thus...

And yet, he was amazed how the passage of centuries never seemed to diminish Areshria's splendor. Made of glistening white pearl, the palace's tallest tower had no rival in all the galaxy, its pointed spire pinnacling ten miles above its cloudy foundation. That it was made of something solid was sometimes hard to believe, for in certain lights, its smooth walls looked to be flowing like curtains of white silk buffeted in a gentle breeze. Giant crystal dragons carved into the four corners of the spire's base glinted with reflections of the crescent moons, and their eyes blazed like white fires.

Adjoining towers tapered down from the main one in a wide, closed ring, guarding the sprawling city that slept within. Vu Verian flew between two towers and dipped low over the city. There was little to see, for over time, the unattended cloud bank had reached up and swamped the streets with mist. The sapphire libraries and platinum halls and silver forges had all but sunk into the clouds.

"Such a shame," whispered the white owl.

Such a shame indeed. Once this place had been a sanctuary for the world's most gifted artists and musicians, the capital city to ten million sky elves, the realized vision of an entire race's labors drifting over a world of unimaginable wonders. Now it was a place of forgotten dreams, forgotten hopes. Now, like so many other places on Phate, it was empty.

Vu Verian could see its inhabitants in his mind's eye, could feel the warmth of their souls flitting through his heart. How he sorely missed them... How he sorely missed long vanished days... "Areshria," he muttered, "the one-time Spire of the Sky, a jewel in the eye of a bygone world."

He flew across the city, curled around to the outside wall of the main tower, then flew miles up its side, passing through flocks of vaporous spirit dragons as he went. He ascended to the topmost terrace, and touched softly to the floor, arcane songs slipping from his beak.

And for the second time this morning, Vu Verian transformed.

Once as large as a small dragon, his owl form now shrank to humanoid size. His feathers smoothed over into silky skin and long satiny robes. Luxuriant hair sprouted from his head to flow straight down his back. The features that formed on his face were both delicate and strong. Everything about him was pristine white—everything except his eyes. Slit wide beneath a gently sloping brow, they remained a solid sky blue, beautiful wells of enduring sorrow.

Here was the true incarnation of Vu Verian.

Here was the last sky elf on Phate.

Now he observed things from the highest viewpoint in the world. The roof of clouds below him looked like a carpet, stained here and there with storms. The horizon's curve was so dramatic, the world looked as though it was rolling away from him. Had the crescent moons been steps, he felt as if he could have lifted his foot over the railing and climbed them to the stars.

It was a singular, solitary feeling, being alone above the clouds—a feeling he well knew. He silently gazed at the sky for a short while, just standing there as wind whipped hair into his face. Eventually he slid his hair aside and said, "Herard, how could you leave me?" Then he turned on his heels and strode to the terrace's twin crystal doors.

The sigils of protection inscribed in the doors' molding brightened upon his arrival, but dimmed just as fast, recognizing the spirit of the one who had placed them there.

Vu Verian grasped the latch with a quivering hand.

He began to turn it...then stopped.

He closed his eyes, brought his head to rest gently upon the door.

"Damn," he quietly swore.

Then he lifted his head and conjured his Cloak of Winds, a mystical mantle that masked him within an invisible shroud. With a resigned sigh, he opened the doors and slipped inside like a fog come to darken a forest wrapped in sunny dreams...

Sleep.

Night after night it had escaped Drinwor Fang, and this night had been no different. Try as he might, he could find no respite from tireless thought. How the body could be so exhausted, yet the mind so filled with energy, was beyond him. Why must one peruse the meanings of existence and mortality when one simply wanted to sleep? What was it about the night that brought out these inner demons? It was torture, really. Each sleepless night seemed like a little eternity in itself.

Sleep! Please! he screamed in his mind.

He grumbled and tossed about, ending up in a position so awkward it ensured he would stay wide awake while his left arm went completely numb. Seconds later, he grumbled again and flipped to his other side. Oh, this was perfect; now he was even more uncomfortable! His right arm, bent in a most awkward angle as it pinched beneath his chest, began to tingle with the onset of numbness.

He was defeated.

Sleep would elude him again.

Yes, my earthling reader, sleepless nights have haunted countless souls in countless ages on countless worlds... In this, at least, you are not alone.

Anyway, Drinwor rolled onto his back and propped his head upon a stack of silk pillows.

"All right," he said to the dark, "you win. I don't need sleep... no, really...I'm fine."

An hour went by.

"Still awake."

Another hour. "Is it the end of the universe yet?"

Another.

"Suffering...sleepless...stupidity..."

He yawned. And then, finally, just as the sun broke its crimson beams across the horizon, just as the morning began to snuff the light of the stars, Drinwor's mind hushed for something longer than a moment, and he immediately fell into deep dreams.

Only to be awakened mere seconds later.

Someone was there.

Drinwor sat up with a start. "Hello?" He blinked, rubbed his eyes.

The space beyond the foot of his bed glittered with tiny sparkles.

Drinwor smiled through a yawn.

The Cloak of Winds.

"Vu Verian! It's been a long time. Wha—"

"Forgive the intrusion Drinwor, I didn't mean to startle you." The mystic sky elf loosened the magical cloak, and his outline appeared—a thin, clear light, like that of the crescent moons', surrounding the sparkles within his frame.

"No, you didn't startle me…appearing out of nowhere at the foot of my bed…" Drinwor looked around, "…at dawn." He yawned again. "No, not startling at all…"

"I apologize."

The Cloak of Winds disappeared. Vu Verian, in full sight now, brought his arm up in front of his chest and bowed.

Drinwor shook his head, stretched his limbs. "Please don't do that, it doesn't feel right. I mean—aren't you at least a thousand years older than I am?"

"You needn't remind me."

"How long have you been standing there?"

"Not long." *Watching you in your last moments of innocence, my dear prince.*

"That's a bit…unnerving." Drinwor shot him a playfully peculiar look, then smiled.

Vu Verian couldn't help but smile, too. It was nice to break the seriousness that perpetually plagued his face these days; but unfortunately, the expression subsided as quickly as it had appeared. How in the Gods' names was he supposed to proceed? *Oh, Herard!* His heart quaked and his nerve faltered. The voice that next fled his lips was not the commanding voice of an immortal, but the quivering voice of one unready to pass on such terrible tidings.

"Drinwor, I have some unpleasant things to tell you." He cringed. Unpleasant? That was the understatement of the ages.

Drinwor, still barely awake, stepped from his canopied bed. "Oh?"

"I'm afraid so…" The words fell like tears.

Vu Verian went silent, wishing he could forever forestall the coming moments. He just stood there, taking in Herard's beloved son one more time before his terrible news changed the boy forever…

Drinwor's large midnight blue eyes shone like moonlit pools from his young elvish face. His features were smooth but strong, recalling the purer beauty of elves from the distant past. His skin was greyish-black, his silver hair like wisps of starlight curling over his shoulders to fall halfway down his back. Beneath his black tunic, his limbs were long, his muscles sleek and tight. His natural posture had him leaned forward, making him look something like a supernatural panther ready to pounce. His expression held a childlike quality that belied his animal-like appearance, though, and one could say his beautiful eyes glittered with hope.

He was a creature of the twilight, a reflection of the evening, an echo of emerging stars.

He was a dusk elf, the only one of his kind in all the universe.

Innocently unaware of what he was, of what was in store, he looked on Vu Verian with a hesitant inquisitiveness.

But now Vu Verian could bear to look on him no longer. He turned away, said, "Get dressed and meet me on the terrace." Then he stepped outside, leaving the crystal doors open behind him.

The harsh light of Phate's sun filtered into the room, and Drinwor squinted. "Uh...all right, we'll talk there."

Well, Vu Verian was acting especially odd, Drinwor thought. Had his father sent him here to lecture him on how to act like a prince again? It had been a while since that had last happened, but he wouldn't be surprised. Drinwor knew he'd been acting strange of late—kind of distant, kind of lazy. He couldn't help it. He hadn't been sleeping, and his nightly ruminations had been chasing him into the day. Something was tugging at his soul, some growing desire to fulfill some purpose or find some greater meaning to his life.

"Oh, I've just been thinking about...everything."

He laughed at himself. Ah, perhaps these feelings had simply been brought on by loneliness. Or perhaps it was because the older he became, the more he yearned to know about his mysterious origins.

That was something that had always bothered him.

You see, Drinwor's very existence was an enigma. No one had ever been able to tell him where he'd come from, nor could anyone recollect the exact moment he'd appeared. He hadn't been born and he hadn't arrived. One day he was simply there, in Areshria, with his father. Upon reflection, Herard had never for a moment questioned his inexplicable appearance or existence, never doubted that he had anything else to do but to take him on as his own son. Drinwor was accepted into his home and into his heart. For Herard, it was a primal calling, an instinct for unconditional love that had been bestowed upon his soul by the universe itself. *Oh, blessed Herard!*

His father.

"Yes, my father, who's never here! Back to the loneliness..." He sighed, grasped the silver sword-charm dangling from a chain around his neck. It was glowing blue, just like the sword it mimicked. Curious. He wondered where his father was now, wondered—

"Drinwor? Are you coming out here?"

Drinwor blinked, looked to the terrace.

Oh, yes, Vu Verian. *Might as well get the sky elf's lecture over with.*

"I'll be right there!"

Drinwor stepped to the ivory bureau near his bed and pulled a small black bundle from one of its drawers.

This was his usual attire, his demonskin armor.

He brought it to his chest, and with but a whispered command it unfolded over his limbs. Smoothly accentuating his muscular frame with shining, leathery black, it left only his head uncovered (and his sword-charm, after he pulled it from the choking neckline). Large blue sigils glowed on the chest, imbuing the armor with magical protective powers—powers Drinwor had yet to discover...

Now fully garbed, he breathed in deeply, exhaled, and moved onto the terrace.

By now, the bud of dawn had blossomed into morning, and the sky was a solid bloody red. An energetic wind was pushing a continent of clouds past Areshria, and the terrace flickered with passing shadows. Drinwor looked across the way, spotted Vu Verian leaning on the railing, and strode up to join him. As he approached, he was struck with a strange sensation. He realized he had dreamed this scene not moments before, in the ten seconds or so he'd actually slept. He gazed at the sky and thought what an odd morning this had been.

The two elves stood in silence for some time before Drinwor asked: "Soooo...how are things in cloudform?"

Vu Verian smiled, then turned to the younger elf. "You know, your father hated it when I gave you that demonskin. He thought it made you look too much like a dark elf." He laughed. "It took quite a bit of convincing, but I assured him it was safe, and despite its vile origins, that armor could protect your life. He finally agreed to let you have it (obviously), on the condition that I would take it back should the first sign of any demonic possession take place." He laughed again, shook his head. "He was rigid, your father, but also accommodating."

Then Vu Verian looked away, his face growing as grey and cold as the rain that fell miles beneath them. His tone lessened to a whisper, and he said, "Drinwor, your father never told you why he last left Areshria for the surface world."

"Well, he rarely told me anything of his quests. But he did seem especially nervous this time, almost like he was afraid."

"Yes, I'm certain he was."

The young dusk elf patted the railing anxiously. "Please tell me what's going on."

"Many things, but for now, you must know that there are evil forces after your father's sword. The Dark Forever wants Surassis."

"The Dark Forever? Why?"

"Because the demons are coming, and the sword poses a great threat to their ascension."

"My father said some things, said a great war is soon to begin, a war like the one centuries ago. But I didn't know his sword was involved. That's rather unsettling to say the least."

"Yes, well, your father went to retrieve an artifact that would have allowed the demons to use the sword against us. But he..." Vu Verian's voice trailed off. He stepped from the railing, walked some paces away.

Drinwor swiveled at the waist, glanced over his shoulder. "Vu Verian, what is it?"

"Your father..."

Vu Verian's breathing quickened and his body trembled. He couldn't bear to hold the terrible truth in any longer, but Gods, he couldn't bear to tell him either! *I have to tell him!* "Drinwor, your father wanted you to know..."

The dusk elf sprang forward, grabbed the sky elf's sleeve. "Something's happened."

Vu Verian gasped. "He said he loves you, and ever will he watch over you."

Drinwor shook his head. Nauseating chills seized him and he moaned. "No... What are you saying? What do you mean *'he'll watch over me?'* I don't understand." He let go of the sleeve, stumbled back into the railing.

Vu Verian looked straight into his eyes. "Drinwor Fang, you are now the Emperor of the Sky."

"No...no... I...I can't hear this. May the Gods return, this isn't happening."

Drinwor crumpled to the floor as if his heart had just burst in his chest. The glorious light of his spirit dimmed as if someone had snuffed the fires of his life force. The universe felt his pain and, for a split second, the sun darkened, casting a planet-sized shadow that swept all across the surface of Phate. Of all the scars Drinwor would ever receive, of all the pains, triumphs, and losses that destiny had in store for him, nothing would ever affect him so much as the soul-crushing revelation of the loss of the man who had lovingly received him as his own son.

Drinwor Fang was broken, with some parts of himself to never fully mend. His mouth opened, but there was no sound. His eyes searched, but they saw nothing. He went limp, his body a shell of emotional pain.

Vu Verian stood over him, silently cursing the cruel neutrality of fate. He had no sorcery to stem the flow of tears; all he could do was stand there and watch him.

After some time, Drinwor stirred from his shock. He was still lying flat on his back, liquid crystal tears rolling into his silver hair and glinting it. His lips parted and a barely audible whisper escaped him.

"Vu Verian...how?"

"He was murdered by Warloove."

"Who?"

"Warloove, the Lord of the Dark Elves, a thousand year old demonic vampire who conspires with the Dark Forever to steal your father's sword. He's the one."

"How do you know?"

"I know." Vu Verian's voice was stern. He didn't want to fill the dusk elf with any false hopes. "Your father made contact with me. He said he'd do that if…if it happened."

"What of Zraz?"

"I don't know, but I have neither seen nor heard from her. I can only imagine she joins him in the Forever. You know her, she never would have left his side."

Drinwor sat up, crossed his legs, and hung his head over his lap. "A worse nightmare I couldn't have had if I'd slept." He sat like this for a few more moments, grappling with his tears. Then he lifted his face and through gritted teeth said, "Where is this…Warloove?"

Vu Verian shook his head. "No, Drinwor, you mustn't even think of it! He is a creature of unending power, a servant to forces beyond your reckoning. Now is not the time for revenge."

"Oh? There will come a time…"

"Perhaps. But not now."

Drinwor twirled his sword-charm through his fingers. "You claim I'm the Emperor of the Sky? How can this be?"

Vu Verian knelt, gently grasped the grieving youth by the chin. "You were the Prince of Areshria, the heir to the sky."

Drinwor shook his face from Vu Verian's grasp. "No, no, it should be you, I know nothing! I can't!"

"My time has long passed," Vu Verian said. "It is you. As your father wished, it is you. And," he added, "only the Emperor of the Sky may keep the Sunsword Surassis."

"What?"

"The sword is yours now."

Drinwor wiped his eyes. "It is?"

Vu Verian stood up straight. "There is much to tell, but little time. The enemy will soon be coming."

"Coming where? *Here?*"

"Yes. We must take Surassis and leave Areshria today. It is not safe for us here any longer."

"Leave? Today? Vu Verian, I've never been away from this palace in my life! I don't know what to do with the sword!"

"I know someone who does." Vu Verian took a step back and conjured the Cloak of Winds. "Stay here, I'll return in a moment." Then he faded behind a cover of dwindling sparkles.

"Where—" Vu Verian was gone before Drinwor could finish the inquiry. "This is all insane!" He pushed himself up from the floor and went back to the railing, his gaze wandering about the sky. *Is this all real?* It didn't seem so. It couldn't be. His father dead? The Sunsword Surassis entrusted to him, the newly proclaimed Emperor of the Sky? It was all unimaginable. And now, after all this, Vu Verian was going to have him abandon his home. If his father had been killed out there in the world, what chance did he have?

He stood there in disbelief, hoping it was all a dream.

I wish it was. For his sake, I wish it was…

After a couple minutes, Vu Verian reappeared. His magical cloak came down from around his tall frame, and he stood there with his hand outstretched. Hovering inches over his palm was the most exquisite sword hilt Drinwor had ever seen.

"The Sunsword Surassis," Vu Verian proclaimed, "the pinnacle of sky elf weaponry."

Drinwor, despite his grief, couldn't help but to be astounded by it and whistle with awe. "I've never actually seen it."

The hilt was made of a burnished white-gold that emitted a glowing enchanted aura. Spots of color shone upon it, for jewels of incalculable worth were set perfectly smooth within the concave impressions of the ivory finger grips. The pommel was a large round crystal grasped by a golden dragon claw. Drinwor's eyes were drawn to that crystal, for it held the most astonishing detail of all: inside it was trapped the lifeless form of a miniature solar dragon.

It *was* the legendary Sunsword Surassis.

"You must take it," Vu Verian said.

"If you say so."

The dusk elf drew in a breath, reached out with his hands, and grasped the handle. He was instantly filled with a tingling warmth. And even though the handle was much longer than the width of both of his hands, it fit perfectly into his palms. After turning it over, he noticed a wide indentation in the top of the finger guard. That had to be where the sunfire blade erupted from, he surmised. The craftsmanship was astonishing. He imagined the countless demons the sword had vanquished, and wondered if it had yet more to claim.

"Good," Vu Verian said, "it has taken to you, as your father knew it would. You must keep it secret, though. Put it into one of your armor pouches."

Drinwor slid the sword into a slit in his demonskin. Although the pocket's mouth appeared as a barely discernible crease lining the outside of his upper thigh, the space within it could hold the contents of a large chest without encumbering him in the slightest. With the sword secured, he looked up to Vu Verian. "Well, I still can't believe you're going to trust me with this! I wouldn't! I'd—"

He was startled to silence by an uneasy pang in his chest. At first he attributed it to the anxiety brought on by his grief and shock, but then he had a sinking feeling something else was the cause. He looked around. The large group of clouds had passed the terrace, and the sky was now clear all the way to the sun. The sun... Something was in front of it. He squinted, cupped a hand over his eyes.

"What are you looking at?" Vu Verian asked.

Drinwor pointed. "You don't see it?"

Vu Verian moved beside him and looked outward. The first thing he noticed was a large cluster of daytime stars flickering over the five moons. "Ah, those are the Shards of Zyrinthia, the shattered remains of our sister world. Every few hundred years they rain like cosmic fire upon our own world." He sighed. "As foretold, their coming has coincided with the ascension of the Dark Forever."

Having no idea what Vu Verian was talking about, Drinwor shook his head. "Vu Verian! I'm not looking at the stars. What is *that?*" He shook his finger, trying to emphasize where he was pointing. "There, right in front of the sun."

Vu Verian saw it. It was a wavering dot, difficult to stare at for too long with the sun glaring behind it. The sky elf sang a sorcerous little song. His vision darkened and tightened into a funnel, and the distance between him and the mysterious thing seemed to close. Now he saw details... He saw...

Wings.

Huge, black wings.

He dismissed his sorcery, muttered under his breath, "May the Gods return, already?"

Drinwor didn't think Vu Verian could turn any whiter than he already was. "What's going on now?"

"I had hoped we would've been safe at least until nightfall, but apparently not."

"What in the Seven Glories is it?" Drinwor asked.

"It's Geeter." Vu Verian said, "and I can assure you—it is not from the Seven Glories."

"It's a what?"

"Its name is Geeter. It's a Greater Demonic Dragon. It's Warloove's mount."

"Warloove," Drinwor growled.

Although still relatively far away, Geeter was no longer a little dot, and Drinwor began to suspect that he was actually quite huge. And he was oh, so black! as black as a night sky in a starless dimension, black enough for his details to be lost in his own shadows. And strangely, the closer he came, the blurrier he appeared...and the more terrifying. Unable to stomach looking upon him any longer, Drinwor turned away.

Vu Verian shouted, "We must get you out of here!" He opened his fingers, and a small object appeared in his palm. "Take this, put it on." Drinwor was given little choice, for while Vu Verian spoke, he grabbed Drinwor's hand and slid a silver ring upon his finger.

Geeter's wicked shriek cut through the air.

Drinwor was struck with unholy dragonfear.

It petrified him like nothing in his life ever had. His heart skipped a beat and he fought just to remain conscious.

Vu Verian yelled, "Drinwor!"

The dusk elf flinched with fright. For a moment, he had forgotten the mystic sky elf was there. He composed himself the best that he was able, and said, "What?"

"I'm going to ask you to do something that will likely scare the light right out of you."

Drinwor pointed to the approaching dragon. "Scare me more than that?"

Vu Verian's skin turned bronzy and his eyes shimmered, reflecting the spells brewing in his mind. With a deep voice he said, "I want you to jump off this terrace, right now, immediately."

Of course, Drinwor thought, why not? His father was dead, he had been entrusted with the most powerful weapon in the world's history, a giant black dragon-thing was coming to kill them, and now Vu Verian was asking him to leap from the terrace of his home and plunge countless miles to his death upon the face of a hostile world he had never set foot upon.

Fantastic.

"Vu Verian, I really wish you'd left me alone today!"

"I've given you a Ring of Floating, you'll be safe, but you must jump, NOW!"

Although Vu Verian's magically enhanced command didn't quite hold the conviction to convince Drinwor to jump, the creature's second scream tipped the argument toward the mystic's side. The scream was so shrill and piercing, it hurt Drinwor's ears.

The dusk elf sat on the railing and swung his legs over the side.

Insanity.

He looked back at Vu Verian to make one final plea.

He didn't get the chance. Vu Verian yelled at him again. "Go, now! I won't be able to hold it off for long! Jump, Drinwor! I'll meet you on the ground, but by the Gods, JUMP NOW!"

Vu Verian sang a song that belied his usual sweet voice, a song that riled up the strongest reservoir of power within him. He waved his arms wildly about, and sections of his body flew in and out of sight as the Cloak of Winds flailed around him like an enraged ghost.

Drinwor couldn't bear to look upon him any longer. He looked away, cast his gaze down into the mass of sorcerous storms swirling below. Well, that sight wasn't much better! Forks of scarlet lightning illuminated the black clouds with explosions of electrified fire, and thunder's booming bellows accompanied the shrieking of the Greater Demonic Dragon.

Quite an introduction for Herard's son into our story, wouldn't you say?

"Oh, father, help me," Drinwor whispered, "this is ludicrous." He grasped his glowing sword charm, closed his eyes, and pushed himself off the railing.

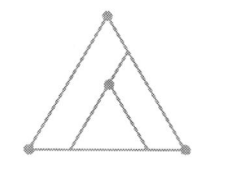

CHAPTER SEVEN
THE WALLS RESURRECTED

It is the selfishness of evil that allows it to survive, for the foolishness of good says to fight until one dies.

Syndreck the Brooding
Master Necromancer, Emissary of the Dark Forever

Drekklor knew if the sun had the strength it would have burned his shadowy form from around his evil soul as he burst from the surface of the Raging Sea. But the sun was weak, dying. The effects of its radiance were negligible. Light leaked from it like blood from a lingering wound. It seemed as if every star in this portion of the galaxy was wounded thus. Here, light was struggling to merely survive. Here, the most brilliant stars were black…at least in the eyes of a demon.

Drekklor scoffed at the sun and soared onward.

He soon came to the Cliffs of Moaning Wishes, which were crowned with the Dead Towers of Ulith Urn.

"So, here is the intended lair of the necromancer! Not so impressive…"

Well, perhaps not so impressive to a shadow demon; but to some, the sight might have been a supernatural marvel. Although it was morning, the compound was shrouded in a deep dark, as if the remnants of night itself clung to the spectral walls. A thick concentration of sorcerous storms was about, and the wavering blue outlines of the ghostly towers were lost within.

Drekklor sped up over the cliffs, then slowed and slunk through the wraith-filled winds.

As he drew closer to Ulith Urn, his supernatural eyes discerned a Glyph of Multiversal Guarding—an invisible, sorcerous semi-sphere that covered the entire compound. He had to be cautious. The glyph itself wasn't impassable or inherently dangerous, but if disturbed, its creators would be aware of his coming.

But Drekklor was a devious one.

As he approached, he condensed his shadowy form, became thinner…and thinner…and thinner…

Now he was but a black needle.

He pierced the glyph with a quick jab, then filled in the miniscule hole with his own substance. A tiny ripple coursed over the glyph's surface as he passed through, but no sorcerous alarms sounded. The tiny hole sealed itself behind him, and he was inside. He enlarged, reassumed his favored demonic shape, and flew unchallenged toward the towers.

"Yes, my demon, go! Raise them!"

Drekklor wasn't certain whether his mind played tricks on him, or if he had actually heard the voice of Nenockra Rool urging him on from the other side. Nevertheless, he was ever haunted by that voice, haunted by the vision of that moon-sized eye glaring at him, demanding his obedience. And always he remembered the ten seconds of agony.

Whether it was his master or his own conscious commanding him, it mattered not. He obeyed.

He flew to the spectral towers and saw what was left of the actual physical ruins. Splintered stones lay everywhere in dusty, spider-ridden heaps; piles of twisted skeletons were scattered about; and lonely ghosts flitted where halls had once stood. When the ghosts saw Drekklor, they thought he was the visage of death finally come to take them to the Forever after their thousand year wait in limbo. Drekklor paid these lost souls no mind. They mattered to no one.

He flew deeper into the compound, and made for the heart of the towers.

He came to a cracked round chamber that sat atop a particularly large pile of rubble. He descended through the large break in its domed peak, and came to hover over a wide, flagstone-capped platform that resided in its center. He remained there for some time, just wondering what in the Dark Forever he was supposed to do next. "Now I would actually appreciate Nenockra Rool's guttural words of instruction!" he grumbled. But no words came.

An inexplicable compulsion struck him, though, when he looked up through the broken ceiling and saw the twinkling crescents of Rong and the Four Apostles shining through the storm clouds.

The sight of the moons compelled him to sing.

What was this? What were these strange sounding words? Incantations? Whatever they were, they flowed through him easily and quickly. He became aware that these words carried some influence, for as he continued singing, thick, bright shafts of moonlight shot down through the broken ceiling, immersing him. Not particularly comfortable in this light, he backed out of it. Henceforth, the light intensified, splashed like a waterfall onto the platform. It streamed across the floor, leaked out the cracks in the walls, and spread throughout the ruins. Before long, the entire compound was flooded in a gleaming lake of liquid moonlight.

And so it was that Drekklor learned he could utilize sorcery.

He tilted his head back and hissed, "Thank you dark master for yet another glorious gift! Now I understand the obsession of wizards and warlocks. The wielding of magic is gloriously satisfying, like…like the unleashing of lust upon a long-desired lover! Thank you, oh great one!"

And now, submerged beneath the moonlight lake, the ruins of Ulith Urn began to rumble and shake. Above, the ghostly walls began to brighten and solidify. Enraptured by his newfound power, Drekklor sang so loudly he screamed. His own chamber shuddered and lifted into the air, the tower beneath it resurrected and rising out of its own moonlight-slathered ruins. Everything was being rebuilt. Where rubble once reigned, twisted towers of iron and onyx now arose. Where wreckage had piled, temples took shape. Stone blocks stacked themselves, splintered beams straightened in reforming rafters, and moonlight filled in every crack, crevice and imperfection, solidifying into whatever substance it had repaired.

The resident ghosts were terrified. They fled down into newly hollowed dungeons, their confused moans bouncing off the restored walls. And then…

It was done.

Drekklor went silent.

The moonlight dimmed, the lake of liquid light receded, and the rumbling ceased.

No longer dead, the Dying Towers of Ulith Urn had awakened after a thousand year sleep. The surrounding sorcerous storms, half-existing in another dimension, slipped through the Glyph of Multiversal Guarding unimpeded and, as if in celebration, illuminated the place with lightning.

Drekklor looked back through the hole in the domed ceiling. It was smooth now, perfectly circular. Rain came through it and he could see the crescent moons shining softly through the clouds. "Fascinating!" Before this, he never would have considered the moons for allies. And they still had one more little favor to impart upon him.

While he gazed through the hole, moonlight glinted the wavering spaces just above his tower. *Ah, yes, the glyph!* He'd almost forgotten about it. Using his newfound gift of sorcery, he sang another song, and perverted the glyph's power into something more useful. The invisible semi-sphere thickened to translucency, turned into a magical shield that could protect Ulith Urn against high energy attacks. And it was rendered useless to those who had created it; it would never again alert anyone of anything.

Now that all was prepared for the coming of the necromancer, Drekklor sent these words into the winds: "Ulith Urn stands ready."

The sorcerously tinged words carried over the cliffs, plunged into the Raging Sea, and fled far down into the abyss. Soon they echoed in the ears of the deep elf sorcerers who had secured Syndreck's ancient soul in Tatoc's young body.

Moments later, black flames erupted on the platform in Drekklor's chamber. The flames flickered violently, grew denser, then receded and solidified into something shaped like an elf.

Here was Syndreck the Brooding.

The necromancer was home.

Finally, after a thousand years of insufferable torment in the bowels of a black hole, he was home.

"The towers are raised?" he asked the shadow demon.

Drekklor nodded and hissed, *"Yesssss."*

His uplifted arms still flickering with black fire, Syndreck tilted his head back and laughed. Now he was truly free! Free within the smooth wrap of taut, young muscle. Free within the beloved walls of a place he never dreamed he would see again... No, that wasn't true, he *had* dreamed of it, every day, every waking moment for a thousand years. He had dreamed of it and, finally, he was here. He looked upon the shadow demon and was again seized with uncontrollable laughter. He laughed until the laughter became weeping, then fell to the platform, grasping at the cool, slick stone.

He fell unconscious right there, and dreamed of wonderful nightmares...

Syndreck stood on the edge of a mile-high cliff that overlooked a sea of writhing souls. Waiting in the sea was an army of a billion demons. A billion—all his to command. Above them, floating through clouds of fire, came massive fortresses of obsidian, with hundreds of thousands of demonic dragons encircling them.

Here were the armies of the Dark Forever.

And appearing on the horizon, his black silhouette encompassing the whole of the sky itself, was the supreme ruler of it all, the Devil King, Nenockra Rool. In eternal servitude, Syndreck fell groveling to the ground. Blood poured from his mouth, preceding words enwrapped within the shaky timbre of ecstasy. "Master, I will open the gate between this world and the Dark Forever. I will lead your eminence's armies to the primary universe, where you will conquer time and space. Before this system's star dies, I will tear the skies apart! I swear it..."

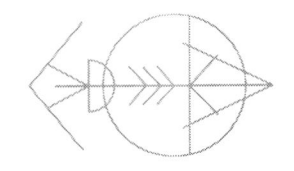

CHAPTER EIGHT
UPON THE FACE OF PHATE

Some men must first pass through the depths of hell before ascending to heaven.
Garg Ogregone
Part-time mercenary, full-time drunk patron of the Hog Harrow Inn

His heart a heavy stone of sorrow, his limbs numb with dragonfear, Drinwor Fang tumbled from the only place he had ever known, his sacred sanctuary and home, the pearly palace of Areshria.

"Oh, how could my beloved sky turn on me so?" he called to the wind.

But the wind only roared back at him like some vengeful banshee, then stole the air right from his mouth. That didn't stop him from yelling, "Brilliant idea, Vu Verian!"

Breathing was a chore, and all was blurry. The storms appeared as naught but flashing black smears, for his tumbling rolled him over ever faster. A wave of nausea passed over him. His sweat was freezing, yet it burned the skin beneath his armor. His hair speared the tears from his cheeks as soon as grief and fear pushed them from between his fluttering eyelids.

"*This is suicide!*"

Indeed, it would seem that it was.

But the farther he fell, the more the effects of the dragonfear diminished, and a portion of his panic abated. Soon his head cleared enough for him to rationalize that it was time for him to at least try and control his wild descent.

Slowly he spread his arms wide, cupped his hands, and, after a short struggle, managed to straighten his legs. He stopped tumbling. Now he faced upward, his body splayed on a bed of more agreeable winds. Breathing came easier, and he voraciously inhaled mouthfuls of air. Feeling a little bit better, he pulled the hair from his face and looked up.

He saw the bottom of Areshria's cloud bank...and the Greater Demonic Dragon approaching it.

"So much for feeling better."

The dragon still appeared much as it had from the terrace—a giant, wavering black blur that looked awfully out of place in the morning sky. The visage was just as terrifying as it had been before, and he wondered why his usually excellent eyesight couldn't clearly see the beast. (He didn't realize it was simply because his blessed vision hadn't yet grown accustomed to viewing something so purely evil.)

For now, Geeter would remain but a wicked shadow in our hero's eyes...

While Drinwor watched, Geeter angled in toward the palace, let loose a soul-rattling scream, then belched a burst of crackling black flames.

A section of the main tower was blasted into shards.

Drinwor was mortified. *My home...* He called out, "Vu Verian! Vu Verian!" praying the sky elf hadn't been killed in the fiery strike. This was just terrible! He felt so helpless. All he could do was cringe as Geeter swung around and dove in for another attack.

But this time the attack came to the dragon. A shimmering flash of blue energy shot from the palace and struck the beast in the side. Enraged, Geeter sounded his horrific cry again and veered aside, his massive wings furiously pounding the air.

Vu Verian was alive and fighting back!

"Yes!" Drinwor shouted.

And then everything disappeared behind swirling billows of blackness.

"No..."

Drinwor had fallen into a lightning storm.

Immediately thereafter, jagged, bent beams of electrified light stabbed the inky spaces all around him, and the ensuing cracks nearly burst his eardrums. He threw his hands over his ears and squeezed his eyes shut, hoping he wouldn't be blasted out of the sky. Well, as you might have guessed, it wasn't yet time for him to depart our tale... The lightning continued to strike, but its branches mercifully missed him. After a short time, the intensity of the strikes lessened, and Drinwor tentatively opened his eyes and uncovered his ears.

He had passed through the bottom of the storm. The black clouds hung flashing above him, eclipsing Areshria, and the sights and sounds of Vu Verian's battle with the dragon were gone. Drinwor craned his neck, moved his head about, trying to see anything around the clouds, but the effort was futile. He couldn't see a thing. For now, Vu Verian's fate would have to remain a mystery.

Resigned, Drinwor decided to focus his attention on his own immediate destiny.

He carefully turned himself over...

...and gasped, for here was a sight he had seen only in his dreams.

Having spent his entire life in the lofty perch of Areshria, the world below had been too far away to see, and nearly always covered with clouds, anyway. Now he was closer to the ground than he'd ever been, and he could see everything. The Continent Isle of Volcar spread beneath him like a jeweled tapestry laid by the Gods. For the first time this morning, his heart fluttered with something besides grief or fear.

"What a sight!"

Forests of crystal trees glittered from within roving fields of violet mist. Silver rivers slid like bespeckled snakes down emerald mountainsides, then fell a thousand feet into lakes of liquid light. There were inland seas of azure fire lapping shores of granule gold. There were jade towers rising out of low flying clouds, their opal spires spinning and glinting in the rays of the bleeding sun. And in the dreamy distance, phantasmal nations lay in the haze of the horizon, their palaces fading from view as lonely dragons flew above them.

It was all so wondrous.

But Drinwor also came to notice that every landscape was plowed through with blackened gullies, as if the world had long ago been scratched by giant flaming claws. (In actuality, it had.) The gullies stretched for miles, then converged on a mighty range of dark mountains that dominated all others, mountains whose sundered peaks spewed liquid fire that trickled down and lined the surrounding lands with molten rivers.

You know of these mountains, of course...

Drinwor shook his head, wondering how Phate must have shone before the first war with the Dark Forever. As fantastic as he'd always thought the upper reaches of the sky to be, the lands seemed even more incredible, despite the burned-out gullies. And with every moment he was getting a closer look.

A closer look.

For all its glorious wonder, Drinwor suddenly reacquainted himself with the growing likelihood of smashing into the ground.

"Well, that's one way to experience the surface."

Soon the mountains weren't below him, but beside, and the details of the world were growing denser. And to make matters worse, it felt as if his descent was accelerating.

"What do I do?" he asked the nearby clouds.

When they refused to answer, he thought of Vu Verian. The sky elf mystic had told him to jump, told him he'd be safe. Seriously? Drinwor quickly mulled over the last moment on the terrace. There was Geeter, the sunsword...and something else.

"The Ring of Floating!"

He grasped the ring, realizing he had no idea how it worked. Did he need to activate it in some way? He twirled it around his finger, said, "So, 'the Ring of Floating,' I guess I'm supposed to... float? Think of floating? Flying? Eagles...dragons...flying things... I don't know!"

Nothing happened. He shook his hand. Still nothing.

The ring...

"Is useless!"

The winds grew more violent. He lost control of his stability, started to tumble again. Terror struck him. He had no doubt—he was going to die! Directly below, the landscape glinted in thousands of places, and he was convinced he was falling onto a huge bed of broken glass.

Again he called out to whatever entity would listen. "What do I do?"

He needn't do anything, for at that moment, the ring released its store of magical power. A soft humming, almost singing, emanated from it, and it glowed. Drinwor felt his limbs lighten as the effects of gravity lessened around him. His tumbling stopped and the speed of his descent rapidly diminished.

He yelled, "By the Gods, what a morning!" and floated down into an ivory forest replete with crystal leaves. He never noticed, but the glimmering boughs retracted just enough to allow him to drift through them untouched.

He landed softly, and heaved a massive sigh of relief.

He knelt to the ground, sifted the cool, dark soil through his fingers, murmuring, "I'm alive…I'm alive…"

Drinwor Fang had landed in the Forest of Chanting Angels. He looked up, and for the first time in his life saw his sky through the interwoven jumble of a forest's branches. It was something to behold. From here, the clouds were like colorful streaks painted on a faraway canvas, and the harshness of the sun was softened. And, oh, the trees themselves! Though inanimate, they seemed more alive than he ever would have imagined, like a huge crowd of rooted elders who looked upon him with curious, hidden eyes. Now that sounds like a thing that might have made Drinwor feel uncomfortable, but it was just the opposite. Something about these trees made him feel snug, as one does when wrapped in the covers of their own bed. And he noticed though each tree was shaped somewhat differently, with various configurations of branches and such, they all shared the same basic attributes. They were knobby yet fluid, intricate yet simple. The air about them was thick and fresh with the scents of sorcery and nature. Shafts of crimson light were turned blue by their azure crystal boughs, and large patches of ground by their bases were darkened with circles of tangled shadows.

Drinwor's mouth hung open and he whispered, "Beautiful."

And then a sunbeam swallow leaped from a nearby branch, startling him. He watched it slap its rainbow wings against the air and vanish into the trees like a dream disappearing upon awakening.

Had Drinwor known the name of the forest, he would have now understood how it got its name. The branch the bird had leaped from shook, and its leaves struck one another like tuned chimes, delivering a harmonious song. A passing breeze encouraged yet more leaves to stir, and the song became a symphony of sorrow.

The Forest of Chanting Angels indeed...

A tear trickled down Drinwor's cheek. He sadly smiled and said, "For you, father."

And then, just as he began to wonder just what in the Seven Glories to do next, his ears perked to a new sound. It was steadily rising over the leaves' song, an airy whistle coming from...from... He couldn't place it—

Wait. Yes, he could.

He went still as stone.

The sound was coming from directly overhead.

He peeked up through the trees just as a great shadow covered the forest, dimming all the sparkling beauty beneath it.

Realization dawned on him.

"Gods, no!"

He hadn't been the only thing falling from the sky.

A huge chunk of Areshria's dragon-blasted tower came wailing down as if to destroy the world!

Drinwor Fang exploded into movement.

He shot through the forest with a speed and dexterity that rivaled any two-legged being in the universe, covering enormous amounts of ground in seconds. A perfectly timed dive sent him flying just as the wreckage smashed into the spot where he'd just been standing. Dozens of trees were pulverized. The entire forest shuddered. The symphony of leaves erupted into a shattering scream. The piece of blasted tower speared the soil and stood like a heinous monument, rising hundreds of feet over the treetops. It teetered there for a moment, then toppled over, destroying many more trees as it slammed to the ground with a roaring thud!

Drinwor sat there for a few moments, catching his breath, staring with astonishment through the dusty white cloud of devastation. Then he slowly stood up, brushed himself off...

And discovered the storm of ruin wasn't over.

Now debris of all sizes and shapes hailed down in a blizzard of burning rubble. Drinwor covered his head with his hands. Small rocks struck his fingers, and a particularly large jagged fragment of stone scraped the front of his armor, pushing him backward before lodging into the ground. Drinwor stumbled but didn't go down. When he regained his balance, he looked at his chest in terrified amazement. The stone left a thin white line that slowly disappeared into the blackness of his demonskin.

He didn't realize it, but his mysterious armor had just saved his life for what would be the first of many times.

He peered upward and wondered if the sky had any further insults to impose upon him. Thankfully, it didn't. Things finally began to calm. Even the chattering leaves quieted, as if granting their shattered brothers a moment of silence.

The dusk elf let out a long exhale. "Welcome to Phate, Drinwor."

"Yes, Drinwor Fang, welcome to Phate."

"What?!" Drinwor nearly jumped out of his demonskin. He whirled around and looked about.

There, in the midst of the murdered trees, a misshapen black figure shuffled through the settling haze. Backlit by the rays of the dying sun, it looked like a specter of the forest, perhaps come to seek revenge against the deliverer of the trees' destruction.

Drinwor froze, unsure if what he saw was alive or dead. Well, the thing certainly wasn't moving with the grace of a ghost, there was no such fluidity about it. It seemed to trip and stumble with every other step, and he swore he heard curses uttered beneath its rasping breath. It *had* to be alive. There was some comfort in that...though little.

The thing stuck a gnarled staff into the ground and pulled itself closer to him.

Drinwor slowly backed away.

The stranger raised his staff and sputtered with disjointed words. "The weather of this cursed world never ceases to amaze me, next it'll be raining cities. Ha! At least these damned, chatty trees have quieted!" The figure tripped over an exposed root, cursed and coughed as it righted itself, then said, "So, Emperor, what finds you, unbidden as you are, amongst this forsaken forest?"

Drinwor, continued to back away, made ready to run. "How do you know me as Emperor?"

The figure cackled. "Who else, if not you, elfling? Not your father, certainly, unless he means to rule from the Dark Forever!"

"Take one step closer to him and that is just where you will find yourself."

The voice that answered came from behind them.

Again Drinwor whirled around in surprise. He was getting awfully tired of this! But at least this time the surprise was a great relief, for there, not ten paces from him, stood a tall radiant being swathed in white robes.

"Vu Verian!" Drinwor shouted. "Thank the Gods!"

"Ah, the last of the sky elves!" the dark-robed figure said. "And not so much the worse for wear after mixing fire with a Greater Demonic Dragon. You did leave poor Geeter alive, did you not? Or was it the other way around?" Then he cackled through a fit of coughs.

Vu Verian stepped forward. He acknowledged Drinwor with a quick nod, then fixed his attention on the dark stranger. "I'm in no mood. Tell me who you are before I scatter your atoms."

The stranger bowed his head. "I am Morigos of the Moom, once a mage of Kroon and High Councilor of the Cold-Blooded Caves, now renegade. I am the Punished One, cursed with the Ever Dying."

"I know of you," Vu Verian said, "you're a dark elf."

"No darker than you, my forsaken brother." Morigos dared to move closer.

Vu Verian matched his steps. "I am no brother of yours, no relation. Your kind of elf is a desecration to everything my people stand for."

Now the two very different mages were standing right before one another, burning each other with stares. Vu Verian towered over this new nemesis, his fingers twitching, ready to unleash blue lightning. Morigos' bent form appeared as the total antithesis to the sky elf's elegance. If not for his crooked staff's support, it seemed as if he would fall in pieces to the ground. And yet something belied his guise of frailty. Drinwor guessed there was some measure of power lurking beneath the trappings of his shattered exterior.

"Come," Vu Verian said with a sneer, "let me be done with all my battles before morning's end!" He lifted his brightening hands.

Anticipating the fires to come, Drinwor cowered.

But then Morigos backed down. He cradled his staff close to his body, said, "Wait! You must know—I, too, have been summoned to Vren Adiri. That is where you're taking the young Emperor, is it not?"

Vu Verian stayed his sorcery, lowered his hands. He considered the words for a moment, then said, "You lie. No being such as you will ever take a single step inside Vren Adiri."

"Oh, I've already been there," Morigos returned. "Herard didn't acquire the Gauntlets of Loathing Light all on his own, you know! No, no, in these, the last of our times, good must conspire with... me! Ha! For now, doom comes even to those who consider themselves dark."

Vu Verian shook his head. "What know you of Herard? And for you to credit yourself in the acquisition of the gauntlets is ludicrous."

"We shall see," Morigos grumbled. Then he turned to Drinwor. "You must know, young elf, without my help, *he* will have you."

Drinwor was taken aback. "What? Who will have me?"

The crumpled mage continued with, "He knows you have the sword, and he'll find you once he has the Gauntlets of Loathing Light...and he *will* have them, soon."

Drinwor's face was marked with apprehension. He turned to Vu Verian. "Who's he talking about?"

Vu Verian's gaze was locked on Morigos as he answered, "He speaks of the murderous demon, Warloove. But don't trust a thing he says, for he is in league with that fiend."

"I no longer serve the one who has afflicted me so!" Morigos declared, motioning to his own crinkled body.

Drinwor cast Morigos a dark look. "Warloove… That's a name I've already grown to hate."

"It's a name I have long hated, young elf," Morigos noted, "a name many hate."

Drinwor picked up a small piece of rubble and threw it into the trees. "I've never had an enemy before."

The dark elf lifted a crooked finger. "Ah, be careful who you count as an enemy, for simply naming one as such is enough to invite their wrath upon thyself! And I promise you, Warloove's wrath will already be plenty severe, for he will chase the one with the sunsword around this entire world if he has to."

"Fool," Vu Verian shot back, "be silent!"

Morigos chortled, then brought his finger before his cowl, mockingly shushing himself.

Drinwor froze in place. "You think I have the sunsword?"

"Share nothing with this creature," Vu Verian urged, "he will betray you to darkness."

A cackling like the crackling of fire shot from Morigos' charred lungs. "We're all pawns in fate's game, young Emperor. You, most of all. It's long been known the Sunsword Surassis was 'hidden' in your palace of Areshria. Oh, I know you keep it, Emperor, for who else if not you?"

Vu Verian stepped forth, shaking his fists. "I told you to be silent!"

Morigos waved him off. "Fear not, sky elf, there is no one else here, and there's no need to disguise the truths we share. Soon, you will both learn it is a time for unlikely allies."

"Are *you* my ally?" Drinwor asked.

"Ha!" Morigos laughed. "Good question!" He flashed a look to Vu Verian, said, "I like this one, he's more transparent than you!" Then he turned back to Drinwor. "Yes, I tell you, I am your ally. But if you don't believe me, you can ask the orchestrator of your fate, the Fallen Angel. Oh, and before I forget, she has a message for both of you. The message is this: the One Soul awaits."

Drinwor's expression went blank. "The One Soul?"

Vu Verian's eyes narrowed with suspicion. How did this being know of such secretive things? How did he know so much of Herard and the gauntlets, of the sword and Vren Adiri? And what of the Fallen Angel? If Morigos' contentions were true, then what had brought the most holy being on Phate to conspire with a dark elf? Vu Verian's mind was awhirl. Was it possible Morigos was actually being truthful...? No, it wasn't possible. He was a Mage of the Moom, an enemy of light, a master of trickery and deceit. It was all a ruse. It had to be. And, Vu Verian realized, it was no coincidence that Morigos had been here waiting for them while Warloove's own dragon was attacking above.

Enough. He had entertained Morigos' lies for long enough. His brow creased and he said, "Evil, wretched being, I don't believe any of this. You're a servant of darkness hoping to despoil the sunsword for yourself!"

Morigos shook his head and sighed. "You sky elves, always so righteous and always so wrong."

"I'm not wrong!" Vu Verian lifted his arms, his fingers flashing with blue energy. "I give you this one, last chance. Leave now, or I swear there will be nothing left of you."

"No," Morigos replied, "for it is by the will of your angel that I stay...fool."

Vu Verian snickered, then began to sing.

Drinwor shrunk back.

Morigos raised his staff. "For my part, I care nothing for your accursed sword, but I'll be glad to exchange fire with an ivory imbecile!" The runes on his robe glowing green, he stood ready to match the sky elf's onslaught.

"Then fire you shall have," Vu Verian muttered. He thrust his fingers forward...

But no sorcery came.

The magic vanished from his fingertips, and the runes on Morigos' robes dimmed. The whole forest suddenly brightened and a clanging patter began to sound. All looked around, and the sound grew louder. It was the leaves; they were ringing beneath a newly kindled rain. But it wasn't the heavy drops of acidic water that typically poured from Phate's punishing skies.

It was raining silver.

Drinwor looked up, and a million little drops of liquid silver, each shining light, bright, and beautiful, bathed the Forest of Chanting Angels with glimmering hope. All the smoke and dust of the day's destruction was vanquished, and even the sun's rays, breaking through the forest's boughs in patchy rows, shone with some vigor of old.

Drinwor was awestruck. "How?"

Vu Verian closed his eyes and words slipped from between his fine lips. But the words didn't seem to be his; they sounded like the voice of the ringing leaves, the voice of the forest. They said:

"Once, long ago, many forests like this one filled the valleys surrounding the Mountains of Might with sweeping lushness. Their wardens were the shadowlight elves, elves whose beauty was matched only by the trees they cultivated. For many ages their sorcerous songs conjured showers of silver rain to nourish the trees. But now the shadowlight elves are gone. Their magic wanes and most of their forests have disappeared. What trees are left stand with lonely trepidation in this dark land. They are innocent casualties, another feature of Phate's beauty almost lost. But all is *not* yet lost and, as you can see, the sun still holds some glory for the morning."

Then Vu Verian opened his eyes and lowered his arms. His voice returning to his own tone, he said, "This rain falls by the power of the Fallen Angel. Although Vren Adiri is some distance away, her spirit must be near..." He quietly added, "I haven't heard of her leaving the safety of the palace for hundreds of years, though." Then he turned to the dark elf mage. "I say again, begone. You have no place with us."

Morigos grumbled unintelligibly. He gripped his staff with both hands and planted it firmly onto the ground, apparently resolute on staying put.

Drinwor was convinced a sorcerous battle would commence, but then the world went white, the forest suddenly swamped over as if by a low-strolling cloud. The only thing Drinwor could see were the silhouettes of the opposing mages. Then they, too, faded to white, and Drinwor suddenly felt very sleepy...

CHAPTER NINE
EMANATING EVIL

The philosopher asks why. The scientist asks how. The faithful do not ask...
Synnethic Innadon
Warlord Ruler, High Priest of the Fezzonian Monks

The Raging Sea was riled by Ulith Urn's reawakening. A ceaseless line of colossal waves broke upon the Cliffs of Moaning Wishes like sacrificial slaves come to honor the reemergence of their dark master. Above, the sorcerous storms in the compound intensified. Roiling black clouds lashed the newly raised towers with whirlwinds of blood rain. The spires were stung with scarlet lightning. The wind howled, frightened ghosts cried, and even the sun could not see through the stormy shroud of Ulith Urn's perpetual necromantic night.

It was the dawning of a new chaos.

In the tallest tower, Syndreck the Brooding was awakened by rain that poured through the circular space in the ceiling. His face slicked with blood, he flicked out his tongue and licked a few drops. "Ah, so sweet."

He opened his eyes. He was on his side, his limbs hanging over the lip of the platform. He rolled over, sat up...and a loud, echoing ring sounded as he slammed his head into the cauldron. His forehead throbbing with pain, he cried out, "Ah! What is this?"

From somewhere in the chamber, Drekklor answered, "Your cauldron. I excavated it from the ruins below."

"What cauldron? And why do you put it right on top of me?"

"I put it where it's supposed to be."

"I'll banish you to the netherworlds, put *you* where you're supposed to be, dark demon of trickery!" Syndreck stood up, rubbed his forehead. "Cauldron in my face...I'll incinerate his..." He mumbled some more, turned around, and his eyes widened with remembrance.

There, taking up nearly half the space on the platform, was the Cauldron of Carcass Control, Syndreck's once beloved pot of necromancy. "Ah, yes, my cauldron!"

He reached forward and lovingly caressed its rumpled sides. Molded from corroded iron, it was large, dull, and dark. Syndreck was pleased to note its innards were already filled with a bubbling swill whose surfaced sizzled with every drop of blood rain. He continued to drag his hand around it, reminiscing about the glory of viler times...

"You have no idea, demon. Within this cauldron, a thousand years ago, I brewed the magic that tore down the dimensional walls. Within this cauldron, I wove the spells that sent armies of undead against the legions of light. And, within this very cauldron, I will again find my power!"

Drekklor floated up to him, bearing a large tarnished goblet whose once pristine silver surface had corroded beneath the grimy grip of ancient oily fingers.

"Give it here!" Syndreck seized the vessel and dipped it into the swill. Then he brought it to his lips and poured the froth down his throat. It was disgustingly foul. Syndreck, of course, found it delectable. That he drank the stuff was unnecessary, but, oh, how it intoxicated him so! He belched, his anticipation brimming like the cauldron's froth.

"Now," he said, "we shall begin!"

And with that, he threw the goblet past Drekklor and laughed. Then he grabbed a long ladle from a hanger affixed to the side of the cauldron, plunged it into the swill and dragged it round. A necromantic song soon slipped from his lips, and he lulled himself into a trance. Minutes passed by. Then hours. Still he stirred and sang. The liquid bubbled and simmered and glowed. As the putrid froth spilled over the brim, Syndreck could feel his soul's inherent powers rekindling, could feel the slumbering bear of sorcery within awakening from a thousand year winter.

Oh, it was wonderful!

And now he was ready to go to work.

With spectral fingers he reached into the cauldron and groped the space surrounding Phate. He nodded, for as expected, the dimensional walls surrounding the world were weak; and lo, as he probed deeper, he discovered that the skies surrounding Ulith Urn were even weaker! "Ah, perfect! Just as I had hoped!" He peered intently into the vile liquid and discerned the exact places where the walls would most easily break. They were right behind him, hanging over the Raging Sea like curtains of frail silk waiting to be torn. Soon he would tear through them, and the Dark Forever's denizens would flood the universe like water racing from a broken dam. Soon, Nenockra Rool would be free.

Syndreck's sorcerous energy surged with his adrenaline.

"Do you feel it?" he said to himself.

"Feel...?" The shadow demon, beset with boredom, had been startled by the necromancer's words.

"I speak not to you, slave!"

"I thought not."

Syndreck looked at the demon and laughed in that uncontrollable way of his. Then he looked back into his cauldron. He was eager to begin. But before he started tearing through the dimensional walls, he wanted to test his burgeoning necromantic abilities. They would be useful, for who knew when he would need slaves, or guardians of the compound? And he was dying to know just how strong he was becoming. He sang a little song, cast a little spell. The cauldron gurgled in response, its glow flickering. Syndreck was ecstatic, for his spell was instantly coming to fruition.

"Come, witness the birth of a new age!" he exclaimed.

Drekklor said nothing.

"Fool, I said come!"

"You speak to me?"

"Yes, fool! What sort of a demon are you? That Nenockra Rool created you I sometimes cannot believe." He shook his head, muttered ancient curses.

Drekklor floated up to the edge of the cauldron. He looked into it, detected nothing unusual. There were swirls of rotten bubbling liquid, and he experienced some foul sensation he later determined to be an awful smell.

But then a hand broke through the surface.

A beautiful, decaying, wretchedly-rotted hand, and a clawed hand at that.

It was a significant event.

For the first time in a thousand years, something dead had been purposefully returned to the world of the living.

Syndreck's eyes widened with jubilation. "You see, demon, you see?"

Drekklor looked to Syndreck. Although the shadow demon had learned to never doubt the will of Nenockra Rool, it was still difficult to understand how this deranged mortal could wield so much power.

The necromancer lifted his arms triumphantly into the air. "I've done it!"

He had done it indeed.

Although the accomplishment itself was minuscule, the weight of its implications would burden the universe. He had successfully tapped into the power of the Dark Forever and leaked some of its influence into the primary plane of existence. He screamed, "Yes! I am to be a destroyer of dimensions again, and a master necromancer! Because of me, the skies will be torn apart, dead things will rise, and Nenockra Rool will stomp the face of Phate!"

He lowered his arms and stared into the cauldron, tears of joy welling up in his eyes as he noticed the hand extend out to the wrist and open its clawed fingers. The liquid around it steamed, and light poured from lacerations in its palm as it grasped at the air. Syndreck mimicked the movements with his own hand like a father encouraging the movements of his newborn son. Then he burst into some strange, twisted dance.

"What a wonderful instrument this body has proven to be!" Indeed it was. Magic flowed through it as smoothly as could have been desired. Its trappings were heavy and clumsy, though. Syndreck ceased dancing, discarded Tatoc's suit of invisible-steel armor, and conjured himself some nice dark green robes. Satisfied and comfortable, he resumed his dancing, thinking how pleased Nenockra Rool would be. How—

"The hand disintegrates."

Drekklor's scathing voice.

Syndreck ceased his revelry and looked into the cauldron. The hand was indeed breaking apart, crumbling into the bubbling filth. "Bah, it doesn't matter!" Syndreck kicked a disapproving foot toward the shadow demon. The specimen itself hadn't been important, just the result of the incantation. This had just been an experiment, a test, and Syndreck considered it a resounding success.

Yes, all would unfold as he had foreseen in his dreams.

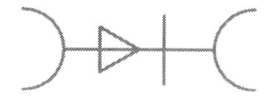

CHAPTER TEN
ALL THINGS CONSIDERED

The only thing more precious than time is the life that exists within it.

Azurion
Keeper of the Sorcerous Tomes of Time

Drinwor Fang was asleep, yet his midnight blues were wide open, glistening with reflections of the paradisial dream that played out behind them. He was dreaming of thousands of golden comets, their contrails sparkling like the ends of so many magicians' wands. They streaked past his head, flew into the distance, and faded, revealing a universe unlike any Drinwor had ever dreamed of before. Giant spiral galaxies dotted with colorful stars were everywhere. Each star was surrounded by life-sustaining worlds, each world surrounded by oceanic moons, all swirling through a void of perfect white.

May the Gods return, my faithful reader, can you imagine a cosmos of pure white?

It was a universe bereft of evil, a universe where darkness had been utterly defeated. And somehow Drinwor knew it was *he* who had defeated darkness, *he* who had bestowed everyone with such everlasting hope. Armed with the Sunsword Surassis, he was the savior of it all.

It was so splendid, so overwhelmingly splendid.

He let out a soft moan and sank deeper into the dream. He perceived that he flew across the universe like an angel, and soon came upon the center of a shining galaxy of golden stars. And there, in front of the largest star he had ever seen, the image of a giant face was materializing. The features formed…the face was his.

"What is this?"

He flew in closer, reached out to it…

The face erupted with blood and fire, then crumbled to dust. Drinwor's consciousness spiraled down into darkness, and for a single, terrifying second, he experienced nonexistence…

His eyelids fluttered and he awoke, screaming, "My stolen soul!"

"My Lord, I was trying to wake you."

"Wha? Who…?" Drinwor sat up, shook his head, and looked about.

It was Vu Verian. The sky elf's silhouette towered over him, a greyish shadow surrounded by a thick white haze. *Ah, yes, the haze.* This was the haze that had appeared in those last moments in the Forest of Chanting Angels. Drinwor was fairly certain they weren't in the forest now, for although he couldn't see much of anything beyond Vu Verian's silhouette, the ground was hard and there was no breeze. Vu Verian leaned over, offered his hand, and Drinwor pulled himself to his feet.

"Were you having a bad dream?" the mystic asked.

Drinwor narrowed his eyes. "I don't know, I can't quite remember. There's flashes, little images flitting through my mind, but…" He stretched his arms, breathed in deeply, then exhaled. "Where are we?"

"Vren Adiri."

"Vren Adiri… How long was I asleep?"

"A couple hours."

"Really? Feels like longer."

Vu Verian motioned around him. "It's this place. It's a place of healing, resting, rejuvenating."

"Nice. I should move here."

Vu Verian evinced a little smile while Drinwor waved off his jesting comment. Then the dusk elf's eyes grew suddenly wide, and he blurted, "Oh, may the Gods return, that reminds me! When we were in the forest I never got a chance to ask you: what happened to my home?! I mean, I'm glad to see you unharmed, but by the Seven Glories, was Areshria destroyed?"

"No, no. It was damaged, but nothing too severe. It still flies."

"That's a relief! It seemed like half of it fell on top of me after my fall."

Vu Verian placed his hand on Drinwor's shoulder. "About your fall—I'm sorry I sent you off like that, but I had to get you out of there as quickly as possible."

"Oh, I know, that dragon would have killed me. I mean, if my father wasn't able to—" Drinwor choked on his words. Trembling, he reached up, grabbed Vu Verian's shoulder and looked deep into the sky elf's eyes. "Oh, Vu Verian, my father…"

Vu Verian took Drinwor's hand, brought it down between them, and grasped it tight. In a low voice he said, "Drinwor, tell me all about your fall. Areshria is so lofty a perch, you must have seen many things." He realized the fall had been a most harrowing experience in itself, but was willing to bet its recollection would at least momentarily steer Drinwor away from dwelling on his father.

He was right.

Drinwor immediately perked up, gasped, "My fall! Oh, Vu Verian, it was crazy! I was tumbling over and over and then I saw the dragon and I was worried about you and then I fell into a storm and…and then I turned over and got a glimpse of the world. It was incredible! But then I thought I was going to crash into these glassy trees and—" He abruptly stopped, his eyes alight with some new thought. "I just remembered something else, I meant to give back your…" He took his hand from Vu Verian's grasp and reached for one of his fingers. Surprised to find nothing wrapping it but the taut material of his demonskin's glove, he hesitated, looked around, and then said, "I must have lost it in the forest. Vu Verian, I'm sorry, I—"

"Lost what?"

"Your ring, the Ring of Floating."

"Oh, you didn't lose it."

"You already took it back?"

Vu Verian paused for a moment, then said, "Drinwor, the ring was an illusion."

Drinwor, in obvious shock, took a step back. "What? What do you mean it was an illusion? Then how—"

The mystic sky elf gestured for him to calm. "Don't concern yourself with this now. Many things will soon be revealed."

Drinwor looked on Vu Verian curiously, almost suspiciously, but presently decided to let the matter of the illusionary ring go. He circled around, swirled the haze with his hands. "So, Vren Adiri is another sky elf palace, isn't it?"

"Yes."

"Is the whole place filled with mist? I wish we could actually see something."

And then, right on cue with Drinwor's words, the haze thinned out. It swirled into itself and quickly faded away. The revealed scene made Drinwor think he had stepped into another dream.

Vu Verian spread out his arms. "Behold, the Chamber of the Staring Sun."

Drinwor tilted his head back and swiveled on his heels. His eyes wide with awe, he said, "It's even more beautiful than Areshria."

The elves beheld a massive tower whose hollowed-out interior mimicked the ancient sky. The silken walls were a soothing shade of blue—a blue Drinwor had only ever seen in the eyes of his sky elf friend. Clouds drifted above. Puffy, clean and white, their densities increased as they climbed toward the ceiling, which hung thousands of feet overhead. And there, embedded in the center of the ceiling, shining with starlike brilliance, was a giant jewel called the Sun's Remembrance. It was a crafted representation of the sun of old, a polished round gemstone that caught Drinwor's eyes and sparkled them. While he gazed at it, it issued shafts of scintillating yellow light that shot through the clouds, all the way down to the white marble floor, surrounding the two elves in glowing columns.

Now, with the Sun's Remembrance beaming, Drinwor noticed the telltale glint of scales amongst the clouds.

"Vu Verian, are those...?"

"Yes, Drinwor, you look upon dragons."

Dozens of them, actually, gliding in long, slow spirals, gracefully slipping in and out of the clouds around the upper reaches of the chamber—cloud dragons and spirit dragons; lightning dragons and crystalfire dragons; even the sparkling tinge of lesser translucent dragons was evident. They were magnificent. I get misty-eyed just writing about them, and cannot wait for you to meet my favorite one of all...

Drinwor shook his head. "I must be still dreaming, for where else could such beauty exist?"

Vu Verian nodded. "It's the home of the Fallen Angel, a sanctuary for the dreams of yore."

And then, as if the place wasn't surreal enough, music arose from some indiscernible place, the low melodies of phantom flutes accompanying high pitched, female voices. The sounds were lulling, emotional, the long-drawn-out notes dragged like a caressing hand across the soul.

Drinwor turned to him. "Listen to that... You know, I never took music for much of a companion. But this...this makes me believe I've truly missed something. There's a sadness but also a solace in the sound. To hear someone or something else produce this makes me think there are others who feel as I do, makes me feel like I'm not alone."

"Here, the songs of the spirit elves ever sing. I'm glad you get to hear them, my Emperor. I'm glad you get to see this. I hope this place comforts you on your most difficult day."

Drinwor made to answer, but was distracted, for a strange sound, like a dragon's inhalation, was emanating from the space right beside him. Instinctively, he leaped backward. Vu Verian swiftly but smoothly stepped aside, then remained still and ready.

The sound rose in pitch and volume...then silenced.

Drinwor muttered, "What was—"

Suddenly, a small cloud of crackling black vapor appeared in the air between them. Within it, glowing blue and white light poured like liquid lightning over a shape that was composing itself into some kind of humanoid form. And then, just as quickly as it had appeared, the cloud vanished, leaving only a few puffs of dwindling vapor at the feet of the newly arrived figure.

Morigos of the Moom stepped forth and cackled. "His most difficult day? I think not. That is yet to come!"

Vu Verian's expression evinced both shock and rage. "How dare you enter this place! For your tainted eyes to even set their gaze upon the grace of this palace is blasphemy! Begone, dark fiend!"

Morigos coughed through his retort. "As I've already told you, I was summoned, invited; just like you."

"Invited to Vren Adiri?" Vu Verian snickered. "You speak nothing but lies."

Morigos dipped his cowled head. "For an ancient owl, you are not very wise."

"I should separate the skin from your bones!"

"Thank you, but it's already been done."

"Then it should be done again, vile deceiver!"

Black blood dripped from the corners of Morigos' mouth, but with his face hidden in the shadows of his cowl, this went unseen. He struck back at Vu Verian with biting words. "And what of you, sky elf? Your continued threats and insults do nothing to disguise what you really are."

Vu Verian was stunned by the statement. "What I really am? What does that mean?"

Morigos shook his gnarled staff. "Oh, you know what it means! Tell me, who do you see when you look in the mirror?"

Vu Verian's whole body shook with rage and he roared in a voice that echoed to the very top of the chamber, "**I should have destroyed you!**"

Morigos looked to Drinwor. "How easily irritated your companion is."

Drinwor was at a loss. "I've never known anyone to anger him so. You have a singular gift."

"Irritating snobbish sky elves is one of the few things I still enjoy."

Vu Verian was seething. "Do not entertain his foolishness, Drinwor!"

"Sorry," the dusk elf said, "I'll be quiet."

Vu Verian smirked. "It is not *you* who needs to be quiet." Red vessels threaded his eyes and his countenance darkened as if it was swathed in some passing shadow. He mumbled to himself, then nodded, apparently having come to some decision.

He pointed at the dark elf sorcerer.

Morigos brought up his staff.

"No, please!" Drinwor begged, his hands raised and waving as he backed away.

Too late.

Vu Verian sang out. Blue streams of condensed fire blasted from his fingertips.

With a speed defying his fractured frame, Morigos spun around and punched the space behind him with a backhanded thrust of his staff. A shield of glowing green magic sprang into the air right in front of Vu Verian's fire, but the fire never touched the shield, for a more potent power interceded.

Both spells were diffused as a little cloud of dim light materialized around the opposing mages.

It was a Fog of Power Quenching

The two mages dropped their arms in futility.

"What's this?" Drinwor asked.

"Someone besides me doesn't appreciate the sky elf's persistent attacks," Morigos suggested.

"Oh, be silent," Vu Verian returned.

The magic-dousing fog faded. After it disappeared, everyone noticed a glimmering white light tracing the outline of a door in the wall closest to them. The space inside the door vanished, and something radiant emerged from within.

Here was the Fallen Angel.

She glided from the doorway, her golden wings aglow as she slid through the shafts of light thrown by the Sun's Remembrance. Drinwor thought she looked like the solid light within the center of a candle's otherwise blurry flame. She was singing as she came. The phantom flutes matched her melody and the spirit elves delicately accompanied her lead. When she came up to the group, Drinwor was compelled to kneel. Vu Verian was silent and Morigos coughed, both still shaken from having their sorcery seized.

She spoke, her words as fluid as her song. "Welcome, Drinwor Fang; Keeper of the Sunsword Surassis; Emperor of the Sky. I extend my sincerest condolences, for your father was a friend to all who fight for the side of light. Few beings, mortal or immortal, possessed the character of Herard. He was a good man...a good man. Come, now, rise."

Drinwor stood up. "Thank you, angel, you and your palace are more beautiful than a heavenly dream."

The Fallen Angel nodded in appreciation, said, "Thank you, Drinwor Fang, you *are* a heavenly dream." Then she turned to regard Vu Verian. The sky elf sank to a knee, bowed his head. The angel placed her luminous hand upon his shoulder, and golden light crept from her fingers. The anger in Vu Verian's eyes subsided and some healthy whiteness returned to his flushed face. Slowly, ashamedly, he lifted his head back up.

The angel said, "Once again I've had to extinguish your anger."

Vu Verian's voice was tremulous. "Forgive me, radiant one. I meant only to defend the sanctity of this kingdom. This is one of the last places still untouched by darkness." He motioned to Morigos. "For this...*being*...to walk in these halls is blasphemous."

Morigos, struggling to remain silent, rolled his unseen eyes.

The Fallen Angel took her hand from Vu Verian's shoulder and motioned to the Mage of the Moom. "This one has seen the futility of darkness and, from this wisdom, there shines a new light within him. He is bound by a new covenant."

"So, he *is* welcome here?" Vu Verian's look was quizzical.

"Yes, he is," the angel said, "and we owe him a debt of gratitude for helping us with the acquisition of the Gauntlets of Loathing Light. Now he stands here willing to aid us with the resurrection of the sunsword."

"Ha!" Morigos thrust his staff in the sky elf's direction. "Told you so!"

"And just how will he help us?" Vu Verian wondered aloud.

"When the time is right," the angel replied, "you will see."

Vu Verian rose from the floor, straightening his sleeves and shaking his head. "Forgive me, again, but I don't trust him. His people are as gifted in deception as you are in foresight. I know this. I have seen dark elves stab their own kings in the back. I have seen their children burn in fires of their own mother's making. I have seen slaves executed, then resurrected to be tormented again. I...oh..." He sighed, unable to continue with whatever dark memories flooded his mind. "I'm sorry, your holiness, but in my heart I know he will betray us."

Morigos, supporting himself with his staff, leaned forward and said, "Well then, with such accusations, I find it amusing that it was *you* who attacked *me*. So much for the alleged graciousness of good!" Then he straightened up as much as he was able and pointed to Drinwor. "I could have killed this one. I'm *supposed* to kill him!" (Drinwor flinched at this.) "But I did not. I stayed the 'hand of darkness,' as you would say." He cackled, waved his arm around melodramatically.

"I don't understand," Vu Verian said, "why does a dark elf suddenly care so much for light?"

Morigos banged the floor with his staff. "Understand this: I care for neither light nor darkness. But I'm not unwitting to the desires of the Dark Forever. Now *all* destinies are headed toward ruin. The demons will come, and they'll swallow whole galaxies. Myself, my lunatic people, we will enjoy no more favor than you." He coughed, then sputtered, "Though you don't believe this, my aims are no longer driven by the ignorance of evil."

"Is that so?" Vu Verian smiled sardonically. "But what of your master's aims? What of Warloove?"

"Bah, he's no longer my master, and his aims are paltry."

"Paltry?" Vu Verian laughed. "Stealing the sunsword and leading the armies of the Dark Forever against us is paltry?"

Morigos yelled, "Fool! Warloove cares nothing for the Dark Forever, nor does he care anything of Phate!"

"No?"

"No!" Morigos let out an exasperated huff. "You despise the dark elves, yet you're as easily deceived as they are. Warloove serves an alien master, a being long ago condemned to our forsaken world." Vu Verian cast him a disbelieving look, but Morigos continued undaunted. "Yes, I have seen this alien. It wants the sunsword's energy to power its *starship*, or whatever it calls that crazy contraption it has hidden away in Warloove's dungeon. It has power cells, crystals, *engines*, that need reigniting. Bah, I don't know the terms! But I do know it desperately desires flight from Phate, for it believes our dying sun is ready to explode—" It seemed as if he meant to say more, but the word "explode" caught in this throat and he gagged.

Vu Verian laughed. "This is a fantasy you describe!" He looked to the Fallen Angel. "You believe this?"

The angel nodded. "It is true. I know of this being. It calls itself Darkis. And I believe Nenockra Rool *wants* it to acquire the sword, for then the forces of light will be rendered helpless. In fact, it is a distinct possibility that Warloove is somehow being aided by agents of the Dark Forever in acquisition of the sword. With Surassis gone, not even the One Life can stand against Nenockra Rool."

Vu Verian mumbled something incoherent, then said: "Well, whatever his aims, Warloove must acquire neither the gauntlets nor the sword."

"He will not," the angel assured, "for we have the sword, and the gauntlets have been sent far away from here."

"You sent the gauntlets away?" Vu Verian looked dismayed. "When? Where?"

"I sent them at morning's first light. They travel to a secret fortified location as we speak. They should arrive before dusk. Fear not, even should Warloove discover their location, they will not be easily acquired."

"Do not be so certain of that," Morigos pointed and shook an unnaturally bent finger at the angel. "As I told you before, oh, light one, Warloove is tenacious. Despite your deception, he *will* find the black gloves, and then he'll likely steal *my* soul to empower your sacred sword!"

"Well," the angel responded, "Warloove will have to travel far to find the gauntlets. And while he searches for them, we can go forth and infuse the sword with the *pure* soul, the One Soul."

"What are you all talking about?"

It was Drinwor. He stepped forward, and all looked to him as if he they had forgotten he was there. "The One Soul? You mean a soul for my father's sword? What does that mean? I'm afraid to acknowledge it, but I feel like it has something to do with me."

Drinwor was met with blank and speechless stares. *Something to do with you, indeed,* they all thought at once.

Everyone looked to the Fallen Angel. She was gazing at the dusk elf, thinking of her last conversation with Herard… A few quiet moments went by before she said: "It is long past time for you to understand what you are, and what your purpose is."

"If I understand correctly," Drinwor said, "I'm now the Emperor of the Sky."

"Yes," said the angel, "and that is an honorable charge. But you are so much more than that. Tell me, have you heard the saying, 'One Life, One Soul, One Sword'?"

Drinwor shifted in his stance, gulped nervously. "Yes, I think I've heard my father say that, but I don't know what it refers to."

The angel nodded. "In order for Surassis to realize its full potential of power, all three attributes must work in concert: the One Life, the One Soul, and the sword itself. But for you, for your part…" And then the angel paused, for her next words stood Drinwor as if on the edge of a cliff, and to utter them would send him plummeting into an unavoidable fate. But there was nothing else to do, for indeed, his fate *was* unavoidable. It simply needed to be explained, so she said: "Drinwor, *you* are the One Life, the Son and Savior of the Stars, destined to wield the Sunsword Surassis against Nenockra Rool and defeat the Dark Forever. It is you. By the grace of the Seven Glories, by the will of the living universe, it is you."

Drinwor's knees weakened and he stepped backward to catch himself from collapsing to the floor. "What? Me…? Supposed to wield the sword? Against the Dark Forever, you say?"

"Yes, the stars created you for this."

Drinwor shot a quick glance to Vu Verian, who was regarding him with a rather blank stare, then he looked back to the angel. "The stars *created me*? What? I've never heard anything of this. Are you certain?"

"I am," the angel replied, "but more importantly, *you* must be certain."

Drinwor laughed. "Well, by all the infernal hells I most assuredly am not! I...I don't know what to say..."

For the second time today, Drinwor was shaken to his core. May the Gods return, he had long suspected he was destined for something greater, but this? It was all too much. Can you imagine being told that you are destined to stand against the most powerful evil force in the history of the universe on the same day that you learned of your father's death? Well, I cannot, and neither could poor Drinwor. All this time, the innocent boy who struggled to sleep every night had actually been the Son and Savior of the Stars, the wielder of the Sunsword Surassis. It was profoundly overwhelming. With these admissions, it was as if the angel had in one moment torn down the walls that had until now sheltered his entire existence.

"This has been quite a morning!" Drinwor exclaimed. He looked around and saw Vu Verian and Morigos staring at him as if the angel's words had cast him in an entirely new light. Undoubtedly, they had.

Now, before the stars, before himself, Drinwor Fang was laid bare.

As the information sunk in, his smoky-colored face went flush. The sigils on his demonskin armor glowed, and his eyes blazed the deepest blue. His silver hair fluttered in some spectral wind, perhaps in the breezy breath of the spirit elves' song, and something warmed inside him. He wrapped a hand around his sword charm and a soft blue light suffused the spaces between his fingers. *"Father..."*

"Drinwor, are you all right?" the Fallen Angel asked.

In a voice barely above a whisper, Drinwor answered, "No, I'm not. And if this is all true, then I have, oh, a thousand questions or so to ask."

"Let's try starting with just one," the angel suggested.

Drinwor nodded. "All right. Well, first, I'm wondering why, in the name of the Seven Glories, didn't my father say anything."

Vu Verian shifted uncomfortably, looked away, and Morigos suddenly feigned an interest in the clouds. A few seconds passed before the angel said, "I will answer that question, but not now. That is something you and I will discuss later."

Drinwor looked dejected. "All right. Then I'll ask this: if I'm the One Life, then who's the One Soul?"

The angel bowed. "The One Soul is a glorious and great one, imbued with purity and strength. It is the soul of the one who wielded Surassis a thousand years ago."

Vu Verian shot his glance back to the angel, blurted, "Drakana?"

"Yes," the angel confirmed, "the Lord Dragon of Phate."

"But he was lost in the war," Vu Verian pointed out.

"Lost, but not utterly destroyed." The Fallen Angel lifted her sunlight arms. "His soul, along with countless others, remains in limbo between this world and the Seven Glories. He awaits the coming of the One Life in the Hall of Voices."

Vu Verian shuddered, rippling his silken white robes. "The Hall of Voices, may the Gods return..."

"What exactly is the purpose of the soul?" Drinwor asked.

"You see," the angel explained, "the One Soul will resurrect Sillithian Synnstrike, the solar dragon in the sword's pommel. With the dragon resurrected, the sword is resurrected, and the power of Surassis' sunblade may blaze forth. The dragon is the source of the sun's fire."

"Sill-ith...ian Synnstrike?" Drinwor attempted to pronounce.

"Yes, Sillithian Synnstrike," the angel said a bit more articulately. "And this is the task that is laid before you all: On the morrow, at morning's first light, you must journey to the Hall of Voices, where Drakana waits to infuse the sword."

"Isn't the Hall of Voices guarded by the Lord Banshee?" Vu Verian asked. "Are we to—"

Suddenly, a high-pitched cry of alarm sounded from above. Everyone looked up. The chamber's upper regions were stirring with activity. The dragons were nettled, the Sun's Remembrance flickering behind their beating wings. One of the dragons broke through the bottom of the clouds and spiraled down like a glinting leaf fallen from the Forest of Chanting Angels, cawing as it came.

Drinwor had never seen its like.

It was an insect dragon, a breed nearly extinct.

Its four transparent wings were buzzing so fast as to be almost invisible except for the blur of the blue at the tips. Six legs extending from the silvery-white, green-striped body trembled as it neared.

Drinwor could see its globular eyes smoldering with worry. It continued cawing as it came down, landing close by. The Fallen Angel glided up to greet it, and the two exchanged indecipherable words. After a brief discussion, the dragon leaped back into the air to rejoin its kin amongst the clouds. The angel watched it depart, and then returned to the three elves.

"Well, what was that all about?" asked Morigos.

"The dragons have seen something a trifle bit disturbing," the angel replied. "Although the Glyph of Multiversal Guarding has not cried out, it is unmistakable—Ulith Urn is occupied. Its walls thicken and its towers come back to unholy life."

Morigos reached out, shook a fist. "It must be the necromancer, Syndreck the Brooding, returned through time and space to bring the Dark Forever back into the primary universe! Your sword is not the only thing that deals with souls. The deep elves must have successfully transplanted Syndreck's soul into the body of my nephew." Morigos leaned to the side and moaned, "Even in death, my bastard nephew manages to annoy!"

Vu Verian's shoulders slumped in defeat. "We've not moved fast enough. Nenockra Rool will step onto Phate before we even have a chance to resurrect the sword."

"The necromancer is the key to all," Morigos proclaimed, "He must be destroyed as quickly as possible!"

"In this, I actually agree with him," Vu Verian said. (Morigos shivered with shock.) "We must try to kill this necromancer before he rips through the dimensional walls."

Drinwor's face lightened with hope. "If this Syndreck was killed, would we not have to fight, then? Would we even need the sunsword? What if—"

Drinwor quieted, for the Fallen Angel was gesturing for silence. Then the being of light said, "The necromancer's defeat cannot be guaranteed in time, and we *must* prepare the sunsword for any eventuality. As long as Nenockra Rool exists, the Dark Forever threatens the universe. It is fated; sooner or later, one way or another, the Devil King will come, and the One must face him." (Drinwor felt his chest tighten at this.) "However, I will endeavor to have Syndreck destroyed as soon as possible. And if we can at least delay him, we'll grant ourselves the time to resurrect the sword and gather the forces of light."

"How will you fight him?" Vu Verian asked. "With all due respect, are your powers not limited when beyond range of Vren Adiri's realm? Frankly, I was surprised you were able to reach out and bring us here."

The angel stepped back, her radiance brightening and expanding. "Yes, it is true: my powers have waned. But it is not I who will fight the necromancer. There is another, someone not of Phate. I will call to the stars, and he will come."

Vu Verian muttered, "Of whom do you speak?"

"I speak of the ageless defender of the universe, of the last centurion of the stars, of the warrior from before time."

The sky elf gasped, "A centurion still exists?"

Morigos shook his staff. "He will not come here! With your Gods gone, this world has fallen out of favor. Light and dark, good and evil, we are all imperiled!"

"It is because of this imperilment that he will come!" the Fallen Angel declared. "For we do not just speak of the destruction of this world, but of *all* worlds! I still have some influence over the heavens. As a star's light travels, so will my voice. He will hear me, and he will come. I swear it..."

Vu Verian stepped forward. "Even if you can find him, even if he comes, suppose this warrior fails? If Syndreck successfully breaches the dimensional walls, you expect us three to fight the Dark Forever alone?" He motioned to Drinwor and Morigos. "Surassis is mighty in legend, but can it hold off an entire dimension of demons? What chance do we have?"

The angel's wings unfolded, her arms raised, and the phantom flutes accentuated her words as she said, "You will not fight alone. In the Hall of Voices you will find not only Drakana, but the spirits of all the dragons who have passed from our world in the last thousand years. Indeed, as I've indicated, the forces of light are gathering, and thus the spirit dragons of Phate await you. Go to the hall and see that the light that defends all things is not as weak as you presume."

"And you will see that the power of the Dark Forever is as endless and undying as the blackness of the universe," Morigos shot back.

And with that, all fell silent as the mage's prophetic words echoed to the top of the chamber.

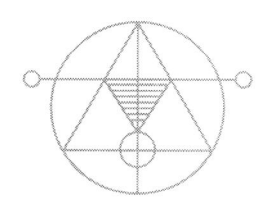

CHAPTER ELEVEN
DIS+AN+ VOICES CRY

The most lethal words are those that go unspoken.
Slayzian
Spy, Commander of Moorgrey Thake's Cyclops Slave Riders

The day drew closer to dusk, the coming night lingering like a dark thought in the back of the world's mind. In Ulith Urn, Syndreck the Brooding continued gathering his strength, reviving his necromantic abilities; while in Vren Adiri, the elder elves' continued their tireless conversing about…well, about everything (including their misgivings with each other). The Fallen Angel repeatedly reminded them to have faith, to not kill each other, and to concentrate solely on delivering the sunsword to the Hall of Voices.

Our dear Drinwor Fang spent the latter half of the day in silence. He just stared at the ceiling, his eyes lost in the clouds as the others chattered around him. He had heard them mention his name a few times, but he hadn't paid particularly close attention to what was spoken about. His own thoughts had kept him plenty occupied. Sometimes he'd thought about the sunsword and everything the angel had revealed to him, but mostly he'd spent the afternoon thinking about his father.

His father, gone forever.

It was still sinking in.

It was beyond despair…

Now, outside, evening took hold, and the Sun's Remembrance dimmed to resemble something like a moon. As the interior clouds darkened and the glint of dragon scales disappeared, Drinwor worried that certain memories of his father were slipping away with the day. He struggled just to see his father's face in his mind's eye. After a minute's concentration, he could only recall one still image of him, as if his father's portrait had been stamped upon the edges of his memory. In this mental picture, his father was looking aside, his expression serene yet serious, as if he held some hope against the likelihood of despair.

Yes, that one image was all Drinwor could presently see. He deemed his father deserved far better than this, so he strained to fill his mind with as many visions of him as he could.

A short time later, a brightening light appeared right before him, rousing him from his thoughts. It was the Fallen Angel, glowing brilliantly against the duskiness of all else. Drinwor looked around, only then realizing how late it had become. The marble floor was strewn with shadows, and Vu Verian and Morigos were gone.

"Where are the others?" Drinwor asked.

"They've retired for the evening. Vu Verian seemed especially anxious to escape the night's darkness. After all this time, I'm surprised he is still so bound to sunlight. He assumed cloudform some while ago, and now slumbers over our heads." The angel pointed to a silvery cloud that hovered halfway up the tower, then swept her arm to the side. "Morigos was shown to a bedchamber. It may be the last time he gets to rest in comfort for quite a while."

Drinwor smiled sheepishly. "I didn't even notice them leave."

"Nevertheless, they both wished Emperor Fang a goodnight, and they look forward to seeing you tomorrow morning. I bid you to retire as well, but first I wanted to tell you something."

"Oh?"

"I want you to know that I have all the faith in the universe in you."

"Do you?"

"Yes, I do. Within you resides incredible strength and power."

"I do not feel strong," Drinwor whispered.

The angel further brightened. "Oh, but you are! You were created from the universe's very soul, your spirit molded in the fires of the oldest stars. I tell you, you are stronger than you know. And with the Sunsword Surassis resurrected and in your hands, there is no force of darkness that can defeat you. Believe in yourself, Drinwor Fang. Believe that you can do extraordinary things, and you will."

"Until this day, I'd never even stepped foot from Areshria, and now I'm the *'Savior of the Universe.'*" Drinwor chuckled, then let out a long, descending whistle. "Me, fighting the Dark Forever. It's unimaginable."

"You were created for this. You're more than capable, you just haven't discovered your abilities. Your father believed in you, and so do I."

"My father..." Drinwor exhaled, tilted his head to the side. "I've been waiting all day to ask you: why didn't he say anything?"

The angel's surging radiance fluxed as she gazed into Drinwor's pleading eyes. "He meant to, he really did. It's complicated, difficult to explain exactly why he didn't say anything, but he just couldn't bring himself to burden you. He wanted your life to be happy, wanted you to feel safe, to not have to think on any of this for as long as possible. And then it all began—the gauntlets, Warloove, the appearance of the shards..." She sighed. "By then I don't think he knew how to tell you. Such little time is allotted to mortals...such precious little time." The angel paused, saw the glint of emotion flickering in Drinwor's eyes. Then she softly said, "He just wanted to protect you, protect your happiness and well-being for as long as he could. He bore so much in his life, so much... Please don't be angry with him, not now."

Drinwor sniffled, blinked his eyes, fought to withhold an ocean of tears. "I'm not angry," he whispered. "I could never be angry at him. But I'm suffocated by sadness. I... Somehow I knew we wouldn't be together forever, but I just wish he would've told me. Told me anything of this. I could have dealt with it, maybe even helped him."

"He feared for your life. He didn't want you to get involved with Warloove."

Warloove.

With the utterance of that name, grim shadows passed over Drinwor's face, and anger darkened his eyes to near black. Through gritted teeth he swore: "I'll kill him. I don't know how I'll react to the perils ahead, to the Dark Forever or whatever else is in store; but I swear I will have no fear of that demon or dark elf or whatever he is…"

To this, the angel said nothing.

Drinwor bowed his head.

As he watched the Fallen Angel's reflection flicker upon the shiny floor, his mind smoldered with hate. Oh, how the mere mention of the name Warloove riled him! He grumbled incoherently, slapped his arms to his sides, and then closed his eyes as if in an effort to escape his rage.

After a short time, he sensed the Fallen Angel's soothing presence close to him, and his anger subsided. He opened his eyes and lifted his head to see her radiance surrounding him like a heavenly golden cloud.

Drinwor chuckled sardonically. "I don't know. I don't know how to feel or react to any of this, honestly. I'm angry at Warloove, sad about my father, and scared at what lies ahead. I believe you when you tell me what I am; I've always known I wasn't *'normal.'* But I don't believe I'm as strong as you think. I just can't picture defeating Nen… Nenock— whatever in the Dark Forever he's called! I mean, I'm not completely inept with a sword, but…uh, I don't know. I just don't understand how I can possibly do all of this."

"You *will* understand," the Fallen Angel assured, "when you learn more about yourself. With experience will come wisdom, and from that wisdom will come confidence. I know you are grieving, and I know you have doubts, but for now, take comfort in this: you are capable of anything you set your heart to, I promise you."

"My heart…" Drinwor clutched at the space before his chest. "My heart was lost the moment Vu Verian told me about my father."

"You will find it again, and you will mend, when the grief settles."

"Will it ever settle?" Drinwor stared at her with desperate eyes.

"It will…it will."

His mouth spread into a sad little smile. "It doesn't feel like it." He ran his hand through his hair, perhaps in an effort to smooth away all the conflicting feelings that battled for dominance in the forefront of his mind. If only it was that easy. He took a deep breath, considered for a moment, and then steered the conversation toward something else.

"Earlier you spoke of help in the coming conflict, of spirit dragons in waiting; but I must ask: where are all the wizards and warriors of the world? Aren't there any armies to battle the Dark Forever? I've seen so little of Phate, but what I have seen seems so empty. In a way, it all reminds me of the halls of my home."

The Fallen Angel nodded. "The world *is* empty. It is from the effects of war, war and time. I shall tell you more about this, more about Phate." She stretched her wings to their full extension and lifted into the air, suspending herself many feet from the floor. Ripples of golden light radiated from her as she loosed these melodious words: "Once, long ago, Phate was the most wondrous place in all the universe. Constructed by the galaxy's most powerful sorcerers, this world gleamed in the eyes of the Gods. It was a world of hope and imagination, a world of endless possibilities, where dragons and dreams were tightly intertwined. Many ages passed with prosperity and all beings flourished in peace.

"But alas, such goodness and grace cannot forever go unchallenged, for the darkest things go after that which is most bright. One day, Phate was infiltrated by evil. Sinister minds arose from the most serene places. Demons came from other dimensions. Aliens visited their afflictions upon the residents of this planet, and the burdens of mistrust and hate weighed upon all. Over time, peace unraveled. Beings once unified were divided, and all suffered with the outbreak of countless wars. These dark times took their toll. Phate's beauty and wonder were lost.

"And worst of all, hope became a thing remembered, not a thing realized..." With this, the angel paused.

"And then what happened?" Drinwor was transfixed, fascinated, for he so desperately wanted to know more about the world his father had hidden from him.

"And then, a mere thousand years ago, the final war came, the last conflict with the Dark Forever, when what was left of the great civilizations was totally destroyed. Where are the armies, the warriors, you wonder? When the Dark Forever came, the iron skull dwarves disappeared, their silver forges purged from the Mountains of Might. The shadowlight elves, with their invisible wizards and flights of translucent dragons, were driven from their crystal forests and wiped into extinction. Vu Verian's people, the sky elves, defeated and reeling, abandoned Phate for the stars, seeking solace on some distant world. And the deep elves, their minds over time delving into darkness as their cities sank into the seas, forsook the light that birthed them and claimed allegiance to the demon lords. Now they are as good as gone…

"Yes, Drinwor, Phate's history is a story of tremendous loss. It's a terrible shame. So many civilizations, so many cities…crumbled like the pages of the books that held their accounts.

With a thoughtful look on his face, Drinwor asked, "If the destruction was so complete, then how come the Dark Forever isn't here? I mean…it sounds like they won. What happened?"

The angel seemed to exhale as if with mortal breath. "Just as defeat was imminent, Drakana, the One Life, unleashed the full power of the One Sword. A great blast issued forth, countless millions of demons were slain, and what was left of the Devil King's army was forced back into the Dark Forever. But, as the fates would have it, when Surassis expelled its energy, the Devil King himself had not yet fully stepped into the primary universe. He was wounded, banished, but *not* destroyed. And thus, the bane of the universe endures." She took a moment, moaned as if in pain. "The One Life used the power too soon, but it was not his fault. He had no choice, for Phate was all but lost."

Drinwor's eyes glittered with visions of what it must have been like, so long ago. He whispered: "And now?"

"And now, when the Dark Forever again threatens to return and destroy all creation, it has come down to us, just we few beings, stranded in the darkest region of the universe, with nearly no one to aid us but the spirits of those who have already sacrificed."

"*Already sacrificed...*" Drinwor echoed.

The Fallen Angel floated back down to the floor, continued with, "What we will we do? Will we let the fires of hatred that seem to burn in the hearts of reckless beings consume us all? Will we let all the worlds, all the galaxies, all the histories, and all those who have lived and loved and died for something beyond themselves perish in flames? No...never. Should one being of light stand against a billion dark foes, then let him stand strong, with faith and hope in one hand—"

"And the Sunsword Surassis in the other," Drinwor finished for her, his gaze wandering to his hand whose fingers clenched as if around an invisible hilt.

"One Life, One Soul, One Sword," the Fallen Angel said.

"One Life...I *am* that One Life," Drinwor murmured.

"Yes, it is you, the Son and Savior of the Stars, the One Life, meant to wield the One Sword. You are the hope for us all."

At that moment, the phantom flutes rose up and the spirit elves began to sing. Dragon cries filtered down from the chamber's upper reaches and the angel's light shone as brightly as ever. Drinwor's face was washed with warmth. His eyes glistened and he felt a burning inside, a wanting to unleash all those feelings, old and new, that had him so unsettled. Unmistakably, the angel's words had awakened something within him and, in that moment, he felt a small inkling of his potential power.

He looked to her, said, "I do have a yearning I never understood. Perhaps it is the desire to help, But I feel so alone now...so alone."

"No, Drinwor, you will never be alone!" the angel avowed. "I promised your father, and I will promise you now—you will *never* be alone. And that's the one final thing I wanted to tell you...a companion awaits you."

Drinwor perked up. "Companion?"

"Oh, yes, for what is the Emperor of the Sky without a dragon?"

"A dragon?"

Although her face had no features, Drinwor had the distinct impression the Fallen Angel was smiling when she said, "Yes, Emperor. The universe has provided you a mount of your own, and a glorious one at that. Tomorrow morning, when you awaken, you'll meet your dragon. And I must say, of all the dragons I have ever seen, there are none greater than yours. She is truly special. She knows about you, and she's anxious to meet you."

"She?"

"You shall see." The angel slowly leaned her head back, and looked straight up. "Find the soul of the sword, Drinwor, and you will find yourself. Worry not about the chaos around you, just conquer the uncertainty within, and all will be resolved as light has dictated since the beginning of time."

Suddenly, the Sun's Remembrance lit like an explosion, issuing brilliant shafts of golden light that were much brighter than the ones it had emitted before. They shot down through the darkness and converged on the Fallen Angel, immersing her in a final surge of borrowed power.

Drinwor backed away, and the angel, glittering in the jewel's spectacular radiance, began to transform. Her outline sizzled, bloomed outward, and she fell to all fours. Her limbs lengthened, her wings expanded, and a tail extended from her hind quarters. She soon grew to be so large, she took up a sizable portion of the expansive floor.

When the transformation was complete, she had metamorphosed into something even the fantastical world of Phate had never seen. The light from the Sun's Remembrance waned, the shafts dimmed, but the bottom of the chamber was aglow with the blazing visage of a Greater Angelic Dragon.

Drinwor was astounded.

To him she looked like a dragon composed of heavenly white fire—and that's exactly what she was now: a dragon of sunlight, a dragon of faith, and, most importantly, a dragon of unimaginable speed. She curled her shining head down to him and said, "And now, Drinwor Fang, I must bid you farewell, for it is time for me to fulfill my part in things, and find help amongst the stars. Remember, believe in yourself, have faith in the universe, and you will never be alone."

"Thank you, Blessed Angel," the dusk elf stammered, "I will remember."

And with that, the Fallen Angel left the Chamber of the Staring Sun. She floated down a massive corridor that led to the grand entrance hall, her radiance flickering on the walls behind her like the reflections of a thousand torches.

And then she disappeared.

Drinwor felt as if another chapter in Phate's history had disappeared with her. Overcome with emotion, he slumped to the floor. There he stayed for some time, watching the shadows of evening further darken the walls. The spirit elves' songs fell away, the phantom flutes faded, and he thought this night would be the loneliest of his life, for the brightest two beings he'd ever known were gone from the world.

Eventually, out of the corner of his eye, he noticed a glowing light carving the outline of a door in the wall to the side of him. The space inside the door faded, and two pairs of misty, disembodied hands appeared within, beckoning him forward. Spirit elves? *Hopefully!* Drinwor stood up, stared at them curiously. They kept up the gentle encouragement until he walked over and passed through the doorway. Once inside, the hands faded.

He was in a bedchamber. It was softly lit by a pair of candelabra that were affixed to the wall. The furnishings were pristine white, perfectly smooth, reminding Drinwor of his own room in Areshria. The bed itself was an ivory-framed bundle of large silken pillows; an inviting refuge for his wearied self. He didn't have to think twice before exhaustion sent him sprawling to it, where, uncharacteristically, he immediately fell into a deep sleep.

And on this eve, his sleep was deep and peaceful, for unbeknownst to him, his dragon was right outside the chamber, where she silently watched over him throughout the entire night, guarding his dreams until the coming of dawn...

The Greater Angelic Dragon drifted out of Vren Adiri's crystal doors.

She coasted over the gemstone floor and landed on the spot where Zraz had lain the day before. She winced upon noticing traces of the cloud dragon's blood, and sorcerously dissolved the stains with a wave of her foreclaw. Then she regarded all about her. Night had fully fallen. The cloudwall wrapped the realm like a shadowy shawl. A cool wind brushed up against her luminous face, and the steady moan of faraway thunder sounded like some distant warning. Glints caught her eye and she looked to the enclosed sky.

Vren Adiri's guardian dragons had leaped from their perches and swooped in over her head. They sang to her. It was unutterably beautiful. No song the angel had ever heard moved her like this farewell chorus of dragons.

She watched the dragons for another minute, then turned to view the palace one last time. Wrapped in ribbons of cloud, its towers looked peaceful, the spires glittering with tiny points of pale light.

The dragons' beautiful song, the sight of her palace... She was moved to fiery tears.

"So, I have come to my end," she whispered. "I give the universe my spirit and my soul, and in the name of the Sunsword Surassis, may my story be remembered and ever told. I swear, oh, guardian of the stars, I will find you."

Her eyes ablaze with conviction, she looked back at the singing dragons. "Goodbye, my dragonkin. And goodbye, blessed Herard. May your son forgive us, and may *she* watch over his soul for all eternity. Farewell forever, Phate..."

And then she spread her fiery wings and leaped up toward the stars.

The guardian dragons gasped.

There were some dragons even the skies couldn't contain.

Now but a streak of golden light, the heavenly dragon shot out of the atmosphere. She wove through the destroyed remains of Phate's sister world, then curled around Rong and the Four Apostles, accelerating as she went. Soon she surpassed the dying sun and left the solar system far behind.

When she came to the edge of the galaxy, the black holes tried to seize her, but she was too quick for them to grab hold. She escaped their tremendous pull and flew on even faster. Traversing pathways that distorted both time and space, pathways only angels knew, she achieved speeds few machines or beings had ever dared, and eventually came to the heart of the universe, where the oldest galaxies lay.

There she curled around many suns, skimmed the skies of numerous worlds, searching, searching for the one. Many beings saw the most brilliant of shooting stars that night, and thereafter swore it had a voice. It had, for the angel cried out to the cosmos as she flew, calling for the centurion of the stars.

She searched and searched and called and called, but could neither find him nor get him to respond. She began to despair.

"Where are you? I must find you! My strength ebbs, my spiritual light fades."

Indeed, her time was running out. Where in all the galaxies could the centurion be?

She carried on, her desperate voice but a ripple in a sea of infinite silence...

Eventually she was heard by other angels. They hadn't expected this. Hadn't Phate's angels fled with all the others? What was she doing? There was no defying or defeating the Dark Forever! Nenockra Rool's power was absolute. Let him be, and pray he didn't enslave them all.

And yet, this lone, dying angel continued to call.

She was daring to hope, and that was something the rest of them had forgotten how to do.

Their immortal heads hung in shame, the other angels knew they at least had to help her, so they gave her a clue... The Greater Angelic Dragon saw all the stars in the galaxy fade.

All save one.

This one star remained shining true.

With all the strength she had left, she flew to this star, and found a world that had recently been embroiled in the center of a cosmic war.

Oh, what a battle it must have been!

Destruction was everywhere, the surrounding space bespattered with swirling nebulae. The world itself was damaged. The exploded remains of a hundred thousand capital starships encircled it like a metallic asteroid field, and its moons were split and spiraling out of their orbits. Redirected comets were crashing into its polar caps, and its continents flashed with massive fires.

But the angel heeded none of this, for upon its surface she saw the last centurion of the stars.

She called out one final time.

"My Lord! The universe needs you once again, for all that is light might yet diminish into eternal dark, and the trillions of souls you have saved might be lost. I beg you, oh guardian of the heart of the universe, seek out Phate."

And then, with her energy spent, her radiant form dispersed across the atmosphere, a glittering cloud of golden sparkles fading against the pitch black backdrop of eternal night.

She was gone.

No living eyes ever saw the Fallen Angel or the Greater Angelic Dragon again, but her spirit was not forgotten, nor did it completely fade. It remained in the hearts of those who held onto the side of light in our Cosmic Fairytale...

Soular Centurion 7 stood on the shore of a synthetic sea.

Beneath his feet lay the ruined body of Oloron Vah, the self-proclaimed Dark Overlord of the Universe, who had terrorized the neighboring galaxies for over six hundred years. Moments before, Soular Centurion 7 had cut him down while the last of his destroyers burned up in the atmosphere.

The battle was over, the war had been won, and the celebration had begun.

Behind the centurion, millions of beings revelled in the streets of a crystal-steel city. Before him, artificial dolphins leaped from the sea, and a legion of spirit warriors danced on the waves, their laser weapons creating a holographic show that mimicked the final fight in the twilight sky above them. The planet's defender starfighters returned through the atmosphere, and its naval warships set courses back to their bases.

And then something curious happened.

Although the buzz of battle chatter had disappeared from the airwaves, the centurion now detected some new transmission coming through. It was weak, riding on some strange frequency. Having no further need to communicate with this system's military commanders, he was going to disregard it. But the little transmission persisted. After some investigation, he discovered its signature didn't match any associated with the surrounding worlds. With nothing left to do, the centurion decided to receive and analyze it.

Although the transmission contained the literal last words of the Fallen Angel, his microprocessors edited the emotion out of it and turned it into something he could more easily understand. To his surprise, it contained relevant data. A line of digital code flashed from right to left across his field of vision.

(From now on, for the sake of understanding, I will do for you what the centurion's microprocessors essentially did for him. I will translate and edit the text he saw into something readable.)

In basic terms, this is what he read:

– ANOTHER TARGET NEEDS DESTROYING ON THE OTHER SIDE OF THE UNIVERSE; COORDINATES CURRENTLY BEING CALCULATED, SITUATION BEING ASSESSED...–

When the calculation was finished, he was given the location of a planetary system whose galaxy was being consumed by invader black holes. He learned that upon this system was a necromancer, a being who intended to utilize the crude yet efficient power of sorcery to tear through the dimensional walls and release the Dark Forever into the primary universe.

This necromancer was the target.

The world was known as Phate.

Soular Centurion 7 computed all the possible outcomes should the target fail to be neutralized. The outcomes were all the same...

–TOTAL UNIVERSAL ANNIHILATION–

If the necromancer succeeded, the Dark Forever would overrun the universe, thus enslaving all creation within an everlasting torment.

And (of course) there was little time.

The centurion stepped from Oloron Vah's body and leaped into the sky, leaving a million worlds to revel and rejoice in a victory they never could have imagined as being so insignificant on the scale of all things.

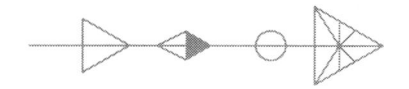

CHAPTER TWELVE
WARLOOVE UNLEASHED

Life is but a momentary spark, snuffed between the fingertips of eternity.

Darkis
Condemned Alien Overlord, Warloove's Master

"Master, I can see the trail of the Gauntlets of Loathing Light!"

Retrieve them, Warloove, and feast your fangs on the fools of Phate. The blood of any who defy you is yours, their souls are the Dark Forever's, and the sunsword is mine. Do not fail me again. Go now, and feast your fangs on the fools of Phate!

Geeter flew like a dagger through the throat of the night.

His hulking wings struck the air so hard it sizzled. That such a massive creature could fly so fast was unbelievable to those few who glanced in fear toward the sky and saw him. With his master solidified and standing atop his back, he sped across the Wicked Plains, dove over the Cliffs of Moaning Wishes, and skimmed the surface of the Raging Sea, plunging unhindered through the tips of its titanic waves.

"May the sun never seize my dark freedom!" Warloove cackled as he flung black fire from his claws, disintegrating the mists that dared to douse his face. "Fly, my demon, through the oceans of the night, fly!"

And fly they did, chasing the trail of the Gauntlets of Loathing Light—a fading vaporous line that led them northwest across the sea, far from the Continent Isle of Volcar.

Although the Fallen Angel had sent the gauntlets away from Vren Adiri early that morning, she had not counted on them tracing a lasting line in the sky that only those who dwelled in darkness could see. Apparently, even she did not know the full measure of their myriad mysterious powers.

And now she would never know of her oversight.

Warloove and Geeter followed the trail into the forsaken realm of Vorz Abyzz. Warloove knew of this place. It was perilous. Here, gigantic oceanic wars had long ago raged, and the waves and skies were still wild with lingering sorcery. He wondered if whomever they pursued hoped that some tragic fate would befall them should they venture into this dangerous realm.

"I think not!" Warloove screamed ahead. "There is no danger *any* being on Phate can endure that I cannot!" And with that, he urged his dragon forward.

Into peril they went.

Seas of blue fire rose up beneath them, and through swirling clouds of noxious vapor did they chase. They smashed aside the suspended corpses of decaying dragons, and darted over haunted warships crewed by burning ghosts. They curled around sentient tornadoes that clashed with spectral typhoons. Abyssal beasts leaped from the waves to devour them, but nothing could seize nor slow them—Geeter was too fast; Warloove was too strong.

Through all this wild realm, they never strayed from the gauntlets' trail.

When they finally surpassed Vorz Abyzz, it was as if the sea and sky sighed in relief. The sorcery that had everything in such an uproar subsided. The fiery waves gave to serene waters, and the dead no longer danced upon the surface, but merely lay still and silent far beneath.

"Onward, my pet, do not slow," Warloove insisted; for who knew how much farther they would have to fly? Geeter acquiesced, continued to shred the skies with his wings, and swiftly did he carry them forth.

After a time, the gauntlets' trail curved straight north, to a land even more desolate than any I have yet described. Directly ahead, the rocky rim of its deserted shoreline lay beneath a dense cluster of rain clouds. The temperature rapidly dropped as they approached. The icy wind's wrath was relatively mild, but strong enough to dash the straight trail into a fast dispersing swirl.

Warloove was alarmed, for he knew time was growing short. "By all the stars I yearn to see," he said through a whispered hiss, "do not lose the trail, or we forsake my eternity!"

Geeter launched them into the rain clouds.

Once concealed, they glided inland like a storm within a storm, their eyes fixed on the gauntlets' dwindling trail. Warloove squinted with a sudden suspicion. "I just realized—there is only one stronghold left in this region of the world. Could the gauntlets have been taken there? It is no place for an angel; no place that would harbor... Wait a minute..." He lifted his head, spread his arms, and spoke as if to some god. "Master, is it possible that others have the same ambition as we?"

A monotone voice colder than the winds sounded in Warloove's spectral ears.

If that is so, then be quick, and stop at nothing to retrieve the gauntlets. Unleash all of your rage upon those who stand against us! Go, for my patience is at its end, and my galaxy awaits!

"Yes, Darkis!" Warloove brought his gaze ahead. "Faster, my demonic dragon! We must find them before the trail is lost, before the night escapes us! I must hold the Gauntlets of Loathing Light before the dawn!"

And then came a clue. A ring of flickering purple lights appeared through the clouds straight ahead. Ah, Warloove's suspicion was right! He pointed forward, called out, "There! I knew it, they've taken the gauntlets to Forn Forlidor!" Now his eyes flickered like fires, and he thrust his arms up through his cloak of smoke. "So, Sorciuss, you, too, dare to betray me."

In the depths of his mind, he began composing a song of sorcery. It was to be an especially diabolical song, and he couldn't help but laugh. His voice rolled like thunder over the ears of all he would slay. Geeter joined in his master's elation, and let loose a shrieking wail.

Now the night itself would grow fangs and strike...

To some, the Iron Fortress of Forn Forlidor appeared as if it floated on the surface of an invisible lake. In actuality, it floated in midair, hovering over the center of a mile wide crater. Long ago, an enemy sorcerer's meteor had blasted away all the ground beneath its foundation, but its protective magic had held it in its exact space.

Forn Forlidor's enemies and emissaries had since been forced to fly...

The octagonal foundation was rimmed with a battlement that rose four hundred feet. Eight silver towers curled up and inward from each corner like giant scimitars, their spires nearly touching at the tips. Giant braziers at the top of each spire stung the sky with violet fires that had ceaselessly blazed through ages of wind and rain and storm. The fortress itself was set in the center of the courtyard, a ten-tiered pyramid of onyx whose nine ascending levels were sorcerously separated and suspended above one another. The pyramidal peak pinnacled some six hundred feet above the base. With the exception of the fixed base and motionless peak, all the sections slowly rotated in opposing directions to one another.

Once the fortress had glistened with dark magnificence, but the molecule-shifting wizard warriors who had constructed and cared for the place had long vanished from the world. Now it was dingy, lifeless and dull.

King of a lifeless land floating over its own waiting grave, the burning black crown of Forn Forlidor was soon to be tested by our story's most vile...

Typically, the fortress was as lively as a graveyard, its current inhabitants concealed inside; but on this fateful night, hundreds of combat mages patrolled the top of the battlement.

They were soulless, decrepit things, these mages, indistinguishable from each other but for the rank symbols burned into their otherwise plain black robes. They were tall and ungainly, their hoods a void from which nothing seemed to stare. Their staves floated in the air beside them—long, shriveled sticks whose heads were ablaze with flaring jewels. Once these mages had moved with the vigor of individual purpose, but now their ambitions were as vacant as their souls. With mindlessness they heeded their master, for they knew not what else to do.

And tonight their master had told them to prepare for a fight…

"Look sharp!" the eldest mage commanded, one of the few still retaining some wit of his own.

Hooded heads turned slowly about.

"The night may be mild," the mage said, "the weather weak, but you can feel the tension hanging heavily in the air! Make no mistake, the master expects a confrontation." He looked to his subordinates, but they did not acknowledge him. Into the night they silently stared.

It was quiet…oh, yes, very quiet…

And then…

Laughter struck their ears.

Echoing, low-pitched, drawn-out, laughter.

The mages crammed forward, nervously peeked through the parapet's embrasures, their sizzling fingers asseverating their sorcery. A gust of wind hit them and a high-pitched shriek tore through the clouds, overriding the laughter. It was a maddening sound, accompanied by some debilitating dread. It darkened hearts already black, and wilted the wills of all.

There was no mistaking…

Dragonfear.

"Gather formations against the wind!" the mage commander called.

Now the soulless mages showed they were not quite devoid of all life. With surprising haste they spread out across the southeastern portion of the battlement, their feet heavily thumping the floor, their floating staves clinging to their sides like loyal pets. They organized themselves into three rows: the front row continued peering through the embrasures, ready to assault the space below them; the two back rows readied to spread fire across the greater portions of the sky.

"Steady...steady..." the lead mage charged.

Suddenly, the stars were extinguished as supernatural clouds streamed in, swathing Forn Forlidor in thick, greyish-black bunches of lightning-wracked vapor. The spire's violet fires were snuffed with a whining whoosh. The moons vanished, the winds uplifted, and faraway, some lonely wolfish creature cried.

And then the world hushed...

But the silence did not last. A twisted song came from somewhere in the clouds.

Warloove released his spell.

On came the Winds of Hurricane Force.

It was as if Nenockra Rool had descended in front of the fortress, opened up his moon-sized mouth and unleashed a terrible scream! Four hundred mile an hour winds, laden with millions of jagged fangs, flew out of the spectral clouds and blasted into the battlement. This was the punishment for those who dared give shelter to Warloove's prize of the Gauntlets of Loathing Light!

"Defend! Defend!" cried the commander, but it did not matter, for against such power, the mages were completely unprepared.

Their eardrums ruptured beneath the winds' deafening roar, and those without sorcerous shields were instantly blasted right out of their boots. Those who managed to withstand the initial onslaught panicked. They unleashed wild fireballs that were caught in the winds and blown straight back into their faces, disintegrating themselves. The hurricane's fangs sliced through everything. The lead mage and his subordinates were skewered where they stood. Staves were splintered. Robes were sheared. Throats were cut. Limbs were separated, slashed apart and flung into the crater below.

In less than ten seconds, the fortress's outer defenses were completely annihilated, and all the mages killed.

The sorcerous hurricane next tested the pyramidal keep itself. The winds slammed into the floating sections with a million clicking clatters, causing them to shudder. But the magically reinforced walls were made of sterner stuff than Warloove had anticipated, and the gusts were turned away. The hurricane didn't relent, though, it simply swirled into a tornado in the middle of the courtyard. Bodies that hadn't been blown over the walls were diced to pieces in a screaming funnel of fangs.

It was utter mayhem.

To Warloove, it was total perfection!

Forn Forlidor's King Sorcerer, Lord Dark Sorciuss, calmly stood just behind the iron doors of the pyramid's lowest section as the Winds of Hurricane Force slammed into them. He was ensconced in deep thought, wondering how the long, onerous avenues of his life had led him astray.

"To what end have I wrought?" he whispered, "to what end?"

To what end indeed.

He had reigned over Forn Forlidor for centuries, a cruel ruler held in contempt by all who had served light. Because of him, so many golden lives had been snuffed, because of him, fear had spread through the surrounding lands like a river running wild through already drenched fields. He had been blessed with great power and, as so many in so many times before, he had squandered it.

But some things that never seem to change, do.

Over the last century, the flames of evil within him had slowly burned out. Weary of war, weary of battle, Dark Sorciuss had retreated into his dungeon's dimly lit depths and found he was weary of even himself.

After a million murders, he had bled enough of his soul. And now Warloove was conveniently murdering all of his wretched minions whom he no longer had the heart to murder himself.

Yes, it was all going as anticipated. The moment the Fallen Angel had asked him to safeguard the gauntlets, he knew what was going to happen. In truth, he'd accepted the angel's request only to experience for himself what doing a gracious deed would feel like. It was disappointing. It had been as if he threw a pebble into a sea, so little did his actions ripple the surface of the waters of fate. He knew there was no forestalling the dark forces that now rose up against the universe; he knew the Gauntlets of Loathing Light would inevitably wrap Warloove's claws. And he also knew it was too late for him to atone for a lifetime of evil.

One good deed would not stand him within the light.

His followers had paid, and his own sentence was soon to pass…

Now he heard the Winds of Hurricane Force subside.

He was about to step outside, but upon hearing some scuffling behind him, he paused and glanced around. Far down the hallway, he saw a creature's white hide sparkle within a solitary lantern's light, then disappear. It was the angel's emissary, the one who bore the gauntlets. Realizing the fortress was doomed, she must have been trying to flee. Sorciuss hoped the creature made it, hoped she wouldn't perish between Warloove's fangs. Although it mattered little, he would distract the demonic dark elf vampire for as long as he was able.

"So, after all this time, I've finally learned compassion," he whispered to himself.

He looked ahead and with trembling hands lifted the guard bar and pushed the doors forward. There was a sharp huff, followed by a grating squeal, and for the first time in many years, the keep was opened. Lord Dark Sorciuss slipped outside, closed the doors behind him, and looked over his compound.

As expected, it was devastated.

The battlement had been completely cleared of mages, its walls painted with blood. And though he couldn't see it, he correctly imagined the scene below—the crater beneath the fortress was a bowl of death, a giant open grave that had welcomed yet more deserving bodies.

Sorciuss moved farther out into the courtyard and surveyed the sky.

Although the magical hurricane had diminished, the clouds were still billowing unnaturally. Behind them, the moons were barely visible blurs. A tentative wind blew, the Shards of Zyrinthia blinked into view, but no distant stars could be seen at all. Sorciuss continued to scan around. When he tilted his head back and looked straight up, he noticed two sets of eyes staring back at him from within the center of a great shadow.

A whisper floated down to him. *"Sorciuss."*

And then came the dragonfear.

Sorciuss held fast, his feet firmly planted on the only stone he'd ever considered home. Although he cared little if Warloove took his life, he found himself defensive when concerning his keep.

Again his name came down from the clouds, but firmer, louder: "Sorciuss!"

"You cannot have the Gauntlets of Loathing Light," the king sorcerer responded, immediately regretting the shakiness in his voice, but not the conviction of the words.

The eyes in the sky disappeared, followed by the shadow; but then, from some indeterminable place, Warloove said, "Oh, no? You wish their power for yourself, do you? Hmm… Lord Dark Sorciuss, wielder of the sunsword! Sounds good, doesn't it? But it will never be, for the gauntlets belong to me!"

"They belong to no one, especially not to you."

"Oh? And who are *you* to deny me?!"

"Who I am—who *we* are—matters little now. The world has no use for us."

"I have no use for the world!" The utterance of these words momentarily set the skies alight with lavender lightning.

Sorciuss realized he was speaking more to himself than to Warloove when he said: "With no adversaries left, evil turns inward, and all we have to combat is our own souls."

Warloove laughed. "Nonsensical fool! Where are the gauntlets?"

The king sorcerer pointed to the clouds. "Your darkness is a disease which no light can cure. I hope the others have the strength to contend with you."

"To the Dark Forever with others!" Warloove screamed, his sorcerously enhanced voice sounding like a distorted chorus. "Like you, they will burn in black fire!"

"We will *all* burn in fire."

"No, not all...just you!"

"You are as empty in evil as I am."

"Empty?" the elusive vampire returned, "I think not. I'm about to fill myself with whatever is left of you."

"Then you'll be filled with nothing, for I have expended all my atrocities."

"Expended all atrocities?" Warloove laughed again. "Sorciuss, what is this? Are you so defeated? How disappointing! Long have I looked forward to mixing fire with you. You're something of a legend to this world! You and this *mighty* fortress!"

"If fire is all you truly desire, then you needn't look to Forn Forlidor. Simply wait. Fire is coming for us all, it will come for you, too. The sun is dying, and the Dark Forever will—"

"Yes, yes, yes," Warloove cut in with an exasperated huff, "the sun dies, and the Dark Forever is coming for us all. I grow bored of prophecy and...oh, I grow bored of *you*. You've gone mad, locked up in that dungeon of yours for so long. Sorciuss, this is unconscionable. I give you this last chance—give me the gauntlets, and I might leave you with your pathetic undead life. But do this now. I have much to attend to."

The King of Forn Forlidor closed his eyes, drew in a breath, and said, "With all that is left of my ravaged heart...no."

A growl like a rabid beast's echoed all over the sky. "Fool! If I had the time, you'd suffer for *eons*! As it is, you will be reduced to a pile of ash and blown away!"

Suddenly, a sense of invasion overwhelmed the king sorcerer. He pivoted, and looked up over his keep.

Against a backdrop of swirling black clouds, the largest demonic dragon in the primary universe was diving straight down at him. A flash of lightning illuminated the beast and, for a split second, Sorciuss got this tale's first clear glimpse of Geeter. It was a horrifying sight! Geeter was indeed massive, even larger than the keep, his wings like sails stolen from an evil titan's ship. He had no scales; he looked to be carved from satiny black stone. He had huge pincers and six insect-like legs. His hundred foot long tail curled over his back, the poison-tipped barb eager to skewer anything. Eyes like burning embers blazed from the shadows of his demonic face, and his acid-stained snout was overlong and oversized, the terrible maw agape.

And then there was Warloove...

The vampiric fiend was a little shadow on Geeter's back, but Sorciuss knew him to be the handle of the dragon's blade. He could feel Warloove's stare upon him, could hear the vampire spew archaic curses, releasing a millennium of pent up hatred from the dark pit of his infernal being!

Now Warloove pointed his finger and sent a laser-like beam of black fire shooting straight down, burning the air itself, screeching like a thing alive.

Dark Sorciuss sidestepped the strike.

It was close.

Warloove's fire exploded the stone right beside him, showering him with charred little fragments.

"Good!" Sorciuss cried out. "Let us mix fire, then!"

He threw his hands into the air and slapped his wrists together, his arms igniting like an enkindled torch. Then he pulled his wrists apart, releasing a geyser of purple flames just as Geeter came screaming down to devour him. Sorciuss dove aside, and the dragon got a mouthful of fire before smashing headfirst into the courtyard, missing his prey but lodging his burning fangs deep into the stone. All Forn Forlidor shuddered as if it had been struck by an earthquake. Geeter shrieked with pain. His colossal body toppled over onto the battlement wall, his neck bent back most uncomfortably to accommodate his stuck head.

Sorciuss rolled out of his dive and sprang to his feet, expecting Warloove to be right on top of him.

But the demonic dark elf was nowhere to be seen.

"Damn!" Sorciuss exclaimed.

Warloove could be anywhere: in the sky above or beyond the battlement; disguised as a shadow flitting across the walls; or perhaps standing invisible right next to him.

Sorciuss backed away from Geeter's thrashing body, and moved into the shadows of the battlement's wall, all-the-while looking all around.

A minute went by, then another, but still there was no sign of Warloove. "Come for me!" the king sorcerer called out, the unknown whereabouts of his opponent becoming increasingly insufferable.

No answer. Just the whistling wind and the grunting dragon who was still struggling to unstick his fangs from the courtyard's stone.

Where are you, dammit?

Eventually, while Sorciuss continued to slink and scan about, Geeter managed to free his fangs and flip over, his tail whipping into the base of the battlement's wall. A hundred foot wide section was smashed. It caved in and crashed down into the crater, the rumbling echoing for miles around. Geeter paid it no mind. He perked up his head, then leaped into the air and disappeared into the clouds.

Sorciuss tentatively stepped from the shadows, his hands raised, a sorcerous song tickling the tip of his tongue. From above came a rumble of thunder, a dash of lightning, and then…

Death.

With supernatural speed, Warloove shot down out of the clouds, a smoky, shadowy blur of savage darkness! His body solidified, then landed with a deafening thud directly in front of Sorciuss. His claws stabbed outward, erupting with searing black flames.

Dark Sorciuss stumbled backward, his own hands discharging a translucent energy shield before him.

It was futile.

His shield was instantly disintegrated and he was smothered in fire.

Warloove stepped forward, his abominable white child face leering through his cloak of smoke, his fangs extended; yellow eyes burning with enkindled rage. He spit on the king sorcerer, yelled, "You know *nothing* of what I've endured! A sobriety that spans beyond all time! I'll have the gauntlets, weakling, and you will suffer!"

Sorciuss's knees gave and he knelt as one humbled before the avatar of a dark god. Such fear he had never expected! Such pain! He moaned, "Plea— Pleeeease!" but the fire wouldn't relent; it completely engulfed him, seemed to curse at him in some crackling, molten language. The pain went from awful to excruciating. Sorciuss screamed and screamed, but Warloove showed him no mercy.

And now Warloove's face sprang out of his smoky shroud to bury its fangs into the king sorcerer's neck. Oh, how Warloove howled and cackled while he drank! His bloodstained lips quivering as he sucked away what poisoned life was left of the burning, half-dead king of Forn Forlidor. Then both his claws stabbed forward, puncturing Sorciuss's chest, his fingertips still spewing flames that licked the king's insides like a hundred fiery tongues.

Unable to withstand the strain of such heat, Lord Dark Sorciuss's bones exploded.

For several seconds he swam in a sea of agony, then his consciousness spiraled down into the utter darkness of nonbeing. Reduced to a dried up bag of burning flesh, his body slid from Warloove's fangs and fingers and slapped to the floor.

"Suffer! Suffer! Suffer!" the demonic vampire screamed, throwing his fire at the flaming corpse.

As promised, what was left of Sorciuss turned into ash and was blown away.

And *still* Warloove's flames flowed.

Seized with the ecstasy of murder, he burned Sorciuss's spot until the heat melted the stone. He would have burned right through the bottom of the courtyard had Geeter's cries not distracted him. He ceased his sorcery and looked at his smoking claws, his chest heaving, his fangs dripping reddish-black blood.

The gauntlets!

He let his seething settle, then turned about, his face receding into his cloak of smoke, his fangs retracting into his mouth.

Geeter glided down, this time gently landing in the courtyard. Warloove strode up to him and whispered, "Clear the keep."

The dragon faced the front doors of the fortress, then bowed his head and drove it forward like a battering ram. The doors gave as easily as a melon beneath a mallet, exploding inward in crumpled pile of metal. Geeter stretched his great maw over the smashed entrance. He sucked in his breath, rolled back his eyes, and exhaled acidic fire. The level's interior burned like an oven. Everything within melted—wood, stone, and steel alike.

Finally, after a full minute of exhalation, Geeter checked his scorching breath and pulled his head back. Burning smoke poured from the entrance like the defeated fortress's final gasp. This did not deter Warloove from entering. Heedless of the smoke, he marched into the fortress as if he was its newly crowned king, disappearing into the charred corridors.

Outside, Geeter halfheartedly looked over the grounds for something else to incinerate, but found nothing. Then, after some minutes had gone by, he heard a wretched cry emanate from deep within the burned-out structure.

It was a cry he well knew.

His master was displeased.

Warloove came bounding out of the keep, screaming, "Curse this world, they're not here! Their trail leads through a trapdoor! Now, to the sky!"

And with that, he leaped onto his dragon's back. Geeter took flight, and they soared over the battlement, ready to give chase to whatever creature had fled with the gauntlets. But to Warloove's pleasant surprise, there would be no need for a chase, for the gauntlets' trail spiraled right into the recesses of the crater.

"Go, go!" Warloove commanded.

Down, down, down into the ghastly darkness they went, where the walls were lined with ancient stones and forgotten bones, where the remains of all those murdered over the last millennium lay unrested, where the wall's crumbled ruins smoked, and the victims of Warloove's wrath still bled. And there, half a mile down, in the exact center of the crater's bottom, at the very end of the dimming, vaporous trail, the Gauntlets of Loathing Light were precariously perched atop a battle mage's broken back.

Warloove's eyes bulged. "At last!"

As Geeter hovered over the delicate dead, Warloove jumped atop them, landing as softly as he was able (not out of any respect, you know, but for fear of disturbing the gauntlets). He clambered over the pile of bodies and seized the evil artifacts.

"Master!" he screamed to the unsettled sky, "I have them!"

Good…good… came the monotone voice in his head.

He lifted the gauntlets high, beheld them against the obscured moons' beclouded light. They were even more glorious than he had imagined! He slipped them on, their black material snugly wrapping his flexing claws, their red runes brightening and pulsing. The gauntlets seemed as eager to find Warloove as Warloove was to find them. They had not wrapped the hands of one so powerful for so long! A warmth like nothing Warloove had ever known swept over him, and in that moment he foresaw his dominion over all of Phate. In that moment, he was assured that he indeed held the power to wield the Sunsword Surassis. Finally, the Gauntlets of Loathing Light were his, and in another dimension, all the Dark Forever's demons squirmed with anticipation, for they believed now the accursed sunsword would not stop them from fulfilling their destiny.

Warloove remounted his dragon and flew cackling into the night, stealing toward the Castle Krypt before the red sun's cruel eye could find him and set his dark dreams aflame.

And it was a relief for this writer when Warloove flew away, for as you can see, when particularly riled, he's out of even my control…

※※※

Warloove was so overcome with joy when he acquired the gauntlets, he never noticed the loyal servant of the Fallen Angel, a starlit unicorn named Arcynn Ahnna Jha, whose body was half-buried not twenty paces away from him.

It was she who had flown the gauntlets from Vren Adiri. Overcome by the exhaustive power of the dreadful gloves, she'd fallen unconscious as soon as she'd escaped from Forn Forlidor. Now she lay helpless, her silky hide shrouded by the grey gloom of old gore.

Swollen with sweet, immortal blood, she would have been delectable to the vampire.

But she was a feast unrealized. And, ironically, she would have died had Warloove not arrived and taken the gauntlets away, for the gauntlets had nearly drained her life force. But minutes after he had gone, her eyes fluttered open, and her strength slowly returned. And when dawn's light crept over the crater's rim, she arose to fly, and forever fled this cursed, lifeless land.

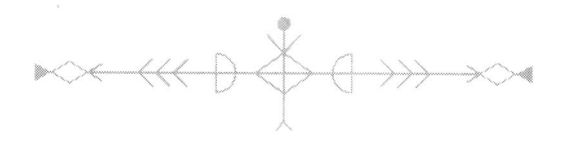

CHAPTER THIRTEEN
MORNING'S HOPE

The eyes of those who love me have a strength that's all their own, and when they look upon me, I know I'm not alone. And in my darkest hours when my life has grown so dim, I gaze into those loving eyes and find a peace within.

Lornalicia
Sorceress of the Northern Spires of Icyndia

"Wake up, my Emperor, wake up…"

A clear ringing voice invaded Drinwor's dreams, but he was reluctant to listen to it, for on this night there were no nightmares, no frightening visions. No, on this night there was only peace. This night, his dreams were as loving arms about him.

He drew out a long moan and turned over, subconsciously fighting the urge to rouse.

But the voice persisted.

"Wake up, my Emperor, wake up…"

Drinwor stirred.

His dreams dimmed and he ascended into the bleary haze that lay just before awakening. He exhaled a deep, rousing sigh, and gently came awake.

When he sat up and looked around, he experienced something that occasionally afflicts all sentient creatures of the universe in their first minute of wakefulness—for the life of him he couldn't figure out where he was. He wasn't frightened, though. He was actually quite comfortable, sitting on an island of silk pillows, surrounded by satiny curtains and smooth furniture all made of the purest white. The candelabra affixed to the wall across from him gave a soft, flickering light, and it was pleasantly cool.

Ah, yes, now he remembered where he was.

"I'm in Vren Adiri."

Indeed he was. But there was something different about the room, something he didn't think had been there the night before. He couldn't quite put his finger on it. Perhaps it was just a feeling. Dismissing it, he shook his head and got out of bed.

Before he took his first step, there was the faintest sizzling sound, and a tray of food materialized atop the hope chest which stood at the foot of the bed. Interesting. He looked behind the satiny drapes, trying to find whatever wizard was responsible.

"Hello?"

There was no one there (well, no one visible, anyway). No matter, he was starving, and the tray was laden with exotic fruits, loaves of fresh smelling bread, and a pitcher of blue fluid. Being fairly confident the food's origin was benign, he sat next to the tray and went right to ingesting all he was able. The food was delicious, the blue beverage very refreshing, filling him with warm energy.

He felt good...until memories of yesterday's conversations started trickling into his mind, that is. He felt a slight tug of anxiety. His thoughts strayed to Vu Verian and Morigos, and his conversation with the Fallen Angel. He remembered how she had proclaimed him the "Son and Savior of the Stars." Was it all a dream? He truly wished it was. He looked down, grasped the silver sword charm dangling around his neck, and held it tight.

His father's sword charm.

"May the Gods return...father."

Oh, our dear Drinwor. In those brief, waking minutes, he'd forgotten. Now guilt collapsed like a mountain upon him, and that familiar feeling of utter hollowness consumed his spirit. He fell back onto the bed and lay there in silence for long moments.

Eventually, without realizing what he was doing, his hand slid into his armor's leg pouch. He felt the warmth of enchanted metal, and slowly pulled out the sunsword. He held it up over his face, beautiful as it was, gleaming and glinting within its own mystical light. He turned it over in his hands, and Sillithian Synnstrike's limp, lifeless body rolled over in the pommel. He brought the pommel close to his eyes, staring at the little solar dragon. It seemed to be resting peacefully, as if patiently waiting for him to return it to life. He looked closer, closer...

"It is something to behold, the Sunsword Surassis."

Drinwor sat up with a start, smacking his nose into the pommel. "Hello there?"

"Hello, I'm here."

"Who's where?" He quickly put Surassis back into his leg pouch, his head darting from side to side. The bedchamber appeared to be empty, but anything was possible in the magical world of Phate. The "food wizard" could have been right there in the room with him all this time. He stood from the bed, still looking about.

"I'm right here," the voice came, "outside."

Drinwor peered through the semi-transparent veil of scintillating white magic that draped the chamber's doorway. From beyond it, a huge eye was staring back at him. He was immediately transfixed. This was no ordinary eye! It was brilliant, glowing through the doorway like a star peering out of the cosmic dust that swirls in the center of a newborn galaxy.

This was the eye of a dragon.

Drinwor wondered if it was real or imagined.

"You slept well, my Lord?"

The words seemed to come from right outside the doorway. Drinwor recognized the voice. As smooth as a swift running stream, flowing clear and soft, yet resounding and strong, it was the voice he had heard in his dreams.

"Yes," the dusk elf said, "I guess I slept well...considering my world has fallen apart." He gave that slight, sheepish smile of his, the smile that tried to ward off the seriousness of the feelings behind it.

"I'm glad, Drinwor."

Drinwor squinted in trying to get a better fix on the eye. "Are you...well...are you her?" he asked.

There was a small laugh. "Yes, I'm *her*. I'm sorry if I interrupted your sleep, I was just anxious to see you, and we have much to do."

"Oh, it's fine, I never get a full night's sleep, and everyone seems to be anxious these days."

"Indeed they do."

Drinwor stepped closer to the doorway. "So, you're really my dragon?"

"Yes."

Drinwor pondered for a moment, then said, "I've flown them before, you know. My father used to let me take his cloud dragon out for a short flight from time to time."

The eye blinked. "Zraz could not have asked for a finer rider."

Upon hearing the name, Drinwor lifted a brow. "You knew Zraz?"

"Yes, I met her a long time ago. She was beautiful and kind."

"If you knew Zraz, then—" Drinwor cut himself off, turned his face toward the floor. He was silent for a few seconds, his mouth hanging open, hesitant to let fall delicate words. Then he slowly brought his head back up and asked, "Did you know my father?"

"Yes," the dragon answered with an airy whisper, "a nobler being there never was."

Drinwor turned, and with shoulders slumped sat back down next to the now empty tray. "You don't mind talking like this, do you?"

"No, absolutely not."

"It's been a very difficult time."

The eye drew closer to the door. "Drinwor, I'm here for you, in whatever capacity you need."

"I appreciate that, though, to be honest, I'm not really sure what I need right now."

"Perhaps just a friend."

"I haven't had many of those. That would be nice."

The dusk elf pushed a tuft of hair from his face and his midnight blue eyes twinkled in the candlelight. He then folded his hands together and set them upon his lap. With lips scarcely parted, he asked, "How did you know him?"

The dragon looked away, reminiscing for a short time. A smile slowly broadened on her snout, but to Drinwor went unseen. She looked back through the doorway, back to Drinwor, who was patiently waiting for her response.

I can tell you that Herard Avari Fang would have been honored to know that this is what she said: "I was here when the Fallen Angel appointed him as Emperor of the Sky. It was a proud moment. He was the only human to ever hold that title, you know. It had always been held by either elves or dragons. But in these times, with the dragon nations broken, and so much infighting amongst the remaining elves, it was a wise choice." She nodded at this, then continued. "Oh, Drinwor, Herard was so young! But he brought levelheadedness where before there had been only pettiness and bickering. It was something to see, this young mortal repairing immortal divides that had spanned for a thousand years. That one so young could see what so many others refused too; that one so young held a wisdom they'd long abandoned…well, his example helped bring them back together." She laughed. "Some of the dragons were convinced Herard had to be one of their own—a dragon spirit reborn in a human body. For only a dragon could have had the patience to deal with an elf!" Her voice dipped back down to nearly a whisper and she concluded with: "Yes, I knew Herard Avari Fang. He was a triumph of the human spirit, of all spirits, and ever will his memory endure in my heart."

And then she was quiet, her eye sparkling with remembrance.

Drinwor looked up to her. "I don't know what to say, except, thank you." He brought his hands to his face, catching liquid crystal tears. "Ah, I'm sorry. I really need to control my feelings. I can't break down every time I hear about my father. It's just—"

"My Emperor," said the dragon, "there's no need to justify or explain. I'm the one who's sorry. I've been insensitive. In your delicate state, I went a little bit too far. I shall not speak of him like that again."

Drinwor took his hands from his face and waved them. "No, no, don't be sorry, *I asked you* to tell me how you knew him! No, please, it's good to hear these things, actually. Good to hear…well…good things about him." He laughed through a sniffle.

"I know you've endured a lot already. If you would like, I can ease your sorrow, at least a little."

Drinwor tilted his head. "How would you do this?"

"I will show you."

She began to sing.

Mystical characters composed of sparkling blue dust slipped through the doorway to dance about Drinwor's head. They were magical notes, accompanying the dragon's tune and reminding Drinwor of the crystal leaves in the Forest of Chanting Angels. Their intertwining melodies were soft, resonating, pleading for the assuaging of his soul. That such a sound didn't emanate from an instrument would have been disbelieved by the symphonic masters of the universe's most artistic civilizations.

This was the Dragons' Song of Solacing.

It was effective.

Drinwor sat with eyes closed, listening as one does to the breaking of waves upon the shore. His breathing deepened and slowed, and an ample portion of his despair was gently turned aside. He still bore it, was still very much conscious of it, but for now, he was better able to cope.

The song carried on for a couple minutes, then slowly sank beneath audibility.

Drinwor exhaled, opened his eyes, and stood up. "Thank you," he said, "I do feel better."

"You're welcome, my Lord," the dragon returned. "Would you like to come out of your bedchamber now, so we can really meet?"

Drinwor said, "I'd like that," then moved toward the door.

The eye remained hovering just on the other side.

"Uh, I might need some room, there," Drinwor noted.

A small laugh ensued. "Yes, yes of course." The eye backed out of view.

Drinwor strode through the doorway. There was a quick, painless little sizzle as he passed through the magical veil, then he was back in the Chamber of the Staring Sun. It was dimly lit. The Sun's Remembrance was shadowy, for outside, dawn had yet to fully awaken; the sky was bluish-black, still flecked with weary stars, and the horizon was just beginning to glow. Inside, all was quiet. Vren Adiri itself seemed to be sleeping.

Something about the chamber was rather odd, though. It was dim, yes, but Drinwor discerned a strange blear that covered all the space before him. Little twinkles shone here and there, and as his eyes adjusted to the chamber's light, he noticed a barely perceptible network of thin red and blue lines threading the very air. "This is strange." He tentatively reached out to the blear, and it was as if his fingers touched some invisible wall that was both warm and tender.

"What *is* this?" he cried, quickly withdrawing his hand.

"Hello, Drinwor Fang, you are even more beautiful that I had imagined."

The dragon's voice sounded from directly above.

Drinwor glanced up, and there, looking down on him, was a pair of those mesmerizing eyes. Now unhindered by the door, he could see them in their full radiance. Indeed they were glorious, like bluish-green worlds fully imbued in a healthy sun's light. They were expressive, compassionate; although their gaze bore into him, they somehow didn't seem intrusive. They came down closer and Drinwor realized—the dragon was right in front of him.

"Oh, I was wondering what that was. It was you!" He laughed.

"Yes." She smiled.

Drinwor had seen dragons in his time, but none like this. He circled around, taking in her full form.

Ah, finally, my reader, a time I have long awaited has come! Beneath this very sentence lies my favorite dragon's description...

She was huge, much bigger than Zraz, over two hundred feet long from the tip of her snout to the end of her spaded tail. She was clear. Her body looked as if it was made of perfectly still spring water. The red and blue threads were her veins, which spread out from the soft golden impression of her heart. The rest of her organs were barely discernible blurs. She twinkled here and there, briefly revealing some feature or another. Drinwor caught a glimpse of the long, curving horns arcing back from just behind her eyes. And for a second he saw her scimitar-like talons, and the tips of her glistening, pearl-like fangs. Her wings looked like great ethereal leaves folded across her back, and she was as sleek and smooth as a creature born to slip through liquid crystal seas.

She was of a world unknown, a creature from brighter times. She projected an air of quiet power, of royal, immortal, and ancient majesty.

She was a Greater Translucent Dragon.

She was purring now, her breath's deep rhythmic hush manifesting only a hint of the heat of the fires that lay behind it. She brought her head down and her facial features sparkled like wintery stars, illuminating the expression on her glorious face.

She looked on Drinwor with what could only be described as love.

Drinwor gasped. "*You* are beautiful." And at that moment, something occurred to him. "Wait a minute…I don't even know your name!"

The spirit elves' first song of the day rose up to accompany her voice when she said: "I am called Morning's Hope."

"*Morning's Hope,*" Drinwor echoed, "I like that. I like that a lot."

"I'm glad you do, my Emperor, for I am yours forever."

Drinwor shifted in his stance. "Why would you do this? I mean, why would you so willingly offer yourself to someone you've never met?"

Morning's Hope didn't answer him right away. She straightened up, her prodigious head lifting so that she could look at the Sun's Remembrance, which was still asleep. While she stared at it, her mouth moved as if she silently conversed with some invisible entity.

At length she curled her neck back down, bringing her head right before his, and she said, "I offer myself because you are the Emperor of the Sky, the Son and Savior of the Stars, the wielder of Surassis destined to defeat the Dark Forever. I offer myself because there is no charge, no mission, no destiny more worthy or righteous.

"But most of all, if I may be so bold to say, I offer myself because you are Herard's son. And for that alone, I would fly with you into the Dark Forever itself. It is my eternal honor, Drinwor Fang, to serve the Son of Light; the Emperor of the Sky; the Savior of all Souls."

And with that she bent her forelegs and bowed, her snout nearly brushing the floor.

Drinwor was compelled to bow back. "I'm overwhelmed, and truly humbled. All I can do is continue to thank you." He straightened back up. "You know, it's been strange, everyone referring to me as Emperor. With everything else going on, I guess it just hasn't sunk in yet. I don't even know what it means, really. I have no idea how to rule."

"It's about faith."

"Faith?"

"Yes," Morning's Hope said. "Have faith that what you think and do is good and true, and go courageously forward. I, and all who serve you, will also have faith in what you do, and will follow. To rule well is to *be* well, and to selflessly extend the will of your heart to all you serve." She paused for just a second, nodded, and continued. "I can already see you have great character, Drinwor. And you will come to learn that consideration and compassion have a strength no darkness can ever defeat."

"We shall see," Drinwor whispered.

Then his glance was drawn to the upper reaches of the chamber. The whole place was brightening, for outside, darkness was being defeated by the dawn. The Sun's Remembrance flickered awake. The interior clouds glittered with dragon scales, the blue walls lightened, and shafts of light shot down to the floor, immersing Morning's Hope just as they had last evening immersed the Fallen Angel. The dragon's interior flared. Her veins lit as if her heart was pumping lightning through them. Her full outline appeared, and she became even more glorious: an Empress herself, Drinwor thought.

It was marvelous. *She* was marvelous.

Drinwor, like so many beings on so many worlds in so many times, took the artistic stroke of nature as a sign. He believed the sun had just spoken to him.

And he believed so had his father.

He grasped his sword-charm (which was now glowing a soft blue) and felt a warming in his heart. Even though he felt undeserving of this incredible dragon's loyalty, he felt exceedingly grateful. And although he didn't yet realize it, some small healing had begun in the guise of companionship.

He thought now on what Morning's Hope had just said—*Have faith that what you think and do is good and true, and go courageously forward*—and took it to heart.

Go courageously forward indeed.

Drinwor stepped closer to Morning's Hope and reached up to touch her. She brought her face down to his, and he patted her snout.

She smiled, then lifted her head back up. "The others should be waking now. Morning has come, and we should already be making for the Hall of Voices."

And just as she finished speaking, a cloud broke from the cluster near the ceiling and floated down. It was silky, silvery-white, like a pillow from Drinwor's room. It neared the bottom of the chamber and dispersed into a million silver specks. The specks spilled onto the floor, piling like sand filling a humanoid shaped glass, and soon a recognizable image formed.

It was Vu Verian, coming together molecule by molecule.

When he was whole, he blinked and wiggled his fingers. His sky blue eyes were wild with the light of the Sun's Remembrance, and he walked up to the dusk elf and his dragon.

"Good morning, Emperor Fang," he said.

Drinwor flashed a playful little smile to Morning's Hope, but resisted the urge to sarcastically comment on being addressed as Emperor. He simply returned the greeting. "Good morning, Vu Verian."

Vu Verian nodded to him, then bowed his head to Morning's Hope. "Milady."

"Good morning," she returned. "Was your night restful?"

The sky elf considered this for a moment. "Yes, yes it was. I dreamed of some faraway place." He smiled faintly. "I believe it was where my people have gone."

"I see." Morning's Hope then motioned to Drinwor. "You may want to move a few paces away from there." Drinwor took some quick steps to his right, and a little cloud of billowing smoke exploded in the space he had just been standing in. A myriad of colors coalesced in its center, then the smoke dissolved downward, as if sucked into vents in the floor.

Standing in the smoke's place, coughing and wheezing, was the deformed figure of Morigos of the Moom. Holding onto his crooked staff as if for dear life, he exclaimed, "Damn this Ever Dying and the vampire demon who gave it to me! I wish it would just finally kill me so I could be done with all this nonsense!"

"*I concur,*" Vu Verian whispered beneath his breath. Then he raised his voice, said, "And good morning to you, too."

"Yes, yes," Morigos said, lifting his staff and waving it around. "Good morning to you all." He looked to the sky elf. "Well...maybe not *all*." He cackled and brought his staff back down.

Vu Verian sighed, shook his head, but said nothing.

Drinwor looked at this diverse group of companions that was to accompany him to the Hall of Voices. Despite the little back-and-forth chiding, the elder elves seemed relatively peaceful now, almost lighthearted toward one another (at least in comparison to their previous encounters). It was as if yesterday's hostilities had softened with the dawn. Perhaps, Drinwor thought, they both deemed the journey ahead was going to be difficult enough without them constantly trying to kill each other.

Drinwor looked to Morning's Hope. "Are we all flying? I don't recall anyone telling me exactly how we're going to get to the hall, wherever it is..."

"Yes," Morning's Hope answered, "we are flying. I will carry you, Vu Verian will fly himself, and as for Morigos, I've offered a trusted friend as a mount."

Morigos shook as if chilled. "Eh, I'd still prefer a Kroon bat. Faster than any behemoth dragon, I'd wager. And if we're going to go down, I'd rather be astride my own cr—"

"Morigos," Morning's Hope cut in, "we've already discussed this."

"Yes, yes, let's see this creature."

Morning's Hope reared on her hind legs and called upward in the complex yet smooth tongue of the dragonkind.

Her call was answered, for something immediately flew down from out of the clouds. As it closed, they recognized it as the creature that had alerted them of Ulith Urn's awakening the day before, the insect dragon. Its wings fluttering in a blur, it came down and landed beside them.

"Fleeting Shadow." Morning's Hope said to the dark elf mage.

"What?" Morigos sputtered.

"He's called Fleeting Shadow, and I trust you will find him plenty agile."

"If you say so," Morigos grumbled. "Certainly is one ugly beast!"

Morning's Hope gave the dark elf a less than genial look. "Come, it is long past time for us to leave."

Vu Verian looked about, lifted his hand. "Wait. Where's the Fallen Angel? I had hoped to see her before we left."

"She is gone," Drinwor informed him. "I saw her leave last evening."

"Ah, I see," Vu Verian said, the light in his eyes dimming ever so slightly. "So, she's already made for the stars. Well then, who's to look after Vren Adiri while she's away?"

"The dragons and spirit elves will watch over Vren Adiri for Drinwor," Morning's Hope replied.

Drinwor's forehead crinkled with surprise. "For me?"

Morning's Hope nodded. "You are the Emperor of the Sky. All the sky elf palaces are yours now, for the Fallen Angel will not be returning. Her time on Phate is finished, may she be blessed by the Seven Glories." Then she turned away and strode toward the large corridor that led to the main entrance hall.

The group followed her, but not before the two elder elves cast quick glances to a rather shocked looking Drinwor. Drinwor shrugged, said: "My life continues to get more and more insane."

Morigos chuckled, and they exited the chamber.

Morning's Hope led them outside.

They walked until they were halfway across the gemstone floor, then paused to take in the morning. It was bright. The cloudwall was serene, its innards bereft of lightning, for nothing ill or evil flew in the surrounding skies. The wind was cool but comfortable, the air between its gusts delicious and warm. Behind them, Vren Adiri's spires were aglow, for a ray of sunlight had slipped inside the realm to bathe the tops of the twining towers.

"It is as I knew it would be," Morning's Hope declared.

"And how is that?" Morigos inquired.

"I prayed last night. I asked the sun to imbue the sky with the brightness of old…if only for today." She turned to them. "You see? All light is not defeated! Hope still remains."

Though somewhat somber, Vu Verian was moved enough to admit, "It does look to be unusually bright this day."

"Yes, it does," Morning's Hope agreed. Then she set down a wing and said, "Come my Emperor, let us roam your sky!"

Drinwor's insides fluttered with excited chills, and he bounded up her wing. To his surprise, a throne materialized in the center of her broad back that appeared to be made of the same translucent substance as her skin.

"I hope you are comfortable in it, my Lord," Morning's Hope said. "If not, I can change its shape and consistency until it pleases."

Drinwor shrugged. "I'm sure it will be fine!"

It certainly appeared fine. It was as royal looking as it was magical, its silvery ornamentations twinkling in the sunlight. Its arms were sculpted dragons, its high back like a great shield whose angelic crest was etched with glowing white runes. Drinwor eased into it, and he himself seemed to glow in its embrace. His hands gained a firm grasp on the dragons' heads and conjured straps looped around the base to enwrap his ankles. Now sitting in his throne, the dusk elf truly felt like an Emperor!

"Fine indeed!" he cried.

The wind lifted his hair, his eyes blazed their deepest blue, and for a moment he was compelled to raise high his sword of waiting fire. But he didn't. Instead he took a deep breath, calmed himself down, and looked aside, to where Vu Verian was transforming.

The sky elf's long white hair melded into his robes and his robes transformed into feathers. His body enlarged and his eyes spread wide and round upon his face, his head expanding around them. He was the Great White Owl again. He shook his tail and tested his wings. He was ready.

"Oh, let's get on with it!" Morigos grumbled.

Fleeting Shadow lowered himself and stretched out a multi-jointed leg, offering its gradient as a stair. Morigos huffed, "Bah, I'd just as soon sprout my own wings than fly such a creature as this," but climbed onto the creature's back.

All were ready.

Morning's Hope looked upon them and loosed these words: "Remember, there is peril everywhere. Although the sun watches over us, her radiant light cannot hide us from all evil. Ever will the observing eyes of the Dark Forever be upon us. The sunsword, even secured as it is, will beam like a beacon in the dark. We must be strong, we must be swift, and to those who would do us harm, we must be unmerciful."

And with that, she spread her great wings and leaped into the sky.

Vu Verian jumped into the air and flew up beside her, with Fleeting Shadow flying behind him. They soared through the upper eastern corner of the cloudwall, then burst out the other side, gaining speed as they made their way into the high skies of Phate.

And all the universe held its breath, for the quest of the Son and Savior of the Stars had at long last begun.

CHAPTER FOURTEEN
A COSMIC ARRIVAL

Better to cross the finish line burned, beaten, and broken, than to never finish at all.
Vol Drokion of the Memnion Observers
Wizards of the City of Exalta

The universe parted for Soular Centurion 7 like a sea before a savior.

He shot past starships made of light, raced comets through the Cloven Streams, and surpassed solar dragons on the outskirts of the Angelic Spheres. He wove through the Ionizz Nebulae Cluster, then curled around the galaxy of the Draxiah Meeh—vicious aliens whose technology was so terrible it could destroy time. Now the centurion flew so fast he himself manipulated time, leaping through self-made wormholes in an attempt to get to Phate before it was too late. He was seldom driven so. He knew it was no small matter of a single civilization at stake. The Dark Forever was threatening to consume all the universe!

His universe.

Soular Centurion 7 would not see it burn.

He flew on yet faster, reaching speeds even the Fallen Angel hadn't achieved.

Finally, after flying through a seemingly endless stretch of empty space, he came to the darkest region of the universe.

–TARGET COSMIC SECTOR ACQUIRED–

In that sector he found a lone galaxy curtained by a tightening wall of predator black holes. It was galactic genocide. Hundreds of stars were being swallowed every second. Had any angels actually seen the death of so many hopes and dreams firsthand, they would have wept for all time. But the centurion wasn't concerned about the trillions who were perishing, for his energies were devoted to all eternity; he could not pause for those unlucky few doomed to sacrifice their lives in the face of Total Universal Annihilation.

He evaded the black holes and flew to the far arm of the galaxy, where, at last, he found the sorcerous world of Phate.

The planet was shrouded. The fragmented remains of its exploded sister stretched a veil of asteroids across its face—asteroids whose arcs were failing.

–SEVERE METEOR STORM IMMINENT, CALCULATIONS FOR TIME OF IMPACTS PROCEEDING–

But the centurion summarily ceased his calculations, for the cosmic bombardment didn't concern him, either. The damage the meteors would reap was inconsequential. That the necromancer be destroyed as quickly as possible was his sole objective. In fact, Phate itself could perish so long as the Dark Forever didn't step into the primary universe.

He carried on through the asteroid belt, his fists pulverizing anything in his path, and came to hover just over Phate's atmosphere. There he took a moment to view the world. It if were a hide, it looked as if it had long ago been lashed by a burning whip, and the wounds had never completely healed. Great black gashes streaked across entire continents and the lands bled lava. Some parts of the world were on fire. Some places were covered with storms so fierce their lightning strikes were blinding even from space.

So, this was Phate, such as it was…

Its characteristics were noted, but of little importance, for the centurion need only pinpoint one particular location. He set his scanners upon its lands and quickly located the landmass known to Phatians as the Continent Isle of Volcar. And there, clinging to the edge of a mile high cliff, were the Dying Towers of Ulith Urn.

The lair of the necromancer.

The centurion conducted a scan of the towers...

-97.2 PERCENT CHANCE THE ONLY LIVING BEING INSIDE IS THE TARGET: SYNDRECK THE BROODING-

Only ninety seven percent...?

Good enough.

Soular Centurion 7 blasted down through the atmosphere with nearly enough force to cleave the planet in two. He was a meteor himself, a streaking blur of blue fire slicing through Phate's morning sky. He reasoned if he impacted the towers at this speed, his power cells would ignite, thus causing an explosion so mighty it would completely annihilate Ulith Urn (and likely take out the western half of Volcar with it).

But alas this was not to be. For you see, one second before he would have hit, he detected a shield of sorts, some strange sorcerous conjuration that surrounded the towers with multidimensional clumps of translucent matter. The clumps weren't impenetrable, but their effectiveness increased as the energy that assaulted them intensified. To impact them at the speed he'd obtained would be like smashing into a reinforced iron wall a thousand feet thick.

Ironically, Drekklor had never perceived anything like the centurion attacking Ulith Urn when he'd converted the Glyph of Multiversal Guarding into something more useful.

Soular Centurion 7 veered aside and descended onto the once grassy hillocks that rimmed the inland edge of the Wicked Plains.

He didn't go unnoticed....

"Ah! What's this?"

In Ulith Urn's highest chamber, Syndreck the Brooding stared into the bubbling swill of the Cauldron of Carcass Control. Along with its other uses, the cauldron acted as a crystal ball; and now, in its depths, Syndreck descried an intruder on the edge of the Wicked Plains.

"How annoying!" He *knew* this intruder was going to end up being a nuisance. (Indeed he would be!) "Why now? *Why, why, why?* I'm *just* starting to scratch at the dimensional walls, *just* starting to utilize my newly-kindled powers!"

Syndreck grumbled, mumbled, and cursed. He squeezed more sorcery into his eyes, and looked deeper into the cauldron…

Soular Centurion 7 stepped onto the plains and into the necromancer's scrying eyes. That he wasn't indigenous to Phate was obvious. He was concealed in a suit of supra-steel armor whose design was angular and alien, its silvery coverings dented and damaged from a million interstellar wars, but still reflective enough to glint in the morning sun. From head to toe, he stood over twenty feet tall. He was comprised of one third flesh, one third machine, and one third ghost. His cybernetic eyes were gloomy grey, but occasionally glinted red, peering from deep within the thin slit of his helm's visor. Clear tubes ran all across him, then disappeared into small gaps in the armor-joints. The fluid in the tubes was translucent, flecked with gold, and flowing at the speed of light, casting the centurion within a golden god-like glow.

Although many knew of him, whether by legend or confrontation, no one had ever known him personally. And if he had a voice, it had never been heard. Of his heart and mind, none had ever known…

Older than most galaxies, a power incalculable, this was Soular Centurion 7, the warrior from the stars.

Now a myriad of tiny lights came to life on various parts of his body. Some blinked in even intervals, some shone steady, and some failed. He surveyed the Wicked Plains, then strode slowly, purposefully forward, his movements smoothly robotic; his head rhythmically swaying from side to side.

He looked to Ulith Urn and, through the cauldron's murky liquid, stared back into Syndreck's astonished eyes.

Syndreck recoiled.

"So, the intruder is an alien enemy!"

Although Nenockra Rool had forewarned him, he was still surprised. A universal centurion? Here on lowly Phate?

"Now the stars themselves oppose us!" Syndreck clapped his hands together. "Drekklor, come." The shadow demon appeared as if from nowhere. The necromancer pointed to the centurion's brightening image. "Destroy this creature."

Drekklor made a gesture that could only be interpreted as an adamant "no."

"What? Why always with this 'no'?"

The "*no*" this time was because Nenockra Rool needed Drekklor for another matter, but Syndreck was yet to understand this. The necromancer pointed at the image in the cauldron, shouted, "Look! *There!* There is the enemy at hand! Kill it!"

Again the adamant "no."

Syndreck was confounded. "Why not? *Why not?!*"

Drekklor hissed, "Look deeper."

Syndreck cursed at him, but leaned over and stared into the depths of his putrid pot.

There was a light in the sky beyond the plains.

Syndreck gasped.

It was a shimmering object, as bright as a birthing star, rising higher and higher into the clouds. He shuddered, for he had seen this light once before, a thousand years ago, when all his demonic empire had vanished, when his own soul had been sucked from the primary universe.

It was the unmistakable imprint of the dreaded Sunsword Surassis. That the sword was inactive and yet still so blinding to his evil eyes...

"Sooooo...*all* of our enemies are upon us! And that fool Warloove has not yet been able to acquire the sunsword!" Syndreck swiveled his head toward the shadow demon. "I understand now. The master tasks you to chase the sword, doesn't he?"

"Yes."

"Then go! Go forth and do as our master wishes! I will contend with this alien invader!"

Drekklor's form blurred and he blasted away, a streak of black wind shooting straight through the walls.

Syndreck looked back into the cauldron. He squeezed his eyes shut and thrust his hands over the bubbling surface. The cauldron churned and sizzled. The liquid darkened and thickened to look like black blood. Syndreck's mouth came open and a dark song of the dead stole from the bowels of his accursed being. The song's evil influence was felt all across time and space. In the distant past, men walking on faraway worlds felt their hearts burst in their chests; in the far future, seas exploded with titanic waves that consumed coastal cities. From the trivial to the catastrophic, dire things happened all over the universe, in all times.

This was the price of Syndreck's dark magic!

And now, on Phate, the Dying Towers of Ulith Urn trembled and shook. The entire compound writhed and wriggled and all about it the Wicked Plains quaked. The tremors could be felt for miles around. There was rumbling and booming...then all went silent.

Syndreck brought his head forward and opened his eyes. He spoke as much to *you*, my brave reader, as anyone, when he said, "It is time for the slaves to arise, the dead upon the plains, the specters in the sky...

"Now, I command you, arise!"

And though but a whisper it was, it was loud enough to open the eyes of a million corpses.

CHAPTER FIFTEEN
SPECTERS OF A FORGOTTEN SKY

That mortals murder is baffling to my immortal mind. They have no conception of the immeasurable fragility and preciousness of existence. It is a treasure to be guarded at all costs; for how long is a mortal life when compared to the span of eternity?

Syrellian Syn
Soothsayer of the Seventh Kind

There was no sun, no spirit, nor any radiant goddess of light that could have outshone Morning's Hope as she soared through the Phatian sky. When the sun hit her just right, her translucent body refracted its rays into little dancing rainbows, and her tail shimmered like a stream of golden stars, and her outline twinkled like a dragon constellation come to life.

Drinwor found it hard to believe she was anything but an angel. She was so swift, so graceful! Not a movement of her wings was wasted. With Vu Verian keeping pace just off her left flank, and Morigos' buzzing beast behind and to her right, she sped away from Vren Adiri, continuing to accelerate even as she ascended.

She wasn't the only beautiful thing emblazing the morning. The sky they traversed was unlike any Drinwor had ever seen. A widespread cover of silvery-red cirrus clouds hung high over their heads, but beneath that, not a sorcerous storm was in sight. It was as if a new realm had been unveiled, and it was wondrous. Airborne seas of multicolored vapor floated in the northern distance, with suspended forests of green shadow trees encircling their shores. The ghosts of sky elf castles could be seen to the southeast; and to the southwest, flights of gemstone dragons flitted, their jeweled wings scintillating, their tuneful voices accompanying the whistling gusts.

Drinwor soaked it all in, then twisted to look around the back of his saddle-throne. Vren Adiri's cloudwall was already a tiny distant puff, but beyond that, just over the amaranthine haze of the western horizon, tendrils of blue sky clung to the vanished tail of night. Now *that* was something to see. For the first time in a thousand years, not all about the sky was bloody or black.

Drinwor, shuddering with excited chills, called over his shoulder, "Morning's Hope, there's blue in the sky!"

She smiled, turned her head and said, "Yes, indeed there is. Savor it, my Emperor, savor it with your eyes and with your heart."

Drinwor did. He took it in until finally he grew uncomfortable from stretching around. Then he faced forward and breathed in an air that had a freshness he had never before experienced. "Truly, this morning has somehow been granted by the Gods, for who else has the power to defy the darkness of recent days?"

Morning's Hope smiled.

Eventually she leveled at a very high altitude, and led the companions on.

Riveted by Volcar's endlessly fascinating features, Drinwor was constantly looking down. There were new lands to see, new forests. There were cities of silver and turbid molten lakes. There were ruins of lordly estates and bones of beasts so huge their rib cages reached into the sky like curving ivory towers. There were the Mountains of Might and their molten rivers and, oh, so many different sights!

But nothing was as spectacular as that which now climbed into the sky and with glory claimed dominance over the day.

Drinwor pointed forward. "Morning's Hope, look!"

"Behold," Morning's Hope cried out, "our sacred star, shining with the vigor of yore!"

Whether by some sorcerous trick or effect of prayer, the ascending sun was brightening from red to white. May the Gods return, it was brightening to white! And all the lands were illuminated as they had been in times of old. The mountains' blackness went from bleak to gleaming, the surfaces of crystal lakes glittered with a million speckled points, and the whole world seemed to crawl out from under the shadows in which it had lived for a thousand years.

"I don't believe my eyes," Vu Verian said from aside.

"Bah, cursed, blinding star!" Morigos complained as he shaded his eyes.

"Be it blessed," Morning's Hope said.

Drinwor shook his head. "I've never seen the world look like this. How is all this possible?"

His dragon looked back, said: "The sun is a child of the universe, Drinwor, just like you, and it has a soul, just like you. And despite what everyone seems to think, not all the sun's strength is gone. No!" With conviction she clenched a foreclaw into a fist. "Today it rises in defiance of the darkness set against it. Today it rises to fight. It's a sign and a reminder: not all prayers go unanswered, and not all hope is lost. And by the grace of the universe, may this light last... may it last."

And then, just as Morning's Hope finished speaking, a great flash shone from directly above, a flash that for an instant rivaled the brilliance of the invigorated sun.

Everyone shot a glance upward.

A bolt of blue light burst out of the clouds directly above, then streaked straight down behind them. Drinwor whirled about, watched it descend. It arced toward the Cliffs of Moaning Wishes, then suddenly turned aside and sped across the Wicked Plains. There it disappeared, somewhere on the edge of the dead fields, its tail fading beneath the sun's greater light.

"What was that, now?" Drinwor asked. This was turning into quite a day for strange wonders!

"It was a Shard of Zyrinthia," Vu Verian replied.

Morning's Hope considered for a moment, then said, "I don't think that was a shard."

"It was," Vu Verian maintained. "Look, their bombardment begins!" He motioned upward with the tip of his wing.

Drinwor looked back up, and when he did, his gaze was met with a vision so breathtaking, so frighteningly awe-inspiring, he could only utter, "Impossible…"

The blue streak of light had sundered the cover of cirrus clouds; each side of the split was burning away like the edge of a piece of enkindled parchment, revealing the heavens. And there, in full view, were the Shards of Zyrinthia. They were close now, crawling right over the atmosphere like a blazing band of fiery little moons. The largest shards were in the lead directly over their heads, heading due east, the same course as the companions. The countless thousands of smaller ones trailed into the distance behind them, fading out of sight as they angled up into unseeable space.

Morigos laughed. "Well, there's one thing my idiot nephew was right about: the shards! Phate is inheriting its own ring of asteroids."

Drinwor was astounded. "But they seemed much farther away just a day ago. How did this happen?"

"They were closer than they seemed," Vu Verian replied. "They fell into orbit overnight, and our world's embrace pulls them ever closer."

"What happened to Zyrinthia?" Drinwor asked. "Do you know, Morning's Hope? My father knew very little about it, said it's mostly unknown."

"I'm afraid I don't know much more than your father did," Morning's Hope replied. "We believe our sister world was destroyed by some alien means. Whether it played a part in an intergalactic war, or was just an innocent bystander, we will likely never know. We can only pray for the billions lost…" And then she dipped her head, whispered a little prayer.

"But now we look forward to Zyrinthia's vengeance," Morigos said from behind. He guided Fleeting Shadow closer to the translucent dragon, added, "Soon, burning fury will rain down upon all of the lands."

Vu Verian reluctantly concurred with the dark elf mage. "Indeed, fate has long proclaimed that the coming of the shards would coincide with the coming of the Dark Forever. The meteors will come, and so will Nenockra Rool."

"No!" Morning's Hope defiantly declared. "We don't know that for certain! And the shards are not our concern, anyway, for there is nothing we can do about them. And remember, as much as fate foresees the coming of darkness, it also speaks of the ascension of light—*our* light. Of all the beings in the universe, it is not for us to brood on darkness, for we journey with the Son and Savior of the Stars! *Drinwor and the sunsword are our only concern.* Never forget this!"

Then she sighed, fearing her tone had been too strong. In a considerably calmer voice, she said, "Forgive my ire, it's just so important that we stand fast against all darkness and despair. The shards will come as they may. Let them, I say. We've survived their wrath before, we will survive them again." She curled her head around. "Drinwor?"

Drinwor smiled at her. "I'm with you."

Vu Verian added, "We're *all* with you, milady, and I shall not speak of such doom again."

"It's all right Vu Verian, I'm glad you're with us," said the translucent dragon.

Morigos snickered, made to comment, but abstained when he caught his companions' glares.

Morning's Hope looked ahead, slapped her wings, and flew forward with all speed. Vu Verian glided out to her left, Fleeting Shadow flew into his spot behind and to the right, and they all kept pace and raced on through the morning.

The hours before midday passed swiftly, with the rhythmic beating and buzzing of wings upon the wind the only sound. Drinwor couldn't bring himself to look up, but from time to time brought his glance down. There was little to see now, for the landscape was shrouded beneath a yellowish haze cast by the sun's rays. Here and there, some mountain peak or tower top broke through the blur like an isolated island, but otherwise the surrounding sky was bare. Far away, the horizon was but a silver slit separating the oceans from the stars. Drinwor wondered what lands lay beyond sight, and what mysteries they held.

Perhaps he would soon see...

As they flew, he realized he was actually enjoying the flight. Despite feeling guilty for even allowing himself to entertain any kind of joy in this time of greiving, he often caught himself smiling. He couldn't help it. He had never before ridden a dragon like Morning's Hope. Simply put, it was exhilarating. She seemed to have no end of energy; he couldn't get over how fast she was. He noticed the faster she flew, the more translucent she became.

Yes, Morning's Hope was a blessing. In such a short time, her strength and wisdom had soothed his sorrow and eased his despair. She had filled a place in his heart that had long been barren, a place he didn't even know was there.

The sky was his kingdom, but in Morning's Hope his heart was finding a home.

They flew on, with hints of blue behind them, and ahead a future unknown...

Many miles passed beneath them and Drinwor realized he had absolutely no idea where they were. How could he? All his life he'd only seen Phate from the miles high perch of an Areshrian terrace, and his father had never shared anything of the world's geography with him (perhaps in an effort to dissuade him from adventuring on its surface, he now thought).

He called ahead, "Where are we? Are we close to the hall?"

Morning's Hope smiled to herself. *He is young.* She turned her head back, said, "We're still some distance away, but keeping an acceptable pace. We should reach the Hall of Voices before nightfall."

Then, right after she had uttered the words, the world darkened.

Drinwor braved a look up, and gasped.

Of course!

It hadn't occurred to him until now—the sun's path was leading it straight for the shards. And now, at the stroke of midday, the lead and largest shard was passing directly in front of the dying star, eclipsing it. It was like dusk now. The sky lost its clarity and depth. All around, above and below, as if encouraged to come out of hiding by the disappearance of the sun, clouds crept into view. They methodically filled their familiar spaces and darkened with storms.

The once soothing winds now lashed. The cool air became icy. With a booming voice thunder made its presence known, and multicolored lightning branched out below. The earlier day's light seemed like a distant memory, or perhaps a dream. The hints of blue were lost, and what sections of sky weren't shrouded by clouds deepened to maroon.

As tactful as ever, Morigos coughed and sputtered with, "Ah, much better! I can see again...barely." He cupped his hands over his cowl's brim.

Vu Verian shook his owl head. "It was beautiful while it lasted."

"*Drah ool layana less ratan ravasha, oh meis inzivita,*" whispered Morning's Hope, invoking a long-unused dragon tongue.

Drinwor barely heard her. "What was that?"

May my mother's eyes again brighten you, my beloved star, Morning's Hope thought. "Nothing, my Lord, nothing."

The group's enthusiasm (with the exception of Morigos) dimmed with the daylight, and a disappointed Drinwor felt his heart darken with the world. He had never before realized how strongly the appearance of everything affected his general mood. Now he understood why his father had always uttered, "*Ah, but for blue skies.*" It wasn't so much the color he was yearning for, but for the feeling that the color imbued.

"For blues skies, indeed," Drinwor whispered.

Apparently, Morning's Hope heard him, for she said, "We fight for blue skies, Drinwor, not just for ourselves, but for all the universe. And I swear, we will see them again."

Drinwor hoped she was right.

Half an hour or so later, the sun moved out from behind the largest shards. Its hue returned to its usual bloody red, and the sky brightened a bit. The whole world flickered, though, for the sun was still partially obscured behind the smaller shards. The clouds around the companions were speckled with dancing shadows.

Drinwor grew more and more anxious about reaching the hall, and began to wonder if they truly were going to arrive before nightfall. He leaned forward to again inquire of Morning's Hope, but before his first words passed his lips, Vu Verian cried out, "Ahead! There! Do you see that?"

Drinwor looked straight ahead, squinting his eyes.

Off in the distance, about at their level of altitude, there were some widespread greyish shapes. A bank of oddly symmetrical rain clouds perhaps. Not surprising, they were beginning to crop up everywhere. Drinwor didn't see anything too unusual, but a suddenly jittery Vu Verian bolted out in front of the group. Morning's Hope and Fleeting Shadow flew in behind him. The clouds quickly grew larger, reminding Drinwor of just how fast they had been flying. Soon they all came up right in front of the shapes and stopped.

Vu Verian sighed. "It's been a long time since I've seen one of these places. I didn't know they still existed."

"This place stinks of foul sorcery," Morigos grumbled.

"Morigos," Morning's Hope said, "be quiet."

Amazingly, Morigos did manage to go quiet. Drinwor stayed silent, too, just staring at the strange sight before him.

It was as if a fleet of alien vessels had descended from the stars to hover in perfect formation in Phate's high sky. All told, there were hundreds of the things, arranged in dozens of rows that took up nearly half a square mile. Although they appeared to be cloudlike in substance, each held a perfectly rectangular shape. They were flat, featureless, and completely motionless, as impervious to the wind as Dreadships are to the sea. There was an ominous placidity about them. They looked drab, unhealthy in a way, as if they were—

Drinwor was struck with chills as he suddenly realized: these were dead clouds.

To look upon a field of dead clouds would be immensely unsettling, wouldn't you say? Nevertheless, some inexplicable force compelled our Drinwor to hold his stare. "What is this place?" he asked anyone.

Vu Verian bowed his head. "It is a sky elf graveyard."

"I mean no disrespect," Morigos said, "but I believe we should leave, now."

Vu Verian shot the dark elf a spiteful glare. "I don't know, for some reason I wish to stay."

"We will stay for a minute," Morning's Hope said, "and pay our respects, for I have never had the chance to honor our noble, sky elven dead."

Morigos shook his head. "I tell you, that is unwise, for I'm fairly certain my people have over the years cursed all such places. And Syndreck may have—" He coughed, then choked on his words. The runes on his robes brightened, but no one, including himself, seemed to notice.

"No, it isn't cursed," Vu Verian disagreed. "I can sense them."

"Sense whom?" Drinwor asked.

"My people," the owl answered. "I can feel their presence… and…may the Gods return, they speak to me now."

Vu Verian looked as if he meant to say more, but whatever words were to follow were lost as if they had soundlessly tumbled from his beak. His eyes widened and he went very still, with the exception of his wings which began to flutter faster.

Morning's Hope looked confounded. "I can't sense anything, I'm sorry to say." She turned to Morigos. "You believe this place to be cursed?"

The dark elf cleared his throat the best he was able, then managed: "After the war, dark elves delighted in defiling anything of sky elf origin, especially the remains of the sky elves themselves. If any souls reside here, they will not be welcoming to us…well, certainly not to me!" Then he leaned forward in his saddle, looked to the dead clouds like a nervous tower watcher peering through the fog of a foreboding night, and added with a whisper, "My people's sacrilege aside, the dead, any dead, are to be avoided as much as possible so long as Syndreck the Brooding resides on this world."

Morning's Hope nodded. "In this I heartily agree." Then she turned away, began to ascend. "Let us leave."

"No, not yet." Vu Verian said, his voice strangely monotone. He slowly drifted closer to the dead clouds.

Morning's Hope said, "Vu Verian, I don't want to take any chances, and if you want to see the Emperor safely into the hall, we need to get there before nightfall."

Vu Verian didn't acknowledge her.

He was listening to something else...

Out over the dead clouds he flew, his talons skimming their smooth surfaces, riling up little swirling plumes. The maneuver unnerved the rest of the group. It felt as if Vu Verian was lingering on the edge of a volcano whose innards were soon to unleash with molten horror, and he didn't seem to care.

"He's been cursed!" Morigos exclaimed, his green runes now glowing brightly, his staff held high and leaking similarly colored vapors. "It is as I feared."

All looked grave.

Drinwor knew something bad was about to happen. Oh, he could just feel it! A jolt of fear surged through him and this was now the last place on Phate he wanted to be.

"Vu Verian!" Morning's Hope called out. "We must leave!"

Vu Verian still wouldn't respond to her. He floated farther out over the clouds.

"He's not listening to us," Morigos keenly observed.

"Then by the Gods we'll go get him," the translucent dragon declared. "Morigos, assist me."

"No! I'll *never* mingle with sky elven spirits!" Morigos pulled back on Fleeting Shadow's reins.

Morning's Hope loosed some quick, sharp words in an ancient draconic dialect, and Fleeting Shadow immediately flew forward.

"We'll be glad to assist you!" Morigos said.

Morning's Hope flapped her wings and both dragons coasted toward Vu Verian.

Drinwor looked at the dead clouds and noticed a little ripple pass over each. They billowed, expanded upward and outward.

"Morning's Hope..."

"I see it," she responded, though her eyes were fixed solely on the sky elf.

Suddenly, a lightning-like crack shot through the air, the temperature plummeted, and behold, the dead arose!

"Morning's Hope!" Drinwor yelled

The spectral corpses of a thousand long dead sky elves streamed like smoke from a fire as they climbed from their cloudy beds. They quickly formed into tall greyish-black apparitions with wickedly-pointed ears, and eyes that were sinisterly angled slits of flaring orange. Their arms grew overlong and their claws grew even longer, like sets of curving spectral blades, if you will. They had no legs; the clouds they formed from lengthened into shadowy tails that curled up behind them.

"Away, away!" Morigos screamed, thrusting his staff down as Fleeting Shadow flew over them.

"Careful!" Morning's Hope warned, her stare never leaving Vu Verian as she flew closer to him.

Now mouths broke open on the apparitions' faces, mouths like crooked caverns filled with stalagmites of smoke. A low, breathy rasp came from each, and a thousand evil hisses joined as one.

"They don't seem happy to make our acquaintance," Drinwor observed.

"No, they certainly do not," Morning's Hope agreed.

She reached Vu Verian and swung around in front of him. But the owl didn't appear to notice her. His eyes were vacant and he seemed to be chattering to himself, his beak moving, but with no audible words. And now the apparitions were on the move, closing in all around the companions. They lifted their cloudy claws, ready to reap whatever souls they could steal.

Morning's Hope shouted, "Vu Verian! Gain control of yourself!"

Nothing. No response.

Morigos cried, "He's lost!"

The apparitions drew in even closer, some putting themselves between the dragons and the owl. More hisses arose, and one swiped at Fleeting Shadow's flank. The insect dragon let loose a high-pitched whine and, with wings buzzing, lifted himself higher into the air.

Morning's Hope was out of patience.

This had gone on long enough.

"Drinwor," she cried, "be wary and hang on!" Then she dove straight for Vu Verian, slicing right through a score of apparitions and scattering their forms with the tip of her snout. They quickly reformed behind her, but not before she reached the sky elf owl.

She slid her snout beneath him and heaved upward, unceremoniously catapulting him high into the air, far from the reach of the awakened dead. Then she exhaled with a satisfied but most un-dragon-like grunt.

That task was finally done.

"Watch out!"

It was Drinwor. His high pitched voice warned her of that which she was expecting—the reprisal. She swung her head around and saw the reformed specters gathering about her. The closest one swiped her with its long claws, cutting her just below the right eye. This seemed to spur the rest on, and they came at her in a charge.

But Morning's Hope wouldn't have it.

She thrust her wings down and twisted upward, her spaded tail whipping around, slashing the closest apparitions apart as she tore away from their grasp. She darted up past Fleeting Shadow, where Morigos was standing with his green glowing staff held high above his head. The dark elf mage was making magic, his voice humming like his dragon's wings. He was about to unleash acidic fire!

"No!" Morning's Hope roared. "Not yet! Not here! Fly up, get over them!"

Morigos' spell trickled from the tip of his tongue and was lost. "Bah!" He was then seated in his saddle as Fleeting Shadow leaped up after his translucent kin.

Vu Verian seemed to finally break out of his trance when Morning's Hope came blasting by him, yelling, "Up, up! Fly for the high sky!" He flashed a horrified look down, then immediately followed suit, dashing up behind the translucent dragon.

The spectral corpses were right on their tails. With their hisses turned into snarls, they had merged into a heaving mass of snapping maws and swinging claws that was fast rising into the sky.

The dragons and owl beat their wings with all they had. But compared to the speeds they had earlier achieved, it felt was as if they were barely moving. And now the air was thinning. It quickly went from cold to freezing, making it harder to breathe. Ice formed on the tips of their wings, but still they climbed higher and higher.

Our Drinwor was pressed into the back of his saddle-throne, his chest heavy with what felt like the weight of a full night's anxiety. Now forced to look straight up, his entire field of vision was filled with the Shards of Zyrinthia. They seemed so close! He could see through their fiery sheens, discern the craggy craters on their ruined husks. They truly were like moons on fire. For a moment he wondered if it was the Dark Forever already unleashed, spit from the pit of space to wreak its hellish havoc upon his beloved sky.

He couldn't bear it. He looked off to the side.

They were so high now, the edge of the atmosphere looked like a horizon itself. "Oh...that didn't help." This was getting insane! How high were they going to go?

Apparently, he wasn't the only one wondering this, for Morigos called out, "Do you mean to take us into space?"

"Perhaps!" Morning's Hope replied. But then she pitched forward and leveled.

Drinwor's world tilted over and he thought he was going to be sick. But the feeling quickly passed, and he was able to reclaim some of the air that had been stolen from his icy lungs. They all came to a stop and hovered beside one another.

Unholy cries came from below.

The dead were flying up fast.

Morigos pointed down, said, "We're trapped against the roof of the sky. Why did we ascend so?"

"If they caught us in that swarm," Morning's Hope replied, "they would have torn us to pieces. They're condensed now, we can destroy them!"

Drinwor looked at her with a modicum of surprise. For some reason, he never thought he'd see her so adamantly fixed on another's destruction. Her blue-green eyes lit like a warrior's as she shouted, "We must dive! Straight down! Dive at them!"

Vu Verian looked on her with shock. "What?"

"Do it!" she cried. Then she rolled forward, streamlined her wings. "Hold on, my Emperor!"

197

"Oh, I am," Drinwor assured, his hands sore from clenching the arms of the saddle-throne, his ankles firmly secured in the sorcerous straps.

Morigos cackled, coughed, and then whispered: "Again I lock stares with death…"

"Dive! Dive!" Morning's Hope commanded.

And dive they did, the dragons and owl pitching over and shooting straight down, Drinwor shouting, "Wooooah!" over the winds.

"Here they come!" Morigos yelled.

The thousand cursed sky elf spirits came roaring upward like a screaming spectral spear intent on impaling the companions upon the moons! Drinwor thought if they were to collide, all the skies would explode.

Morning's Hope looked out to her right and yelled, "Morigos, douse them in fire!" Then she looked out left. "Vu Verian, unleash whatever volatile sorcery you have!"

Vu Verian shook his head, screamed over the winds, "I cannot! I cannot!"

"Do what I tell you! Release these people from pain!"

"These people have no heaven to go to!"

"Neither do we! Do it *NOW!*"

Certain impact was imminent, Drinwor hunched down, lifted his hands in front of his face…

But then the dragons and elves released their magical might.

Morigos was the first to fire.

Screaming his scabrous song of sorcery, the tip of his staff ignited in a blaze of dark green flames that shot down and slathered the spectral corpses in a crackling acidic coat.

Fleeting Shadow came spiraling down behind the burst, breathing his own salvo, a spewed fountain of red fire that scorched apparitions already engulfed in Morigos' broiling wrath.

And then Morning's Hope unleashed her barrage.

Drinwor had seen it brewing right under his feet, for moments before, her innards had begun to glow. Now her entire body lit up as she spit out a dense, electrified burst of white energy. Thick as an oak's trunk, the beam blasted right through the center of the spectral mass with all the power of a sorcerous storm! Its effects were devastating. The burning apparitional geyser ruptured. The dead sky elves were blown into sparking strands. The explosion seemed to fill the entire sky, and the ensuing tormented screams pierced all of their ears.

Drinwor was amazed and mortified.

So this was the unbridled power of a Greater Translucent Dragon!

After unleashing their barrages, the dragons twisted over and veered out to opposite sides, avoiding the exploding mass.

Unable to come to grips with firing on his own people, Vu Verian had hesitated. He hadn't unleashed sorcery, nor had he adjusted his course. Now it was too late to avoid the explosion. With no alternative, he tucked in his wings and shot straight down, blue energy beams passing from his irises into the air, vaporizing his tears as they came. Although he justified in his mind that his beams were purely defensive, they were nonetheless quite potent. As they surged into the remaining apparitions, the sky elf ghosts spit their last curses at him before their very souls were vaporized.

Vu Verian was horrified.

All around him, the burning souls of his brethren screamed as they perished. He screamed himself just to silence their cries. He felt the sting of sorcery, the heat of his own fires, but came out of the bottom of the fiery mass virtually unscathed.

Only his heart had been wounded, and ever would those cries echo in his memory.

He flew to Morning's Hope, and Fleeting Shadow flew to them. Together they all watched as a last series of little explosions dissipated and died.

The sky elf apparitions were gone.

Drinwor was panting, his heart racing. Despite countless hours of sparring against sorcerously animated foes, he'd never before been involved in any sort of actual combat. He swallowed hard, clutched his chest, and breathed in deeply, trying to control his adrenaline.

Morning's Hope heard his sighs. "My Lord?"

Drinwor lifted his head. Through his gasping, he said, "I'm fine… I just need a minute…a minute to calm down."

"We have some power among us," Morigos noted.

"We have nothing," Vu Verian said, his glazed eyes staring aside.

Morning's Hope shook her head with exasperation. "We *must* be more careful. *I* must be more careful. This whole ordeal was foolish, reckless. We need no such unwarranted expeditions. We risk so much."

They hovered in a silence for a minute, all eyes slowly drifting to the Great White Owl. Vu Verian noticed them and whispered, "No one need say anything. I was charmed, yes, but I let myself be so." He looked to Morning's Hope. "They welcomed me. They spoke to me with voices I've not heard in a thousand years. It was them."

"It was *not* them." Morning's Hope said firmly, "It was a fouled, haunted shadow of what they once were, my friend."

Vu Verian shook his head in disagreement. "Oh, it was them. I could sense them struggling to break through the barriers that block their ascension to the Seven Glories. I tried to tell them…tell them that the way to heaven is closed, but they refused to listen. They were cursed, yes, and in confusion turned malicious, but there was no evil there." He turned to Morigos. "I hope you delighted in dousing them in fire."

"I delight in nothing," Morigos returned, "I'm not a child, and I do not unleash sorcery just to amuse myself. If you recall, if you *all* recall, I said from the moment we came to this place that we should leave."

Morning's Hope spread her wings and coasted down. "Come, let us continue on to the hall."

And with that, they followed her down through a sky vanquished of all evil spirits.

Vanquished of all…except one.

Drekklor the Shadow Demon had caught up to them. Now riding in their wake of winds, he slid silent and unseen behind them. Through his eyes the Dark Forever watched, and a billion demons growled with disdain.

The warriors of light had escaped Syndreck's deadly illusion…

CHAPTER SIXTEEN
MARCH OF A MILLION DEAD

Invest half as much hope in your life as you've invested desperation and despair, and you may find your future to be even brighter than your past has been dark.

Morning's Hope
Greater Translucent Dragon, Sworn Protector of Drinwor Fang

—SYNDRECK THE BROODING LOCKED ON TARGET—

The necromancer appeared as a glowing reddish blur in Soular Centurion 7's cybernetic eyes. His soul seething with stolen power, the necromancer was either unaware he stood in glaring contrast to the dark swirl of sorcerous storms and spectral towers that surrounded him, or he simply didn't care. There was no stealth, no deception to his doings. He made magic in full view of his enemy, in full view of the universe for that matter.

"My challenge is open to any who dare oppose me!" he shouted toward the sky.

Such was the brashness of evil.

Soular Centurion 7 strode slowly, purposefully forward.

Haunted winds swept low over the Wicked Plains, bending what few reeds still dared to protrude out of ground otherwise bereft of life. Raspy voices filled the air. They whispered to the warrior from the stars, whispered things like *death* and *torture*, *failure* and *horror*... but it had absolutely no effect on him. He was part ghost himself, and it would be *he* who did the haunting here. Had he possessed any sense of humor, he might have laughed at the crude attempt to rattle his will. Now it merely emboldened his purpose.

Suddenly, Syndreck's image brightened, and his sorcerous singing arose. The song carried forth from the towers like a cold winter's gale. A bluish blanket of magic spread far and wide, then settled down, soaking all the plains. The ground then trembled and churned. A rumble like that of an oncoming army's arose.

Soular Centurion 7 slowed.

All the land before him seemed to be quaking now.

The centurion stopped…

…and for miles around, the plains split apart with a booming crackle. Fissures exhausted their stinking breath into the air. Black hills pushed upward, and crevices deepened between them, sprinkling the upper caverns of Kroon with dirt. The slivered plains overturned. Old bones were exposed and the curiosity of the lingering carrion crows was aroused.

Then Syndreck's song ended as suddenly as it had begun. The rumbling stopped, the wind calmed, and the dust of ruin settled down. For a moment there was stillness, an eerie soundlessness…

…until the clattering began.

After a night that had lasted a thousand years, dawn was finally breaking on the dead. Syndreck's necromantic song had awakened the great graveyard of the Wicked Plains. Corpses stirred. Eyes broke open. Bloodless hearts began to beat. Tortured moans filtered up through the ground like a miserable chorus, a tormented, confused sound that grew louder and louder and louder.

And then the ravenous dead arose.

"*Yes, yes!*" Syndreck screamed.

The dead thrust their hands through the dirt, their decayed, wriggling fingers grasping at roots, weeds, reeds or stones—whatever they could find to pull their bodies from their disturbed graves. They climbed up from miles around, from every crevice in the plains, hundreds of thousands of them, then hundreds of thousands more. They clambered over one another, the broken corpses of elves and demons and men, the casualties of war come to be victims again.

All told, they were a million strong, a blasphemous army stolen from a different age!

Some were wholly fleshed, while others were completely skeletal. Some had no heads. Some had no arms. Some were mangled beyond being recognizable as anything that had ever lived at all. Limbs crawled beside them and severed fingers inched through the dirt like worms. Eyes rolled about and swollen tongues wagged with no words. Not a shred of remains was wasted. Syndreck's necromantic song had given life to every scrap, scrape, and ounce of rotted flesh.

Although the corpses had no wit about them, they were infused with some dull sense of aggression. It was a nagging desire to hit, to kill, and, if they were lucky, to eat. For a short time they stumbled about in confusion, looking blankly at one another. But then Syndreck commanded their heads to turn toward the gleaming galactic guardian. "Ah, look there, you dimwitted dead! There lies satisfaction to end all desire!"

Now, with limbs hanging, flesh dripping, and bones clattering, the corpses came staggering and stumbling toward the centurion.

-INTRUDERS APPROACHING-

Soular Centurion 7's defenses went on alert.

A row of tiny red lights illuminated on his chest-plate, and the gold-flecked fluid racing through his exterior veins accelerated, thus granting him more energy. A small panel on his armored leg-covering opened. He reached into the compartment, unclasped an object from a small clip, and brought it to bear.

Simple, smooth, and silver, it was the hilt of his cosmic sword. It was relatively small, just long enough to be held in both hands. A transparent circular hand guard was set atop it, with a barely discernible crease across the center. By all appearances, it didn't appear to be a weapon of extraordinary potency. But when the centurion flicked the little switch near the pommel, a massive, double-edged plane of pointed energy sizzled forth. Crafted from the compacted matter of a black hole, the blade was a sliver of the most hardened space. A supernova-like swirl of purple vapor wrapped its edges and within twinkled a thousand tiny stars.

Once fully extended, the blade's sizzle lowered to a hum. It was a strange sound, more like a voice, like a single solemn monk perpetually drawing out a note so low, it rode just on the fringe of mortal perception.

Here was a sword as alien as its owner.

Here was a power that had destroyed stars and Gods.

Here was the Sword of Molecular Destruction.

Whatever this blade touched disintegrated into nothingness. Whatever it passed through completely disappeared. And now upon the Wicked Plains it was unleashed like some hellish cosmic beast!

On came the miles wide mass of undead slaves. Oddly, they seemed encouraged by the sight of the centurion's sword. Snarling, screaming, and flexing their serrated claws, they picked up their pace, broke into a trot. The first wave lunged forward, ready to rip out whatever heart lay in that silver chest!

Soular Centurion 7's servos whined as he raised high his sword and literally flew into action. He leaped a hundred feet into the sky, a silver flash against the fading traces of blue, then soared down, sweeping his starsword across the fouled fields faster than Syndreck's disbelieving eyes could perceive. Five hundred undead were instantaneously vaporized. What little dust of them remained settled like fertilizer upon the plains.

But more undead poured into their place.

So again Soular Centurion 7 bounded into the air.

And again he came down fast, like a dragon setting flame to a keep, the Sword of Molecular Destruction arcing over and slashing through all before it. Hundreds more undead disappeared in a blinding black flash. Then the centurion leaped from side to side, his arms whipping faster than a sorcerous wind. Thousands more were slashed into nonbeing.

Yet still they came—thousands, then tens of thousands, heedless of their own demise. All were destroyed, the centurion twirling like a cosmic tornado as he eradicated his enemies from the fields!

Thus the day drew on.

As the Shards of Zyrinthia stretched around the planet, as the sky lost its blue and the lands were once again clouded over, as the keeper of the Sunsword Surassis and his companions fended off their own undead, Soular Centurion 7 battled on.

"How can this be?" Syndreck the Brooding said as he peered into the Cauldron of Carcass Control. "What power holds this being?"

Throughout the day, he had watched the battle out of the corner of his eye, all-the-while preparing his most important incantations. The centurion had indeed proved to be quite a distraction! Syndreck had presumed his sea of insensate warriors would overwhelm this one, mighty as he may be. But presumption had proven to be as foolish as presumption often is.

Now he gazed deeper into his cauldron and looked right into Soular Centurion 7's eyes. There was no fear in them, no hesitance, no doubt. No, those eyes held the straightforward intent of the dead that marched against him. Those eyes were purposeful to a fault, as emotionless as a spider's.

Syndreck nodded, whispering, "So, I have underestimated you. Well, no more..." He stepped from the cauldron, threw back his head and screamed the shrillest of sorcerous songs.

Arcane anger came ripping over the Wicked Plains.

The undead masses were instilled with heightened savagery, their limbs imbued with unholy strength. Their incessant snarls elevated to roars, they charged the centurion like starving lions.

It did not matter.

As the undead ramped up their savagery, so, too, did Soular Centurion 7.

The warrior from the stars fought like a cornered beast on fire.

He whipped the Sword of Molecular Destruction around so hard it created a vortex. (Ironically, the vortex's creation nearly tore open the very dimensional walls Syndreck was currently trying to break through.) The air around the centurion swirled inward, and the surrounding undead were pulled over the ground, right into his starsword's plane. Their torsos were sliced in half before what was left was sucked into the depths of the black hole blade.

The sword's hum heightened to a wail. The vortex intensified into a violent maelstrom. Solar winds gusted all over the Wicked

Plains. The remaining corpses uplifted, thousands of bodies whipping around the centurion like tattered rags. There were screams and moans and curses, limbs and legs and cosmic lightning! Then everything was pulled into the storm's center, spiraling down, down, down into the blade's tip. The galactic warrior held his hands high over his head, and the Sword of Molecular Destruction sucked the atoms from the last of the undead!

It was done.

The undead were gone.

The maelstrom dissipated, its winds following the bodies into the blade with a roaring whoosh. The centurion flipped the little switch near the pommel, and the blade disappeared.

But not all had been defeated...

A lone eye rolled up to Soular Centurion 7. Still instilled with arcane aggression, it bobbled at his boots. He lifted his foot and squashed it. *Now* the Wicked Plains were purged.

The one had defeated a million.

And slowly, purposefully, the centurion of the stars strode closer to Ulith Urn.

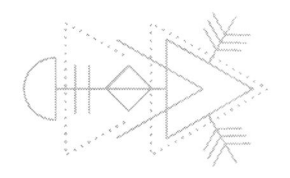

CHAPTER SEVENTEEN
THE MYRIAD FEATURES OF PHATE

It is difficult to climb a mountain when one carries the weight of the world on his shoulders.

Sharl Lindrayl
Queen of the Spirit Elves

Morning's Hope flew down through a layer of sorcerous storms.

She descended rapidly, banking this way and that, with Fleeting Shadow buzzing behind her, and the Great White Owl just off her left flank. Arcs of emerald lightning leaped over them, wind whistled in their ears, and rain nipped them from all sides. It was as if Phate was reminding them that the earlier day's brilliance was an aberration, and the skies would always belong to the storms.

Let it rain, Drinwor thought, *for these rainstorms are much preferable to the storm of apparitions that just tried to kill us.*

Now that the encounter was over, he realized just how much it had shaken him. He tried not to think about it, but alas, how could our sensitive Drinwor not? When he scrutinized the possibilities if just one of those haunted beings had gotten to him…well…he realized he could have died. But such imperilment was a part of his life now, and he'd have to get used to it, have to thicken his skin and suppress his overly contemplative mind. He knew if he constantly dwelled on his fear, he would be tentative in the face of confrontation, thus endangering himself, thus endangering them all. Yes, for everyone's sake, he must learn to be mentally strong.

He was Drinwor Fang, Emperor of the Sky, Son and Savior of the Stars...

The companions broke through the bottom of the storms and continued eastward. The rain was steady but light, the world before them drained of color, as if it had been sheathed in a dreary grey sheet.

Drinwor, still grappling with his thoughts, shivering in a chill wind, leaned forward and called out, "Morning's Hope?"

"My Lord?"

"Are you all right?"

The Greater Translucent Dragon smiled sympathetically, for she understood—the boy was reaching out.

She tilted her head slightly aside, said: "I'm fine, Drinwor, *we* are fine."

"Morning's Hope?"

She waited for the question...

"Back there, should I have done something more? I mean...as Emperor, should I have led us? I just wasn't certain..."

Morning's Hope looked forward, checked her bearings, and then swung her head back around. "All of our lives we learn Drinwor, from our first steps to our last flight. You can do nothing more than what you know to do from your experiences. In time, you'll be able to lead us when such situations arise."

Drinwor looked away, fixed his eyes on the distant gloom of dark clouds. "Those things wanted to kill us. I'm honestly not certain what I should have done."

"Do not dwell on what happened." The translucent huffed, rolled her eyes. "It was more my fault than anyone else's. I made the initial decision to stay."

Drinwor didn't seem to hear her. He mumbled, "If I do something wrong, or command someone to do something and they get hurt, or—"

"My Emperor, listen to me," Morning's Hope interjected, her commanding tone snapping him out of his contemplation, demanding his full attention. "Do not worry about such things. You are the keeper and protector of the Sunsword Surassis and, for now, that is burden enough."

Drinwor shook his head, brought his gaze back to her. "I just hope when the time comes, I make the right decisions."

"You will." Her voice softened. "Remember, listen to your heart and trust the good within you. You will learn to make good decisions. Have you ever before encountered a sky elf graveyard?"

"Well, no."

"Well, now you have. What will you do should you see such clouds again?"

"Command you to fly far away from them?"

Morning's Hope laughed. "There, you see, you *are* becoming a wise Emperor!"

Drinwor laughed too, then quickly quieted down. He grasped his glowing sword charm, looked at it, and asked, "Why *did* you want to linger with the dead clouds?"

Morning's Hope didn't answer immediately, but when she did, she said, "I was fairly certain that place was as Morigos claimed: cursed. But if there was even the slightest possibility that it wasn't, I didn't want to deny Vu Verian the chance to honor his people. He's been lonely for so long. I..." She glanced to the sky elf owl, made sure he hadn't heard her. Then she sighed, quietly said, "Sometimes circumstances dictate that you knowingly make a wrong decision. But that is something we will talk about later." And then she said nothing more.

Drinwor sat back and mulled over his dragon's words, the continent isle flowing by beneath them.

The afternoon aged.

By the time they crossed into eastern Volcar, the sun had fallen far behind them. Its rays, still filtering through the Shards of Zyrinthia, cast a flickering pall across all the wilted lands. Shadows flourished both in the air and on the ground. Some were natural... and some were not.

There was so much to see, so much to take in. As Morning's Hope continued to descend, Drinwor was once again captivated by the myriad features of Phate.

I shall do my best to describe even just a fraction of what he saw...

They passed high over the Lion Lands of Irixx Een, a realm of hundred foot tall silver reeds whose shining city of platinum pillars was ruled by an undead lion-like beast. Amongst the reeds Drinwor caught glimpses of the gilded backs of some giant creatures, which crept to and fro the city. The companions passed over this place quickly, and once having flown beyond its borders, they heard from behind them a roar of such frightening, domineering might, they were one and all instilled with the will to never return.

None of them ever did.

They next came to a place where the air was laden with wispy white ribbons. Whether it was cloud-stuff or some magical vapor, Drinwor could not tell. But soon before them a faded structure came into view, and Morning's Hope bore straight for it. Thus they flew through the corridors of the Multidimensional Mansion of Veeryk Vyne, a mountain-sized house that was stuck between dimensions and floating in the sky. Its origin was unknown even ages ago, for it had occupied the same space before Phate's galaxy had even existed. Drinwor was speechless as they swept through the mile tall halls, wondering just what sort of beings had inhabited the place so long, long ago...

Out of the mansion they came. Morning's Hope carried on with what appeared to be a predetermined path, such was the confidence with which she flew. She guided them farther down, soared through Scimiton, an invisible forest of birches that stood thousands of feet tall. The great boughs supported a forsaken city of invisible elves who had disappeared from existence not long after they had disappeared from sight.

Drinwor was profoundly taken in by it all "I did not know such places like these existed," he uttered, for he could contain his reverent silence no longer.

"There is more," said Morning's Hope, "the most fascinating landscapes lay ahead. You will see."

And that he did.

Now they came down close to the ground and flew over Cygorgia, a rocky plateau that was dotted with the ancient ruins of a cyclops warlord's warrior state. (Time had proven to be an adversary even a military nation couldn't defeat.) Broken ebony stones were strewn in great circles, as if some god had flattened the realm with his palm, then smeared the remains. Rivers, once rushing with liquid gold, were now dull and leaden, slogging through cracks and crevices that lined the ruins like wrinkles on an ancient face. Groves of withered trees were scattered about, their sparse, limp leaves hanging with cloudy broken crystal. Abandoned by its inhabitants, abandoned by nature itself, all the glimmer of the land was gone. And it was deathly quiet. The wind held no whispers, for even Cygorgia's ghosts had long fled.

Drinwor, craning his neck to see everything, uttered, "Such a shame to see so much ruin and emptiness. I can only imagine the beauty these lands must have once held."

"Then imagine all you can," Morning's Hope said, "for imagination is the foundation of hope and progress. If something can be dreamed of, then it can be so. Yes, Drinwor, as Emperor, see not a ruined city as a thing abandoned, but as a city that might one day thrive!"

Drinwor smiled. "Do you always speak so hopefully?"

"Would it befit me not to, named as I am?"

Drinwor laughed. "No, no it wouldn't. I'm glad you do."

"Good! Then I shall never stop." She paused, tilted her head, and said, "I truly believe hope shines brightest where it is most dark."

"And what hope do I have?" Vu Verian wondered aloud. His words came as a surprise, for he hadn't spoken since the confrontation with the sky elf spirits. Now his flight path had wandered him close to his companions, and he looked on Morning's Hope with vacant eyes, eyes whose blue had fled with the sky's and fallen grey.

"You have the same hope that we all do," Morning's Hope declared, "that you will serve the Son and Savior of the Stars well and, by doing so, secure the safety of the universe. That is your hope."

"Then that is all that I have," Vu Verian stated, his eyes further dimming.

"Then you are lucky," Morning's Hope said, her eyes brightening, "for you have more than most."

Vu Verian slowly nodded. "I suppose I do."

Fleeting Shadow flitted up beside them, taking position just off of the translucent's right flank, opposite Vu Verian. Morigos was standing in his saddle, pointing his staff down. He was shaking, and his grating voice flew like a crow from his cowl. "What hope can we have for a land that melts beneath us! Look!"

They all looked down.

Astonishingly, the dark elf's claim wasn't far from true. Past the ruins, where the plateau's rocky features flattened, some strange substance gushed from numerous fissures in the ground. The substance spread out for miles, covering all the eastern section of the uplifted plains. It issued like something molten, but the air above it was cool. The companions flew down, skimmed its surface, the dragons nearly dipping their wings in its flows. Upon closer inspection, the substance looked like a viscous vapor; it was bluish-white, yellow flecked, and glinting like a lake beneath a noonday sun. A metallic scent stole into their nostrils, and Drinwor felt a tingle of energy course through him. "What is this?" he asked.

"It is called Syrox," Morning's Hope answered.

"I've been to eastern Volcar," Morigos said, "but have never seen this. What sort of sorcery produced this place?"

"That's exactly what it is," Morning's Hope remarked, "pure sorcery."

"I don't understand what I'm looking at," Drinwor said. "It's like a misty morning sky crawling across the ground, or like what Morigos said—the land melting…"

Morning's Hope pointed down with her foreclaw. "What you see is sorcery in one of its rawest forms. Essentially, Syrox is an abandoned mine of magic, created by wizards who long ago passed through the gates to the Seven Glories. Now unattended, the magical ore flows freely."

"Can it be harnessed?" Morigos asked, seemingly enthralled with the possibility.

Morning's Hope shook her head. "No. At least not by any means that I'm aware of. And it would take a tremendous amount of this substance to affect even the smallest incantations, anyway." She went on to explain, "Taking into account that Phate was constructed by sorcery, the Wizards of Syrox were attempting to mine magic right out of the ground. But they soon discovered that this flowing ore was diluted, not very potent. No, true sorcery has always come from within, from our spirits drawing power from beyond the physical planes of the universe, filtering it through our hearts, and releasing it with a song. The wizards were weak of heart, their magical voices feeble. They thought Syrox would empower them, but, for the most part, they failed."

"*For the most part...*" Morigos echoed, waiting for some additional explanation.

"Well, they did succeed in one thing," Morning's Hope added.

"Well? What would that *be*?" the mage impatiently inquired.

"Although the wizards failed in their pursuit of power, they inadvertently provided Phate with one of its more spectacular features. Come, I will show you!" And with that, Morning's Hope accelerated toward the edge of the plateau.

Drinwor was mildly unnerved, for it rather looked like they'd come to the end of the world. The plateau ended abruptly, the edge looming in the near distance like a horizon itself, with nothing but a greyish-purple void beyond.

Morning's Hope came up to it and dove over the side, her companions following suit. They swung out, banked around, and she called out, "Behold, the Phantom Falls!"

And lo, the Son and Savior of the Stars saw that indeed, all beauty and might had not fled these barren lands!

As tall and broad as a mountain range, the Phantom Falls spanned the entire eastern side of the plateau. The vaporous ore fell down for miles, cascading over a series of massive ledges before finally splashing into a little sea. The Phantom Falls were so huge, they dwarfed the Cliffs of Moaning Wishes. In fact, the whole scene was so vast, it was difficult for Drinwor to comprehend, and a touch of lightheadedness swayed him in his saddle-throne. He thought his earlier impression was accurate, for indeed it looked as if a glittering ocean was spilling over the very edge of the world.

Morning's Hope guided the group right in front of the flows, and they were all sprayed with sparkling flecks of silver and gold. "Drinwor," she called back, "look through the gaps in the flows."

Drinwor peered through the spaces in the falls. At first it was difficult to discern what he viewed, but little by little he came to realize that an entire nation had been carved into the black crystal undercutting. Each tremendous shelf was a city in itself; a sprawling complex of onyx towers, ebony chapels and night stone keeps. Palaces were embedded in the ledge's sidewalls, their curved spires slicing through the magical fluid and segmenting it into thousands of individual falls. Every structure glittered with every splash, and Drinwor thought the whole realm might have been pulled from some heavenly god's starry dream.

But for all its splendor, it was lifeless. No beings were about. No activity could be detected. The shelf-cities were suffused with that eerie hollowness that seems to haunt all abandoned places to some degree. But the emptiness only intensified Drinwor's fascination with the place, made him wonder about the inhabitants' fate.

"This is incredible," he said. "I'm guessing the wizards lived here?"

"Yes," Morning's Hope replied. She slowed to a hover, the others flying right up to her side. "They literally showered themselves in their ore; although, in their time, long ago, the falls weren't much stronger than a light mist."

"How many wizards were there?" Drinwor couldn't help asking questions; it was such a curiously astounding sight!

"Millions," his dragon replied, "perhaps more, before they were defeated by—"

"The Dark Forever," Morigos finished.

Drinwor frowned. "Is there any place on Phate that hasn't been annihilated by the Dark Forever?"

"No," Vu Verian quipped, "even in the throes of defeat, the Dark Forever managed to devastate nearly all of our world's cultures and history."

"What the Wizards of Syrox lacked in sorcerous skill," Morning's Hope said, "they more than made up for in numbers—or so they thought. The demons wiped them out in seconds."

Drinwor whistled. "Millions, wiped out in seconds, you say…"

Morigos pointed at the falls. "Perhaps they should have imbibed the stuff rather than bathed in it!"

Morning's Hope shook her head and sighed.

"Perhaps you should be quiet," Vu Verian suggested.

"Perhaps!" Morigos cackled, "But then I'd be as boring as a sky elf! If—"

"Enough, you two," Morning's Hope interjected.

The mages glared at each other, but no more words were exchanged. Morning's Hope, satisfied with their silence, beckoned them all to move on.

They coasted down, glided over the cities, fully imbuing themselves in the splashing sorcery's glittering spray.

Now Morning's Hope looked much the same as when she had first risen into the morning sky. Her translucent body lit as if a thousand fireflies buzzed inside her, her heart their glowing hive. All the companions' appearances were affected. Vu Verian's feathers looked as if they were gilded with metallic gold. Fleeting Shadow's wingtips left a sparkling little trail. Even Morigos' ruined robes were enlivened with balmy light, their green runes alive with uncharacteristic brightness.

But Drinwor Fang outshone them all.

His silver hair might have been silver fire, and his eyes, oh, how they blazed! Even his smoky skin was luminous; he looked as if a scintillating veil had been pulled tight about his face. His black demonskin gleamed and its blue sigils blazed. Had he reached into his leg pouch, he would have found the sunsword beaming like a hilt of solid light. As it was, its radiance seeped through his legging.

Magical beings on a world where sorcery overflowed, the companions shone as beacons of hope in the imaginative eyes of the universe…

As they continued to glide down, a welcoming calmness came over Drinwor. For although he felt the hollowness of the shelf-cities, there was also a peace and serenity about the place. The flecks of magic chimed like quiet little bells over the hushed whisper of the splashing flows. The soothing sound settled the more nettled parts of his spirit.

He leaned forward, called out, "I'll be very disappointed if this place turns out be cursed."

"No, I promise you, this place is a blessing." Morning's Hope returned. "Although it's just an accidental byproduct of the wizard's failed efforts, Syrox has turned out to be a beautiful memorial to a world that once was. Yes, all of Phate used to be like this—beautiful; magical; serene. That was a long time ago…a long time…" She turned her head, flashed Drinwor a little smile.

Her features glinted, and Drinwor caught a glimpse of her expression. Her eyes were bright and wide, but sad. He could only imagine the memories that were now flowing through her mind.

Out of the blue, he asked, "Did my father ever see this place?"

"Yes," she confirmed, "he spent some time here, actually. It was a place of contemplation for him."

Drinwor nodded, whispered: "Good, good."

A raspy cough from nearby broke the serenity and warned them that Morigos was about to speak. Fleeting Shadow drew close to Morning's Hope, and Morigos said, "Forgive me for interrupting such sentimentalities, but our destination awaits, and we should pick up the pace."

"Why are *you* in such a hurry?" Vu Verian snapped from aside.

"We wouldn't want you to disappear into cloudform before we even arrive at the hall, would we, now?" Morigos retorted.

Vu Verian scowled. "I'm sure you'd like nothing more, but what care you how fast we go?"

Morigos said nothing to this.

"Come on!" urged Vu Verian, "out with it!"

Morigos shrugged. "Well, I didn't want to say anything after what happened in the high sky, but if you really want to know, I think we should leave because I believe that here, too, we are not alone." Now his cowl was aimed upward, his hidden eyes staring into the falls, far, far above. "I'm afraid this place is not so serene as it seems, and ever will we travel with curses in tow. Something trails us. I'm almost certain."

"Oh, stop this ceaseless torment of me!" Vu Verian demanded.

"What trails us?" Morning's Hope straightened her neck, tried to aim her gaze and pinpoint the exact location where Morigos stared.

"I do not know," Morigos replied, "but I saw a shadow not of natural making move amongst the onyx towers on our way down. I saw it move forward. It made a small distortion that disturbed the otherwise smooth falling ore; and for a moment I felt *cold*, like when we used to conjure up old Kroon ghosts."

"More ghosts?" Drinwor cringed at the thought. "So much for feeling pleasant!"

Morning's Hope looked all around, but could see nothing. "It is quite possible some ghosts may be about, but I wouldn't worry, for not all who have passed from life are rife with malcontent."

"Think of the sky elf clouds, dragon." Morigos looked Morning's Hope straight in the eye. "Something tracks us."

Inwardly, Morning's Hope agreed with the dark elf's assessment, or, at least, she reluctantly acknowledged that it was a distinct possibility. But she saw no point in further belaboring the issue, for her companions were spooked enough, and there was nothing to be done without delaying their quest. It was getting late, and they still had some distance to travel. Who knew what lay in store, and what other obstacles awaited?

She gave Morigos a frustrated little look that sat somewhere between agreement and incredulity, and said, "Worry not, for if indeed something trails us, I shall be aware. Now let us be on our way."

And with that she glided forward, led them down over the last ledge, passing through the spray caused by the fall's final splash into the waiting sea. When they moved out of the spray, all their countenances dimmed to normalness.

To Drinwor's surprise, the sea of magical vapor that caught the falls was perfectly still and smooth. Beyond where the falls splashed into it, nary a ripple marred its glossy surface. It was like gazing at the reflection of a clear blue sky in a mirror. Looking out to either side, he concluded it was more like a wide river than a sea. It snaked the whole length of the falls—well, at least as far as he could see, anyway, which was quite far. He wondered…

"The Syroxian Sea," Morning's Hope said. "That's what it's called."

"Ah," was all the dusk elf gave in response. *She is something, this dragon!* He shook his head and looked forward.

They flew across the far shore, and an entirely different environment unraveled beneath them.

Now below were rolling fields of tall silken grass. Although residing in the Phantom Fall's far-reaching shadow, the grass was shiny and bright, imbuing the fields with a liveliness Drinwor hadn't perceived in any other landscape. The surrounding air was rich and nourishing; the wind didn't blow so much as it breathed. As the owl and dragons swept low over the grasses, the blades bowed like a crowd of peasants before the passing of royalty.

And beyond was an even greater greenery.

In the near distance lay a vast forest of lush evergreens, their boughs abundant with natural green leaves, and spotted with a spectrum of sorcerously colored ones as well. Standing tall and straight, the trees loomed like the guardians of the fields. The companions flew toward them, then soared up over their crowns. They were so numerous, so dense! Drinwor envisioned them as the younger, more energetic brethren of the trees in the Forest of Chanting Angels.

The fields, the trees—this whole country had…a soul? Yes, there was a presence here, a vitality that belied the otherwise dead landscapes that encapsulated most of Volcar. Drinwor realized he had felt this presence many times before, back home, in Areshria. He had become aware of it on those solitary afternoons when he'd stood on his terrace and gazed at the clouds. There had been a presence there, too, though until this moment he'd never thought of it like that.

"There's something about this place that reminds me of the sky," Drinwor called to his dragon. "It's almost as if the forest is alive."

"Oh, indeed it is," Morning's Hope said. "It is the soul of nature you feel. Although Phate was constructed by sorcery, much of its surface was imbued with natural life." She swung her head about, took in all the landscape. "Yes, there's a presence in this forest and behind us in those fields. Unfortunately, places like these are rare now. Most natural forests have been destroyed by war, or slain for evil means."

Drinwor pondered for a moment, then asked, "Is the sky *connected* to the forest in some way?"

"Most definitely," Morning's Hope affirmed. "Everything in the world is connected, everything in the galaxy. The land and sky and even the sun and stars are all one. In essence, the whole universe is one flowing entity."

"And we are all a part of it," Vu Verian added, "a part of the universe."

"Yes," Morning's Hope concurred, "all of us bonded together in life, charged with the guardianship of one another's souls." She looked to the sky, saw the blurry glare of the shards shining through some low-flying rain clouds. "Though so many have forgotten…"

Morigos emitted his usual uncouth noises that warned everyone he was about to speak, but Morning's Hope flashed him her now recognizable look that warned she was going to shut him up. He took the hint, and said nothing (for now), and Vu Verian said nothing more. Drinwor stayed quiet, too, but thought he could faintly hear some windy voice in his head, as if the spirit of the world was whispering to him. He froze, suddenly afflicted with the idea that it was Morigos' specter, who was hot on their tail. He twisted round, peered behind them, but could see nothing save the features from whence they came. The falls loomed like a great dark wall, and the skies above the fields and forest were barren of all but the wind and clouds. It was nothing, he mused, just a byproduct of his overactive imagination.

"Fear not," said Morning's Hope, "it is unlikely that we are being pursued. All is well."

Drinwor smiled. "I know."

Onward they flew.

The evergreens' bunched peaks bristled beneath them like a breezy valley of pine bushes, and Drinwor caught a whiff of their brisk, sweet scent. The scent vanished almost instantly, though, for a heavy moisture came and squeezed the sweetness from the air. What was once a light drizzle was becoming a driving rain.

Drinwor glanced upward and for a moment frowned at the clouds. When he looked back down, he noticed something peculiar straight ahead. A wall of fog was billowing out of the forest not quite a mile in front of them. It was so tall it rose all the way up into the rain clouds. He opened his mouth to ask Morning's Hope about it, but from behind, Morigos suddenly spewed with words. "We near the edge of Volcar! You dragons are not so slow after all. Ha!" Then he cackled as only he could, with that gurgling, half-choking accompanying it.

"Yes," Morning's Hope said, "now again we come to a place that is not so natural."

"What do you mean?" the dusk elf Emperor asked.

"You will see," she returned, "you will see."

They flew straight toward the fog-wall, and Drinwor began to shift with unease. With consternation trembling his voice, he said, "Morning's Hope?"

"All will be well," she assured with a gentle tone.

Then she streamlined her body and dashed right into the fog, the owl and insect dragon flying in behind her.

The trees disappeared beneath them and all the world was a swirling greyish-white void. Drinwor had no sense of their altitude and, strangely, the farther into the fog they flew, the hotter it got. Morigos complained from behind and Fleeting Shadow whined. But it wasn't long until Morning's Hope cried, "Almost through!" It was true, for moments later she shot clear of the fog.

Drinwor was dumbstruck by the revealed scene.

"It's as impressive as I remember!" Morigos said.

"It is a sight to see," Morning's Hope agreed.

Drinwor whispered, "This is baffling to me..."

He thought they had flown right into another world.

Sprawled before them was a sea of purple fire.

Beyond a beach of crushed crimson crystals, mountainous waves of violet flames roared beneath a sky filled with floating volcanic islands. Drinwor thought it looked as if the Volcanoes of Volcar had been torn from the ground and suspended in midair. (He was soon to learn he was essentially right.) Some islands were whole and huge, while others were sundered in many places, with some sections clinging close together and others drifting many leagues apart. Some islands had been reduced to nothing more than roaming heaps of molten rubble. But whether split or whole, most of the volcanoes on these islands were active. Lava falls were everywhere, often cascading over multiple islands, then plunging down thousands of feet into the sea, riling up the fiery waves that swept all across the flaming deep. The winds were hot, the still air sweltering, the sky a reddish-purple stain. The horizon was but a burning, blurry slash on the far edge of sight.

It was a realm even immortal eyes could not believe!

Morning's Hope led them higher into the sky, maneuvering through the maze of airborne islands. She banked around and behind the lava falls, with Drinwor clinging tight to both arms of the saddle-throne. "Where in the world are we?" he asked as they ascended.

"We've crossed over Volcar," his dragon answered, "and have come to Pyrlovos, the realm at its eastern edge."

"Peer-low-vose..." Drinwor slowly pronounced.

"Yes." She went on to explain: "Constructed and overseen by sky elf wizards, this place was once a prison state for the most diabolical criminals on Phate. These volcanic islands were lifted from the coastal waters of the Pyrlovian Sea, and suspended in much the same way the sky elf palaces were, with a sorcery that defied our world's gravity. Fortresses were built on the central islands, iron barracks whose walls were imbued with magic dampening wards and surrounded by molten moats. Below, the Pyrlovian Sea was covered over with flames, thus making Pyrlovos virtually inescapable. But then—"

"Let me guess," Drinwor cut in, "the Dark Forever came."

Morning's Hope nodded. "Yes, the war. The demons destroyed the guardian wizards of Pyrlovos, and the sorcery that held this place together went wild. The islands broke up, drifted apart, and the volcanic activity intensified. The prisoners died, escaped, or otherwise disappeared. Now it is a reckless, uncontrolled place."

"We should be especially cautious of confrontation here," Morigos suggested, "for it is said that not all of the inhabitants have fled, and demons might still be lurking about. And," he added, "this would be the perfect place for an ambush by those who seek to thwart our journey to the hall."

"We will be on guard," promised Morning's Hope.

They flew on.

The concentration of islands thickened, and so did the lava falls. All around, wavy ribbons of glowing heat plunged down and splashed onto the islands below, severing them, or disintegrating them all together. Clusters of glowing rock wandered about, suspended storms of burning stone that pelted the walls of black iron fortresses whose ruins floated all around. Fire dragons darted through the wreckage, flaming little creatures with skeletal heads that cackled like haunted fiends. They leered at the companions, but never engaged them.

Morning's Hope guided them safely through it all. As always, she seemed to know her way, flying swiftly and confidently, always managing to avoid the hanging ruins and scorching flows.

Eventually the concentration of islands thinned out, and she turned her head aside, said to Drinwor, "We're almost through Pyrlovos, not too far from the Hall of Voices."

"Anywhere is better than this place!" Drinwor's frightful eyes darted all around.

Moments later, Morigos called out, "Look there!" his tattered sleeve fluttering as he thrust his arm out and pointed his staff down. "Something I do not like makes itself known!"

"For someone who's supposedly so broken, you seem to have very keen eyes!" Drinwor noted.

"Nothing to do with my eyes, boy," Morigos replied, "I have a knack for sensing trouble!"

And trouble they may have found, for directly below them, many dozens of dark shapes were appearing in the fiery waves. Drinwor couldn't make out what they were, but was fairly certain they weren't some phenomenon native to the sea. Could they be some sort of ships? Maybe. But they had no sails, no decks. They looked like fat, legless insects. Whenever a wave rolled over them, they emitted a green aura, but otherwise seemed completely unaffected by the sea's fury.

Morning's Hope turned to the dark elf mage. "Are those—"

"Dreadships," Morigos confirmed. "Strange. I've never seen them in this sea."

"Nor me," whispered Morning's Hope, with a tinge of concern.

Drinwor was confounded. "Dreadships? I thought deep elves were beings of the water."

"Oh, there's water beneath those flaming waves," Vu Verian chimed in, "but make no mistake, the deep elves have the power to exist anywhere. Fire. Water. It doesn't matter. Some say that when Phate is gone they'll live in space because it is most like the sea. A frightening prospect, that, because within the abyss...they're unconquerable."

Drinwor patted his leg pouch. "Are they looking for the sunsword?"

Vu Verian looked perplexed. "I don't know."

"They must be!" Morigos declared.

Morning's Hope looked to Vu Verian, said, "Perhaps you should cloak us."

"Yes," the mystic owl replied, "perhaps I should."

"Hurry!" Morigos urged.

Vu Verian flew up over the dragons and directed them to gather closely together. Then he conjured the Cloak of Winds. The mystical cover spread out from his wingtips, curled down, and surrounded them all, rendering the group virtually invisible. The spell was timely, for at that moment, more Dreadships sprang into sight. Soon there were hundreds of them.

Morigos spewed curses at them, then said, "Bah, deep elves! They should burn in those waves or sink back into their dark abyss!"

"Why would deep elves be interested in the sunsword?" Vu Verian asked.

"Remember," Morigos replied, "it is *they* who offered the Gauntlets of Loathing Light to Warloove, *they* who would see the sunsword in his hands, and *they* who will align themselves with Nenockra Rool!"

His feathers ruffling, Vu Verian snapped back with, "And it was *your* people who conspired with them."

Morigos scoffed at the comment. "My people have become fanatical sheep, senselessly following that which they think will bring them to dark glory. They're children in need of discipline, nothing more. But the deep elves…they have a collective mind like a dagger, aimed at the hearts of all. They're just waiting for the armor of the world to fall away."

"Well it is the deep elves who will foolishly perish," Morning's Hope added, "or anyone else who allies themselves with the Dark Forever." She sighed. "Has history taught them nothing? Evil holds no allegiance, especially to those who aid them. The deep elves will be the first to fall should the demons breach our skies."

"Well, whatever the case may be," Morigos said, "let's just get away from here."

And so they soared forth, the mystic owl as the hood of their protective cloak, the violet fires of the Pyrolvian Sea dancing in their eyes.

Drinwor was glad Vu Verian was playing a part in helping them now. The sky elf had been so distant of late. Perhaps his involvement would reaffirm that he was among friends, fighting alongside allies with whom he truly belonged—Drinwor and Morning's Hope, at least, if not Morigos (though Drinwor was finding he rather enjoyed the dark elf's company, despite any skepticism he had about the mage's true intentions).

It was well-known to those few who knew Vu Verian that he had long regretted his decision to remain on Phate when, a thousand years ago, the rest of his people had taken to the stars. Oh, initially, he had proudly volunteered to be the caretaker of Areshria, the honorary Emperor of the Sky; but he had been totally oblivious to the backlash he would eventually receive. After the war, all of

Phate had denounced the sky elves for abandoning the world, and Vu Verian had been a constant target for racial hatred. As a result, he had grown increasingly more reclusive over the years. Even after Herard had befriended him and taken the responsibilities of emperorship away from him, Vu Verian ended up spending most of his time floating through Phate's skies as a cloud.

And now Herard, his only true friend, was gone.

Drinwor had no doubt Vu Verian bore the weight of his father's death as much as he did, and it pained him to see his sky elf friend so distressed. At least he wasn't alone, though. Drinwor resolved to stay close by his side, no matter what happened.

They flew on, and left the Dreadships far behind.

Morning's Hope eventually called to Vu Verian, "I don't think we need the cloak any longer, my friend."

The Great White Owl nodded. "We should be out of range of the deep elves' detection now."

"Wait!" Morigos crooned, "Perhaps it would be wise to keep the cloak about us, hide us from *all* enemy eyes."

"If, as you suggest," Morning's Hope said, "a shadow follows us, there is no cloak through which it cannot see."

Morigos merely grumbled and shrugged in response to this.

Vu Verian snickered, and the Cloak of Winds swiftly seeped back into his wingtips. He looped down to his usual position off the translucent's left flank, and Fleeting Shadow took his place out to the right.

Thus they left the realm of Pyrlovos.

The waves of violet fire faded into the haze of heat behind them, and dark waters crawled out from beneath the fringes of the flames. But the inevitability of all things fated stood like a fiery tower in the forefront of their minds, for the afternoon was old, and soon the menace of night would take hold.

A lump of fear found Drinwor's throat.

For him, the coming night had a name.

And that name was Warloove.

The first stars began to twinkle in the sky, and for a moment Drinwor thought they were the awakening eyes of the murderous vampire, gazing at him from across the world....

※※※

Silently Drekklor the Shadow Demon slid through the clouds, coasting just out of the range of the translucent dragon's detection. He was more cautious now, having some inkling that he might have been detected by another, by one who was somewhat familiar with his kind. These beings he trailed had some sharp perception, and he need not jeopardize his mission. Destiny beckoned in the skies above and soon the shards would strike. When the world fell to night, and the moment was right, he would steal away their most hope filled dreams.

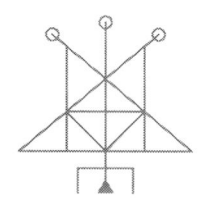

CHAPTER EIGHTEEN
THE DARK EYES OF THE ENEMY

It is the horror of war that it repeats itself, for freedom has long been paid for.
Herard Avari Fang
Emperor of the Sky, Ruler of Areshria, Last Human on Phate

Droplets of spittle flew like darts from Syndreck the Brooding's frothing mouth as he cursed in languages he thought he had long forgotten. He stared into the Cauldron of Carcass Control, his eyes wide with disbelief, for out on the Wicked Plains, the cosmic warrior had defeated his million undead minions.

It was unconscionable.

"This is unconscionable!"

And to make matters worse, the beautiful body of Tatoc of the Black Claw had begun to decay. It was a shame, really, but Syndreck knew a body so young could not hold a soul so vile and old without repercussions. Alas, with sorcerous anger came aging. The smooth ebony of his face had greyed and crinkled. His once clear eyes were becoming bloodshot pools. And the onset of self-mutilation was simply inevitable, for with no other living bodies around, hence no other way to indulge his cannibalistic tendencies, Syndreck had discovered the delightful delicacy of himself. He had become prone to taking a little dagger and carving off slices of his own skin, then savoring them between his rotting teeth. He couldn't help it! He was stressed and his skin tasted so good…ah, so good…

"I'm glad Tatoc saved all of himself for me! Ha!"

Oh, well, anyway, with his gaze still fixed in the bowels of the cauldron, he thoughtfully thrummed his fingers on his chin. "My new pets...all gone."

Such a waste. Soular Centurion 7 had no respect for the damned.

Syndreck flicked the cauldron's surface with his finger, and the image of the interstellar warrior dispersed. He took a deep breath, shook his head. "How annoying, how...irritating!"

It was quite a quandary. To get involved in a prolonged confrontation with this alien invader *and* concentrate on freeing the Dark Forever at the same time would demand too much of even him. Once the dimensional breach was open, most of his energy would be required to sustain it.

"Nothing is ever easy!" he complained to his cauldron. Indeed, nothing ever was, not even for our story's exceedingly powerful evil necromancer.

He sighed, with more curses riding on the breeze of his breath. He contemplated, thought hard, and that was something he was good at. You see, although his body was deteriorating, his mind was as sharp as it had been since his awakening from his thousand year sleep. After only a minute or so, he was struck with a wild idea.

"Yes, I *do* have an idea! Perhaps I can tear open the dimensions and destroy the enemy with the same stroke?! Hmmm... It's a bit premature to use such force, for I'm not certain the dimensional walls are yet weak enough to rip through." He contemplated for another minute, his mind filling with increasingly confident thoughts. "But then again, if I could manage to create even the slightest dimensional tear, those demon hordes on the other side should have the strength to widen the breach themselves. *And,* using the method I'm thinking of, I could annihilate the galactic warrior in the process!"

Yes...it just might work...

Syndreck cackled.

"Yes, it *will* work! Let the skies rain demons, and let my enemy perish beneath the crushing weight of falling stars!"

He raised his arms, blinked his eyes, and tears saturated by sorcery dribbled down his face. Now his vision was all-encompassing.

He could see through his walls, through the sorcerous storms that surrounded them. And when he looked high above, he saw the skies blazing with cosmic fire.

The Shards of Zyrinthia.

He bent his mind to them, and the strongest song he had yet sung erupted from his lips. Dark sorcery coursed through him like lightning through a flagpole. The Cauldron of Carcass Control bubbled and gurgled. Syndreck lifted off of the floor, his toes dangling like tassels. Bright crimson light leaked from the orifices of his face, and his song elevated into a thousand shrill screams. The incantation was so strong its words could be seen—glowing, cursive red letters of arcana scrawling themselves in the air above him. The letters entwined about one another, then dashed like evil spirits into the sky. They rose through the storms, through the high-flown clouds, ascending beyond the atmosphere itself.

The words struck a small pocket of shards.

Soon thereafter, the asteroids trembled, flared, and broke from their paths and plunged down through the atmosphere!

Syndreck's voice went silent. He dropped back to his feet. The effort had nearly drained him, but his spell casting wasn't quite complete.

Now he closed his eyes and thrust his arms forward, his fingers jabbing and scratching as if at some unseen assailant. With every last ounce of energy, he tore at the dimensional walls he had been steadily weakening. Huffing and panting, he slumped to the platform's stone and crumpled beside his cauldron, his fingers continuing to jab. Black blood poured from his mouth, and he could feel his consciousness slipping away.

But before his awareness fully fled, he thought of the centurion, and these words escaped the chasm of his bloody mouth: "From the stars you have come, so shall the stars come for you…"

Then he sank into unconsciousness, his face stamped with a smile.

Meteors fell through the sky over the Continent Isle of Volcar. Those who witnessed this were stunned, for all prediction and prophecy had not prepared them for the visage of the falling shards. Prophets wept, seers sobbed, and mystics called out to the unhearing Gods. They supposed it was the beginning of the end of all history.

They didn't realize it was only a small taste of what was yet to come...

...but we'll get to that a little later...

The shards swooped down and leveled over the Raging Sea. They flew so fast they scalded the sky they passed through and boiled the waters beneath them. Silken sails caught on fire, birds and whales burned in their wakes, and the world was reminded of its wounding a thousand years before.

With Ulith Urn beckoning them like a dimly lit lantern in the distance, the shards approached the space Syndreck had been scraping with his spectral fingers. Weakened by his malicious meddling, the walls of the planes affixed to that space were ripe to rip.

And rip they did.

The group of shards shot through that weakened space with such force, their passage tore open the sky. The tearing emitted a sound so fierce, the thousands who heard it would never hear again. A hundred forks of black lightning sprang from the breach and spread out with an electrifying web that disintegrated the surrounding clouds. The lightning quickly dissipated, but the damage had been done.

The sky looked as if it had been wounded.

In essence, it had been.

A red gash hung over the sea, bleeding thin wisps of an even redder light. So small, but so substantial, the door to the Dark Forever had been opened a crack.

A billion demons went berserk with glee.

On the Wicked Plains, Soular Centurion 7 paused.

His silver-helmeted head tilted as he received alarming new data. Something had disrupted the normal flow of the space-time continuum, and his proximity sensors were pulsing with a beat whose intervals were rapidly decreasing.

-OBJECTS APPROACHING: MULTIPLE SIGNALS INCOMING FROM OVER THE NEARBY SEA-

They were large, these objects, moving fast.

Their trajectories were calculated, their destinations computed.

They were coming right for him.

He looked to the sky.

Dozens of meteors came wailing at him like a fleet of suicidal starships.

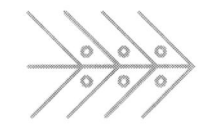

CHAPTER NINETEEN
OCEANS OF ECHOING DARKNESS

> *Morbidity is a disease that robs contentment from the mind.*
> Moorgrey Thake
> Warlord Ruler of Serpentia, Prisoner of the Dark Forever

Though a night that was sure to be thick with darkness was close at hand, much of the sky was still alive with brilliant colors. Enhanced by the burning haze of Pyrlovos, the sunset blazing behind the companions was splashed with spectacular shades of scarlet and lilac. Overhead, the sparse cover of clouds could do little to conceal the reddish-orange glare of the fiery shards, whose brilliant belt now drew all the way back over the conflagrant horizon. In some small way, this dusk was reminiscent of brighter dawns from, oh, so long ago.

But not all was so bright, for ahead the world was slipping into shadows; and directly below sprawled a rippling texture of blue. It was alive, this blue, and yet so deep and dark it was nearly black.

It was a blue like that of the dusk elf's eyes.

This was the blue of a natural sea.

Drinwor had never been this close to such waters. He had no idea how deep the abyss went, had no inkling of its power. He never would have imagined its depths held the strength to crush the mightiest of metals, or madden the mettle of any mind. He didn't realize that most races had gone farther into space than they'd delved into their own oceans.

Now the Emperor of the Sky was to learn of the empires of the sea...

Morning's Hope flew down so fast and so close to the waves, Drinwor thought they might plummet beneath the surface. But the dragon leveled and straightened just before they would have submerged. She turned her head aside, her fluid voice carrying on the winds. "Know your neighbor, my Emperor. As much as you understand your own dominion, understand all those around you. Indeed, mark well the sea. Although the sky often disputes the sea, never will they war...until the end."

"You know what I'm going to ask," Drinwor said with a little smile.

"I do," Morning's Hope replied, "but I cannot answer, for these waters have no name. It was lost in history, lost like the race of beings who named it. It is now known simply as the nameless sea."

Fascinated, Drinwor looked all around.

It was as if they maneuvered through an endless valley of undulating hills. And the air was thick, even thicker than the air that hovered over the trees. Drinwor inhaled deeply, savored the salty richness in his nostrils. It was invigorating. He leaned forward, said, "Morning's Hope, I can feel that presence, the one that inhabits the sky and forest. It's here, too."

"Yes, it is in all natural things," she said, "and some would say it is strongest in the sea." She was going to comment further, but suddenly she lifted her head and blurted: "Ah, finally, we've come to the Hall of Voices!"

Drinwor looked ahead.

There, in the near distance, a great bank of mist was sliding across the water's surface, slowly revealing a massive mountain island. Drinwor thought it odd he hadn't noticed the mist or the island before. It was as if the whole scene had just materialized out of invisibility.

"That was a long, perilous day," said Vu Verian, "but we've made it!"

"The day is not over," Morigos noted, "and the night will be longer still..."

Morning's Hope flew forward, then swung out and arced around, making for the island's far side.

The whole island was a drab, dull white that seemed to slink across the water like some decrepit, ancient iceberg. Drinwor thought the mountainous center resembled the giant skull of some ferocious beast, and he had the distinct impression that it was looking at him. All about the mountain's base foothills piled like burial mounds. The mounds gently flattened as they spread toward the shore, which was rimmed by a short beach.

The most notable feature of the island, though, was the ivory castle that crowned the mountain's peak. The castle was impressively huge—like so many of Phate's structures you've already encountered, my reader; but there were some features that made this particular castle quite unique…

The the towers weren't standing even close to straight. Well, that's putting it mildly. In actuality, they leaned at a staggeringly severe angle. Curious, Drinwor thought. He called ahead, "Morning's Hope, it looks like…I don't know, it looks like some *titan* tried to push the castle from the summit, then in frustration stopped long after it should have toppled over."

She chortled, "That's a good way of putting it. And that's not even the most distinctive thing about it. Notice anything else?"

Drinwor scanned the structure up and down its length, and as they got closer, he detected an even greater peculiarity. The castle was *upside down*, as if it had speared the mountain from the sky. The spires' conical tops were buried like arrow points in the peak. Thousands of feet above, the castle's base was lost in a heaving mass of violent storms that swirled the calmer clouds around them.

Drinwor said to Morning's Hope, "That is something indeed! Is it a sky elf stronghold?"

"Yes," Morning's Hope responded. "It's Shirian Shirion, loosed from its miles high perch and sent crashing to the bones."

"The bones?"

"I'll show you."

With the insect dragon and owl sticking to her flanks, Morning's Hope dipped close to the shore. Although Drinwor had never seen a beach, he just knew something wasn't right about this one. It was uneven, jagged, and when the waves met the shoreline, it rattled like a windswept field of prehistoric chimes. Rattled like...

Bones.

Drinwor gasped with realization. The entire island was made of bones, beach, mountain, and all.

Vu Verian called out, "It's the sight of yet another atrocity we must bear witness to on this day."

"Yes," Morning's Hope agreed, "it *is* another atrocity, another sad story of unrelenting violence, of incalculable loss...another sad story of war. So many dragons I knew were lost here, so many..." Her words trailed off, her head swaying from side to side as if she was trying to shake the memories from her mind.

"I'd like to hear this story," said Drinwor.

Vu Verian cast Morning's Hope a questioning look. The translucent dragon nodded and, with the beach of bones not fifty feet beneath them, they all slowed to a hover. The Great White Owl nervously glanced to the fiery stars, then said, "I will tell you the story, Drinwor Fang, Emperor of the Sky. I will tell you, and then I will have to leave, for night is nearly upon us, and my spirit urges me to seek the safety of cloudform."

"No time for stories!" Morigos warned.

"You're afraid of the dark?" Vu Verian posed.

The mage cackled. "You *do* have a sense of humor, after all, my sour sky elf friend." He pointed his staff toward the sinking sun. "You all wish to see the Emperor safely into the hall? Better do so before nightfall, or else our adversaries on this eve will multiply. There are far greater shadows than the one that has chased us across Volcar..."

"You speak of Warloove, don't you?" Morning's Hope said plainly.

Warloove.

All went silent upon the voicing of that name.

To Drinwor, it was as if she had cursed, and the name echoed through his mind. *Warloove...Warloove...* Now, on the brink of night, when the possibility of a confrontation loomed, the name stepped out from under the grieving gloom of his consciousness. Now, with its utterance, his inner demons of sorrow and anger were reawakened, and he felt a little prickle of fear…

Morning's Hope asked the dark elf, "Do you sincerely believe that Warloove has already obtained the Gauntlets of Loathing Light?"

Morigos nodded.

Morning's Hope frowned. "Even if that's true, he'd have to fly all the way across the continent to catch us. We'll be long gone before he tracks us here."

Grumbling, Morigos bowed his head and shook his staff in frustration. "Oh, you beings of light, sometimes your faith blinds you." Then he lifted his head back up, said, "Warloove could fly to the moons and back in the blink of an eye. I tell you, we should get the boy into to the Hall of Voices at once."

Vu Verian glared at Morigos. "Need we always do exactly as *you* wish?"

"We needn't do anything," the mage returned with a cough. "We can hover here and wait for the sun to explode if you'd like. I'd like nothing more, quite honestly."

Morning's Hope rolled her eyes.

Vu Verian's feathers ruffled, and he lifted up over the little group. "We will do as the Emperor wishes!" (Morning's Hope looked to Drinwor, and he met her glance with a shrug.) With wings fluttering, Vu Verian asked, "Drinwor, do you still want me to tell you the story?"

"Well, yes, but if—"

"Then I will," Vu Verian avowed, casting Morigos a condescending glare.

"You're the Emperor," Morigos chortled at Vu Verian.

The sky elf mystic ignored the sarcastic comment. He turned his attention to the air before him, and whispered a fluid, gentle song. Sparkling streams of blue sorcery fled his beak and gathered into a little cloud. The cloud brightened, and in its center a window of images came to life.

Vu Verian had cast the Eyes of Time.

And now his sorcerous song sounded like a lullaby as the incantation invited them all to look into the past. Drinwor's mouth fell open like a captivated child's, and oh, so silent and still he remained while the sorcery construed its story before him.

And in less time than it takes to describe, this is what he saw...

A thousand years ago, the war with the Dark Forever was raging. Swarms of dragons shot through the sky, spitting many shades of fire as a million clawing demons etched their hides with blood. Branches of black lightning cracked the clouds, spectral storms surged over the roiling seas, and a lashing wind, filled with newly damned souls, carried the sorcerous songs of battle. It was a hurricane of combat. And right here, over the nameless sea, where the fighting was the most furious...it happened.

The sky elven battle castle of Shirian Shirion floated into the thick of the fray. It was a mighty fortress, called 'The Bastion of Gods' by those who'd fought alongside it. It floated over this very spot and bolstered the reeling dragons. A thousand warrior-wizards strong, the fortress was able to turn the tide of battle toward the side of light.

But good fortune was not long to last, and a new host of demons flew to meet it. They were led by a cruel, taunting succubus, Zyllandria. She encircled Shirian Shirion, and one by one picked its wizards off the parapets with her enchanted whip. She teased them, laughed in the face of their pathetic volleys, thinking they'd swoon under her seductive powers. But lo, she underestimated their strength!

The warrior-wizards of Shirian Shirion raised their collective voice and their songs converged into a sorcerous symphony. A thousand white fires conjoined as one, then sizzled through the sky and struck Zyllandria. Never expecting such a powerful reprisal, she was overwhelmed. Her head afire, her heart ablaze in her breast, she shrieked and fell lifeless, down, down into the sea. There, the waters broke open as if to claim her for themselves.

But rising from the rent in the bloody waves was an abyssal force of demonic deep elves. Leading them into the sky was the newly proclaimed ruler of the oceans, Murdraniuss, he who was betrothed to Zyllandria herself. As he arose from the waves, Zyllandria fell into his arms. He was astonished, appalled. In a hundred thousand years he'd loved nothing but her. And now her burning body broke apart in his hands. She was gone. Enraged, he flung her remains into the murk of the blackened sea.

Then all time seemed to stop.

All the dark stars awaited.

Murdraniuss opened wide his maw and unleashed a cry of utter despair. His scream carried on and on and on, a guttural howl sired from the very pits of the Dark Forever! The sound pierced the soul like a spectral spear, killing all who heard it. His massive horde of demonic deep elves fell to pieces and the pieces piled about him. Above, thousands of dragons lost their spirits and fell from the sky. The warrior-wizards of Shirian Shirion felt their brains burst in their heads before they toppled from their towers, and the sorcery sustaining their fortress fled. Bereft of its magic, Shirian Shirion overturned and came wailing down, its spires plunging into the massive pile of dead.

And still Murdraniuss screamed.

Buried beneath an island of bodies, he screamed until the demonkind were vanquished from the world, screamed until the flesh from the bodies about him rotted to bone, until the substance of his own skin had been purged from the primary universe and all that remained was a specter of his forgotten self.

Eventually, finally, over a hundred years, his voice faded. But always does it echo…always. And in this place his stubborn specter still haunts. For within the mountain of bones lies the doorway to the only heavenly haven a good soul of Phate might find, the Hall of Voices. And as long as his spirit endures, as long as he is alone, he will admit no living soul.

He is Murdraniuss, the Lord Banshee.

And with that, the window to the Eyes of Time closed.

The little cloud evaporated, its magic dispersing into sorcerous dust that settled on the bony beach and dimmed.

"Well, I'll give you this," Morigos piped up, "for a snobbish albino bore, you tell quite a story!"

Drinwor shook his head, wiped a strand of hair from his face. To his surprise, he also wiped away some tears. Vu Verian, who was staring at Drinwor, said, "Shed no tears for no demon, Drinwor Fang, son of he who was slain by such a beast. Shed no tears for Murdraniuss, the murderer of millions."

Drinwor dried his face, but his midnight blues still glittered with moisture, for he was unable to shake the image of Zyllandria falling dead into the arms of the forsaken, unable to keep his mind from imagining the unfathomable despair that followed. He could still hear the banshee's cry echoing in his ears, and it filled him with sadness and fright.

He said: "I didn't think evil beings were capable of love."

Morning's Hope looked to Drinwor as if with surprise. "It wasn't true love, for Murdraniuss only cared about himself and his own desires. Zyllandria was to him but a slave. That is *not* true love. True love is a thing given more than it is a thing received. Murdraniuss had no heart for anyone but himself."

"Nevertheless," Drinwor said, "lives and love were lost…" He looked past his companions, to the mountain of bones. It looked different now. Now it loomed like a foreboding monument, a powerful reminder of what had happened here. And while he looked at it, an image of the story flashed through his mind. He saw the mountainous pile of bodies…all those bodies… And then he saw them suddenly decay down to their bones…so many bones…

And somewhere beneath those bones was Murdraniuss, the Lord Banshee.

In that moment, Drinwor realized he was soon to become a part of the demon's story.

"How do I fight Murdraniuss?" he whispered in a monotone voice.

"You? Fight?" Morigos sputtered. "Fight *we* may have to,"—he motioned to himself and Morning's Hope—"but *you* will not. You must flee into the hall after I draw Murdraniuss away from the entrance. What happens next, only the fates can tell!" he added with his telltale cackle.

"Draw him away?" Morning's Hope glanced to the mage. "How do you propose to do that?"

"I will offer myself to him."

Vu Verian's voice echoed with laughter. "You'll offer yourself to the Lord Banshee?"

"Yes," Morigos said. "For long ago, he demanded my life so that he might enslave my soul."

Vu Verian couldn't help asking, "Under what circumstances, pray tell?"

Morigos bent his arms about his crooked staff, held it in a close embrace. He spit, chortled, then said: "There was a time when my former master desired entrance into the Hall of Voices. He tried several times, but could never get past the banshee. And then, the last time he tried, he asked…er…commanded that I accompany him. Unbeknownst to me, he had already made a bargain with Murdraniuss that would allow him to enter the hall."

"What was the price?" Drinwor asked.

"The soul of his slave," Morigos grunted in response.

"You," Morning's Hope surmised.

"Yes," the dark elf confirmed. "My master entered the hall and the banshee came for me. But I was not so willing in those days to surrender my life. Before the screaming demon could unleash his unholy voice, I fled!" The mage cackled and choked for a few seconds before continuing. "Then my master returned from the hall, having been turned back by those beings of light that guard it on the other side. And he fled, too! We both escaped, having never paid our price to Murdraniuss. But now—"

"Your *master?*" Vu Verian exclaimed. He turned to Morning's Hope. "Do you realize what he's saying? May the Gods return! He's lead our enemy right to—"

"Be silent for one second!" Morigos snarled, causing the mystic owl's feathers to ruffle. "Before I was so rudely interrupted, I was going to say—I will offer myself to the banshee, and he will come for me, for he will not be able to resist the prize that has so long ago escaped him. That should give you the chance to bring the boy to the hall's entrance."

"Did *you* conceive this plan?" the translucent dragon asked.

"I suggested it to your Fallen Angel, and she agreed. This is why I accompany you."

"I see…" Morning's Hope said.

"Where's the entrance?" Drinwor inquired, his eyes tracking all over the island.

"It's at the base of the mountain," Morigos replied, pointing to the center of the island, "at the end of a pathway that starts at the beach and leads through the—"

"Listen to me!" an infuriated Vu Verian demanded, unwilling to remain silent while the dark elf spewed his lies. He flew between Fleeting Shadow and Morning's Hope, screaming, "I knew Morigos would betray us, but I didn't think he'd be so bold as to openly defy us!"

"He has?" Morning's Hope wasn't so sure.

"Yes!" Vu Verian shouted. "The traitorous, lecherous, vile, rotten bastard! Whom do you think he speaks of when he speaks of his master? Don't you all understand? *Warloove knows of this place!* He's been here!"

"Do you not listen to anything?!" Morigos squealed. "I've made it quite clear! It matters not where we fly, Warloove could find us *anywhere*, fool!"

Oh, you can believe that Vu Verian had heard enough out of the dark elf mage! A thousand spells of violence coursed through his mind, and it didn't take long for him to choose one.

But before he could unleash any sorcery, the sun fell completely behind the horizon. The change to the world was sudden and dramatic. As the black ghost of night arrived to haunt the sky, the Shards of Zyrinthia brightened, and the clouds beneath them swirled into wraithlike shadows that wept with storms. Howling gusts of wind came whipping across the sea, and the bone mountain flickered with reflections of lightning.

Vu Verian groaned in agony, for the now the darkness of night itself scorched him. His whole body wavered and in some places turned into mist. But he resisted the urge to go to cloudform, for he desperately wanted to lash out at Morigos and burn his atoms right out of the sky. But the pain of night was so unbearable it was disabling. He was unable to act, but continued to struggle, the awful sound of his groaning disturbing them all.

"Vu Verian," Morning's Hope said, "you've done enough today. Do not suffer the night. Let go, my friend, go to cloudform, go to sleep!"

Vu Verian did, but only because he absolutely had to. He could resist the night no more. But before his disappearance, he managed to utter: "What's this? Morning's Hope, beware...there *is* a shad—"

And then he slipped completely away, as if his body had been devoured by the dark. Now but a cloud, he shot into the sky and was quickly lost amongst the swirl of storms.

"I am *not* rotten!" the dark elf yelled after him. Then he looked down upon himself. "Oh…well…yes I am."

Morning's Hope regarded Morigos with a vacant stare. "Warloove has been to this place?" she stated more than asked.

The dark elf mage nodded. "Yes."

The translucent dragon looked worriedly to the sky. "So, he may find us after all."

Morigos failed to stifle a little chuckle, then shook his crooked finger at the dragon. "Are you sincerely so surprised by this? How many times do I have to say it? *It doesn't matter where in the world we flee, Warloove will find us.* Did everyone get that this time?"

"It is not so much that I don't believe he can find us," said Morning's Hope, "but I cannot believe the Fallen Angel would have allowed the gauntlets to have been acquired so soon, or so easily."

"If he comes, I will help you fight him." It was Drinwor, his tone meek but determined. "I have more reason to fight him than anyone."

Morigos cackled. "Anxious to fight something, aren't you?"

Morning's Hope whipped her head around. "Drinwor, no!" Her mind instantly filled with numerous reasons to dissuade him, and they poured out of her in a streaming torrent of rambling statements, some of which were: "He's more powerful than anything you've ever encountered!" "You must infuse the sword with a soul!" "You're too important!" "We cannot endanger your destiny!"

Then she ceased, horrified to silence by the look on Drinwor's face.

The dusk elf looked like he was undergoing some kind of demonic possession. The emotions that had begun to simmer with the utterance of Warloove's name now boiled over, and angry tears exploded from his eyes. Rage crumpled his features and his smoky skin paled to white. His chest heaving, he stood up and screamed with all fury:

"**He murdered** *my father!*"

It was a primal hatred he unleashed, an adrenaline-fueled utterance more growled than spoken, surprising even Drinwor himself. Never in his life had he vocalized with such an indignant tone. His words still echoing across the sea, he followed the statement with a quieter but equally intense inquiry. "How am I to fight all the Dark Forever if I cannot even face this one foe?"

"Good question!" Morigos observed.

"Morigos!" Morning's Hope whipped her head about. "Silence yourself, or I swear you will bathe in flames!" She raised a single talon, intending to scold him further, but checked herself. With the collective sanity of the little group all but unraveling, she needed to exercise at least some measure of restraint over her own emotions. She closed her eyes, slowly exhaled, and silently reassured herself.

She was dragonkind, and she was woman.

She would calmly retain control.

She reopened her eyes, looked to Drinwor. He was slumped in his saddle-throne. His chest was still heaving, but the anger appeared to have fled his face. *Bless the boy, he's settling himself down.*

He looked up at her, shaking his head. He dropped his hands on his lap, said, "I'm sorry. That was...insanity."

"Sometimes a little insanity keeps one sane!" Morigos couldn't help but point out.

Morning's Hope cringed, barely restrained herself from swiping the mage right off of his dragon. "Drinwor, it's all right."

The dusk elf averted his gaze from her, fixed his stare in the clouds traipsing over the nameless sea. "The truth is, I've been struggling to suppress my anger all day. And there's something else, something else inside. I can't describe it. It's a desire, a yearning that goes beyond revenge." He drooped his head. "I don't know, I just want to get this hatred out of me. *Warloove.* Every time I hear that name, my heart sinks a little deeper into my chest. I want to rip him apart...I..." He shuddered, unable to continue.

Morning's Hope moved her head closer to him. "I know, my Emperor, but for now, you must not get entangled in a confrontation with War—with *him*. You must leave him for me and Morigos to deal with."

Drinwor bowed his head, whispered, "I understand."

"Actually," Morigos chimed in, "if we can finally stop wasting precious time and get the boy into the damned hall, neither one of you will have to deal with *him*. If he does come here, he'll likely come straight for me."

"Why will he come for you?" Morning's Hope asked.

"Because your sky elf friend was right—I *am* a traitorous bastard!"

"So you mean to hold off all of our enemies by yourself?"

Morigos shrugged. "If it comes to that."

Morning's Hope tilted her head, pondered the mysterious dark elf's intent. "What is it with you? Why are you so anxious to die?"

Morigos snickered. "I'm not anxious for anything. Though cursed with the annoying encumbrance of this disease-ridden body, I refuse to succumb to Warloove's infliction. No…no sickness will ever claim me. But if I should be so lucky as to meet my doom in fire, then I welcome it. I *deserve* it. I want it!" He looked straight into the eyes of Morning's Hope and concluded with: "Fear not for my fate, it was signed and sealed hundreds of years ago, scrawled and stamped in the blood of those unfortunate innocents who crossed my murderous path."

To this, Morning's Hope only nodded. Then she flapped her wings and lifted a little higher from the beach of bones. Fleeting Shadow matched her, and Morigos lightened his tone, said, "I go now to draw out Murdraniuss. Listen for my signal, noble dragon, it will sound right before the banshee's cry. When you hear it, you must protect your young Emperor, and then, if you survive, with all speed bring him to the hall."

Morning's Hope nodded. "I will. And protect yourself, you—"

And then a soul-shivering shriek came from somewhere within the storms, echoing across the nameless sea and rattling the beach of bones.

All flinched, for a split second thinking Murdraniuss had released his wail.

But it wasn't the banshee.

No, Drinwor recognized this shriek. It was the sound that had convinced him to leap from his home and come tumbling to the unknown world. It was the sound of the dawning of his fear, the musical accompaniment for the first truly horrific thing he'd ever experienced.

He would never get used to it…

Morning's Hope uttered, "I can't believe it…"

Grumbled words crept from Morigos' cowl. "No one listens to me, the *lunatic* dark elf! Despite my repeated warnings, we've wasted too much time. Now we are under attack."

And may the Gods return, he was right, for although they couldn't yet see their enemies, on came Geeter's dragonfear.

CHAPTER TWENTY
THE CENTURION AND THE STARS

The burden of a thousand failures can be utterly vanquished beneath the weight of one success.

Fyrax Ooshoa
Veteran of the Iron Skull Wars, Sage of the Levitating Marshes

The sky over the Raging Sea was bleeding. Poisonous red vapor leaked from the rift torn open by the shards and flowed into the waves. Hence, before a single demon stepped foot onto Phate, the Dark Forever claimed its first victims. The abyssal creatures that swam through the tainted waters came dying to the surface, their bodies bloated, their insides exploded by the infiltration of the deadly substance.

And soon more cracks appeared in the sky.

Just as Syndreck had hoped, the encouraged demons were tearing at the dimensional walls from the other side. They grasped the edges of the rents and pulled…and pulled…and pulled. It took the energy of a million black holes to widen the creases by the width of a needle's point, but widen they did…enough for the first legion of demons to slip into Phate's sky. But these were not the club-clawed behemoths that would rip the world to pieces; no, these were the most subtle amongst them.

These were the specter demons.

Gliding through the sky like sentient gusts of wind, they looked to the heavens and for a moment were lost in something akin to mortal wonder; for out there were the stars, out there was the universe they had waited so long to conquer. Oh, how pleasant the coolness of space would feel! Such vast emptiness, such unrestricted freedom! They squirmed with pleasure just thinking about it. They looked on the night a little while longer, then set their sights on the world around them.

Upon the edge of the obsidian cliffs they saw a shadowy complex of writhing towers. They knew within one of those towers resided the mortal who allegedly commanded immortal power: the necromancer, Syndreck the Brooding. It was *he* who had freed the vast legions a thousand years ago. The demons observed him with curious eyes. Although he was slumped unconscious on his platform, the echoes of his sorcerous voice still trembled all the plains before him, and the sky around his towers was filled with meteors that he himself had commandeered.

The demons were impressed. Indeed, his power *was* substantial. And there was something else... Beyond the towers there strode a being unlike any they'd ever seen. Its broken body and weary soul ensnared in a worn wrap of technological armor, it moved slowly but purposefully forward, toward Syndreck's towers.

Apparently, Syndreck didn't hold this being in high regard, for while the demons watched, the necromancer's meteors went screaming toward it. Surprisingly, the alien didn't move. It stood in stern defiance as the cosmic boulders approached.

Now fascinated, the demons took another moment to watch the confrontation unfold...

Soular Centurion 7 displayed no fear, his grey eyes staring unblinking at the incoming volley of shooting stars. His batteries surging with power, his translucent veins glowing with the light speed flow of cybernetic blood, he reactivated his sword and stood at the ready.

The first shard shot down at him with blistering speed!

–ENGAGE EVASIVE MANEUVER PATTERN CENTURIOUS 5.3–

The centurion leaped aside.

The meteor cratered the plains beside him with a thundering, blazing impact. In an instant, many square miles of overturned reeds were incinerated from the fallowed fields by fire. What little remains were left of the Wicked Plains were also destroyed—bones to ashes, ashes to dust, dust to atoms.

From space it looked as if a country had exploded.

It nearly had.

And yet, Soular Centurion 7 was unblemished as the cloud of dusty ruin settled down around him.

His eyes focused upward.

Another meteoric shard screamed in.

–SYSTEM'S PERFORMANCE ACCEPTABLE. PROCEED WITH ATTACK PATTERN ARTIZIAN 27–

The centurion jumped a hundred feet into the air.

With the Sword of Molecular Destruction held high, he punctured the shard before it angled down atop him, and it blew apart with a sparking explosion. He fell down through the raining rubble and thudded to the ground. He then readied himself as the next shard came whistling in with a disharmonious din. He blasted it into powder, his space-sword a flash of black and purple.

And then another shard came, and another, and another. They streaked in from every direction, diving down like avenging angels come to douse the light of the centurion's immortal soul!

Soular Centurion 7 scanned each of the targets for their size, speed, and distance from one another. With the data computed, he bent his knees and pivoted at the waist, twirling his torso all the way around to end up facing almost forward again. At the turn's apex, there was the slightest pause, then he whipped around and sprang into the sky like a loosed coil. His starsword's low murmur elevated into a howl, and with a swift upward thrust, he cleaved a shard in two. He then angled his trajectory aside and swung down from straight overtop, vaporizing another meteor, the molecular remains swallowed by his black hole blade.

Thus he proceeded to dance across the sky, vanquishing all of the attacking shards. The Wicked Plains, immersed in a storm of melted stones, soon looked like the surface of a burning moon.

The stars were waging a war, but Soular Centurion 7 was winning.

Beneath the plains, more of Kroon's caverns and corridors crumbled and caved in as the meteoric shards the centurion had evaded smashed down their ceilings. Many dark elves were lost. Those who survived fled into the cave port then bolted up the great shaft. From there they scattered into the many secret passages that led to the terraces and balconies which dotted the cliff side. Dusty and disoriented, they staggered wide-eyed into the night, wondering why the fates were punishing their loyalty.

When they looked to the sky, they understood.

Now had come the fulfillment of prophecy.

The stars were exacting punishment. Red death crept out over the waves. The sounds of battle boomed above, specter demons slipped through the skies, and spectral storms battered the walls of Ulith Urn, its holy walls again solidified.

Indeed, the new age had finally come!

The dark elves sang out with euphoric joy, then they turned savage with ecstasy.

As massive waves pounded the cliffs, as spray doused them in poisoned water, they turned their swords upon one another. Hundreds died, their corpses taken by the sea. It was sensible. They were purging their ranks of all who did not belong or believe. Those who died tonight obviously had no place in the new order. The ritual went on for some time, calming only when the most violent among them had sated their bloody thirst.

(I tell you, I would not want to be close to these dark elves when they found a reason for revelry! Would you?)

"Come," one of the Black Claw called, "come and join with the conquest of eternity! Come and reclaim your rightful place among the Lords of the Dark Forever!

Thousands of consenting cries rose over the cacophony of exploding meteors. The Mages of the Moom levitated up the face of the obsidian cliffs. Some of the Black Claw leaped upon the backs of their bats, and many more began to climb.

There, in the fields surrounding Syndreck's towers, they would gather, ready to kill whatever stood against their god, Nenockra Rool.

And while all this was going on, Syndreck did nothing but snore...

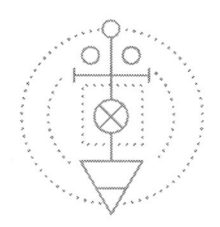

CHAPTER TWENTY-ONE
BATTLEGROUND OF BONES

Sacrifice is a part of every noble story.
Vorlicia
Condemned Empress of Zyrinthia

Although the stormy shroud of night had not yet revealed the beast to their eyes, Geeter's dragonfear intensified. The companions were covered with a cumbersome blanket of dread. No one was immune from its effects, not even brave Morning's Hope. Her wings and limbs weighed down and her vision was momentarily blurred. Morigos felt his throat constrict and he coughed, as if choking on the fear. With his wings weakening, Fleeting Shadow fought just to not drop out of the sky. Drinwor's will was reduced to a wilted, rotted thing. He leaned over the saddle as if sickened, and reached down to touch his dragon, to feel something that belied this suffocating horror.

"How… How do we overcome this?" he barely managed to mumble.

"Have faith my Emperor," Morning's Hope replied, her head swaying about as she scanned the swirling clouds.

Fleeting Shadow whined, drifted in a little circle, his large eyes bulging with fright. Morigos spit over the dragon's side. "Bah, Warloove. It's *always* a show with him. *Always* a charade. Just come and fight us!" he screamed toward the sky.

"I've been so foolish," Morning's Hope muttered, "toying with our precious time throughout the whole day." She looked to Morigos. "You were right. Though I'm aware of his immense power, I underestimated him. I was confident in the Fallen Angel's ability to ensure that he wouldn't acquire the gauntlets so quickly."

"Do not punish yourself too severely," Morigos returned. "Warloove has a habit of foiling even the most carefully laid plans!"

"I can't breathe," Drinwor groaned.

"Easy, easy," Morning's Hope soothed.

"Well, it's still not too late to succeed with our quest if we separate *now!*" the dark elf mage asserted. "Come, my ugly insect dragon, let us make for the mountain!"

And then the world went utterly dark.

The gleam of the bones beneath them faded, the reflection of the stars upon the sea diminished, and above the dull glow of the storm-shrouded shards disappeared.

Drinwor straightened up. "What happened to the sky?"

"It's been stolen!" Morigos yelled. "Move!"

The Emperor of the Sky was snapped into the back of his saddle-throne as Morning's Hope slapped her wings and dove wildly aside. Fleeting Shadow followed suit, his quadruple wings buzzing back to life, propelling him similarly in the opposite direction. Drinwor held on tight to the dragon armrests, and the straps about his ankles constricted. Against all reason he tilted back his head and looked straight up to see the terror that was to befall.

"Gods, I should not have looked!"

Imagine how he must have felt to see a huge black fireball burst out of the storms and come blasting straight down like a moon of burning shadows! It sizzled right through the spot they'd just been hovering, scalding the tips of the dragons' tails before smashing into the shoreline. Bones were blown into slivers, waves were dashed into mist. The companions were soaked by foam and stung by fragments. The fireball never relented. It shot down into the unseen depths, boiling the waters of the nameless sea as it went.

It all happened so quickly.

"Move! Move!" Morigos continued to urge. For he knew, though the fireball had missed them, it was only a promise of impending pain. Morning's Hope didn't need convincing, she continued to dash away.

As expected, on came the demons.

Although Drinwor knew he should look away, he couldn't help but continue to stare upward. He twisted round and watched as Geeter punched through the bottom of the clouds. Now, with Drinwor no longer viewing the world through a veil of complete innocence, he got his first clear look at a Greater Demonic Dragon.

The image was similar to the one Lord Dark Sorciuss had seen before his demise: a devilish dragon of unbelievable size diving straight down for them, its smooth, inky hide glistening, its massive pincers snapping, its ten foot long fangs dripping acid and fire. Its tail curled overtop it like a great black serpent itself, twitching with eagerness to impale and sting anything.

"It's the stuff of nightmares sprung out of some evil sleep to slay us!" Drinwor cried in terror.

But for all of Geeter's horrific traits, the most frightening feature was the shadowy swirl of vampiric smoke upon his back. Although Drinwor caught only a fleeting glimpse of Warloove, he was stricken as if with a seizure. There was his father's killer, projecting the power of a god. If the demonic dragon was the physical embodiment of fear, then Warloove was its heart, a throbbing black core from which all despair arose.

Indeed, as I've earlier described, to look upon him was like being stabbed by darkness, by death itself, even!

And then came Warloove's echoing, distorted cry. "Son of Herard, give me the power of the stars, or suffer in torment and die!"

"Ignore him!" Morning's Hope screamed as she continued to dash away.

Drinwor turned about, brought his head down, squeezed his eyes shut, whispering, "I had no idea...no idea how awful... I can't—" His words were strangled by fear into silence, and he was struck with a strong sense of foreboding. Somehow, he knew: death would now claim one of them. He didn't think it was himself, but he could feel it…one among them was already lost. "No…" he whispered through a mournful moan.

Although Morning's Hope and Fleeting Shadow continued racing away, they were well within Warloove's sorcerous reach. As Geeter plummeted toward them, on came maniacal magic.

Wrapped by the Gauntlets of Loathing Light, Warloove's clawed hands thrust out of his cloak of smoke, the fingers opening, flexing straight. Inharmonic songs of offensive sorcery sprang from his hidden mouth, and a wide swathe of black beams erupted from his fingertips. The beams were loud, crackling like dried leaves beneath a stomping boot as they came blazing down…

…and cut into Fleeting Shadow's hide.

The insect dragon was struck behind the saddle, the beams slicing deep into his body. Warloove cruelly twirled his fingers, then closed them together, scissoring off the dragon's tail. Fleeting Shadow jolted. His tail went spiraling into the sea, green blood gushing from the terrible wound. He loosed a cry that was recognized by all: a cry of suffering, a cry of dying, a cry of death.

Drinwor twisted back around and screamed, "Morigos! No… no…! Fleeting Shadow!"

Morning's Hope also flashed a look behind her. For a moment she considered flying to her kin's aid, but she immediately recognized there was nothing to be done. The insect dragon's fate was already sealed, and in her current position, she was vulnerable to Warloove's fire.

"And, above all," she reminded herself, "I *must* protect the Son and Savior of the Stars."

She continued to dart away.

"Oh, Morning's Hope!" Drinwor cried, flinching as he watched the unfolding of such a wickedly violent fate.

Bleeding and mortally wounded, Fleeting Shadow careened, contorted, then slammed into the beach of bones with a tremendous crunch. The impact broke his own bones, and the last of his blood drained into the nameless sea. His dome-like eyes dimmed, and his fluttering heart and buzzing wings went still. His soul teetered on the precipice before the gaping abyss of eternity…and then fell into it.

Fleeting Shadow of Vren Adiri was dead.

A wave came in and washed his body into the sea. He was gone.

(Although his life was lost, he was spared the eternal damnation of the Dark Forever, for his spirit was met between the planes, joined by those glittering dragon souls who awaited the opening of the gates to the Seven Glories. He was spared joining the coming battle, and led to a shining realm of infinite silver skies, where soon his mortal pains disappeared beneath the gaze of immortal eyes…)

And to Fleeting Shadow, we bid farewell…

Morigos had pitched himself over the dragon's side after Warloove's beams had struck. He'd plummeted down beside his mount, but whispered a levitation spell right before he would've struck the beach. He gently landed on the bones, then scampered from the shoreline, the bones nipping his calves. "You were a fine beast," he quietly uttered, "and it should be me, not you, who bears the sufferance of so pointed a hatred."

Geeter never slowed.

The demonic dragon smashed into the shore with such force, the entire isle shuddered. His head plunged through the bones and into the abyss, garnering him a mouthful of fossils seasoned by seawater. His belly smacked onto the beach, and for a moment he just lay there, watching Fleeting Shadow's body sink into the darkness of the deep.

The reverberation of Geeter's impact sent Morigos flying over the dunes, a cursing, ragged pile of robes. He grunted, "Urgh! Geeter, you're *not* so fine a beast!" when he hit the bones with his bottom.

Warloove solidified and somersaulted onto the shore. His boots firmly planted in the bones, he glanced to the sky. There he saw the translucent dragon soaring out over the sea, saw the dusk elf Son of Herard upon her back, and the blinding white glare of the golden artifact among him.

The glare of the Sunsword Surassis.

"There it is! There it is!" He turned to his dragon. "Come, Geeter, not all bones are so dry. Let us feast on blood and meat, and claim the master's prize!"

The Greater Demonic Dragon pulled his head from the water, and Warloove made to remount him. But then a peculiar feeling struck the vampire, giving him pause. What was this? He felt a familiar presence, as if something or someone he knew was right here on the beach. His head perked up and he sniffed the air. *Could it be?* He twirled about and scampered to the top of the dunes.

"What is this I smell?" he bellowed, scanning the darkness before him. "Smells like a slave!"

Morigos froze. Then he slowly turned around and held up his staff. The gnarled piece of wood emitted a little cloud of magical smoke that he hoped would blend him into the shadows.

It didn't appear to work, for Warloove took a step down the dunes, directly toward him.

Morigos took a step back.

Warloove took another step toward him.

Morigos took another step back. "*Oh, devil*" he whispered.

Warloove thrust his enkindled hands over his head and unleashed a brilliant fire into the air, illuminating all the area. And there before him, contrasting sharply against the drab white of the bones, was a wavering little cloud of smoke.

"By all the Dark Forever," Warloove roared, "I *see* you!"

Now exposed, Morigos lowered his staff in futility and let the smoke screen disappear, putting himself in plain sight. The runes on his robes burned brightly, just as his eyes burned with the visage of the vampire who towered over him like some wind-racked wraith recently raised from the sea.

"You dare hide from me?" Warloove yelled, "dare defy me? What in hell's cursed name are you doing here?"

Morigos shrugged. "Uh…I don't know. I was thinking of building myself a dark little domicile here? You?"

"Imbecilic fool!"

And then Morigos felt Warloove invade his mind.

Such was the strength of Warloove's will, there was little he could do to curtail the vampire's forced entry of his thoughts. Warloove searched though his memories as if he ransacked a shelf of books, tossing each volume aside until he came upon the one he sought. And when he found what he wanted, he tore off the cover, if you will, ripped through the pages, and a scene from the recent past played out like one of Vu Verian's magical stories in the minds of both victim and invader. For Morigos, time seemed to slow; *he* seemed to slow, his limbs feeling like weights, his usually fluttering heart now laboriously chugging beneath his rotting breast.

As simply as I can describe, this is the shadowy scene they saw:

"You'd just love to kill me, wouldn't you, Herard?" The dark elf sorcerer quipped as he looked out into the thundering night. "Or perhaps your dragon would delight in smothering me in flames?"

They both noticed the black silhouette of Zraz passing through the clouds above them, flying watch over the edge of the Cliffs of Moaning Wishes, where the two stood alone in the storms.

"You are unarmed, Morigos," Herard returned, "and I still hold honor, as does Zraz. If it is blood you still crave, return below, to Kroon."

"I am always armed, you know this. Sorcery is my sword." The ancient dark elf sorcerer turned to face the man, his shady eyes flickering with malcontent... and sadness just the same. "It's a shame, in a way, for besides my own kin, I have run out of worthy enemies. A part of me will miss our battles, Skylord."

"I cannot agree with you...but I understand..."

Herard glanced to the Raging Sea. It was so big, and he felt so small now, so exhausted, body, mind, and soul. And despite Morigos' claims, he sensed a similar weariness in his old adversary, a similar dissatisfaction, though his own life had not been wasted in the administration of senseless evil. But, alas, he still didn't trust him, still needed to know—was this wretch going to betray them? He asked plainly, "You have the gauntlets? You will give them to me as planned? They are in Kroon, I presume?"

Morigos hung his head as if the slightest shame was upon him, yet he would not speak of it. When he did talk, his voice was low, practically blending into the sea and waves and wraith-filled winds. "Yes, yes, you shall have them, if all goes as planned. They are not in Kroon, though, but soon will be. Do not worry, Lord of Areshria, though I know my words hold little weight with you, I swear this is true, for by merely being here I risk torture eternal…as do you."

"I know," Herard said, "I know. And because there are no others who will defy the darkness set against the universe, because of the angel's urging, I will trust you. May the Gods return, I am forced to. Though our chances are slim, I must acquire the Gauntlets of Loathing Light. If Warloove obtains them, and the sword—"

"Then this damned and ruined world will meet its dark end even faster!" the mysterious mage finished for him. "For once he has the sunsword, nothing will stop him. I cannot compete with him, his dragon, and his dark master from the sky, not alone." He paused, for one thoughtful moment, then said, "Remember me Herard, remember I am the only of my kind that has even had an inkling to betray them, an inkling of conscience for that matter."

Herard stood still as stone, praying that Morigos was not like the other dark elves, like the thousands he had been forced to kill in his decades as ruler of the sky. "If that is true, then may whatever Gods are out there notice your courage and bravery that are so foreign to your kind. Should I survive, should I claim the gauntlets, then I am in your debt."

Morigos cackled lowly. "So the last human on Phate indeed still holds glory and honor. Good, make sure you have speed, accuracy, and a complete lack of fear when the time comes. For you know I can but assist you little; too many eyes, too many eyes upon me."

"One more favor?" the silver-armored man asked solemnly.

Another favor? Morigos thought. What more could this man want of me?! "I believe I am doing enough, but go ahead," Morigos snarled, his heritage showing a bit now, his patience with the encounter running out as he feared one of his kind would find them.

Herard appeared to look back up at Zraz, but he was actually looking beyond her. He started to choke up a bit, but carried on with his request. "He is up there, the sword is out there. If I fall, do what you can…if you have truly turned to the side of light, see it through and help watch over him. He knows nothing of what he is, what is at stake. Phate is doomed if he does not—"

"Ha!" Morigos tapped his staff to the stone. "So, you say the foreseen dusk elf savior exists! And I am asked to watch over him should the last human on the planet die?" Morigos laughed, covering his mouth with his arm, in case *anyone was near.* "You are bold indeed, Herard Avari Fang. But I'll tell you what, if I like this boy, I accept, for I will have nothing better to do!"

Herard narrowed his eyes. "Not amusing in the least, traitorous elf, not at all. He is—"

"The chosen one born of the stars."

"Yes."

"He is unique. He has all our strengths, none of our flaws, perfect in every way..."

"Yes." *Herard sighed, breathed in deeply, and watched the only dark elf holding a shred of honor start to walk away.* "His name, is Drinwor, Drinwor Fang," *he called after him.*

"As I've just indicated, I know of the legend of the savior. As for what I do about him...we shall see...we shall see..." *Morigos began to enshroud with the haunted shadows of night.* "This meeting never happened, eh?"

"Agreed, and well met, Morigos of Kroon..."

Herard waved.

The dark elf disappeared around one of the dingy crags that dotted the clifftop, his voice an echoing whisper that was barely heard, then drowned by the wind.

"Farewell, Herard, last human of Phate..."

Morigos' awareness was suddenly back on the beach of bones.

Warloove thrust a hand forward, as if throwing his screaming words at the mage. **"Traitorous, lecherous, vile, rotten bastard! I will suck the skin from your bones and keep you alive! I will inflict you with a thousand more diseases and wait long centuries for you to die! Betrayer! Betrayer! Betrayer!"**

"Such unoriginal insults," Morigos remarked. "I swear, in the next life I fight for neither light nor darkness! You're both infinitely annoying!"

Warloove stepped forth. "There will be no next life for you!" he said through gritted fangs. "I will steal your soul for the sword and disintegrate your very spirit!"

Morigos chortled. "You cannot destroy that which I do not have...master."

"We shall see!"

Now Warloove murmured with arcane madness, his fingers aching to unleash yet more flames. Morigos lifted his staff and the vampire laughed, mocking the mage's defensive stance. Then Warloove whispered, and fire erupted.

But it was not his own.

Morning's Hope had arced around and swooped in from the sea like a heavenly guardian of the stars come to douse the fiend with lightning-like flames of white!

Immersed in her breath, Warloove screamed with rage and pain, then whirled to retaliate. The runes on the Gauntlets of Loathing Light ignited, and eagerly did his flames explode upward from the ends of his clawed fingertips! Fire contested fire. The translucent's scorching breath was squelched beneath the stifling punishment of the vampire's own blackened pitch.

Warloove had been stung, but his cloak of smoke had repelled most of the searing force of the flames.

Morning's Hope soared right over him, then curled back out over the sea, screaming, "In the name of Fleeting Shadow, no enemy of light shall ever employ the power of the sun!"

Warloove swiveled to watch her, his hands lowering, his mouth twitching with a smirk. He yelled after her, "You are foolish to be dangling the sword right in front of my face like this! Do you not realize I can in seconds overtake you?" But he did not go after her immediately. *Ah, what a tantalizing moment!* He couldn't help but pause and savor the promise of battle, if even a battle it was going to be. Soon he would feast on sweet immortal blood, and the Sunsword Surassis would be his. Finally he would be free of the fear of the fires of an exploding sun! For a moment he imagined himself and his master aboard their technological dragon, slipping through the cool blackness between the stars...

"Ah, but first, there is one small matter to attend to. One revenge to incur!"

Disloyal, weak, and foolish Morigos was scampering away. Warloove began to stride after him, but stopped almost immediately, for a voice entered his mind. The voice was monotone, soulless...and persuading.

Warloove! Why do you delay? The sword is within your grasp! Seize it!

"Master...yes, of course." Warloove instantly turned around and leaped onto the back of his dragon. His smirk widened. The mischievous mage might escape his own fangs, but he would not escape another's.

Morigos must have known: on this isle they were not alone.

With a sorcerously enhanced voice, Warloove called to the mountain. "Now, after long years, I will fulfill my part of the bargain and leave you your prize! Come Murdraniuss, come hither and take him!"

And then, with a mighty thrust of his wings, Geeter took flight. He shrieked his ear-splitting cry and bolted after Morning's Hope.

Morigos flashed a look to the sea, his eyes tracking the fleeing translucent dragon. And then something peculiar happened to him. He was struck with small pang of...regret? Loneliness? Was that what that was? "Nonsense!" he exclaimed to the dark. He shook his haggard head, pulled the tattered brim of his cowl farther down over his face, and sighed to the bones beneath his feet. "Soon," he whispered, "soon I will join you."

A strange sound came from the base of the mountain, and the sky trembled with cosmic thunder, and auburn lightning scattered through the clouds; and Morigos of the Moom, betrayer of Warloove, outcast dark elf sorcerer afflicted with the Ever Dying, prepared to face the Lord Banshee alone.

CHAPTER TWENTY-TWO
FORWARD WITH FATE

> *Creativity is a fire in which the whims of the soul yearn to burn.*
> Drooviock
> Warlock Sage of the Five Moons

Syndreck the Brooding regained consciousness.

He lifted his face from a pool of his own curdled blood and moaned softly, his joints aching with the soreness of mortality. Apparently, even these nimble limbs could stiffen. Well, no matter, it was time to evaluate what had happened, assess what was going on. His cognizance returning, he pushed himself up with his elbows and attempted to stand. No such luck. His feet, slipping on the blood-slicked flagstone, slid straight out behind him, and his face met the floor with a dull smack.

He laughed at his stupidity, but gave his clumsiness an excuse. "So cumbersome and awkward, these mortal bodies, even the best of them!"

He reached up, grasped the top curve of his bulging cauldron, and carefully pulled himself from the floor. Once standing, he rubbed his eyes and peered into the pot.

The images within were wild.

"Ah, yes!"

Behind his towers, the sky over the Raging Sea was now torn in many places. Red vapor spread out from the cracks, cannibalized the clouds, and polluted the waters with poison. In front of Ulith Urn, the Wicked Plains were barely recognizable. The Shards of Zyrinthia had razed the ground. The soil was as blackened ash. Craters were everywhere, from which streamed endless columns of fire and smoke.

"Glorious!"

Ah, Syndreck. Naturally he'd think it glorious. He went into hysterics, a barrage of grating laughter exploding from his blood-stained mouth. "My sorcery has been successful! The dimensional walls have been breached and the centurion has undoubtedly been destroyed! Oh, Nenockra Rool will be so pleased."

That might have all been true but for one perplexing little detail he was just beginning to notice—Soular Centurion 7's body was nowhere to be seen.

"Where is he?"

Syndreck looked deeper into the bubbling liquid, searching for the centurion's charred body. But it was difficult to discern anything, for even his extrasensory eyes struggled to peer through the wind-swept walls of fire, smoke, and dust. Determined to find the alien carcass, he firmly gripped the edge of the cauldron and hung his head right over the bubbling surface, searching, searching across the devastated plains. Nothing…yet.

"Where—"

Wait. Something moved. He looked closer. Yes, something was there, glimmering where all else was dark.

The necromancer blew a foul breath into the cauldron.

On the plains, a wall of black smoke was dispersed by a sorcerous wind, and there, very much alive, was Soular Centurion 7, walking slowly, purposefully forward, toward Ulith Urn.

He was close.

In that moment of revelation, Syndreck experienced something he hadn't felt in a thousand years.

In that moment, he felt fear.

It trickled into the basin of his mind, a small inkling that Soular Centurion 7 might actually possess the strength to destroy him. Although he commanded extraordinary sorceries, and was favored by the most powerful forces in the universe, Syndreck was *not* invincible. If his bones were shattered or blown apart, his spirit would flee into the very dimension he was trying to free. Now he just stood there, staring into his cauldron with disbelief as the cosmic warrior walked right up to the sorcerous shield surrounding Ulith Urn and squeezed his armored body through it.

"This is preposterous!" Now the alien enemy was actually inside the compound. Consumed by rage, Syndreck slammed his fists on the cauldron's rim. "NO! NO! NO! How is it that the cowering Gods always manage to reach through time and space to torment me? I need to concentrate on the breaches, not on this damned warrior!"

A torrent of rain flew through the circular space in the ceiling, moistening the dried-up blood on his face. Bloody black tears streamed down his cheeks and dripped from his glistening chin. His eyes closed to slivers, and he growled like a stricken beast, pondering what spells to call forth to finally stop the centurion.

But then something new entered his sphere of awareness. He unclenched his fists, shot a look back into the Cauldron of Carcass Control.

Something was crawling up the Cliffs of Moaning Wishes.

On came the dark elves of Kroon.

"YES! YES! YES!"

Two thousand battle mages and at least thrice that many warriors swarmed over the cliff's ledge, a rising tide of fanatical fury devoted to crushing the foes of the Dark Forever.

Syndreck smiled so widely, the scabbed skin around his lips cracked and leaked more blood onto his chin. He waved his arms across the cauldron's surface, temporarily deactivating the shield to allow the elves easier entry into the compound. He considered leaving the shield down, but knew he'd need it to protect his towers from the sky's impending fury—the great onslaught of the Shards of Zyrinthia was about to ensue...

Dark elf commanders on bats soared into the compound and curled around the towers. Mages of the Moom flew through the storms, stealing lightning bolts and sorcerously storing them within their swelling robes. The thousands on foot clambered over the ledge and surged onto the grounds, their silver weapons held high, their echoing chants sounding like an angry dirge. The flying mages sang a foul song, and a wispy shroud of magic blanketed those on the ground. Those with invisible-steel armor became invisible themselves.

Syndreck was beaming. "What a timely army!"

He reactivated the shield, effectively sealing the dark elves in, then telepathically contacted the battle mages, instructing them to destroy the approaching alien warrior immediately.

The command was unnecessary, for the dark elves were already advancing on the metallic intruder.

Soular Centurion 7 stepped into the compound and slowed his advance.

New signals were coming through.

–THOUSANDS OF DARK ELVES APPROACHING–

Dark elves.

That race, though uncommon in the universe, was known to him—intelligence misguided by hate, cunning in cold blood, steel empowered by sorcery. They could pose more of a challenge than any of the previous obstacles he'd dealt with since arriving on Phate. They were not indomitable, though, not to the galactic guardian of the stars.

He was just beginning to formulate his defensive strategy, when suddenly the sky brightened. A series of tremendous booming, thundering, and slamming noises reverberated across the entire world, nearly overloading his auditory sensors. It sounded like thousands of moons exploding in rapid succession directly over his head.

He wasn't the only one whose "auditory sensors" were overloaded.

Every inhabitant of Phate looked up, fearful the Gods had returned to murder the world. It wasn't the Gods, but it might as well have been, for the doom promised by prophecy was now being delivered.

The prophets that had earlier wept now wailed.

The seers that had earlier sobbed now screamed.

The full onslaught of the Shards of Zyrinthia had arrived.

Although Syndreck had managed to pluck a small group of shards from the sky, he had no control over them all, so even he was somewhat stunned as the entire lower portion of the asteroid belt dipped beneath the atmosphere and blasted down to smite the lands!

The dark elves went wild.

As the great meteor storm commenced, they rushed the warrior from the stars.

Soular Centurion 7 stood his ground and silently readied to fight again.

CHAPTER TWENTY-THREE
AGAINST THE FALL OF NIGHT

When your energy has wilted, and you fall to your knees...crawl. Not as a slave, but as a survivor, crawl; for ultimately, it is determination that will carry you into your dreams...

Zravion
Captain of the Silver Fleet,
Avatar King of Solidariuss, the Sentient Sea

It was a night like no other on Phate.

The haunted remnants of a thousand civilizations were dismissed into the dusty pages of history as the vengeful shards came down and consumed them in a great storm of cosmic fire. Not since the last war with the Dark Forever was so much lost in so short a time. Port cities were swallowed by their seas. Obsidian mountains were pounded into plains. Sapphire forests were reduced to ash, and the sky inherited a sea of dust that ever after deepened the darkness of the bloody days.

Indeed, it was a night like no other on Phate.

A night of a thousand forgotten stories. Stories of heroes who saved those who might have perished. Stories of villains who murdered those who might have lived. Stories of courage, and sacrifice, and yes, even love... Ah, so many forgotten stories, reduced to nothing but a passing paragraph on this very page as the Shards of

Zyrinthia burned them from the minds of those who might have remembered.

Yet for all those forgotten stories, there were some tales that stood the test of recorded time. Among them was the tale of Drinwor Fang and Morning's Hope, who we now join as they dash away from the demonic dragon and his master...

The Shards of Zyrinthia streaked down all around Morning's Hope, pummeling the nameless sea and battering the island of bones like great molten fists. Explosions of shattered fossils blew into the air, and the sea erupted with monstrous waves. The rumbling of impacts echoed in the distance, the horizon flared with every strike, and all the world endured this cosmic punishment!

Morning's Hope whispered, "So, Phate has become the drum upon which destiny pounds... Now our paths dash us headlong toward whatever end awaits, be it glorious or vile."

Drinwor was certain he beheld the end of the world, for it looked as if the entire sky was being slashed to fiery ribbons. "Is this the doings of the Dark Forever? My Gods, the burning moons come for us all!"

His dragon looked back to him. "It does appear to be the doings of evil, does it not?"

"Watch out!" Drinwor cried as a shard screamed down at them.

Morning's Hope swung her head forward and dodged aside. The meteor grazed her flank and plunged into the sea. "Hang on, my Emperor!" she yelled whilst evading the ensuing wave.

"I hadn't planned on letting go, I assure you!"

Drinwor Fang held on for dear life while Morning's Hope flew as if to shake him from her back. She angled this way and that, twisting and spiraling, dodging the shards and waves.

And then came Geeter.

The Greater Demonic Dragon swerved around a shard's blazing trail and swooped in behind them. Drinwor knew Geeter was there before he even saw the beast, for dragonfear stifled his breath, and shrieking terror pierced his ears. Against his better judgment, he flashed a look behind him.

Foolishness!

The enemy dragon filled his field of vision, and Drinwor was both horrified and amazed. "How can something so huge be so fast and maneuverable?" Just as he said that, Geeter lunged forward. Eager to dig his massive fangs into the enticing flesh of the translucent's tail, he bit down...but missed, falling short by only a few feet.

Drinwor cringed. "Morning's Hope! He's right on top of us!"

"I know!"

"Gods, he's tremendous!"

"I know!"

The meteor storm intensified.

It seemed as though the sea itself caught on fire as a pair of blazing meteors collided and exploded right over the waves beside them. Morning's Hope flew through a spray of sea and sparks as Geeter snapped at her tail with his maw and pincers. She continued her wild maneuvers, but couldn't shake her larger, faster opponent. The Greater Demonic Dragon was drawing ever closer.

The whole situation was madness, I tell you!

Warloove was ecstatic.

"Concede the sunsword!" he cried through the roar of waves and wind and fire, "for there is no force that can forestall the coming of the Dark Forever! Concede the sword, or I will give you wounds more severe than anything the sea or stars can inflict!"

Apparently he had no intention of waiting for a reply, for then he immediately sang out a malicious song of sorcery.

A host of sparkling silvery-white spears appeared in the air around him, and behold, these spears were actually spirits themselves—the Spears of Stinging Ghosts. Warloove flicked his fingers and the spears whipped toward the translucent dragon, howling as they sliced through a wave and into her hide. Morning's Hope cried out. The ghostly spears shrieked. Warloove cackled, "Yes, burn her! *Burn her!*" The imbedded spears dissolved like ice rapidly turning into liquid, melting into crackling little pools that stung her as they spread across her sides.

Morning's Hope screamed, "Cursed demon!" and swatted at the stinging ghosts.

Drinwor instinctively put his hand to his leg pouch, once again wishing the sunsword had its captured soul. "What do I do?" he shouted through the shrieking and roaring. "How can I help you?"

Through a series of painful grunts, Morning's Hope said, "There's nothing...just keep holding on!" She then sucked in a heavy inhalation. Her insides lit up so brightly, she appeared as a glowing shard herself. She adjusted her course and flew straight for a particularly massive wave that was rising up before them.

Drinwor pointed forward. "Uh, you do see that, right?"

"Yes I do!" Morning's Hope answered.

"And yet still you fly toward it..." Drinwor was taken aback. Apparently, his usually levelheaded dragon had something rather daring in mind. "Good Gods," he muttered to himself, "this is lunacy." Indeed it would seem that it was, with Warloove and Geeter closing in behind them, the wall of water rising up in front, and the stinging ghosts continuing to crawl over his dragon's skin.

Morning's Hope angled her head around, opened her maw, and spit a thin blanket of crackling lightning across her back. A startled Drinwor cried out and, fearing he was about to be electrified, tried to wrench his ankles from their safety straps. The straps held his ankles fast, but the lightning never touched him; it streamed around the saddle-throne and stretched beneath the dragon's body, covering all the stinging ghosts. The ghosts moaned, but their cries were lost by the rushing roar of the oncoming wave as it reached up to slap Morning's Hope from the sky.

She called out, "Hold your breath and hold on!" Then she faced forward.

Drinwor felt the ankle straps tighten even further as a sudden jolt of acceleration pressed him into the back of the throne. He had no idea what was going to happen next, but did as he was told. He grabbed onto the armrests and sucked in a deep breath...

Morning's Hope met the wave head on.

Tucking her wings and twisting her body, she drilled snout-first through its white-capped crest. Immersed in water, the lightning blanket she'd laid over herself crackled and sparked, scorching the stinging ghosts. They shrieked a piercing cry as their forms exploded and dispersed. The lightning fizzled out, and Morning's Hope spiraled out the other side of the wave, her body cleansed of enemy sorcery.

She righted herself, yelled, "Drinwor!" praying her Lord hadn't been electrocuted or lost to the sea.

The sky's Emperor sputtered, spit out a mouthful of water, then said, "I'm still here!" His demonskin had absorbed the electricity. Glistening with seawater, his heart pumping hard, he pointed forward and shouted, "Fly on!"

Behind them, Geeter soared over the wave, his talons skimming its crest as the riled waters passed on beneath him. Letting out an irritated shriek, he came diving down after his translucent prey...

Morigos of the Moom calmly waited for the Lord Banshee.

He knew he didn't need to shout or make some garish show of sorcery to draw Murdraniuss away from the entrance to the Hall of Voices. He need only stand there. Surrounded by dull bones, even his weakened life-force would blaze like a fire in the cursed spirit's eyes.

And now he heard an eerie, long drawn-out moan rise over the roar of meteors and waves—a moan that quickly multiplied into many voices.

Murdraniuss was coming.

"Ghosts!" Morigos said to the dark. "Phate is filled with ghosts! The skies, the seas; is there not a single place where the living reign?" He cackled, but halfheartedly.

Ghosts...

Bah, he didn't care, he had no fear over that which he had once ruled.

"Yes, Murdraniuss, come closer."

And closer the banshee came.

When Morigos saw its bluish vapor-like form flow over a foothill that lay halfway between him and the mountain, he was suddenly seized with chills.

"No fear of ghosts, ha!"

Before he even realized what he was doing, he turned round, scampered over the dunes and onto the beach, retreating until the freezing surf tickled his toes. Then he pivoted to face the mountain again, and went still as stone. A small shard smashing into the mountain's side momentarily caught his attention, and when he looked back down, he saw that he wasn't alone.

The Lord Banshee had arrived.

Morigos' chills returned with a vengeance.

Murdraniuss appeared as a long, sinuous spirit of dark blue, looking somewhat like a cold, misty river spilling onto the beach. Hundreds of smaller spirits clung to him like spectral leeches, each quivering and moaning. These spirits were the captured sounds of defeated souls—the actual screams of the banshee's victims given corporeal form. They were a cloak of shrieks, a coat of cries, forever clinging to their slayer, the grand master of fatal voices.

Morigos gripped his staff as if he was asphyxiating an enemy's throat, so tightly did he squeeze. He whispered a sorcerous little song. Murky green magic sprang from his hands and entwined his arms.

"Yes, come," he uttered, "come for me..."

The Lord Banshee stopped just ten paces in front of him and rose up like a disturbed cobra. The captured screams gathered around his head and fanned out like the cobra's widening hood. Their many moans joined in harmony and Murdraniuss's own voice arose as an airy, raspy murmur, its unworldly sound getting louder with every second. A strange tingling charged the air, and the temperature went from cold to freezing.

A shivering Morigos again whispered sorcery, and the green tendrils of magic entwining his arms expanded to encircle his whole body, surrounding him in his protective magic bubble.

And then the banshee and his captured screams went silent.

Morigos tilted his head, said: "Soooo… Do you, of all beings, have nothing to say?"

The banshee answered with a squawky whisper.

Morigos cackled. "You sound like a little sea nymph!" Then he erupted into a mocking dance in his bubble, twirling about, crunching the bones, waving his staff.

He didn't notice the sea receding from his toes. Didn't notice when the first of the mighty waves caused by the meteor storm came slamming onto the shore…

Morning's Hope desperately wove through a shifting maze of waves.

She couldn't ascend, for Geeter's fire continuously sizzled over her head, pinning her down, coming closer and closer to scoring a direct hit. Warloove constantly hurled threats along with his flames. He called out to Drinwor, said: "So pathetic a thing to bear so mighty a force! What need for the sword do you have, child? Give it to me, or your burned and bloodless body will be given to the sea!"

Drinwor turned around; but before he could respond, Morning's Hope yelled, "No! Don't acknowledge a single thing he says! Don't even look at him!"

"No, Son of Herard," Warloove countered, "look at me! Spare yourself the burden! Give me the sword! Give it to me, and I will *ease* you into eternity!"

"You know nothing of eternity!" Morning's Hope shot back, "it is lost to you!"

"Is it?"

With Geeter closing in, Warloove fired another barrage of black flames—a barrage that shot right toward Drinwor. Morning's Hope spun around and lifted her forelegs, shielding Drinwor with her belly. The fire blasted into her, marring her translucent flesh with more blisters, contorting her with more pain. Her wings folded inward and she faltered.

Geeter was on her.

The Greater Demonic Dragon flew up to her and tipped forward, his tail whipping up over his back, its poison stinger slicing down like a giant scythe. Morning's Hope ducked her head just below the strike, lashed her wings, and dashed forward. The demonic dragon's momentum rolled him right over his prey, and he fell down behind her. Morning's Hope raced away, her wings flapping violently, the swift movements intensifying her pain.

"Curse you!" Warloove bellowed after her. "You will defy no dreadful fate!"

Drinwor couldn't help a little smile at the deftness of his dragon's maneuver. "Good flying, Morning's Hope!" But when he shot a look over his shoulder, his smile vanished. Geeter was right behind them, and Drinwor could see Warloove standing atop his back. The vampire was a ghastly pillar of smoke and darkness, a vaguely humanoid shape whose upraised hands were engulfed in black fire. The space about him rippled; his cloak of smoke distorted the air around it like a mirage. And then his shadowy head appeared; it grew many horns and its ghostly white face brightened with yellow eyes that shone hot with hate.

The eyes…

Drinwor's gaze met those eyes, and he was transfixed.

"Yes, look into me!" Warloove called out, "look into me, Son of Herard!"

"Close your mind to him!" Morning's Hope implored. "Put your focus elsewhere."

Too late.

Morning's Hope continued to call out, but Drinwor was already ensnared in the vampire's stare. Twisted in his saddle, gazing deeper and deeper into those immortal eyes, it felt as if he was falling into the bottomless pit of Warloove's accursed soul…

With Morning's Hope maneuvering through an endless valley of waves, and his gaze sometimes blurred through the back of his translucent throne, Drinwor's line of sight with Warloove's eyes would occasionally break. But the Lord of the Dark Elves would always catch his stare, and our Drinwor was lost in the depths of his twisted mind. And there, Warloove telepathically showed the dusk elf his intentions. Showed him how he would catch him and rip him apart. Showed him how he would imbibe his blood as a heathen imbibes a brew, then spit out the tattered remains of his spirit as he stole the sacred sunsword away. Drinwor hadn't until now realized just how desperately Warloove's flame-flinging fingers desired to entwine the golden hilt of Surassis. The sorcerous vampire would torture the world for its acquisition! Drinwor would die. Morning's Hope would—

"No!" Drinwor suddenly screamed, his primal instincts fighting to break him from the stare's psychic connection. "Let...go! Let go! Ah!" He tried to look away, tried to push Warloove out of his mind—

"Never!" Warloove screamed. "I will sink my fangs into your soul!"

Drinwor's resistance wavered and he sank deeper into the stare. Morning's Hope uttered something akin to a curse, frustrated she couldn't fly far enough away from the demonic dragon to free Drinwor from the trance. So she did the only thing she could—she went in after him with her mind.

Drinwor, Drinwor! she thought, over and over again. *Come back to me, come back!* She continued to press, even as the enemy dragon's fire singed her flanks. Drinwor heard her and drew strength from her, much in the same way Zraz had drawn strength from Herard earlier in our tale. He heard her compassionate voice rise over Warloove's threats, saw her face through the shroud of horrors the vampire placed in front of his mind's eye, and pulled himself from darkness.

Drinwor blinked.

"No!" Warloove yelled, "you are mine eternal!"

Yes! Come back to me, Drinwor!

Drinwor blinked again, then strained to turn his head away from the vampire's stare. He struggled and struggled, then finally managed to look away, lurching back as if someone had just released the other end of a rope he was pulling on. He twisted around and slumped in his saddle-throne, his head throbbing with hot pain.

He was back.

"Can you hear me?" Morning's Hope asked.

"I hear you."

"Good, good."

"Your soul is mine!" an enraged Warloove called from behind. "The sunsword is mine!"

"Don't listen!" Morning's Hope begged. "Don't look!"

"Oh, I won't," a sighing, bleary-eyed Drinwor responded, even though Warloove's booming voice echoed inside of his head.

And so Morning's Hope flew on, ignoring Warloove's incessant threats and evading the waves and meteors and barrages of fire. Noticing the bone mountain in the near distance, she adjusted her course to fly directly toward it, wondering if Morigos was ever going to draw out the banshee and sound the signal that warned of its bloodcurdling cry.

"Come on, mage, do it…"

The titanic wave blasted over the shoreline, but like a Dreadship in a storm, Morigos was unaffected. His bubble-shield completely protected him, and he wasn't even aware of the wave until after it had passed over him. The Lord Banshee was also unaffected. The wave went right through him, then washed over the dunes and receded into the bones of the foothills.

Morigos cackled. Apparently he found all of this rather amusing. He continued dancing, and the banshee resumed rising over him, soon towering to over twenty feet tall.

"Come and unleash your anger upon me," Morigos taunted. "Come and scream like *Zyllaaaandriaaaa!*" His tone rose and fell as he sang through the syllables.

For the first time in thousands of years, the master of screams was speechless.

Zyllandria? The insane mortal dares utter that name?

Now would come a cry that would drive the dragons from the skies and erupt a hundred meteors! Now would come a cry that would shake overturned Shirian Shirion from the mountain!

Now all the world would suffer the cry of the Lord Banshee.

A face appeared on Murdraniuss's peak. It was transparent, looking like a holographic image hovering in between the corporeal screams. It was the face of a man, a man of such intense anger, his eyes boiled, his frown curled down far past his chin, and the bridge of his nose was stabbed by the deeply creased V of his furrowed brow. He sneered at Morigos…then his bottom jaw plunged twenty feet to the ground, revealing a throat like a cavern that led to some dark, awful place. The captured screams all retreated back to the banshee's tail, and there was the rushing roar of a mighty inhalation.

Morigos was pulled forward, shield and all. He reluctantly stopped dancing, then threw himself down to the bones. The bubble of green magic tightened around him, and he curled up into a ball.

The time had come to send the signal.

He sang out, sorcerously sending these words across the sea: "Deathly sounds must not be found by the ears of one and all!"

And then the banshee's inhalation ceased.

Morigos clenched every muscle, and…

"Deathly sounds must not be found by the ears of one and all!"

"Did you hear that?" Drinwor asked. "That wasn't Warloove's voice, was it?"

"No, it wasn't!" Morning's Hope never thought she'd be so happy to hear Morigos' grating tones. "Drinwor, take in the deepest breath you can, and hold it!"

"Oh, no, not again." The dusk elf looked around. They seemed to be chasing the waves this time, not flying directly into them. "What are you—"

"Listen to me! Do it! Do it NOW!"

Drinwor wasn't going to argue any further, for Morning's Hope was already diving down into the sea. He took the deepest breath he could, closed his eyes, and felt the icy waters wash over him…

If all the oceans in the world had in a split second been sucked into space, the sound wouldn't have come within a thousandth of the volume of the blaring shriek that emanated from the Lord Banshee.

The scream was so strong it could be seen.

It blew from his mouth like a storm of specters. It was a flurry of black gusts that blasted across the foreshore and out over the sea, a shrieking, roaring, tortured, crying, deathly scream of unholy horror!

It was the loudest sound Morigos of the Moom had ever heard, and ever would hear. He lay there cringing, his hands pressed so hard against his ears he nearly broke his wrists. Although his protective shield stifled the scream (and ultimately saved his life), it couldn't possibly repel all of the sound. The decibels that found his ears bled them.

And yet, despite the strength of Murdraniuss's cry, it did not go on for too long. Thank the fates, for if it had drawn out any longer than a single breath could hold, the story of those who kept the sunsword would have ended right here, right now…

Morning's Hope had plunged into the sea a split second before the scream reached her. The tip of her tail wriggled as the sound waves plowed into it, then disappeared into the abyss.

Right behind her, Geeter thought the night itself had grown fangs and bit him. Warloove felt as if the Spears of Stinging Ghosts had been multiplied a hundredfold and thrown back in his face. They were too strong with darkness to be slain by the fatal voice, but both fiends cried out as the waves around them exploded. Geeter's wings were weighed down by many tons of water, and he fell smacking to the surface. His ears filled with agony, he whined and thrashed and whipped his tail about. Warloove screamed commands, but it was futile.

Now only one voice could be heard, and it mastered all.

Morning's Hope dove down as fast as she could.

She had all along counted on the cover of the sea to diminish the voice's effects, but there was no way for her to know just how much sound the water would filter. She hoped Drinwor could withstand it, for even she could barely endure it now. It was so loud! so painful! like jabbing needles puncturing the softest parts of her inner ears. That it was excruciating to Drinwor, she had no doubt. She wondered if Geeter still pursued her, hoped Murdraniuss had indeed been drawn from the hall's entrance, and prayed that Drinwor wouldn't lose his life or the sunsword.

Are you still with me? she thought.

Always, my servant, she swore she heard, a weak but determined reply.

She swam on, deeper, deeper, her wings and limbs drawn in, her body undulating like an eel's. Yet the banshee's cry was still growing louder and louder. She couldn't stand it!

Stop! Stop!

And then, just when she thought she couldn't bear it any longer...it ceased.

Thank you, mother!

She immediately changed course, and swam upward.

Stay with me, Drinwor! Hold your breath just a little longer!

And then, in the moments before she surfaced, she became aware of the undersea's serenity. In these moments, things were actually calm...and graciously quiet. Save for the faraway cry of some peaceable beast gently pulsing through the currents, not a sound could be heard. *What a relief!* She looked about. Here and there, the deep blue of the abyss was illuminated by sinking shards, which flickered for a time before burning out like discarded torches as they sank into obscurity. And far, far below, Morning's Hope saw a dim glow of orange rings.

Deep elves.

There was a deep elf city below. She wondered what those mysterious elves were doing about the bombarding shards… No matter, she continued swimming up.

Before long, a whitish mound appeared from out of the darkness directly in front of her.

The island of bones!

The sight of the island spurring her on, she lifted her head, thrust her wings down and darted for the surface, which hung above her like some wavering, magical veil, glittering with reflections of fire and stars. Her graceful snout sliced through it, and she leaped like a dolphin from the water. Fully extending her wings, she caught air and soared free on currents of wind.

She swiveled her head around. "Drinwor! Are you all right?"

The Emperor of the Sky erupted with a gargling scream, regurgitating what he thought was half of the sea from his body.

"Drinwor!" she cried again.

He let out a mighty gasp, then, through a fit of coughs, said, "I think I've had enough going underwater…for a lifetime… I'm fine, I'm—"

"My Lord, the banshee's cry, did it—"

"That was *loud!*" Drinwor put his hands to his head. "I wonder if the ringing in my ears will ever go away?"

"I'm sorry," Morning's Hope said as she dashed for the island, "I had no idea how long we'd be submerged, but the voice would have killed you had you been exposed."

"No, it's all right," Drinwor said, rubbing his bloodshot eyes. "May the Gods return, you've saved my life yet again."

"It is my honorable and sacred duty, my Lord. Now, let's get you into the hall."

Drinwor looked forward and nodded. "Let's go!"

The bone mountain loomed before them, looking more than ever like some giant evil skull. The shards had punched holes like eye sockets in its sides, the orifices flaring as if with pupils of fire. The castle at its crown was lurching, and all the island quaked. Half of the foothills were smashed flat, and steaming fissures pocked the beach. The banshee's cry had given the island a minute's respite from the punishing sea, though, for his voice had leveled all of the waves before it.

Still dodging shards, Morning's Hope dashed across the shoreline. She flew in low over the foothills, following the pathway Morigos had earlier pointed out—a thin cleft that zigzagged like a hairline fracture through the bones, toward the mountain.

She called out, "Are you ready?"

"I am!" the dusk elf returned, his eyes ablaze, his demonskin's sigils aglow. The saddle-throne's ankle straps disappeared, and he stood up. "For my father, for Fleeting Shadow, for the Fallen Angel, let's finally resurrect the sunsword!" He slapped his leg pouch hard.

"Then prepare to leap. When I tell you, jump down and run as fast you can to the mountain." Morning's Hope motioned beneath her. "I'll bring you in closer to the path and—"

She never finished the sentence.

Dragonfear struck a split second before Geeter's foreclaw.

Morning's Hope was hit so hard on her left-rear flank, her tail whipped up over her back and lashed the mainsail of her right wing. The wing crumpled and she pitched over. She recovered as fast as she could, and called out, "Emperor Fang!"

Too late.

The attack had thrown Drinwor from her back.

He instinctively curled up his body and somersaulted forward as he plummeted nearly a hundred feet to the bones. He righted just before he hit, and came down into the side of a particularly steep foothill. Luckily, the bones there were brittle; it felt as though he fell through the boughs of a forgiving tree. His armor saved his skin from lacerations, and the impact was relatively soft. (The mountain island itself would dare not claim the life of the Son and Savior of the Stars.) Unhurt, Drinwor climbed up through the little chasm he had just created, and poked his head through the hole.

Directly above him was a sight he would never forget.

There was Geeter, his huge foreclaws grasping Morning's Hope, his neck intertwined with hers. With wings flapping wildly, they writhed around one another, snapping at each other like dueling snakes. Geeter shrieked and Morning's Hope roared. Each spit fire: Geeter his black, acidic spray; Morning's Hope her white, electrified flames. With their heads so close together, the fires missed their marks, but crossed streams and clashed like the meeting of two overpowered cosmic swords. A puff of greyish smoke emanated from the point of contact, and giant sparks flew everywhere.

"Get away from her!" Drinwor spewed with a guttural cry. He leaped from the chasm onto the more compacted bones near the pathway, his gaze an angry slave to the sky.

Geeter was overcoming his prey.

His limbs wrapped tighter around Morning's Hope, his giant teeth grazing her neck, drawing streams of clear-bluish blood.

Grunting, Morning's Hope managed to twist about in his grasp. She looked down and screamed, "Run, Drinwor!"

Drinwor just stood there.

Liquid crystal tears exploded from his eyes. He knew he must run, but how could he leave her to die? No! He couldn't abandon her, couldn't leave her to die at the hands of these murderous fiends. Emboldened by rage, he stepped forward, called out: "Warloove! I swear on my father's soul, if you harm her you will swim inside a thousand suns!"

"*No!*"

It was Morning's Hope. "Drinwor, go, go, go!"

Warloove, who was seconds away from blasting Morning's Hope into a bloody carcass, turned his head and called down, "Will I, Son of Herard? Will I swim inside the stars?" With a snarl he added, "Would you care to join me?" And with that he threw the fire that had been meant for Morning's Hope at Drinwor.

The dusk elf back-flipped out of the way. The bones before him exploded, and he landed awkwardly on his side, ivory splinters raining down upon him. He stood up slowly, his surge of courage subsiding, his will wilting before the fiery ire of his enemy.

But then he met the eyes of his dragon.

Though meteors screamed down behind her, though blood trickled from her myriad wounds, though claws scraped her beautiful skin and black fire blistered her wings, her eyes shone with hope. And with her features glinting, she flashed Drinwor a little smile.

Drinwor felt his heart warm.

Then Morning's Hope slipped these sorcerously persuasive words down to him: *"Have faith in the light of the universe, and have faith in me. Run, Drinwor. Please. For your father, for yourself, for all creation, run."*

Now the dusk elf Emperor of the Sky was overcome with a single thought.

The Sunsword Surassis.

He whispered, "Beloved creature of light," then turned away, and with all speed dashed for the Hall of Voices.

He never saw the green beams of sorcery blast into Geeter's flanks. Never saw a dark, twisted shape levitating up behind the dragons, trailed by a streaming ribbon of moaning, angered spirits.

Of Morigos and Murdraniuss, Drinwor was not aware.

But of Warloove, Drinwor most certainly was.

The demonic dark elf vampire leaped from Geeter's back, leaving the dragons to wrestle themselves to death for all he cared. A glowing blur of spinning blackness, he shot down and landed hard, his booted feet loudly crunching the bones.

He screamed, "Like father like son, with nowhere to run!"

Drinwor ignored the cruel words and jumped into the cleft. The pathway was tight and deceptively deep, the sides rising to well over his head, streams of seawater splashing at his feet. The confinement was unnerving, but without pause he bolted for the mountain.

Warloove bounded in after him, yelling, "Fool! It is *you* who is fated to die by the fires of the sun!" Invisible lightning erupted from his claws, scattering a smattering of lethal little forks. They branched out, but fell short of their mark, exploding only the bones that jutted from the sides of the path behind the fleeing dusk elf.

Spurred by adrenaline and fear, assisted by the strength of his demonskin's glowing sigils, Drinwor ran as fast as he ever had, ran as he never knew he could. Without realizing what he was doing, he leaned forward, dropped to all fours and sprinted like a supernatural tiger. Growling like a werewolf, Warloove picked up his own pace. His vampiric form was a blur of smoke and shadows, phasing in and out of sight as he half ran, half flew after the dusk elf. He gained ground on Drinwor, bellowed, "Son of Herard! Do you abandon your beloved as your father abandoned his? What is this light you fight for that begets such betrayal?"

The words were swayed with sorcery.

An image of Morning's Hope crushed in Geeter's clutches filled Drinwor's mind, and he faltered a step. In that instant, Warloove caught up to him and swiped at his legs, grazing the back of his calves, the Gauntlets of Loathing Light sizzling as they scraped the demonskin. But the armor absorbed the blow, and Drinwor recovered his stride. He ran even faster down the path, unleashing a guttural cry. "No, damn you! She will survive!"

The dark elf vampire was in disbelief.

How was it possible that this child's swiftness superseded his own immortal speed? He called after Drinwor, "You will die by the very light you uphold!" and tried to keep pace.

But he could not.

The Son and Savior of the Stars was too fast.

With the meteors' final assault bombarding the island, and the rising sea swamping the bones, Drinwor dashed into the shadows at the base of the mountain, and came to the pathway's end. The cleft's sides fell away beside him, and in front a stair of polished ivory led into a cavern carved into the mountainside. A sparkling blue mist poured out of the cavern and spilled down the center of the steps.

Drinwor straightened up, for a moment looked wonderingly at his arms, then raced up the stair, his feet swirling the mist. He stumbled over something, but didn't stop to see what it was. (It was one of many bodies. Concealed by the mist, the victims of the Lord Banshee lay all over the steps—curled, decomposed corpses still clutching unused weapons or grasping unspoken scrolls, the tattered parchments ripped through by death-convulsed fingers.)

With Warloove screaming threats from close behind him, he made it to the top of the stair and bolted into the cavern.

The cavern was dim and serene, its size difficult to discern. Curtains of blue vapor undulated all around like walls of windblown silk. Where the real walls were was a mystery, for beyond the vapor walls, all was dark. Glittering mist covered the floor like a swamp of sparking ghosts. It came up to Drinwor's waist, and in some places reached up to the ceiling in tightly coiled swirls. High above, the chamber was capped by a crystal dome whose glints were dimmed behind a suspended haze.

But Drinwor barely noticed the cavern's features, for his attention was immediately drawn to the middle of the chamber. There, hovering as though it floated upon the surface of the mist, was a huge, humming globe of soft yellow light. It looked like a little sun. Stone steps rose out of the mist before it and disappeared into its lower curve. Rings of intricately scribed glowing blue runes hovered around it, and here and there certain words would flicker brightly. Within its brilliant core, Drinwor saw a shining realm whose sky was bespeckled with the multicolored stars of his dreams. "This is it, the portal doorway to the Hall of Voices," he whispered.

He ran halfway up the steps and stood right beneath the globe, his silver hair fluttering in an undetectable breeze, the sigils on his demonskin flaring as if they were on fire. He knew not why he paused. Perhaps out of fear of entering a realm totally unknown. Perhaps all that had happened was sinking in and he felt terribly alone.

Then he sensed Warloove enter the cavern.

"Stop, Son of Herard! Enter there and doom yourself, for you are no conduit for the sword! Let *me* be the soul you seek, and I will empower you to rule the world!"

Entranced by that distorted yet flowing song of a voice, Drinwor turned to face the black apparitional form.

Warloove stepped slowly toward him, easing his utterances as he came… "No, not just the world, but *all* the universe could be yours. Give me the sword, and spare your father's soul. Give me the Sunsword Surassis, Drinwor Fang, for the sake of us all…"

Drinwor saw eyes of black suddenly blaze to yellow, and he remembered falling into them, into the well of Warloove's soul. It was a place he did not want to return to, a place only Morning's

Hope could have rescued him from. He whispered a single little word. But his voice carried the word like a strong gust across the undulating ocean of mist, and it burned like an ember in the undead ears of his adversary.

The word was: *"No."*

"No?" Warloove crept closer. "Are you certain? Is this what you seek?"

Suddenly, a host of dreadful thoughts and images filled Drinwor's mind, and he had the distinct impression that claws were reaching for his throat.

Warloove crept closer still.

Drinwor turned away from those blazing yellows and cried out, "Morning's Hope!" Then he bolted up the rest of the steps, closed his eyes, and leaped into the portal...never noticing the small, nearly invisible black wisp of Drekklor that accompanied him in.

Warloove screamed, "Bastard child, you are no destroyer of destiny!" then went flying after him.

But the vampire never made it; for you see, when Warloove was only three feet away from the portal's steps, the crystal ceiling came crashing down atop him...

The last shard of the meteor storm shot over the Continent Isle of Volcar, passed over the nameless sea, and as if guided by some meddlesome whimsy of fate, angled down and smashed directly into the sky elf fortress of Shirian Shirion.

The castle was totally destroyed.

The towers exploded, the walls caved in, and the keep crumbled. The mountain couldn't withstand the stress, so it fell into itself. The crushing of ten million bones crackled like the burning of ten thousand trees, and all ruin came thundering down.

The island was lost to the sea.

Waves came in and swept all that remained beneath them.

The portal globe to the Hall of Voices, hanging suspended over the water, flickered, faded, and failed. Nevermore would it be seen, though evermore would it be sought. Thereafter, legends would tell that it had been lost when the sea had defeated the stars.

And I, the scribe of this story, slump in my chair and heave a great sigh of relief, for my precious Drinwor had survived *Against the Fall of Night*.

CHAPTER TWENTY-FOUR
THE BLOOD OF ANOTHER DIMENSION

Our lives are but the eyes of the universe, which ever gazes wonderingly at itself.

Vorlock
Sky Elf Warrior of Shy-Rheem

Syndreck's relentless application of dark magic continued to exact its price. The rate at which his stolen body decayed was accelerating. Now he looked more like he did when his part in our fairytale had begun, when Drekklor had first pulled him from the bowels of the black hole.

Scabby skin fell in flakes from his face. Black blood dripped from the corners of his mouth, for his throat was lacerated by the perpetual passage of scathing sorcerous songs. Even his conjured robes were withering. Their green fabric went grey, the embroidered cuffs unraveled…much like the sanity of the one to whom they belonged, I suppose. The dearly departed Tatoc would have been mortified to see his body in such condition, but Syndreck didn't care, for his bloodshot eyes still held a remarkable light, even as the flesh around them rotted.

His hands splayed above the Cauldron of Carcass Control, he continued to tear the skies over the Raging Sea apart. And then, to his delight, words came from within the cauldron, words that trembled the very foundations of eternity…

Yes, Syndreck, set me free! Set us all free!

His ears twitching, the necromancer paused. "My Lord...? Is that *your* voice?"

Nothing of the Dark Forever must be withheld. With all the power you can muster, tear down the dimensional walls!

"Nenockra Rool!" Syndreck raised his arms, his words issuing slowly and thunderously. "Great One, though I strain against the stars, though I toil against the very fabric of the universe, I am succeeding! Look, Great One! Your vast hordes assist me from the other side!"

Syndreck made a fist, punched the cauldron's surface, and a million demon eyes appeared within the ripples. He called upon them, exhorting them to expend yet more strength. "Pull harder! The Great One *must* be freed!"

The demons acquiesced.

With more energy than ever being focused on ripping the sky apart, the cracks widened and, in some places, the dimensional walls completely gave. Black lightning burst from the breaches and rapid successions of demonic thunder drowned the sounds of all else. Now huge holes hung over the Raging Sea. The red vapor gushed from them like blood from another dimension, and a crimson haze spread out in an ever-enlarging cloud.

"Success!"

The Dark Forever was free!

Syndreck unleashed a moan of ecstasy as thousands of demons came streaming through the rents. There were behemoths with chests like rippling, lava-caked hills; and monstrosities with multitudinous limbs that clenched wickedly jagged weapons; and juggernauts whose maws housed fangs that were so long they continuously cut their own chins as their gibbering mouths spewed with bloody laughter. The demons fell into the Raging Sea, piling like the bones of Murdraniuss's victims. The specter demons that had preceded the others slipped into the four winds and spread across the world like an airborne plague, infecting the lands with extinction.

Indeed, the conquest of the universe was beginning!

Syndreck the Brooding fell weeping to his knees. Words he had waited so long to utter fled the bleeding gates of his lips:

"Master, I have freed your demon horde. The light of the stars will diffuse within flames so dark they will blind those foolish beings who wallow in the ignorance of all they believe to be righteous. I see blood where there was water. I see power where there was weakness. I see your visage where now there are no Gods at all. Yes, master! Come forth and claim the universe! It is yours to shape! Yours to amend! I am your slave, and in servitude will follow you to the ends of existence. I will scribe your declarations with the blood of our enemies, and watch as they hopelessly suffer before thee!"

Then Syndreck heaved a bloody sigh and stood up.

Looking back into his pot of necromancy, he saw the vengeance of Zyrinthia, the meteor storm, blasting down upon the shield that protected Ulith Urn. He heard the impacts, felt his tower shudder as the shards vaporized right over his head. Then the cauldron's images showed him different parts of the world. He saw cities and forests swept over by fire; saw beings and beasts scampering for safety as everything around them turned to ash; saw a thousand struggles for both good and evil unfold before his uncaring eyes...

Then the images changed again, and Syndreck saw his own courtyard.

Between his writhing, storm-battered towers, the dark elves were attacking the centurion from the stars. Floating mages cast emerald, crimson, and azure energy beams. Commanders on giant bats flew over the compound, screaming orders to those on the ground. Invisible warriors, wielding invisible weapons, lunged and stabbed and screamed and died as the spaces above them filled with fire and souls!

In the center of it all was Soular Centurion 7, moving slowly, purposefully forward, even as he slew.

Syndreck thrust a finger into the cauldron. "Nenockra Rool! The one from the stars threatens us! Please, master, please help me destroy this one!"

And though no words came from the Devil King, he answered.

Over the Raging Sea, a thousand winged demons suddenly changed course and raced toward Ulith Urn, all the while mocking the meteors that evaporated like snowflakes before their mighty flames.

A legion of invisible dark elf warriors rushed Soular Centurion 7, their attack supported from above by invisible mages. Their disguise was virtually perfect. Even the glint of their enchanted weapons was intangible, as were the fires that arced over them like a hail of invisible burning arrows. They came straight in, confident their camouflaged advance would herald the centurion's destruction.

And yet, unbeknownst to them, the cosmic warrior could see them all.

To Soular Centurion 7, invisibility was nothing of the sort. It was a feeble trick, a measly mask against mortals who could only see what was firmly affixed to their current plane of existence. The dark elves? Ha! If anything, their invisibility only made them easier for the centurion to perceive. They actually glowed in his eyes.

–INITIATE DEFENSIVE STANCE ANDROMEDEUS 4 ALPHA 5–

He easily repelled their attack, his cosmic sword slashing at supersonic speeds. The hail of fireballs went sputtering down into the depths of the black hole-blade. The legion of warriors had their torsos vaporized, their heads sent tumbling to the ground. Never had these slaves of sorcery encountered a technological warrior such as this.

The dark elves retreated.

They didn't fear this alien foe, but they recognized that he was more formidable than anything they had ever faced. New measures would have to be taken, new strategies employed. The elves regrouped, formed a wide ring around the centurion. They would attack again…but a bit more cautiously. Oh, they knew no matter what they did many of them would die, but they would *not* give Soular Centurion 7 the satisfaction of trouncing them utterly. No. Never that. They were dark elves of Phate, servants of Nenockra Rool!

If nothing else, this invader from the stars would stumble before they themselves would fall.

They screamed unholy war songs and launched another attack. But this time, the Mages of the Moom fired their flames, then flew for the cover of the towers. This time, the bat riders loosed their weapons and spells from farther out, then angled away. This time, the fighters of the Black Claw broke off into smaller groups, then staggered their advances—each wave scurrying in, striking, then darting backward while another wave came in from another side.

It did not matter.

It was the same as before: the Sword of Molecular Destruction claimed all within its range.

The battle mages who veered away were pulled screaming from the sky, the gravitational forces of that devastating blade sucking them into its black oblivion. The waves of fighters helplessly sprawled end over end into the slicing sword's arc. The bats spun down out of control, their wings vaporized, their riders unseated and halved. Wave after wave continued to pour in, but each attack was as futile as the one before it.

For the dark elves, it was an inescapable massacre.

The centurion continued pressing forward, a silvery reaper exacting the death of all.

He was close to vanquishing all of the wicked elves when his proximity alert signal went off, warning him of something new…

   –LARGE HORDE OF INTER-PLANAR BEASTS CLOSING RAPIDLY–

It was distressing. These demons would murder yet more seconds, thereby lessening his chance to neutralize the necromancer before Nenockra Rool himself was free. And he knew for every demon he killed, a thousand more would take their place.

The fate of the universe was in jeopardy, for even Soular Centurion 7 could not defeat the Dark Forever's countless millions alone.

For a fraction of a microsecond he again considered using his atomics. He could easily raze the entire compound and everything in it: the remaining dark elves; the approaching demons; the towers of Ulith Urn and the necromancer they harbored. But that would also mean the destruction of himself. No. It just wasn't feasible. His latest calculations showed that now, more than ever, it was imperative that he survive.

The future needed him just as much as the present.

   –77.3 PERCENT CHANCE RESCUE OPERATION PENDING…–

The microsecond after he decided that the annihilation of himself and everything around him wasn't feasible, he concluded that there *was* another option, albeit one he hadn't utilized in a long, long time.

For the first time in a hundred million years, Soular Centurion 7 sent out a distress signal—a multi-dimensional message that expanded with supra-light speed into many planes of existence.

The chances that anyone or anything capable of aiding him would respond in time to help were infinitesimally small, but such daunting odds didn't dissuade he who had often seen such impossibilities blossom into being.

For Soular Centurion 7, the universe was a place of endless hope.

And lo and behold! his hope was justified.

His distress signal was received immediately after its transmission, and he had his answer soon after that.

-ZEERZEEOZZ CONFIRMATION—REINFORCEMENTS ON THE WAY-

He would not fight alone.

Phate would open its heart to him, and send forth its noblest spirits...

CHAPTER TWENTY-FIVE
ONE LIFE, ONE SOUL, ONE SWORD

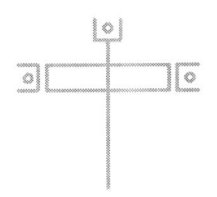

> *To not realize one's dreams is a shame; to not reach for them is a tragedy.*
> Thissian Thisrax
> The Immutable Monk of Mordington

Drinwor Fang opened his eyes.

He was surrounded by colorful stars, thousands of turquoise, saffron, and lavender points twinkling in a milky white sky. As he gazed at these stars, he had the distinct impression he'd seen them before. But where…?

"Ah, yes!" He suddenly remembered—he had seen them in his dreams. "But how can this be?" He stared at the stars for a little while longer, pondering the possibilities until his gaze was drawn downward. Interesting, his feet were fogged over with billowing white vapor. It appeared as though he was standing on a little cloud. Interesting indeed…but a little disconcerting as well.

"Hmm…not feeling very secure about this…"

He tapped his foot, ever so gently, mind you, fearful that even this slight movement would send him plummeting into the white unknown. Relief warmed over him, though, for he felt a spongy but relatively firm surface beneath his soles.

"Well, it seems solid enough."

He noticed his tapping caused little threads of silver energy to spread out from his toes and race to the cloud's ends. Not quite knowing what to make of that, he shrugged, then looked back up to the starry white sky.

It was all so surreal.

"Perhaps I'm dreaming *now*..."

He half expected to hear the fluid voice of Morning's Hope cut through his consciousness and rouse him awake—*Wake up, my Emperor, wake up*—but it never came. No, he knew he wasn't dreaming. And Morning's Hope wasn't with him, she—

Oh, no! Morning's Hope!

That terrible image of her locked in Geeter's grasp suddenly sprang into his mind. Then he recalled the fire flung at his feet, and the ungodly being who had leaped down and chased him through the winding avenue of bones.

"Warloove!"

May the Gods return, had the dark elf vampire followed him through the portal?

Drinwor whirled about, kicking up wisps of vapor. But there was nothing there—no dark figure flitting amongst the colorful stars, no shadows or sizzling funnels of smoke. No, thankfully, Warloove was nowhere to be seen.

That was good, but Drinwor still couldn't help wondering about the fate of his dragon. What had happened to her? Was she even alive? He called out, "Morning's Hope!" his voice reverberating as if through the empty corridors of Areshria. Perhaps she would hear him, just as he had heard her beneath the surface of the nameless sea. Again he cried, "Morning's Hope!" but there was no answer, only the echoes of his own voice rippling into the far reaches of this white infinity.

In defeat, he whispered, "By the grace of the Gods, survive; please, Morning's Hope, be alive." He crouched, reached down and swirled little circles in the cloud. "I wish this *was* all a dream."

"It is no dream, Son and Savior of the Stars."

Drinwor stood with a start. "Who said that?"

There was no response, but when he glanced aside, he saw many luminous spheres of golden light dart up over the cloud's rim, causing him to recoil in surprise. Their glimmering trails crisscrossing one another, the golden lights circled his head like curious fairies, then whisked away to the whiteness beyond. They were enthralling, beautiful; Drinwor imagined they were heavenly spirits, for what else could fly through such a glorious sky?

"Hello?" he called after them.

"They are silent, but not insensate," came the voice from an indeterminable origin.

Drinwor swiveled in his spot. "Who speaks to me? Who are you?"

"He who caught you with a cloud," the voice replied. "But the more important question is: do you know who *you* are?"

Drinwor was hesitant to answer, hesitant to reveal anything about himself to a stranger he couldn't even see. But what else was there to do? Float around on his personal cloud for Gods knew how long? No, he was in the realm that allegedly housed the Hall of Voices; he would trust that the source of the voice was benign. He cleared his throat, lifted his head, and with as much authority as he could muster, said: "I am Drinwor Fang, Emperor of the Sky, Son of Herard. I have traveled far, and I seek the Hall of Voices."

"Greetings, Drinwor Fang, but that does not answer my question."

The dusk elf was taken aback. "What do you mean? I just told you who I am." He spun about, still trying to determine the origin of the soft yet powerful voice. It was impossible to locate, though; it seemed to come from all around.

"You told me what you are called, not who you are."

Drinwor chuckled, then in an exasperated tone said: "I don't know, you tell me—who I am?"

"I have already told you."

Drinwor rolled his eyes. "You've told me nothing. Nothing of yourself, nothing of this place. I ask again—who are you? And what is this white universe?"

"This universe is what your soul chooses to see."

"Chooses?" Drinwor tilted his head. "I don't know about 'chooses,' but I believe I *have* seen it before...though only in my dreams."

"There is nothing that is dreamed that cannot be."

"I've dreamed of many things."

"Then many things you may achieve...perhaps all things, for your sacrifice."

Drinwor echoed the word, "*sacrifice*," then shook his head, tired of the incessant bewildering statements. "I'm weary, and whoever—or whatever—you are, you're confusing me. Apparently I've come a long way to merely wind up in one of my own dreams."

"Do you desire a different setting?"

The dusk elf laughed. "Yes, right, a different setting..."

"Then you shall have it."

Drinwor froze. "Wait a moment, I wasn't serious, I like this—"

The universe changed.

The white sky faded to a blue that passed through many darkening shades before settling into the most hauntingly beautiful black. All the colorful stars brightened to silvery white, and the wispy arms of a thousand galaxies emerged around them.

It was breathtaking.

Drinwor was just beginning to soak it in when his perspective suddenly shifted. Now it was as if he peered at the distant stars through the eye of some interstellar telescope. Oh, I tell you, he saw things even his dreams could not have conjured! He saw starships streaking like comets through the newly blackened void, with supernova dragons chasing their glittering ionic trails. He saw technological titans constructing solar systems around suns of silver fire. He saw watery worlds inhabited by mile-long artificial whales whose innards housed whole societies.

The images instantly snapped back, and Drinwor's perspective was returned to the little cloud.

He was speechless, but he understood—it was a vision of the universe of yore, a universe teeming with life, before the predator black holes had sprung up like a pox to consume all creation.

The voice sounded again. "Do you find this universe pleasing?"

Drinwor trembled, then said, "Yes, I... With my waking eyes I've never seen such things. How can this be? Do I stand in space?"

"No, you peer at it from the inside."

The dusk elf looked down, took a few deep breaths, then lifted his head and said, "Please, I ask one more time, who are you? No more riddles. Not now. And where is the hall?"

The voice said, "You'll soon discover who I am, but first I will show you the Hall of Voices."

Drinwor whistled. "So, I *have* found it…"

Tortuous seconds slipped by, with Drinwor waiting and wondering in silence. A minute, and still no sign of anything that looked like the Hall of Voices (whatever in the Seven Glories the hall was supposed to look like!). Eventually, the impatient dusk elf asked, "Well, where is it?"

"You're standing in it," came the voice.

And with that, thousands of stars leaped from their perches, shot through the heavens, and positioned themselves all around Drinwor's cloud. Oddly, although they had instantly closed a seemingly great distance, the stars were still no more than pinpricks in size. They twinkled brightly, then stretched into fine silvery lines that formed many complex shapes and angles, thus surrounding the cloud with a frame of starlight.

"Does the universe ever cease to unleash with wonder?" Drinwor muttered.

As if in answer, the frame filled in around him.

A complex ribbing of transparent beams stretched above him, and soon thereafter a vaulted ceiling of starlight was formed. Translucent walls substantiated beside him, each laden with rows of clerestory windows whose crystal surfaces were etched with animated depictions of triumphant translucent dragons. Sculpted figures made of millions of tiny stars brightened the shadow galleries that had burrowed themselves into the walls. Spinning crystalline pillars, transparent fountains, and myriad other artistic architectural embellishments appeared all throughout the place, and the entire structure was made whole.

This was the Hall of Voices.

Drinwor's midnight blues, glittering with thousands of tiny reflections, looked like little universes themselves. "A cathedral of starlight…I should have known."

Through the translucent walls, Drinwor saw the golden spheres that had flown around the cloud return to fly around the hall. He saw them and all the cosmos that lay beyond. The Hall of Voices was as much a part of the sky as were the stars. "Have I finally found a place where light reigns unchallenged by those who would destroy hope?"

"Only those who have hope can destroy it," came the voice.

"Perhaps..."

"Come to me, Drinwor Fang, Keeper of the Sunsword Surassis."

With those words, Drinwor finally had some sense of the origin of the voice. It seemed to have come from the far side of the cathedral. He looked ahead, and the cloud beneath his feet summarily billowed forward like a wave rolling toward the shore. Row after row of ethereal pews were left in its wake, as was a wide aisle that cut straight through the nave's center. Drinwor inexplicably found himself striding down the aisle.

He felt as if he strode into a dream within a dream.

But then something distracted him.

He stopped, looked to his left. Just outside the walls, the golden spheres were gathering. One of them dimmed ever so slightly, but only for a moment before returning to its full luster. The other spheres encircled it, then spread out. The one that had dimmed was now the brightest, the largest, a king star amongst a court of lesser suns.

The voice said, "Did you enter this place alone?" The slightest quaver in its tone.

Drinwor shrugged. "I believe so. I *was* being followed, though I'm fairly certain my pursuer didn't make it in here."

"Bestirred by the presence of the Savior, those souls must be. Come."

The spheres quieted, their frenzy calmed, and they resumed their fluid course around the hall, enwrapping the cathedral in rings of streaming gold. Drinwor continued forward. As he passed through the cloudy pews, he had the distinct feeling that they were occupied. He looked around, but didn't see anyone. He disregarded the feeling and pressed on toward the cathedral's sanctuary. There, the head of the cloud had flowed up a trio of wide steps and surged across the dais, its billows bunching together and piling up to shroud the back wall, which was many stories high.

As Drinwor approached, the cloud settled down, dissipated a bit, and the wall was slowly unveiled. Once again our dusk elf was overcome with wonder.

"Spectacular."

The wall was perfectly clear, revealing hundreds of spiral galaxies that drifted through the space beyond. Their radiance tinged by the swirling arm of a nearby nebula, the galaxies illuminated the sanctuary with a soft violet glow. Drinwor was mesmerized. He thought the star-riddled space provided a more beautiful backdrop than any work of mortal artistry ever could have. Slowly, reverently, he climbed the steps to the dais, his footfalls as light as a doe's.

Once upon it, he felt as though he wasn't alone...

He was right.

Directly in front of him, materializing over the mist-covered floor, was a being unlike any he'd ever seen.

Drinwor was compelled to kneel.

The being spoke, and thus the source of the mysterious voice had been found.

"I am ZeerZeeOzz, the Seer Between the Stars, the voice for dragons lost, but soon to be set free. I am the Emissary of Drakana, his servant for all eternity. I know what it is you hold, and what it is you seek, and a soul lies in waiting, the soul for the sword to keep. Welcome to the Hall of Voices."

Drinwor whispered, "Thank you." He slowly lifted his head, and beheld the spectral seer.

ZeerZeeOzz's substance was a thing of transparent brilliance, seemingly comprised of the same thinly stretched starlight that made up the hall. He had no neck. His disembodied head hovered over his torso as if it had been separated by the Sword of Molecular Destruction. He had no legs. His lower half curled beneath him as an effervescent tail of mist, and he hovered five feet above the floor. His eyes were glowing wells of green, windows to a wealth of otherworldly wisdom. His vaporous face was smooth, his features slight, but brimming with unfathomable emotion. He was accoutered in the translucent trappings of an ancient archer. A bow of silver hung across his back, and arrows of starlight were kept in a quiver of gold slung at his side.

Ghostly but not ghastly, he was ZeerZeeOzz, a seer of the stars, a hunter who had found his eternal home.

He floated closer to Drinwor and bid the dusk elf to stand.

Drinwor did so, asking, "What exactly is this place?"

ZeerZeeOzz swiveled, raised an arm and swept it back, his vaporous fingers leaving a glittering wake as he motioned. "This place is the last light seen by dying eyes, a haven for those who have lost their heaven. It is a sanctuary for dragon souls, a place where many await the opening of the gates to the Seven Glories. But now, most importantly, it is the place where you will find the One Soul."

"You've been waiting for me..." Drinwor whispered.

"Yes. One Life, One Soul, One Sword."

"One Sword..." Drinwor echoed.

So, the seer knew the saying. He wondered how much else he knew. Perhaps he could answer some of the myriad questions Drinwor never had the chance to ask the Fallen Angel. The elf patted his leg pouch, asked, "I still don't really understand—how can the One Sword defeat an entire dimension of demons?"

ZeerZeeOzz tilted his disembodied head forward, his expression evincing a small measure of surprise. "There is no more powerful weapon in all the galaxy. Surassis will destroy Nenockra Rool."

"Well, yes, but, I mean..." Drinwor winced. "*How* will it destroy him, exactly?"

ZeerZeeOzz spoke as if the answer was obvious. "While the One Soul provides the energy to light the sunblade, the One Life is the spark to ignite the One Soul. If both of their pure essences conjoin and release themselves through the blade's fire, a supernova-like explosion of pure light ensues. The explosion is so powerful, it will destroy all evil souls for thousands of miles around the sword. Beings of light are immune to this enormous blaze of fire, but for darkness, the destruction is total." ZeerZeeOzz paused, thought for a moment, then concluded with: "For your sacrifice, not even Nenockra Rool will survive."

Drinwor's face went pale. There was that word again. Words slipped hesitantly from his lips. "What do you mean...'*sacrifice*'? Is this the release you speak of? The release of my life?"

ZeerZeeOzz brought his head back, said, "Has the savior of the universe not been prepared for his destiny?"

Feeling somewhat embarrassed for his ignorance, Drinwor turned away. He shuffled around, disturbing the cloudy mist with his feet. "I've only recently discovered my part in things. The Fallen Angel told me the sunsword needs to be resurrected, told me I'm the one destined to wield it. That is all I know."

"I see," ZeerZeeOzz said.

Now the spectral seer took a few moments to ruminate...

He wondered how it was possible that the savior was unaware of his full destiny. How could this child of the stars not know of his mortal fate? *This child....* Ah, perhaps that was it. ZeerZeeOzz stared deep into Drinwor's emotive eyes, probing, probing. There was little experience behind those eyes. Yes, Drinwor indeed *was* a child. Although he was imbued with infinite strength, his inherent purity had left his conscience fragile with innocence and fear. Now ZeerZeeOzz understood—the Fallen Angel had never fully disclosed the responsibilities of the One Life to Drinwor, for if the boy had been cognizant of his impending sacrifice, he might have shied away from such commitment, thereby dooming the universe.

ZeerZeeOzz saw the wisdom of the angel's decision, but now feared he might have just inadvertently clued Drinwor in on his fate prematurely—though it did stand that his fate was close at hand...

Drinwor, who was staring at him with eyes that were slit to suspicious slivers, said, "You are not speaking, you are thinking, and I do not believe that bodes well for me. Please, just tell me—what does my destiny have in store?"

Indeed I have erred. He suspects his fate. Things must be handled most delicately now.

"You have nothing to fear," the seer replied, "the universe will cradle your soul in its loving arms for all eternity. Should you succeed, you yourself shall open the Gates to the Seven Glories."

"Well, that sounds pleasant, but it doesn't exactly answer my question. What of my life?"

ZeeZeeOzz said nothing.

Drinwor stepped forward, his brow lowering, as did the tone of his voice. "Do you mean to lead me astray?"

"I'm a sworn servant of light whose solemn duty is to steer you in the direction of your destiny."

"I'm *asking* you about my destiny."

"Your destiny is to be embraced by light for all time."

Drinwor lifted his hands and with resignation slapped them to his sides. This was not at all what he expected from a being such as this! This treatment was making him feel like the child he knew ZeerZeeOzz suspected he was. "You're accustomed to giving evasive answers, aren't you?"

"It is the truth."

Drinwor looked to the ceiling and sighed. "Perhaps, but it obviously isn't the whole truth. And I think I'm beginning to understand why my father never spoke to me about these things, and why the angel never addressed all of my questions." Seconds of silence passed, with Drinwor's stare stuck on some glowing runes that had etched themselves into the rafters. His lips parted, but were unable to let slip words. Eventually, though, he whispered, "They were afraid to tell me that I was going to die, weren't they?"

ZeerZeeOzz stayed quiet.

Drinwor looked back down to the vaporous seer/hunter, and realized that this being, for all his wisdom, was bereft of compassion. Oh, there was emotion in those deep green eyes, there was feeling, but it was remote, reserved for things Drinwor probably couldn't possibly understand. A hint of loneliness hit the dusk elf then, and he very much wished Morning's Hope was here. With tears threatening to stream down his face, he said, "I don't know if I can do this. I don't know if I'm ready to die."

The seer broke his silence. "I did not say that you will die."

A sad little smile crossed Drinwor's face. "You didn't have to."

As delicately as he could, ZeerZeeOzz said, "Fear nothing, Drinwor Fang. You cannot yet fully understand this, but you are so much more than you can imagine. Your existence is encapsulated by more than the skin that surrounds you."

"I've been told things like this before, and I was beginning to believe them, but now I'm not so sure." And then, as if gently nudged by some invisible hand, Drinwor's face turned slightly aside. He looked past ZeerZeeOzz, to the back wall. The light of a hundred galaxies met his eyes, and he suddenly felt ashamed.

Here he was focusing on his own fate, when out there, precariously dangling before the pitch black face of infinity, were the hopes and dreams of countless precious lives. He was reminded—he wasn't here for himself, he was here for them. For *all* of them. All creation. Now, staring at the stars, he thought of those he fought for, of all those beings who had already paid the ultimate price: his father, Fleeting Shadow; perhaps even Vu Verian, Morigos, and Morning's Hope.

They had all sacrificed for the universe, and for him.

Deep down in his heart, he knew there was no question…he would sacrifice for them.

He suppressed his tears, for he deemed he had no right to let them fall. They were tears that had been appropriated for self-pity, and they suited the Son and Savior of the Stars not at all. He composed himself, his features hardening with resolve. He looked back to the seer and with a trembling yet determined voice said, "Tell me how to wield the Sunsword Surassis. As Emperor of the Sky, as Son and Savior of the Stars, I demand a straight answer."

ZeerZeeOzz nodded, thinking, *Good! Embrace your fate!* Then he replied, "Once imbued with the One Soul, Surassis's fiery blade can be summoned simply by your will, by the mere desire of the One Life. Then it can be wielded like other, lesser swords; although no weapon in all the world can match the power of Surassis! In this way you may defend yourself until you are close to the Devil King, Nenockra Rool."

"And then?"

"And then, when you are close enough, Surassis will call upon you to conjoin with the One Soul, and—"

"And boom! There goes Drinwor…"

"And there goes the infernal ruler of evil in the universe," ZeerZeeOzz added, "while the One Life's soul lives on in the Seven Glories for all eternity."

Drinwor thought for a moment, then asked, "What happens to the One Soul itself?"

"The One Soul sacrifices itself to eternity. The One Soul will be no more."

Drinwor exhaled, shook his head. "Good Gods, I can't believe all of this." He looked once more at the galaxies behind them, thought once more on his father and friends, on all that was at stake, then gasped, sighed, and said, "Let us do this. Let us finally imbue Surassis with a soul."

"So it is said, so let it be done."

ZeerZeeOzz lifted his hands into the air. White vapor streamed from his fingertips, his head lifted many feet above his torso, and he asked, "Who are you?"

Drinwor straightened up, answered, "I'm the One Life, the Son and Savior of the Stars."

"And tell me—why are you here?"

"To imbue the sword with the One Soul."

"And what voice do you hear?"

"The voice of the sword."

"And what does it say?"

"It says: One Life, One Soul, One Sword…for all hope."

"Ah, awareness is awakening within you! You are the One Life, the wielder and keeper of the One Sword. Do you accept this?"

Drinwor whispered, "I…I do."

"Then we will resurrect Sillithian Synnstrike."

ZeerZeeOzz turned around and clapped his hands.

Outside, one of the golden spheres separated from the others. It was the king star! It shot around the cathedral, plunged into the back wall, and slowly seeped into the sanctuary. Once there it spread out over the dais as a cluster of wavy wisps of silvery-gold.

The seer moved backward, motioned for Drinwor to join him at the edge of the steps. As Drinwor did so, the wisps melded together, then expanded into the shape of a large serpentine body. Wings and legs emerged from the sparkling outline, and a tail like a whip of sunlight unfurled. A long neck extended forth, and a head of scintillating silver appeared at its end. The eyes that fluttered open were so brilliant…

…their radiance shrouded the curved black irises evilly slitting their centers…

Drinwor was speechless. Here was yet another extraordinary being.

"The One Life," ZeerZeeOzz called out, "I present to you the One Soul! Behold, Drakana, Lord of the Spirit Dragons!"

Drakana said nothing, but acknowledged Drinwor with a slight bow. Drinwor returned the gesture, said, "Your magnificence."

"And now, bring forth Surassis," ZeerZeeOzz instructed.

Drinwor reached into his leg pouch, withdrew the sunsword, and with both hands hefted it high over his head. Gods, its magical aura was brilliant now! His hands were lost in its golden luster, and the crystal held by the dragon claw pommel glinted so brightly, the limp body of Sillithian Synnstrike within was set aglow. Surassis was splendid indeed, Drinwor thought. He could have pictured it hanging upon the back wall, the holiest relic in this holiest of places in all this dreamy universe. The crystal pommel glinted again, then sent forth a wide swath of blazing light beams, illuminating the entire cathedral.

Drinwor looked over his shoulder.

Thousands of spirit elves were looking back at him.

"May the Gods return!" Drinwor cried.

"May the Gods imbue you with eternal strength," ZeerZeeOzz said.

The spirit elves had been there all along, congregating amongst the misty pews. With the sword's light upon them, their forgotten faces had phased into visibility. Their features were piercing, simple, and strong, shaped from a time long, long ago. All at once, they cried out in song—a smooth stream of echoing notes whose melody soared with a sound no mortal had ever heard. It was inspiring, hopeful, powerful. It grew louder and louder as the light from Surassis grew brighter and brighter.

All told, it was quite a beautiful scene, my devoted reader!

Drinwor turned his head back around, and through his uplifted arms he saw Drakana. The Lord of the Spirit Dragons reared on his hind legs and spread wide his wings, which caught the light of Surassis. The sword's light beams erupted into a wild white fire.

Drinwor called out, "ZeerZeeOzz!" but his voice failed against the singing thousands. Everything disappeared behind the blinding (but thankfully not burning) flames. And gripping the handle as tightly as he was, he was unaware that the sword had lifted him into the air, his feet dangling five feet above the dais.

Drakana's outline reappeared. The spirit dragon's head curled down through the flames, and he enfolded Drinwor with his wings. His eyes twinkled, then seemed to liquefy, the silvery-black fluid trickling into the upheld sword. Huge surges of energy, like vines of lightning, twirled about Drinwor's hands, then fled into the pommel's crystal. Drakana's wings retracted, his whole body condensed, and his flashing form rushed down into Surassis, a gushing stream of sparking soul-fire!

Drinwor screamed.

Such power coursed through him, his eyes brightened to blazing silver and his hair whipped all about his upturned head. In that moment, some long-unsatisfied part of his being was finally sated, as if a long lost passionate love had at last returned to him. In that moment, he felt as if he'd instantly garnered the wisdom of many years. Now he understood more than ever the conviction of light, the certitude of his peers. His fear of death and failure slackened and his doubt diminished, for he felt a power within him that suppressed his mortal concerns. Now he knew his life was but a small portion of a greater entity, an entity that would endure for all time.

Now Drinwor felt immortal.

The soul-fire surged through him for another few seconds, then subsided...for now.

It was done.

The One Sword was resurrected.

Drinwor dropped to the floor, his eyes darkening back to blue. The power that had passed through him settled, but was still there, a reservoir of strength seated in his soul, connecting him to the sword. And though one desire was gone, another, stronger one began to brew…

The song of the spirit elves ceased.

The fire subsided.

The Hall of Voices was gone.

Somewhere in the middle of all of this, the universe had returned to white. Drinwor once again stood upon the little cloud. The colored stars were all around, and below he could see countless thousands of the golden spheres arising. They shot up all around him, placing him in the center of a great geyser of streaming gold.

ZeerZeeOzz reappeared, his barely discernible figure hovering amongst the soaring spheres. His voice came as it had when Drinwor had first heard it—a mysterious echo from some indeterminable place. It said: "Go, Drinwor Fang, go and vanquish all of the dark storms of fate, for you are a mightier storm than all. You are the One Life, the summation of all the dreams of all the souls that have ever been and ever will be. Conquer your uncertainty, and you will conquer all. Have faith that your goodness will prevail. Now go, Son and Savior of the Stars. For every father, for every soul, fight for blue skies, fight for us all!"

And then ZeerZeeOzz was gone.

Drinwor felt his stomach twist in his gut, and his breath left him with a puff.

He knew—something traumatic was about to happen…

"May the Gods return!"

Still holding Surassis high over his head, he shot screaming into the sky, accompanying hundreds of thousands of other souls back onto Phate…

Inside the sunsword's crystal pommel, Sillithian Synnstrike was awakening.

His little dragon wings unfurled.

His little dragon eyes opened...

...and Drekklor the Shadow Demon could see.

All had gone as the Devil King had foreseen. Drekklor had successfully followed Drinwor into the portal door, possessed the spirit dragon lord, and claimed his place inside the sword.

Oh, so wide went the little solar dragon's smile...

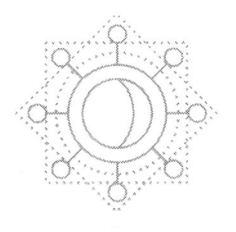

CHAPTER TWENTY-SIX
FACE THE SUN

It is in dreams that mortals will find their higher selves, for only in dreams do their minds dare to dip into the waters of immortality.

Vu Verian
Mystic Sorcerer, Last Sky Elf on Phate

And though it seemed as if there was no force of light capable of diminishing so terrible a night, a light did indeed come to relieve the world of darkness. A dispirited dawn was breaking. The dying sun peeked over the horizon, and had it been capable of shedding fiery tears, it might have blazed as it had in times of old, for once again its last surviving child had been scalded by extrasolar flames. The Shards of Zyrinthia had been merciless, the devastation complete. Everywhere great plumes of smoke rose like spirits escaping the cadaver of the world.

But now all was quiet, eerily calm. Those who had survived gazed silently at the sky, awaiting the end of it all.

And for one, dawn itself was as the coming of death...

Warloove opened his eyes.

He was in the strangest of places. All he could see were decrepit trees that slowly swayed through glowing shafts of mist. "I hallucinate," he whispered. He shook his head, gathered his wits, and looked about. There was something vaguely familiar about this place, something— Wait... He wasn't hallucinating, he *knew* this place! And all too well.

"It is the Forest of Corpsewood. I am home."

But something was very different. The forest was bathed in...

Warloove gasped with a horrific realization.

"*Oh, no! It cannot be*! Do I behold the light?"

Indeed he did. For the first time in a thousand years, he was witnessing the dawn. He groaned, made to move, but couldn't. With widening eyes he looked down upon himself.

"Wha...what is this?"

With his body fully solidified in its dark elf incarnation, he was chained to the front wall of the Castle Krypt with glowing white shackles. Now he seemed not so powerful a thing, for his vestments were torn away from his chest, exposing his emaciated skin, and his cloak of smoke didn't surround him, and the Gauntlets of Loathing Light were gone from his claws. He whispered sorcery, tried to transform into spectral smoke, but it was futile. Some property of the shackles was sapping his supernatural powers and weakening his limbs.

He was helpless.

And then the sky brightened. The daylight's searing heat submerged into the pale sponge of his dead skin. It was excruciating! Hear Warloove now as he tells you what it felt like!

"*It feels like I am being punctured by a million jagged needles, and the needles are slowly twisting, damn you all!*"

He rolled back his head and peered through the wickedly curled branches of the dancing trees, his eyes tracking up the dusky walls of the long-dead volcano. Beyond, through its gaping mouth, he saw something he had not seen for so, so long.

The bluish-black sky was lightening to red.

He groaned, "Daylight!" rather pathetically, I must say, and struggled against his bonds.

But there was no escape.

"Who is holding me?" he muttered as the pain intensified. He deceived himself. He well knew there was only one being on Phate who could hold him so.

"Master!" he screamed. "Please! What is this sorcery that enslaves me?"

Inside his head, the cold, monotone voice of Darkis sounded...

I commanded Geeter to bring you back here because you repeatedly defy me, Warloove. While the Dark Forever breaks into the world, you tease and toy with my eternity! Primitive, barbarous abomination, the sunsword has escaped you! I said to feast your fangs on the fools of Phate, but the fools have feasted on you. Need I again remind you what will happen to us if we are here when the Dark Forever descends upon us? What will happen when the sun goes supernova? We will burn. Oh, we will burn! Our dreams will perish with this world, and we will never swim in the soothing seas of eternal darkness. We must escape! I must ascend to the stars and reclaim my empire, my life! I must wreak revenge upon my enemies! My starship awaits the power of the sunsword, my life beckons me like a specter from some forgotten space, and you, Warloove, you must not fail me again.

Today you will feel something of failure. Today you will realize that you, too, can die. Today you will face the sun. Remember this day. Remember it is but a taste of what will happen to you should you fail me again. It is a punishment, and it is a test. And the test is simple—feel the fringes of a star's light, and see if you can survive.

Warloove was aghast.

"Master," he uttered through lacerated lips, "the sword was in my grasp! But then the bones...the bones fell atop me, and it was lost. All went dark. And then I was here." He tried to lift his arms, but the shackles held them firmly to the wall. "Oh, master, you saved me! ...Master?"

There was no response. It was silent but for the crackle of his flesh. Desperation seized him. "Stop this! Stop! I will acquire the sword, I swear it!" He began to sob, his burning face fizzling with acidic tears. Helpless, tormented, he turned back time in his mind, perusing the hours in which he could have spent his efforts in a more meaningful manner. The sunsword had been his to take! If only he could go back, try again... But it was too late.

No, on this day, our wicked Warloove would face the sun.

"*Oh, grey one!*" he cried, "*hear me! I will never fail you again!*" But still no answer came. His master had left him alone with the sun. And although his heart was dead, his chest throbbed with fear.

The dying sun crawled yet higher into the sky.

Thick shafts of daylight crept over the rim of the volcano, shot down through the trees, and struck him like an enemy sorcerer's powerful beams.

"Master! *Noooooo!*"

It was painful beyond anything he had ever imagined. His eyes smoldered in their sockets. His fingers felt like pokers thrust into a fire. Heat reached down this throat and burned his dried out organs. The light found every crevice between every molecule of his body. His skin was cut, cracked, stung, scorched, and stretched. He tried to thrash, but the shackles further tightened and he was unable to even find any solace in shifting. He was acutely aware of every ounce of pain.

"*Agony! Agony and torment to end all misery!*"

And just when he felt as if his skin had melted from his bones, and perhaps his eyes had been burned from his head, and his insides must have been a smoking, hollow cavern not even suitable for the carrion crows to feast upon, it stopped.

By the grace of the Dark Forever, it finally stopped, and all the world darkened.

A shroud had covered him, a scintillating grey screen blocking out the awful sunlight. It was more of Darkis's technological magic. The screen sang with a lifeless, droning hum, but Warloove didn't notice this, for he was making his own sounds. A loud, guttural wheezing leaked from his crispy lips, and his skin crackled as it broke off in scrimy little flakes. He opened his mouth to unleash an anguished moan, but a silvery flash startled him, causing him to loose a grunt of surprise instead. The grey screen disappeared, and he was teleported into another place. A better place...

Now he was lying in his open coffin, his skin soaking in the coolness of the pitch black chambers deep within the Castle Krypt. The Gauntlets of Loathing Light lay next to him, and he grasped them and pulled them close to his chest like a child clinging to some comforting toy.

It was over.

He had faced the sun, and he had survived.

The agony subsided, but the humiliation remained.

He hissed, *"Massssterrrr..."* as the coffin's cover slammed shut atop him.

Warloove would never be the same.

A new malice had been burned into him, an anger that aroused a level of hatred he had never before experienced. That he should be punished thus was unconscionable! He couldn't be certain how much damage had been inflicted upon him this day, but whatever was left of him would murder the world, he vowed.

He squeezed these words through gritted fangs: "I...hate... *everything!* I will kill you all... You will burn, bastards of Phate. Oh, all of you will burn! If not by my fire, then by the vengeance of the sun you will meet your doom, and I will be far, far away. I will rule worlds draped in the shadows of everlasting night, and the memory of this place will fade with my wounded mind into the forgotten archives of time..."

Then he lost the energy to speak as his thoughts spiraled down into unconsciousness. His eyes closed and he slipped into a vampiric slumber, a slumber so vile the darkest nightmares of others would seem as pleasant dreams in the bowels of his poisoned sleep.

※※※

Across the continent, a more hopeful dawn was breaking, and Drinwor, precious Drinwor, was waking.

As the first strands of awareness seized him, he couldn't discern what had been a dream, and what had actually been real. Visions of dragons lingered in his mind—dragons and demons and spirits and meteors, all swimming in oceans of echoing darkness. But the darkness didn't endure. For as the rising sun broke the back of the night, a compassionate voice emptied the seas of Drinwor's sleep, and guided his consciousness toward the surface of light.

"Wake up, my Emperor, wake up."

Drinwor grumbled and opened his eyes. His vision was blurry. All he could see was a spotted red stain. He blinked a few times, then came to realize his eyes weren't quite as blurry as he'd first suspected. The red stain was the roiled sky; the spots were the Shards of Zyrinthia that had remained in orbit.

He was back on Phate...maybe?

"Do I perceive some fantasy, or is this part of some conniving, clever new dream?"

It didn't feel like a dream when a warm breeze touched his face, and the sound of gentle rustling came from all around. He was lying in tall grass; the rustling was the sound of the blades brushing his demonskin armor. He got up into a crouch and, with all but the top of his head concealed in the grass, carefully peeked around.

The scene that greeted his eyes was somewhat familiar. To his left was a lush forest of evergreens. Backlit by the awakening sun, the dewdrops on the ends of the clustered needles glinted softly, some reflecting a broad spectrum of colors. A modest wind raced through the boughs, causing an elaborate mosaic of shadows to flit across his face. It was a calming, pleasant sensation. He took a few moments to inhale the morning's fresh scent, then shifted his view to the right. There a long field of rolling hills gently sloped down to a shoreline of mist. Beyond the shore was a wall of luminous vapor that was so massive, it stretched from horizon to horizon, dominating all the western sky. The vapor plunged down, its great splashes glittering the spaces before it with golden flecks.

"Ah, yes, I *am* back on Phate, for there lies the Phantom Falls!"

But it wasn't the same.

Enormous plumes of smoke twirled out of a great many giant clefts that sundered the massive ledges holding the cities. The once serene majesty of the place was all but spoiled. It was a disheartening sight.

"So," Drinwor whispered, "even the falls were not impervious to the wrath of the shards..."

But before Drinwor could dwell on it for too long, he was quickly overcome with a strong feeling that he wasn't alone. He whirled about, looked around, but was unable to spot anyone. He was certain someone was close by, though. He could feel it. And then he heard the voice, echoing as if from the beyond.

"*My Emperor…*"

Suddenly reminded of a certain mysterious voice that had sounded from afar, Drinwor stood up straight. "Who's there? Zeer-ZeeOzz? Is that you? Not your voice from nowhere again!" He said that, but knew it was not the spectral seer. No, this voice was smooth, lyrical…and feminine. Realization flushed his face, and his heart grew warm.

"Can it be? Oh, can it?"

And then, soaring out of the splashes that glittered the face of the Phantom Falls, came the clear yet coruscating outline of a Greater Translucent Dragon.

Drinwor held his breath.

The dragon glided closer, swooped down, then gently landed in the field not far from him. It walked toward him like some crystal creature conjured from the waters of the Syroxian Sea, with veins sparkling and golden heart glowing in the center of the clear pool of its breast.

Now there was no doubt…

"Morning's Hope!" Drinwor did not think himself capable of feeling such joy and relief. He leaped into the air, laughing, "Ha! You're alive! I knew it, I knew it, I *knew it*!"

"My Emperor," Morning's Hope said, "there are no words to sufficiently describe the joy I felt when you were safely returned to us."

Drinwor was beaming like the sunsword. "Blessed be the stars, I'm *so* thrilled to see you!" A euphoric tingle of joy coursed through him and he danced about. He soon relented, though. (Despite his fantastic dexterity, dancing wasn't something he was particularly good at…or comfortable with.) He stared at Morning's Hope, soaked her in. It felt as if he hadn't seen her in weeks. But as he gazed at her, his initial euphoria waned. Oh, he was still overjoyed to see her, you can be sure, but something about her wasn't right.

She wasn't…*perfect*.

One of her beautiful blue-green eyes was gone.

Drinwor winced. Where her right eye had been, there was now a small pinkish gash. "Morning's Hope, *no!*" He sprinted up to her.

She dipped her graceful snout to his uplifted hands, said, "It was a worthy exchange, my Lord: an eye for our lives, for certainly death could have taken us all last night."

Drinwor was shaking. He saw now that the missing eye wasn't the only wound she bore. Her translucent hide was raked all over with bloody scrapes, and marked as if with sunspots—sickly black circles where the enemy's fire had scorched her. The Emperor of the Sky was driven near to tears, but alas he forbade them to fall. With as calming and quiet a voice as he could muster, he asked, "What happened?"

"I was going to ask you the same! I have to know! The sword?"

Drinwor put his hands to his head and grimaced, for with even the slightest contemplation of the Hall of Voices, his mind was overwhelmed with many conflicting thoughts. Frightful images and dreadful emptiness wound around feelings of fulfillment and satiated power. It was overwhelming. He instinctively shied away from recollecting anything. "I will tell you in a little while, I promise, I just need to put it all together."

Morning's Hope displayed an obvious look of concern. "Are you all right, my Lord?"

Drinwor took his hands from his head, nodded, and said, "I am, please…please go on."

For a time she said nothing. She simply regarded him as he regarded her, with an impassioned stare. Oh, how her lone eye gleamed as it looked upon him! As if compensating for the loss of its beloved companion, it shone as brightly as ever, a shining testimony to the unending depths of her sympathetic soul.

Eventually she breathed in deeply, then let slip her story.

"For all their devastation, the Shards of Zyrinthia actually saved me. Just as Geeter was overpowering me, a shard came roaring down and smashed into his side. I was jarred free from his lethal grip, but when I spun away from him, his claw caught my eye." (Drinwor flinched at this.) "Oh, and before that even happened, I saw Morigos." A small snicker escaped her maw. "That crafty old dark elf was levitating upward, blasting Geeter with his green flames and leading Murdraniuss right into the shard's path. The banshee was actually struck before Geeter, his captured screams scattering all over the sky. I suspect the fiends were driven into the mountain of bones, but I cannot be sure." She looked to the sky, then closed her eye and sighed. "If only you could imagine how I felt when the shard struck, Drinwor. By the stars, I had no idea if you had made it into the Hall of Voices before the mountain exploded. It was terrible! Splintered bones flew for miles into the air, and the ruins of Shirian Shirion sank into the sea." She opened her eye, its brilliance now dimmed with distress, and looked back down to her Emperor. "I was afraid I had lost you."

Drinwor exhaled with an airy whistle. "So that's why Warloove didn't follow me into the hall." Then, with a hopeful tone, he posed, "Is it possible either he or Geeter was destroyed? If not by the shard, perhaps by the destruction of the mountain of bones?"

Morning's Hope shook her head. "I don't think so. They're immeasurably strong, extraordinarily resilient."

"And we couldn't possibly be so fortunate," Drinwor added.

She let out a sad little laugh. "True." Then she knelt before him, keeping her massive head level with his. "We *are* fortunate in one thing, though."

"Oh?"

"We are still alive!"

A shadow passed over Drinwor's face, and he looked away from her. "For now…"

Morning's Hope narrowed her eye. "What do you mean by that?"

"Nothing, nothing, I'll tell you later." The dusk elf waved off his comment, looked back to her, and patted her snout. "Oh, those evil beings, wounding you like this!"

"Scars are but a reminder that we've faced adversity and conquered it. Do not worry, I will heal. Now, if *you* had been hurt… well, that's a wound I do not think I could have suffered."

Drinwor allowed himself a little smile.

Morning's Hope smiled back. Then she shook out her wings and licked a bruise on her side. She made to speak, but Drinwor blurted, "Wait a minute, where's Morigos and Vu Verian?"

Morning's Hope motioned behind her. "Morigos is back there, immersing himself in the Phantom Falls. He says the vapor soothes him. I warn you, though, he's not the same. He's *worse*. As for Vu Verian, I don't know. I expected him at first light, but so far there's been no sign of him."

Drinwor lifted his hands to the sky. "May the stars be with us." When he brought his hands back down, he noticed Morning's Hope looking at him with a pleading stare. "What is it?" he asked.

"Drinwor, I've told you my story from last night, but by the Seven Glories, what of yours? What of the quest? You must tell me what happened in the hall!"

The dusk elf looked confused. "The quest?"

Morning's Hope let out an exasperated huff. *"The sunsword! Did you imbue Surassis with a soul?!"*

Drinwor inexplicably turned away from her, walked some steps away. He tried to calm the frenzy of thoughts that distorted the memory of his time in the hall. It seemed like a dream, and an elusive one at that. He whispered to himself, "What *did* happen? I feel so empty…and yet…fulfilled." And then he concentrated harder, drew his focus inward. Slowly, the events of last night fell together like pieces of a puzzle. He remembered the cloud, the universe of white. He remembered the starry structure of the hall. Then it all fell into place. He recalled that moment when the Lord of the Spirit Dragons had emptied his soul into the sword. He remembered the power he had felt, and the fulfillment and satisfaction thereof. He felt that power now, lying dormant within him like some sleeping beast, waiting for him to awaken it…

"Drinwor?"

Drinwor shook himself from thought and turned back around. Morning's Hope was still looking on him with that pleading stare, her huge translucent expanse twinkling in the daylight. "Drinwor? The sword?"

He smiled weakly. "I'm sorry. Yes, Surassis has its soul."

"Sillithian Synnstrike lives!"

Drinwor nodded. "He lives."

Morning's Hope shook her head. "It must be magnificent."

A curious expression twisted Drinwor's features; his eyes slit with purpose, and he nodded. "I think it's time for us to find out."

"Drinwor—"

"Yes, let us finally see it as it was meant to be." He reached for his leg pouch.

Consternation crossed his dragon's face.

Drinwor looked puzzled. He stayed his hand. "You don't want to see it?"

"I do, I do. I'm just concerned that revealing the sword might bring us unwanted attention."

Drinwor's face tightened with anger. "I don't care. This is *our* world. *My* sword. If Surassis is ready, then let our enemies cower before its light! I want to see it!"

Morning's Hope bowed. She said, "Then so be it, my Emperor," but thought, *He has changed; he has lost some of his emotions, and acquired others...*

Drinwor pulled forth the Sunsword Surassis.

And just as he had in the Hall of Voices, he gripped it with both hands and hefted it high into the air. The surrounding winds suddenly rose to a wailing whirl, shivering the evergreens, and a lick of red lightning split the sky above them. Grey and black clouds streamed in from the far horizon, and the world darkened as if to brighten the sword all the more.

"By the angel's light, the evil presence of the Dark Forever is about," Morning's Hope stated, "and irritated by the emergence of the One Sword it would seem."

Drinwor heard her, but didn't answer. He was transfixed by Sillithian Synnstrike flying around in the pommel's crystal. While he watched the little solar dragon, an intense desire to unleash the blade struck him, and his heart began to pound, for he knew he needn't suppress this compulsion any longer.

He whispered, "For you, father…"

Then, with but a thought, the Emperor of the Sky set the blade free!

Wild energy erupted like a sparking geyser from the slit on top of the hand guard, in a split second extending to ten feet in length. Finally freed after a thousand year dormancy, it was a wild burst of energy indeed! It soon condensed, though, tightening into a double-edged blade of compacted white fire. Singing with a vociferous sizzle, it illuminated all the area for a hundred feet around. Sillithian Synnstrike brightened to a silhouette of yellowish light, and Drinwor felt such power course through him, he thought he might leap into the sky and fly over the clouds.

Oh, it was quite a sight, the Son and Savior of the Stars wielding his sword!

"Look at the blade!" he cried. "Have you ever seen such a thing?"

"The Halo of the Gods," said Morning's Hope.

Drinwor's expression was quizzical, but he was too entranced with Surassis to pause and ponder the translucent's strange statement. He fell into a crouched stance, then leaped forward, thrusting. Surassis sizzled. Drinwor grinned. He began combating imaginary foes, twisting about and swinging the sword from side to side. Gods the blade was huge! But it was so light, so perfect. He whipped it around so fast, it left a fiery circular trail.

"The Halo of the Gods!" Drinwor yelled through a series of grunts. "I see it! I see it!"

Morning's Hope was enthralled, but she also couldn't completely stifle the sinking feeling that they were now exposed to all who stood against them.

When the dusk elf saw her face, he relented his sparring and commanded the blade to diffuse. The white fire instantly rushed back down into the hilt and disappeared. Then he was struck with a most uncomfortable feeling. Not because of the dragon's expression, but because it suddenly felt as if a billion sets of eyes were upon him...

A billion demons laughed.

Surassis, the most feared weapon in all the universe, the sword of the fated sun that had a thousand years ago vanquished them, was cursed and in the hands of a child who would have no idea of this until it was too late.

The cracks over the Raging Sea opened wider, a million more demons scampered free of the Dark Forever, and the dying sun's light crept through the largest tear and glinted on Nenockra Rool's skin...

Eternity itself wept as if with tears of cold suns, for now it seemed there was no doubt...the Devil King would come.

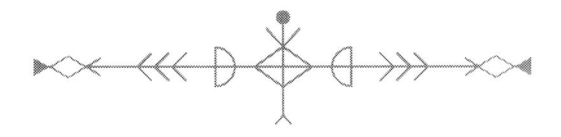

CHAPTER TWENTY-SEVEN
SLOWLY, PURPOSEFULLY FORWARD

You are master of your present, guardian of your future, and survivor of your past. Dwell not on yesterday, for it is but a beast slain by time…

Treeziax
Fighter for the Second Darkness,
Champion of the Whirlwind Wastes

The flesh on Syndreck's face had all but rotted from his skull. Now he resembled the dusty cadavers he had recently pulled from the ground. "Perhaps someday someone will pull *me* from the ground, send me trudging toward some foul purpose!" He chortled, then peeled a slice of skin from his forearm and tossed it into his mouth to nibble on. "Useless trappings but for the snacking, this dying skin!"

His skin might have been dying, but his eyes were still vibrant, still imbuing him with powerfully enhanced sorcerous vision. So powerful, in fact, that when Drinwor ignited the Sunsword Surassis on the other side of the continent, Syndreck saw it, saw it as a little streak of disturbingly intense flame illuminating some distant unknown field. "What's this? The sunsword resurrected? It was supposed to be cursed! Perhaps it is…?" Frustrated by uncertainty, he recoiled from his cauldron and erupted into a tantrum. "No! You promised, master, promised we wouldn't have to contend with the sword! Has the weakling Warloove failed us again? I will—"

The horrific death rattle of a hundred demons distracted him. He turned aside, glimpsed a hail of charred bodies whip around his tower and disappear below.

Another kind of cosmic sword had claimed them.

Syndreck looked down.

Trudging through a mess of dark elf limbs, vanquishing hundreds of demons into the depths of his black hole blade as he came, was Soular Centurion 7. The warrior from the stars seemed unconcerned with anything but his target. Even as a thousand descending demons dispelled the Glyph of Multiversal Guarding, he never took his cybernetic eyes from the necromancer. Even as those demons came wailing in to obliterate him from existence, he strode on with but one thing in mind.

Thus he came right up to the entrance of Syndreck's tower and stopped, his silver-helmeted head tilted upward, his ancient grey eyes gleaming through the sorcerous storms.

Syndreck looked down, saw his own glowing red silhouette in those eyes.

–TARGET ACQUIRED AND LOCKED IN–

Syndreck actually saw that readout, and fingers of fear tickled his psyche.

Unable to contain himself, he erupted with vulgarities, then screamed, "Enough of you! Begone! What sort are you to endure such mighty resistance? Go back to your doomed stars, I say! May the currents of the Dark Forever drown you beneath their unholy waves! BEGONE!"

Then Syndreck squeezed sorcery like sweat from the rag of his soul.

He screamed arcane words, and wild forks of explosive lightning shot out over the top of Ulith Urn and blasted hundreds of demons out of the air. The energy then curled down and swirled around his tower, surrounding it with a tornado-like funnel of purple lightning! The funnel spun so fast, its accompanying winds ripped chunks of stone from the tower's walls and, before long, the entire structure was pulled into the lightning and disintegrated. The only solid things left were the Cauldron of Carcass Control, Syndreck himself, and the sorcerously suspended floor of cracking stone that supported them.

Syndreck continued screaming and the sparking funnel continued to intensify. It wound up tighter, assumed the shape of a tower itself, its winds shredding Syndreck's tattered robes apart and tearing what remained of his skin from his bones.

Now the necromancer was the skeletal master of a vortex tower of purple lightning, his burning, howling eyes leaking a vapor like that of the Dark Forever's!

He lifted his skull back, raised his bony arms, and bellowed with a crazed voice, "I will feast on the light of your soul! I will tear the fabric of this world apart! I will send a billion demons against you!"

And then he laughed.

His laughter sounded above the shrieking demons, above the crackling whoosh of the whirling lightning tower. He lifted an ivory finger and it ignited with translucent red flames. Pointing the finger down, he yelled, "I, too, can make atoms disappear!"

Below, Soular Centurion 7 lifted high the Sword of Molecular Destruction.

Syndreck cackled like a crazed banshee as he unleashed his flames. The fire shot down through the lightning toward the warrior from the stars.

–INITIATE DEFENSIVE MANEUVER CENTURIOUS 8.7 X–

Soular Centurion 7 spun away from the flames and leaped into the sky just as a host of demons landed beside him. Their claws missed him, and their spewed fires fell short, for their enemy flew up hundreds of feet in a second. He blasted through the electrified tower's walls and thudded to Syndreck's suspended floor, his sword whipping down before him, eager to vaporize his necromantic target.

But Syndreck was not there.

The centurion's sword swept through empty space, and hacked a hole into the floor.

"Metal against magic?" Syndreck's echoing voice teased from some indeterminable place. "Tell me, galactic warrior, can you roam beneath the dimensions?" Then he reappeared on the other side of the Cauldron of Carcass Control. With his hands raised, he sang out, and bolts of energy flew from the tower's wall to engulf the cosmic warrior in a mesh of lightning. Then Syndreck disappeared again, slipping back into the space beneath the dimensions, his echoing cackles trailing into inaudibility.

The centurion's mechanical systems sparked. What little flesh he possessed burned. But before any permanent damage was inflicted, a wave of blue energy pulsed through him and doused the lightning with cosmic cold.

-SPIRIT FREEZE COMMENCING-

The ghostly parts of the centurion were taking over, cooling his primary systems. His eyes dimmed to a darker grey, and all he viewed grew hazy.

-TRACKING TARGET THROUGH DIMENSIONAL PHASING-

Soular Centurion 7 faded from the primary universe, his enemy located and locked in his cybernetic eyes…

CHAPTER TWENTY-EIGHT
BEFORE THE END

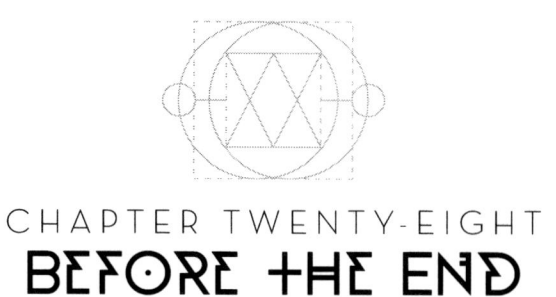

Learning is the one journey whose end should never be reached, and whose road should never be abandoned.

Yorn Illadruss
Sorcerer Seer of the Youthful Scribes

Ever so carefully did Drinwor Fang slip Surassis back into his leg pouch, fearful that any sudden or exaggerated movements would attract the attention of "the billion sets of eyes." He scanned the horizon with an uneasy stare, then looked to Morning's Hope and said, "With the sword revealed, it *did* feel like I was being watched. Perhaps I should have listened to you." He tilted his head back and exhaled an exasperated huff. "I couldn't help it. I've spent my whole life waiting in the clouds, wondering what this urge inside me could be. And now I know... I've been waiting to set the blade free, and thus, take one step closer to my destiny."

Morning's Hope nodded. "You *are* destiny, Drinwor. And worry not about the emergence of the sword, for the wounds of the world have opened, and the eyes of the Dark Forever would have spotted us anyway. And now we know you have it within you to unleash its fiery blade. You needed to know. *I* needed to know. Nevertheless," she added, her unblinking eye fixed on the wild clouds, "I do believe we should be cautious and keep the sword concealed, at least until such time as we need its light to shine. And then you must be ready."

Drinwor cast his gaze to the ground and murmured incoherently, his foot gently brushing the grass. He could sense Morning's Hope turn her stare down to him, and after a minute or so he brought his head back up to face her. "Oh, I'll be ready…"

"Is there something you're not telling me?" she asked. "Since you returned from the Hall of Voices, you seem…"

"Different?" he suggested.

"Well, yes, but that's to be expected. You seem troubled."

"I've been 'troubled' since we first met, wouldn't you say?"

"Well, *yes,* but it seems like there's something else going on, something you're not telling me. Hmm… Perhaps I'm mistaken. But I know the infusion of the soul had to have been a most intense experience."

Drinwor laughed. "Intense? Yes, one could say that. Honestly, I believe the resurrection of the sword has profoundly affected me." Then his face seemed to darken with that shadow that had recently found a home amongst his features, and he looked deep into his dragon's sole surviving eye and said, "I've learned things. The Fallen Angel was right. *I* was right. I am much more than the Emperor of the Sky. And I'm beginning to understand what it means to be the Son and Savior of the Stars. But what I didn't know until recently is just how much I'll have to sacrifice. Like father, like son, with nowhere to run…but headlong into whatever fate has in store." He paused for a moment, then whispered: "I'm not as afraid as I thought I'd be, though, not afraid to give myself, my life, to the sword. I wonder why that is? I'm not afraid of my destiny."

"That's good. You *are* the Son and Savior of the Stars, and you should fear no evil." Morning's Hope said this with conviction, but I must tell you, she was a trifle bit unnerved when she saw what could only be described as a rather villainous grin stretch over Drinwor's chin.

Drinwor half muttered, half growled, "You won't have to worry. When the time comes, *I swear I shall burn evil from the sky!*" And then his grin vanished.

Morning's Hope found his tone as distressing as his expression. "Are you *certain* there isn't something specific you want to talk about?"

He shook his head. "No. Not now."

"As you wish." She moved her head down closer to his, softly said, "But please know—you can tell me anything, at any time, should you desire."

As Drinwor looked upon her glorious face, his own face lightened, the shadow fled, and his expression returned to the one of hopeful innocence Morning's Hope was accustomed to seeing. He matched the softness of her words when he next spoke. "I know, I know. Thank you." And then he patted his leg pouch, said, "We're all right. It's just all been so much to bear. I'll get used to it."

Morning's Hope opened her mouth to comment further, but from somewhere behind them came a raucous cough. The two glanced to the field, and there, on a nearby hill, cloaked in dark, ripped robes, stood a crooked figure clutching an equally crooked staff. A strange little song emanated from the oversized cowl, and the figure disappeared in a puff of black smoke…only to instantly reappear right beside them.

"Morigos!" Drinwor cried out. He was surprised at how happy he was to see the haggard dark elf.

Morigos choked, swiped away the smoke clinging to his robes, then managed: "What in the name of blasphemy went on here? Were you simulating the impending death of our ancient sun? What was all that light?"

Drinwor clenched his fists. "I've succeeded! The sunsword has been imbued with a soul!"

"Succeeded?" Morigos snorted. "You'll vanquish yourself before you vanquish any foes with that thing! At the very least lose a limb or two. Blasted, burning light!"

Drinwor pointed toward the falls. "What were you doing there?"

The mage cupped a hand to the side of his head. "Eh? What is that you say?"

"I told you," Morning's Hope said, "he's worse."

Drinwor smiled, spoke louder and slower. "I asked—*what were you doing in the falls?*"

"Ah, I see. I mean, I hear…barely! Damnable banshee scream probably won't ever completely abandon my ears! No matter.

Anyway, I was salvaging what's left of this broken body, my boy, though little good that'll do me."

Drinwor nodded, though he didn't entirely understand.

Then swiftly did a darkness pass over them, causing everyone to look upward. A velvety black cloud had snuck in over their heads, squirming through the sky like a worm through the dirt. Morning's Hope whispered, "Silence, no one move!" Everyone froze, and the cloud slunk down and twined about them, issuing unintelligible whispers and chilling moans. When it slid around Drinwor, sparks ignited in its innards, sending it shrieking back into the sky, leaving a fading wake of red fire.

"What was that?" Drinwor asked as he watched it fly away.

"Specter demon," Morigos answered. "They bleed fire. Somehow, you wounded it. Nicely done!"

Drinwor let out a little gasp and looked to Morning's Hope. "The sword *does* attract quite a lot of attention."

She shook her head. "It doesn't matter. As I said, sword or no, it was inevitable that we would be seen. But now, with specter demons about, and the Dark Forever freed, time is against us. We must leave."

"Where are we going?" Drinwor asked.

"Where else?" Morigos cried, raising his staff high, "to Ulith Urn, where the doom of eternity awaits!"

"Yes," Morning's Hope concurred. "Nenockra Rool will likely enter the primary universe somewhere close to Ulith Urn. My Emperor, you're going to see some unpleasant things. Phate has endured—"

"I know," he interrupted, "the damage caused by the shards."

"It is not so much the destruction caused by the shards that I speak of," she said. "It is the effects of the Dark Forever that will be difficult to take in. The world will appear…morbid."

Drinwor clasped his hands together and bowed his head. "Wonderful." Then he suddenly perked up, said, "Oh, are we going to leave without Vu Verian?"

Morning's Hope nodded. "Indeed we must, for all fate cannot wait for him! Fear not," she reassured, "I think I know where he is. He will find us."

"I hope not!" Morigos said, cackling even as Morning's Hope glared at him.

"I wonder what he's doing," Drinwor said.

The dark elf's cackling suddenly turned into a painful grunt, and he held up a broken, backward facing finger. He threw down his staff, grabbed the finger with his other hand, and twisted it round. Drinwor grimaced as it crunched back into place. The mage cackled, cursed, and said: "Battle damage." Then he picked up his staff, faced Morning's Hope. "I would never presume to sit with the boy Emperor upon your noble back, but I have not the strength to fly myself across the continent. What strength I have left is reserved for killing demons."

Morning's Hope stared to the west, to the sky over the Phantom Falls. "I have foreseen this. Last night, after our fight, I summoned a loyal emissary of the Fallen Angel. She arrives now."

Drinwor and Morigos looked to where her gaze was fixed, and saw something descend out of the darkening clouds. Thankfully, it was no specter demon. No, no, not at all! It was snowy white, bespeckled all over with silvery glints. The movements of its feathered wings were fluid and graceful. The creature didn't fly so much as it swam through the sky, in a fashion reminding Drinwor of Morning's Hope.

As it approached, Drinwor couldn't help smiling, for indeed it was a creature that could have only come from Vren Adiri.

Bear witness, my faithful reader, here was the last of the starlit unicorns, the last winged steed of the long vanished shadowlight elves! But should I be so lucky as to be afforded the time to continue my tale, I promise you, it will not be the last one you ever see... I know where there are more.

Anyway, the starlit unicorn flew down, unfolded its six legs, and landed before them. It was large, much larger than Drinwor had originally perceived, at least three times bigger than a wild horse, in fact. Its musculature was so perfectly structured, had it been standing still it would've looked like a white marble sculpture. A long crystal horn twisted up from the center of its forehead, and its eyes were wide and white as frozen seas.

Here was Arcynn Ahnna Jha, she who had delivered the Gauntlets of Loathing Light to Forn Forlidor.

To Drinwor's surprise, she strode right up to Morigos.

"If ever there's been a more unlikely pairing, I don't think I've ever seen it," Morning's Hope commented. "You couldn't in a thousand years understand the honor bestowed upon you."

Morigos extended his black-gloved hand to Arcynn Ahnna Jha, who lowered her head and nestled her snout in his palm. "And you cannot understand what this beast means to *me*, my patronizing dragon. I am not so unworthy as you might think. I know this creature, and I am indebted to it."

Drinwor and Morning's Hope were stunned. But before they could press the dark elf for more information, he added, "Ask nothing, for that is a story for another day…"

"Then save your story," Morning's Hope said as she unfurled her wings and shook them out, "and let us fly to secure the day that we might hear it. May we vanquish all threats of darkness, and by doing so add another tale to the tomes of history! For all the dreams and hopes and lives that exist beneath blue skies, let us fly. Blessed be the light, blessed be Drinwor Fang, the glorious Son and Savior of the Stars!"

"You're quite a big fuss, eh?" Morigos quipped to Drinwor with a chortle. "Let's hope your little sword is all it's cracked up to be!"

"Let us hope!" Drinwor agreed.

And with that, Drinwor ran up his dragon's wing and secured himself in his saddle-throne. Arcynn Ahnna Jha knelt, and Morigos struggled but succeeded in climbing atop her back.

They took to the sky.

One and all, they would never forget this flight…

Drinwor's eyes were arrested by atrocity. "May the Gods return, look at that!"

Morning's Hope was right: everything did indeed look morbid. The Continent Isle of Volcar appeared to have in one night gone through an entire age of necromantic despair. The lands were virtually unrecognizable. Craters were everywhere. Rivers overflowed with blood, and mindless masses of undead trudged through burning cities.

What forests had survived the meteor storm were now being strangled by a poisonous red vapor that crept out of cracks in the countryside. Trees withered to dust before the companions' very eyes.

"It's the influence of the Dark Forever!" Morning's Hope yelled. "All the universe will suffer thus should the forces of light stand idly by!"

The red vapor crept into the clouds, curdling the air. All around the companions, sorcerous tornadoes swirled into being like giant evil genies suddenly freed from some other dimension. They had no wishes to grant, but curses they had aplenty, and from their phantom hands did waves of liquid lightning stream through the stormy sea of the sky.

"Watch it!" Morning's Hope called out as a flash of electricity slipped past her.

Arcynn Ahnna Jha angled hard aside and spun over, evading the strike.

"A most wicked weather today!" Morigos yelled as they righted, one hand holding his staff out, using its weight to balance himself, his other hand clamped to the unicorn's silvery mane.

Swifter than the ill winds that chased them, the dragon and unicorn flew on, the bevy of sentient storms a constant pest.

As the day grew longer, I'm afraid the conditions only worsened. There were constant lightning strikes, and clouds that spontaneously erupted into flames. There were gusts of acidic rain, and all around them the spectral tornadoes continued to whirl. Specter demons were everywhere, their hushed hissing as prevalent as the whistling of the winds. It was chaos, with no serenity in sight.

"Has all of Phate turned against us?" Drinwor screamed over the storms. "Morning's Hope, are we losing our world?"

"No!" she cried, "the world is still ours! This is but a show, a masquerade meant to terrify the eyes and heart. Nothing more. We will destroy this blasphemy with the power of the sunsword!"

Seemingly inspired by her own words, she flew on even faster, the starlit unicorn ever staying right behind her. They flew deeper and deeper into the day, desperately trying to get back across Volcar as swiftly as possible. It was a difficult journey indeed, for not only were they targeted by the unnaturally nasty elements, but they were beheld by many a demonic eye. They did their best to avoid confrontation, but sometimes demons strayed too close for them to ignore. Of these encounters, it suffices to simply say that Morning's Hope mercilessly dispatched all blasphemous beings in their path with potent breathes of electrified energy. She was merciless because she had to be. Now she was a warrior dragon, and she led her little group on through this host of horrors.

Thus they crossed Volcar, taking no time to view the myriad features of Phate, which most of them wouldn't have recognized now, anyway.

By the time they approached the western edge of the continent, the red sore of a sun had already crawled over the sky's summit and fallen halfway to its nightly dungeon.

"We're not far from the sea!" Morning's Hope called out. "Be ready!" she bade Drinwor. "We approach the enemies of all the universe!"

Drinwor slipped his hand into his leg pouch, made to withdraw Surassis.

Morning's Hope shot her head around, shouted: "No! Not yet!"

"But you just said to be—"

"Not yet with the sword! At least not until *he* appears..."

"*He?*" Morigos called from behind. He shook his staff and it leaked a trail of glowing green smoke. "Do you mean Warloove or Nenockra Rool?"

Drinwor cringed upon hearing the fiends' names.

The mage was left to wonder which one Morning's Hope meant, for she paid him no mind. She pulled her wings in and slowed. They were many miles in the air, and she seemed to be considering the world beneath them. Everyone wondered if she could actually see anything, for the lands were totally obscured by the storms. After a few seconds, she nodded with satisfaction, then darted down through a thick layer of black clouds, Arcynn Ahnna Jha staying right on her tail. Forks of lightning jabbed at them, but none found their mark; the immortal mounts punched through the bottom of the clouds unscathed.

Totally lost, Drinwor asked, "Where are we?"

"Some Emperor of the sky *you* are!" Morigos snickered from behind.

"We're over the Mountains of Might," Morning's Hope answered before flashing the mage one of her looks.

"We are?" Drinwor trusted his loyal mount, but wondered how she knew that. There was no point of reference, no horizon. The land directly below them was shrouded by low-flying clouds that looked more like aerial flows of fire. In the distance, a colossal, heaving mass of reddish fog had seemingly consumed all the western world. It billowed over the edge of the Cliffs of Moaning Wishes and stretched for miles uncounted to the north and south. This was no wandering sorcerous storm! The bloody fog climbed high into the sky, rising and rising until its lightning-wracked peaks buffeted angrily against the bottom of the atmosphere, as if it insisted on breaking through the claustrophobic confines that separated the skies from the stars.

Drinwor thought it looked like Phate was transforming into its own dying sun. "What in the name of the Seven Glories is that?" he shouted through the winds, pointing to the red mass. "Is it smoke?"

"It is not smoke," his dragon said, her voice stern.

"No? Then—"

"It's the Devil's Wind," Morigos confirmed. "The Dark Forever has come!"

"The Devil's Wind?" Drinwor said.

"You're looking at a gigantic mass of demons," the dark elf mage explained, "shrouded by the misty red air leaked from the Dark Forever."

"May the Gods return!" The dusk elf Emperor stood from his saddle-throne, his eyes as fiery as the scene they beheld, his hair wild with wind. Sweltering sweat drenched his face, but inside his armor he shivered with frightful chills. "I see the demons!" Indeed, the red mist was bursting with millions of gleaming, crimson bodies. Glowering, hateful eyes peered through the fringes, and claws and horns and hoofs stuck out the billowing sides. Drinwor could hear their unholy cries, their cackles of delight, and he himself squirmed when the whole mass writhed. Thunder sounded, the loudest he'd ever heard, and in the midst of the mass he saw huge cracks splitting the sky apart.

And just when he thought he could stand to look on it no longer, his gaze was mercifully drawn away. For Morning's Hope, continuing to descend, had banked sharply around. She deftly evaded the burning clouds, and what was left of the Mountains of Might appeared through the haze below.

"It would appear that the mountains are no longer so mighty," a wheezing Morigos noted.

The mage's declaration was accurate—the range had been totally ravaged by the shards.

With most of them leveled to their bases, the Volcanoes of Volcar spewed lava like the impaled gushed blood, with eruptions splattering everywhere. The mountains sat in the middle of their own molten lake. A smoking tributary trickled from the lake, carving a new valley into the Wicked Plains before plunging over the cliffs and emptying into the poisoned waters of the Raging Sea.

Morning's Hope flew a little farther down, then held her altitude and glided forward, careful to avoid the unpredictable eruptions. "Where is Vren Adiri?" she mused aloud. "It's supposed to be here…I thought perhaps Vu Verian would meet us—"

And then the volcanoes flared with brilliant light.

"Look!" Drinwor shouted, peering over his dragon's side.

"The mountains are exploding!" Morigos yelled.

"Indeed they are," Morning's Hope returned, "but not with fire."

"With what, then?" questioned the mage.

"Dragon souls," she whispered.

It was true: May the Gods return, the Mountains of Might were erupting with spirit dragons!

Freed from the Hall of Voices, answering the call of Soular Centurion 7, and rising to the aid of the Son and Savior of the Stars, thousands upon thousands of golden dragon spirits flew up through the bloody bowels of the ruined mountains, slathered themselves with lava, then shot clear into Phate's haunted sky! Oh, here were dragon ghosts given life again! They'd been jewel dragons and cloud dragons, lesser translucent dragons and insect dragons, forest dragons and lightning dragons, all come from different lands, different realms, and different ages. Some were the size of castles, and some the size of flies. But now they all inherited the same hide—a fluid, reddish-black skin that flowed like a molten coat about their souls. And their eyes, burning with the white fires of eternity, all pierced with the same purpose. Their brazen cries echoed through the skies beyond the Wicked Plains and out across the sea, voices from the past returned to challenge the future's forbidding fate.

On and on they came in a seemingly endless eruption. They flew up behind the companions and soared over them, a great wing of molten beasts that soon amassed into a swarm five hundred thousand volcanic spirit dragons strong!

Drinwor was breathless.

He tilted his head back, trying to take in as many of the dragons as he could. They looked like another meteor storm, a massive hail of living shards. He could feel the heat that they projected, and his nostrils were infiltrated by the metallic and smoky scent of flaming souls.

"Magnificent," he whispered.

Oh, it *was* magnificent, it really was!

Morning's Hope slowed to a stop, hovered in place. With the volcanic beasts streaming overhead, she looked back and offered Drinwor a slight smile that was soon broken by dispirited words. "It is a blessing, but a tragedy all the same."

"How so?" the dusk elf asked.

"That it always comes to war, that there are no more generations to sacrifice, and past generations must sacrifice again...that war now claims not only the lives but the eternal souls of those who have already lost everything..." Her head bowed.

Drinwor's curiosity was piqued by his dragon's solemn statements. "I still don't quite understand. Who's already lost everything?"

Morning's Hope lifted her head and pointed skyward with a wing. "Those who ascended with you from the Hall of Voices. Those dragons. *They* have lost."

Drinwor gasped. "The golden spheres in the white universe were the spirit dragons! The Hall of Voices, of course! I hadn't realized until now."

"Yes, those dragons have already fought and died for light. Now they come to fight and die again. It was your arrival, the arrival of the Son and Savior of the Stars, who bade them back into the living world. Now they will surrender their eternities; for any beings who have died, then venture unborn back into the primary universe, cannot die again. All who perish in this battle will lose their souls to nothingness. One birth for every death: that is the way of all souls. But these dragons will aid us nonetheless, and I will be powerless to abstain from letting many tears fall."

Drinwor's face went pale as he watched the massive dragon swarm fly straight for the Devil's Wind. "They will lose their souls... for me."

Morning's Hope clenched her claws and shook them, uttering, "Yes, they give up their eternities for you, and for everyone. *It must not be in vain!*"

And then a great shaft of heavenly light came slanting down from the high sky as if to accentuate her noble words. It sliced right through a sorcerous storm and illuminated the head of the dragon swarm, which now neared the edge of the cliffs close to the fringes of the Devil's Wind. The winged defenders of Phate bellowed ancient battle cries, then angled to fly around the brilliant shaft. The light thickened, brightened with a flash...then faded away. But something remained in its place, hovering amidst the dragons. At first it was difficult for the companions to tell what it was; the dragon swarm encircled it, obstructing their view. Drinwor squinted trying to discern its details. It was huge, tall, and white. It looked like many things joined together, like a bundle of twining sky elven arms pointing to the stars, like...towers.

It could only be...

"Your Vren Adiri!" Morigos observed.

Morning's Hope was relieved. "The spirit of the Fallen Angel is with us."

The dark elf smirked. "Is it?"

The companions hovered in place as the last of the volcanic dragons passed overhead, and the Devil's Wind continued to spread as Nenockra Rool prepared to put his first foot onto Phate.

Wherever you are, in whatever time, on whatever world, I ask that you take a moment and pray for our heroes' souls, for the great battle was about to begin, and I must admit, I fear my forthcoming words...

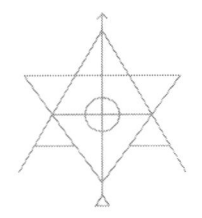

CHAPTER TWENTY-NINE
THE DOOM OF PHATE

My father once told me the persistence of hope is faith, and to be faithful is to be steadfast in the face of despair. If I'm to be faithful, he said, I must be strong. If that is true, then I must gather all courage, defeat the enemies of my soul, and awaken that which has lain dormant within me. I must fear no sacrifice, no darkness, no death. I must believe in the universe, and in myself. I have learned to hope, but for the sake of all eternity I must learn to be faithful...

Drinwor Fang
Emperor of the Sky,
Son and Savior of the Stars, Wielder of the Sunsword Surassis,
Destined Last Hope of the Universe

The universe shuddered as Phate's galaxy plunged deeper into the massive cluster of black holes. More suns were snuffed, more worlds were crushed, and a trillion more lives slipped beneath the surface of the eternal sea of nothingness. Now all destinies were imperiled, and darkness was threatening to endure for all time. As long foreseen, as long foretold, the Emperor of everyone's fears, Nenockra Rool, was returning.

But all hope was not lost.

Not yet...

Although Phate itself had long suffered, and the might of its civilizations had all but disappeared into the cadaverous dust of history, it was this world's inhabitants who would fly high the standards of light, and stand fast against the dark tides of eternity.

And now it was time.

Time for the ultimate battle to save the universe to commence.

Time for the fate of this story to unfold.

And by the grace of the heavens, I hope to see *you*, my courageous reader, safely on the other side…

Once a haven for those who were lost, the resplendent sky elven palace of Vren Adiri now flew as a bastion for those who would fight. Its cloudwall dispersed to but wispy rings, it hovered in plain view over Ulith Urn like a king come home to find his country overrun with evil—an evil Vren Adiri would not tolerate. A thousand spirit elf sorcerers stood upon the terraces of its many towers, their voices lifted in song, their fingers flickering with white flames. The dragon swarm parted before them, and they threw their fires into the heaving head of the Devil's Wind. A tremendous explosion ensued. The dying damned cried out…

…then a million infuriated roars followed.

So, there would be a fight to dominate Phate, after all!

Evil turned its vile eye to Vren Adiri.

Eager to terrorize the attacking palace, hordes of demons clawed their way to the top of the Cliffs of Moaning Wishes and leaped out of the Devil's Wind. As they amassed around the unholy grounds of Ulith Urn, they spewed and spit thousands of streams of black fire up towards Vren Adiri. Explosions rocked the palace's walls, sheets of flame consumed the towers, and the horrific whine of vaporizing souls mingled with the ecstatic cheering of unholy beasts.

Watching from a few miles away, the companions flinched upon viewing the spread of dark fire about the graceful walls of the palace that had so welcomingly harbored them.

"Elf-towers destroyed in one volley!" Morigos cried out.

"No," Morning's Hope returned, "those walls will not so easily fall."

"We must join the fight!" the dark elf urged.

"No!" the dragon shot back. "Not yet! We wait for the one! Others will deal with the demon rabble."

"Rabble?" Morigos laughed. "You call the might of the Dark Forever rabble? Apparently, I am not the most insane among us! Your fortress is destroyed! We fight alone!" But just as his words were sputtering from his mouth, the demons' fire fell away and, to Morigos' surprise, Vren Adiri's towers were still intact. Though heavily damaged and marred with black burns, the palace flew boldly forward. "Well strike me blind as well as deaf! I'd eat my words if they weren't so foul!"

"We will never be alone," Morning's Hope swore, her glorious eye glistening with sparkles of hope.

And then, as if to punctuate her point, a vast number of huge, slanting shafts of white light came down from the heavens and illuminated the entire western edge of the continent. Sorcerous storms were dissipated within those heavenly beams, and the demons climbing over the cliffs gave pause. The shafts of light thickened, brightened...then faded away. Ah, but thousands of sky elf palaces remained in their places, though. Countless thousands. All with colossal towers of scintillating white, and hosts of spirit elf sorcerers anxious to unleash holy fires into that blasphemous demonstorm! The palaces drifted down, lined up and hovered over the cliffs' ledge like the great pillars that guarded the gates to the realm of the Seven Glories itself.

"Your palace has multiplied!" Morigos noted.

"They're here to protect the Son and Savior of the Stars," Morning's Hope said. "*They* are the foundation for the might of Phate! The sky elf kingdoms were abandoned but *not* lost. The spirit elves have taken control!"

"Now do we fight?" Morigos pressed.

"No!"

The dark elf sighed. "You really like to make us wait!"

Drinwor stared forward in silence, unable to believe what he perceived. It was dizzying. The sight of a single sky elf palace was exhilarating enough, but thousands of them? With Morning's Hope still holding position miles away from the fray, he watched the ensuing battle with silent awe, wondering if Areshria was out there...

The five hundred thousand volcanic spirit dragons divided into relatively even-numbered flights and took formation between the palaces, the eldest souls among them cawing to the spirit elf sorcerers for instruction. The sorcerers responded to the dragons in their own draconic tongues, commanding them to maintain their flanking positions until called upon. Then the spirit elves conferred with one another. Their combined wisdom, garnered over ages untold, quickly arrived at a single, simple determination.

The time for assault was at hand.

The elves murmured.

Their murmurs conjoined into a single song.

And before long this song crescendoed into the loudest sorcerous chorus Phatians had ever heard. A million fingers brightened with sorcery and, in a sudden burst, one hundred thousand streams of sparkling energy shot out in front of the palaces. The streams converged and spread out into a great sheet of multicolored flames that formed the surface of a blazing airborne sea. Oh, it was a brilliant beauty, I tell you! Fleets of mystical fire galleons materialized atop this sea and sailed forward, pitching fireballs from catapults of flame. The whole conjuration surged down into the Devil's Wind, ships ramming and waves crashing. A ten-mile wide line of explosions, which burned hotter than any fires the demons had ever danced in, made the edge of the cliffs light up like the surface of a sun. The advancing demons were blown back into the Devil's Wind as a burning shower of charred and bloody limbs!

The demons' advance was stalled...but only for a moment. The next wave instantly lashed back with savagery.

Their hearts lit with hate, their mouths lit with fire, multitudes of demons sprang out of the crimson vapor, poured over the cliffs, and scampered onto the Wicked Plains. The wizard lords among them raised their arms and a new host of sorcerous storms was conjured in the skies above them—tendrils of shadowy mist whipped around the palaces' towers. Massive flocks of flying fiends burst out of these diabolical clouds and flew screaming into battle.

Dear god, the number of demons was staggering!

Each palace was attacked by *tens of thousands*.

With the spirit elves blinded by the spectral storms, multitudes of sorcerers were sliced to pieces before their brethren could even command the flanking dragons to fly in to protect them. When the dragons did come, they flew heedlessly into the vile clouds. Cackling demons slammed into them, ripped off their wings, then splattered their molten husks against the palaces' walls. Specter demons infiltrated them through their ears and skewered their ethereal organs. Larger demons swallowed smaller dragons whole.

And then the battle became even more desperate, for the demons' wizard lords targeted the palaces with precision lightning strikes. Electrified forks of emerald energy erupted from the spectral storms, exploding huge sections of wall. Entire towers crumbled to the ground. Spires blew apart. Some palaces were knocked from their positions and collided into each other.

It was dreadful. A massacre was close at hand!

Ah, but not so fast, for then Vren Adiri's strongest souls refocused their mystical minds and adjusted their strategy. Telepathic commands were henceforth sent into the gloomy winds. The besieged dragons were ordered to flee the storms and reorganize above the palaces. The dragons immediately obeyed, dashing straight up into clearer skies while the palaces floated forward out of the clouds. With the flying demons jeering at them for fleeing, the spirit elves turned about, thrust their glowing arms into the sky and fired thousands of sparking energy bolts into the centers of the storms.

The attack was formidable.

Jeers turned into screams as the demonic clouds burst into flames. The lightning flared out of control and hordes of demons were set ablaze. Then, following the instructions of the spirit elves, all the volcanic dragons simultaneously turned their heads down and breathed molten fire, scorching the already burning storms. The spectral clouds blew completely apart, and demons already dead exploded.

The storms were utterly vaporized.

More commands came from the spirit elf sorcerers. Over two hundred thousand fiery dragons of light dove down like a great squall of molten winds, come to blast the demons that were fast spreading across the Wicked Plains. The dragons all breathed simultaneously again and, in minutes, tens of square miles of plateau were set on fire.

The demons reveled in it.

Although direct contact with the dragons' flames could destroy them, the supplemental fires spreading across the Wicked Plains hadn't quite that strength. Actually, these fires invigorated them. Laughing demons leaped up, snagged dragons who had dared fly too low, and dragged them down into their deadly midst. Burning carcasses falling out of the sky brought yet more dragons down, and melee combat ensued. It was a bloody, snarling, growling, confusing, desperate fight! Claws sliced through heads. Eyes were stabbed with talons. Fires burned limbs and limbs were used to beat out the fires. Demons fought even after their heads were severed from their bodies.

The cries were horrifying...

...but nothing could match the singular sound of a soul being lost.

When a volcanic dragon died, its lava skin would pour down from around its disintegrating spirit, and the pitiable moan of a soul condemned to nothingness would echo across eternity...

Since it had all began, the companions suffered those awful cries over and over again.

Morning's Hope was devastated.

For every dragon destroyed, another piece of her heart was lost, and for every dying soul she shed a tear (though she sorcerously hid those tears).

She glided closer to the battle, but still kept plenty of distance, holding the companions well over a mile away from the sea, where the fringes of the Devil's Wind billowed. It still wasn't exactly a safe place to be, for when the plains beneath them erupted with the dragons' flames, she was forced to guide the little group another thousand feet into the air.

As the companions watched, the battle continued to intensify. A hundred thousand more demons sprang out of the red vapor, and fire and lightning and storms and spells consumed the western edge of the Wicked Plains in a thunderous, violent wall of flashing death! Morigos repeatedly suggested they get it over with, join the fight, and perish in a hail of black fire, but Morning's Hope repeatedly denied him, insisting they still had to wait.

So wait they did, just hovering in the sky, watching it all unfold.

Morning's Hope turned her head slightly aside, said, "Are you still with me?" to her Emperor.

"Oh, I'm with you!" Drinwor returned, his voice trembling with anticipation.

The sight and sounds of battle had the dusk elf's heart pounding. He didn't breathe so much as he seethed. He was anxious with fear, but that fear was suppressed beneath an unbelievably strong urge to fight! What was this? Never before had he felt such an intense desire to engage in combat. No doubt it was to some degree inspired by all the anger he harbored over his father's death coming to the surface, but mostly, it was the sword. He could sense Surassis urging him, almost daring him to rise up and unleash its holy blade. He whispered: "Yes, it is time…time for me to harness the powers that have for so long lain dormant within me; time for me to vent my frustration and rage; time for me to strike these murderous demons from the world!"

The urge became too much to ignore. Too much…

He gave in.

He reached into his leg pouch, slowly withdrew the sword, and said, "I must be ready to fight!"

Morning's Hope turned her head full about. "Drinwor, what are you doing?"

Drinwor freed himself from the saddle-throne, stood up straight, and held his face high. "Darkness, your sufferance shall be my salvation!" he yelled.

And then something happened that shocked Morning's Hope.

Her dusk elf Emperor suddenly appeared to age.

The smooth beauty of Drinwor's face crinkled, and his jaw stiffened and squared with a seasoned warrior's resolve. His silver hair lengthened and lightened, his smoky skin darkened, and the luster of his midnight blue eyes disappeared. For a moment they emptied to soulless black, then a reflective sheen passed over his sockets and orbs of silver emerged. Now his eyes were as shining steel, their wide and distant stare all encompassing.

Morning's Hope stretched her head closer to him. "Drinwor, by the Seven Glories...your eyes..."

Drinwor drew up Surassis and by thought alone commanded its ten foot blade of condensed white fire to surge forth and claim prominence in the dark turmoil of the chaotic sky!

The little band of companions was illuminated.

"It would seem our little Emperor likes his new toy," Morigos posed.

"Are you all right?" Morning's Hope asked the dusk elf, her eye wide with worry.

Drinwor did not answer.

He was looking beyond her by looking *through* her. All he saw, all he heard, was the battle. Grimacing, he defiantly thrust Surassis higher into the air, and it felt as if he was casting his own spirit into the sky. Such strength he felt, such confidence! Now he was invigorated beyond reckoning, himself a sword from which light would carve its signature upon the scrolls of darkness! He stepped forward, his voice loud and rumbling as words erupted from between his lips. "Come, Morning's Hope, let us rid the universe of all murderers! Forth now! Forth with fate! Forth with the sword of my father!"

"Yes!" Morigos concurred, "forward into battle!" He spurred Arcynn Ahnna Jha on. The starlit unicorn reared in midair, her wings spreading, her six legs ready to gallop across the clouds. She leaned forward—

"NOT YET!" Morning's Hope screamed. She whipped her head around to face the dark elf. "I won't tell you again, Morigos! We wait for the coming of Nenockra Rool!"

The unicorn stayed her advance. Morigos, himself bursting with adrenaline, was about to protest when another cry came from close by.

"No! Do not wield the sword."

Everyone looked up.

Diving down through the clouds came a large white creature, its sky blue eyes shot with what Drinwor thought were streaks of fire, its snowy feathers tainted with stains of black blood. It cried out again, "Do not wield the sword!" and its labored, hoarse voice was suddenly recognizable.

"Vu Verian!" the companions all shouted in unison.

Drinwor was shocked, gladdened, and a bit dubious all at once. "Where have you been?" he asked.

The Great White Owl flew down in front of them, looking as if he'd already fought the battle for the fates. "I come from Vren Adiri, and I tell you, the sunsword will not stay the tides of eternity! It has no power against such a mighty force!" He thrust a wingtip toward the Devil's Wind. "*That* is undefeatable! We must preserve the sword!"

Drinwor was confused. His surging adrenaline partially quelled, he lowered Surassis, but did not extinguish the blade.

Morning's Hope said, "Preserve the sword? For what?"

"We must safeguard it against this horde," Vu Verian proclaimed, "hide it until such time as it can be used against Nenockra Rool."

"That time is fast approaching!" Morning's Hope returned.

Vu Verian shook his head. "We'll never get close to the Devil King. The demons will overrun us. Come, let us take Surassis to Areshria. I know a chamber where we can hide it."

Drinwor's eyes widened. "Is Areshria out there? I don't see it."

"It's out there," Vu Verian affirmed.

Morning's Hope was livid. "No!"

"No? Areshria isn't out there?" Morigos chimed in.

Morning's Hope went from livid to enraged. Again she swung her head to face the dark elf. "Morigos! Stop it!" Then she shot her look back to Vu Verian. "And no, we will *not* hide the sword, or preserve it, or whatever it is you're suggesting! Now is the time for the Son and Savior of the Stars to vanquish all evil from the universe!" She motioned to Drinwor, his dark figure blurred behind the radiance of the sword's blazing blade.

"You've always known," Vu Verian calmly stated, "The boy cannot stave off the forces of the Dark Forever."

Drinwor's silver eyes narrowed as he whispered, "I'm a boy no longer…"

Morning's Hope was stunned. "Cannot…? Vu Verian, what madness afflicts you?"

"The sky elf spirits have contaminated him!" Morigos shouted. "He was never the same since the confrontation with his deceased brethren!"

Vu Verian leered at the dark elf, then angled toward the starlit unicorn, screaming, "Traitorous dark elf fiend! I'll spread your atoms into the demonstorm. I'll see your spirit sucked to its core!"

Morigos loosed an irritated sigh. "Oh, bother, not this again."

Morning's Hope flew between the ancient enemies, her huge bulk blocking any straight line of fire. "Fools! Enough! There will be no more discussion. I will—"

Her voice was cut off by a sound like a thousand avalanches set off at once, a tremendous crackling boom that easily drowned out the cacophony of battle. It painfully pierced their ears, and Drinwor thought perhaps the world was splitting apart.

I hesitate to scribe this, but…he was nearly correct.

Many miles out to sea, in the center of the Devil's Wind, an already massive rift was tearing even wider across the sky. It stretched so long it looked as if a new horizon had been suspended above the old one. The legions of the Dark Forever went silent. Struck with a forced penitence, they paused their attack. Everything paused, as a matter of fact, and the forces of both light and darkness watched as a clawed foot the size of a small continent stepped through the rift and stomped into the sea. It splashed down so heavily, the ensuing tsunamis doused the clouds. It was so huge, the sea couldn't even cover the top of its toes after it settled. Drinwor feared the whole world might crumble beneath the weight of that foot.

"It is the devil of all devils," Vu Verian cried, "the doom of us all, the end of the universe!"

"Nenockra Rool," Morigos whispered, his head bowing, "it is he."

"*Now* we can attack!" Morning's Hope shouted over the tumult of the resurgent battle. "Drinwor, are you with me?"

"Let us fly!" the dusk elf replied, his shining eyes doing nothing to disguise the intensity behind them. The saddle-throne disappeared. He began pacing across his dragon's broad back, waving

Surassis around expectantly, readying to fight. The sight of Nenockra Rool had at first astounded him, but now it filled him with purpose—purpose fueled by an immortal energy.

Finally, his destiny had arrived!

Morning's Hope looked to Vu Verian and spread her wings wide as if to remind the sky elf of her superiority. She coldly said, "I don't know what madness has overcome you, but either fly with us as a servant of the stars, or fly away. I will say this only once: do *not* challenge me, or I swear by the Fallen Angel..." She let out an exasperated huff, choosing not to finish the statement. She instead closed with: "Do *not* interfere with the doings of the savior or his servants. It is your choice."

"Don't trust him!" Morigos warned. "Don't!"

Vu Verian gave the dark elf mage a sinister little scowl, then looked away, his eyes darting here and there as he considered the dragon's words.

Morning's Hope said to Morigos, "My instincts tell me that you may very well be right, but my heart and a thousand years of loyalty to the sun cannot turn him aside." Then she swung her head back to Vu Verian, her eye a well of brightening purpose. She spoke softly now, pleading, "We need your strength, my ancient friend, now more than ever."

A moment passed, and then the white owl whispered, "It is yours."

Morning's Hope nodded.

Morigos cackled, slapped his knee. "Then may doom find us all!"

And with that, Morning's Hope led the companions forward, careful to fly high over the fighting and fires raging across the Wicked Plains.

As they soared toward the palaces, a large group of volcanic spirit dragons broke from the melee to meet them. When the molten beasts approached, they called to Morning's Hope. She answered and, after a brief exchange, the dragons moved to surround the companions in a wide triangular phalanx. A smaller yet similarly organized force took point in front of the rest, and the entire group ascended.

"Guardians!" Morigos observed. "Good!"

"*My servants,*" Drinwor murmured as he viewed the volcanic dragons from closer than ever before. He thought them glorious. Their eyes were similar to his, sockets full of silvery-white spirit-fire. They were large and sleek, commanding all the awe and presence of a greater dragon. Their streaming coats of sparking lava gave off a hot orange aura as they flowed around their souls. Though different than Morning's Hope, these dragons didn't seem so out of place among her. Drinwor took some comfort that these beasts had come to serve them…to serve *him*.

And it was a good thing that they had.

Before the group reached the sky elf palaces, a trio of specter demons disguised as storm clouds swept up in front of them. Immediately recognizing them for what they were, the six volcanic spirit dragons in the lead broke formation and dashed forward, spitting molten fire. The barrages slammed into the clouds, igniting them, and the demons shrieked in pain. The dragons, intent on finishing off the vile creatures, extended their talons and continued rushing in. The demons were ready for them. Claws unfurled out of their venomous vapor, and the dragons flew right into their grasp. Necks were squeezed and slashed. Lava erupted from lacerated throats. Soon all the combatants were as one wriggling mass of fire and shadow! The tumbling tumult fell down through the sky, struck the surface of a molten river, and exploded. Nothing was left but the agonizing echo of lost souls, whimpering as they disappeared into nothingness.

Morning's Hope turned to Vu Verian. "Six souls lost."

Vu Verian viewed her with frightful eyes.

"*Six more souls,*" she emphasized.

And then came another earsplitting roar.

Everyone cringed, and Morigos said, "Ah! Deafness take me already so I no longer have to hear the racket of the world!"

This time it was the collective sound of a million demons stabbing the sky with screams as they poured over the cliffs to join the melee on the Wicked Plains. More sorcerous storms were conjured, and coils of black cloud snaked around the sky elf towers to come rushing down toward the companions. The guardian dragons cawed, then shot forward, leading the companions below the storms but into the midst of titanic battle!

Soular Centurion 7 flew beneath the dimensions.

It was a strange place, like one universe hiding in the shadows of another. Stars flickered darkly and worlds were but great translucent spheres floating away from black suns. Purple streams of liquid fire wound through supernova-like clouds, and alien apparitions drifted aimlessly about. But none of this garnered the centurion's attention, for he was searching for the necromancer.

Syndreck shouldn't be difficult to spot, he mused. There should be a telltale tether of magic somewhere close by, because the necromancer had to keep some ties to Phate to maintain control over his evil doings.

Soular Centurion 7 didn't have to search long before he found a sparkling grey line leading into a dying solar system. The line wove through a score of lifeless planets, then disappeared into the shadows of a phantom moon. The centurion slipped around the moon's far side…and found Syndreck's skeletal specter hovering in the darkness near the bottom of a tremendous crater.

-TARGET REACQUIRED. INITIATE APPROACH PATTERN NOVIUSS 6-

The centurion came up quietly, stealthily…

…and then with all speed shot forward, unleashed his sword, and slashed down at his enemy's gleaming skull!

Syndreck flew aside, avoiding the strike, screaming, "Persistent pest!" Then he spun around and vomited fire.

The centurion hacked it away.

"Vile betrayer of the Dark Forever!" Syndreck yelled as he blasted into the void. "What delusion of righteousness motivates you?"

Still having no use for words in this story, the centurion didn't respond. Only the whirring of his mechanical movements and the monk-like chanting of his sword sounded in this lonely realm. For a moment he watched Syndreck fly away, then he gave chase.

And lo the chase was fast!

Flying like a couple of wild comets, the two soon accelerated to near light speed, flying deeper into the depths beneath the dimensions, entering levels of existence that existence itself had forgotten. They saw things no one had seen in a billion years: the dissolving ghosts of forsaken Gods begging for help they knew would never come; lost starships the size of solar systems spinning out of control, their immortal captains slumped and defeated in their metal thrones; galaxy-sized cemeteries of souls stretching into untold distances, their ghosts waiting for the reopening of the Seven Glories. They raced through all of these things, chasing to the very ends of this hidden universe.

And always Soular Centurion 7 was right on his target's tail.

"Come! Come!" Syndreck beckoned, his skeletal fingers constantly flinging fire over his shoulder.

Again and again the Sword of Molecular Destruction swallowed the flames.

"You cannot forestall the coming of the Dark Forever!" Syndreck yelled. "Your soul will burn in the Lakes of Liquid Hate!"

But nothing the necromancer could say slowed his opponent. Soular Centurion 7 was closing.

Drinwor Fang was surrounded by sky elf palaces on fire. Such sights were nearly beyond his ability to believe, but I swear, they happened as I describe. Oh, dear Drinwor! Demons of every conceivable size and shape climbed the towers and slashed spirit elves into soulless shreds. They overtook the palaces and rode them to explosive deaths upon the Wicked Plains. Drinwor fought back crystal tears as he saw graceful towers topple over and plunge down into the Devil's Wind, where the Raging Sea swallowed them like great warships whose hulls had been rent by mighty cleaves. And as much as the sights raced Drinwor's heart, the sounds shivered his soul. Specter demons screeched and thunder storms bellowed as fireballs of every size, color, and consistency blasted everything. Claws sliced volcanic spirit dragons to slivers, and the wailing agony of dying souls was a continuous song amongst it all!

"Drinwor?" called Morning's Hope over the roar of battle.

Upon hearing his dragon's voice, Drinwor shook himself from staring at a disintegrating palace and shouted, "I'm still with you!"

"Good! Let's keep it that way!" Morning's Hope turned her head from side to side. "Morigos, Vu Verian! We fly for Nenockra Rool! Everyone, at all costs, stay close to me!"

Vu Verian said nothing, but Morigos yelled, "Suicidal dragon! The minions of Nenockra Rool have already found us! Look!"

Morning's Hope glanced to where the dark elf pointed. "I see them."

A legion of huge demons appeared through the crimson haze on the edge of the cliffs. They were glistening black and many-limbed, with eyes glowing red and long curved horns extending from atop their broad, flat heads. They climbed over the cliffs, sprinted up piles of burning bodies, then leaped into the air, wings sprouting from their backs. One and all they flew for the glorious glare of the Sunsword Surassis!

Dozens of volcanic dragons dove down to meet them, but it was no contest. The demons' giant claws tore through their wings and ripped their souls from their molten skin. The dragons' screams were horrific; the diabolical laughter of their murderers equally horrifying. The demons punched through the dissolving carcasses and headed straight for the companions.

"Begone vile creatures!" Morning's Hope shouted before she spit a concentrated beam of white fire into the center of the oncoming horde. Many demons burned and exploded, but her powerful burst couldn't slay them all. Those who survived engaged her head on. She shredded most with her foreclaws, but what remained landed on her back...

And met the Son and Savior of the Stars.

"Drinwor!" Morning's Hope yelled.

"**One Life, One Soul, One Sword!**" the dusk elf screamed from the very pits of his being. He raised the massive blade of Surassis high into the air and called out a challenge in a tongue he'd never before heard or uttered.

The demons answered, for here was the enemy of all hell! They surged forward, ready to tear him from the sky.

But oh, I tell you, Surassis might as well have been an extension of Drinwor's soul as he unleashed all the pent up frustrations of his life onto the attacking horde. He leaped across his dragon's back, spinning in midair, whipping the sword around with unimaginable speed. The Halo of the Gods appeared and a host of fireballs was slashed to sparks before the demons that cast them were sliced to fiery pieces. Those who survived Drinwor's initial onslaught rushed him, swinging and snapping as they came, but it was to no avail. Our little elf was much too fast. Drinwor dove forward, rolled beneath the striking pincers and claws, then came up swinging. Surassis swept out in a wide arc, came full around, and the demons were cut into burning halves.

But more demons flew in.

And more…and more…and more.

They came in endless bunches, attacking Drinwor from every angle, but always they were destroyed. The Son and Savior of the Stars dashed back and forth from the base of his dragon's neck to the spaded tip of her tail, running and somersaulting, hacking and swinging his blade with a speed and accuracy unknown to mortal warriors.

"My Lord," Morning's Hope called, "I cannot fight them off *and* balance you on my back!" Five demons flew at her face; she swept them away with a breath of lightning, their crackling bodies sent tumbling to the Wicked Plains.

"Fight them off!" Drinwor commanded. "You won't lose me!"

Guardian volcanic dragons dove in, blasting as many fiends away from Morning's Hope as they could. Morigos' sour singing continuously sounded from her flanks, and his staff's acidic green fire splattered demons with burning pain. "Come, dance with me!" he cried.

"Cover the Emperor!" Morning's Hope ordered the dark elf.

"Who will cover you?" he called back.

"I will!" Drinwor swore as he thrust his blade into the belly of a descending demon. He rolled aside and the beast glanced off his dragon's back and fell.

Arcynn Ahnna Jha flew over Drinwor and stayed with Morning's Hope as best she could, her starry hide barely managing to elude the deadly swipe of dirty claws.

"Where's that blasted sky elf of yours?" Morigos called down to Drinwor.

Drinwor had no idea. Where *was* Vu Verian? Between killing demons, the dusk elf shot glances across the sky. Eventually he spotted the Great White Owl left of their position, fighting amongst the few surviving guardian volcanic dragons. Vu Verian arced smoothly through the air, his blue flames slicing heads from the bodies of any demons foolish enough to approach him.

"I see him!" Drinwor shouted. "He's with us!"

And then, just as Drinwor looked away from the mystic, he heard Morigos scream, "Turn aside, turn aside! Doom from above!"

They all looked up.

Drinwor was mortified. "Morning's Hope!"

"We can't avoid it!" she shrieked.

Directly above them, a sky elf palace was exploding into massive shards. Huge sections of ruined tower, on fire and crumbling, came plummeting down. The ruins were too close and too big to avoid...

So the companions flew up through it.

"Watch out!" Morning's Hope called out as the palace's fragmented foundation fell atop them. She veered aside, followed the starlit unicorn through a large break in the stone, but couldn't avoid getting scraped by the flaming wreckage as it whisked past her. Laden with more wounds, she grunted, but continued to climb. Drinwor ducked, held Surassis protectively over his head. Vu Verian spun away left, disappearing into a haze of burning rubble. Arcynn Ahnna Jha wrenched hard to her right, Morigos cursing as they flew through a shower of fire and dust. There seemed to be no end to the destruction! Sections of burning stairs and shattered windows fell past. The remains of royal chambers stung them all with a rain of crystal shards. The companions continued dodging from side to side, desperately evading the debris.

"Stay with me!" Morning's Hope screamed.

"I'm trying to!" Drinwor returned, leaning his body this way and that. He watched in horror as the flight of volcanic dragons beside them was smashed beneath a tremendous wall and driven toward the ground. The palace's exploded spires fell by them. Demons clinging to the wreckage swiped at Morning's Hope on their way down. In a desperate move to avoid them, she banked left, then dove hard right.

That last maneuver took Drinwor by surprise.

He lost his footing and slid from her back.

"Morning's Hope!" he screamed, his one hand clinging to the sunsword, his other to the edge of her wing. His demonskin gloves slick with blood and sweat, his grip was weak. He was slipping, slipping…

Morning's Hope leveled and folded her wing to her body. Drinwor rolled onto her back, landed on his knees, his breath returning with a deep heave.

The translucent dragon winced. "I'm sorry, my Emperor…it was all I could do to avoid the wreckage."

"No need to apologize," he said, standing up, brushing himself off.

By now they'd flown clear of the falling ruins—all traces of the destroyed palace were gone. But most of the guardian dragons were gone, too, their molten husks lost to the crater-pocked plains far below, their souls lost to eternity.

Morigos, cackling as crazily as ever, flew up to Morning's Hope. "Some allies you have with these spirit elves! Throwing palaces at us!"

Morning's Hope ignored him, cried, "Come, to the Raging Sea we go!"

Arcynn Ahnna Jha retook her position over Morning's Hope. Vu Verian flanked them to their left, and the dozen surviving volcanic spirit dragons spread out around them as they flew over the Cliffs of Moaning Wishes and plunged into the swirling vapors of the Devil's Wind.

Nenockra Rool's second foot stomped into the sea, riling up even higher waves than the first. Then, with most of his body still stuck in the Dark Forever, he leaned down and peered into the universe he intended to tyrannize. A moon-sized eye filled a corner of the cloven sky and regarded the world with a hateful stare, its pupil gleaming with a fire blacker than any that had been thrown in the battle.

The Devil King found the little sea that splashed his toes rather annoying, for he hadn't expected his first steps in the primary universe to be planted in murky water. He looked to the sea and twitched his eye—a single little twitch—and the Raging Sea was overlaid with a shimmering coat of flickering energy.

The sea burned.

And then it disintegrated!

Just as the tidal waves from Nenockra Rool's first step were about to crash into the Cliffs of Moaning Wishes, they vanished. From horizon to horizon, from shore to shore, the entire sea disappeared in a sizzling flash, and millions of species were burned into extinction with the twitch of an eye.

Now the plains of the abyss were exposed.

Jagged rows of sedimentary rock crisscrossed into the distance. Oceanic trenches burrowed like canyons deep into the world. Hydrothermal vents sputtered the last of the sea's liquid like blood from the mouth of the dying, and whatever foliage was left folded to the seafloor. All that remained were the deep elf cities, which now stood as isolated oases on an otherwise dead world, their Dreadship fleets suddenly patrolling the sky. For reasons to be recounted in later tomes, the Devil King had spared the mysterious elves from his burning glare.

Satisfied with the sea's destruction, Nenockra Rool ducked through the rift and lifted his head into the free air of Phate. All the world seemed to gasp. Here was the seed of everyone's darkest dreams, a crimson-black behemoth so terrible, his every feature so wickedly shaped, it hurt the heart just to view him. He was a mountain range of muscle, a devil of stupendously tremendous size, with nothing but death residing in the blackened hollows of his cruelly angled eyes. He was so many miles tall that when he straightened, his horned head rose up through the storms clouds, pushed through the atmosphere, and lifted into space.

For a moment he just stood there, staring at the cowering stars. His look was so loathsome, it unleashed a torrent of hate that spread throughout the universe and froze the hearts of a trillion beings, slaying them wherever they stood.

Nenockra Rool was euphoric.

Here was eternity! *His* eternity! So many souls would he rule! So many beings would he subjugate! He would suck on the stars, chew on their worlds, and crush the moons between his fingers. He made to rise into space…

…but found he was not completely free.

His right arm was still elbow deep in the dimensional breach.

He tugged at it, but couldn't pull it all the way through, for in his hand was his weapon, the Hammer of Battered Souls. The hammer's head was so massive, it couldn't fit through the rent, the handle pushing on the sky from inside of his own realm. Well then. It would seem that Nenockra Rool was in a little quandary, eh? He would not leave the Dark Forever without this weapon—which also served as his scepter and staff—so he leaned down to deal with this bothersome issue.

When his head reappeared within the atmosphere, he was welcomed by a frenzy of dragons.

One hundred thousand volcanic dragons had broken from the battle above the Wicked Plains to converge upon the living embodiment of all of their fears. They screeched at the stars, some begging for help, some for mercy, and some cursing all who hadn't come to aid them. Angered and desperate, with a million demons on the tips of their tails, they swarmed the Devil King, a streaming mass of molten covered souls curling around his tremendous body and attacking.

At first, Nenockra Rool ignored them. They were tiny, inconsequential; they couldn't even scratch his stone-hard skin. And their fire was futile, actually pleasant when compared to the sensation of the Raging Sea between his toes. He was confident that his demon hordes would slay them while he tried to wrench his hammer free. But soon the dragons managed to annoy him enough for him to twist around and swat at them. The dragons parted, half of them diving away, half of them diving closer to his body.

Tens of thousands of them couldn't evade that kingdom-sized claw as it came down like the Continent Isle of Volcar itself falling from the sky.

The dragons were slashed apart, their ruptured lava skins raining down upon the now Disintegrated Sea. Simultaneously, each doomed soul let loose with their last scream, and all the world heard what would be forever remembered as the Dying Chorus of Light.

The Devil King went back to trying to work his hammer free, not yet noticing the little white fire of Surassis coming closer and closer…

"What's this?"

Syndreck the Brooding swore he heard the triumphant cry of the Dark Forever, swore he felt thudding steps tremble the underpinnings of the universe.

It could mean only one thing.

Nenockra Rool was free.

Syndreck's skeletal face stretched with a sinister smile. (For all the things that I've described, I actually find that little image to be one of the most disturbing!)

"Come, wicked warrior!" he taunted Soular Centurion 7 as they chased, "come and mix might with the mightiest!"

Now, as exhilarated as ever, Syndreck rallied all of his sorcerous strength and sped beyond supra-light speed, beyond the reach of the Sword of Molecular Destruction. His echoing laughter haunting the skies of a hundred decaying worlds, he flew faster and faster, until he managed to lose the centurion…and then he stopped.

His blasphemous form faded like the spirit stars about him, and he disappeared.

As the companions drew ever nearer, more and more of Nenockra Rool's nightmarish form became apparent through the choking haze of the Devil's Wind.

Drinwor grimaced.

In Nenockra Rool, he saw the death of his father, the death of dragons, the death of all who didn't deserve to die. Here was the purveyor of the destruction of his once beautiful world, the poisoner of his blessed skies.

Drinwor realized he *hated* Nenockra Rool.

Hated him even more than he hated Warloove. Hated him with such fervor, the desire to burn him from existence right then became an obsession. And he *knew* he could do it. All along the power had been inside of him. The sunsword was merely the wand through which his innate magic would flow.

"Morning's Hope!" he screamed, "take me to him! Take me now!"

"My Lord!" his dragon returned, "we must first defeat these demons!"

Drinwor looked down as a hundred demons shot up from the red vapors below as if they'd been launched from a cannon.

"No time for tea?" Morigos snickered.

"Evade!" Morning's Hope commanded as the demons poured in.

The companions did, but the last of their guardian volcanic spirit dragons didn't. Instead, the brave beasts dove down, tightening their positions to each other in an attempt to obstruct the attack upon the companions. Their sacrifice succeeded, for their bodies blocked a rising wall of greenish-black fire spewed from the demons' mouths. The huge wall engulfed the dragons and exploded. With their molten skin ruptured, the dragons' bluish souls appeared for a second, swirling up out of the fires before they went screaming into eternity and disappeared.

"Cursed devils!" Morning's Hope swore.

"Come to me!" Drinwor challenged the demons.

And came they did, though had they been wise, they would have stayed far away from the Emperor of the Sky. His sword wasn't a blade but a blinding blur to those fiends who found themselves skewered on the end of its fiery tip. He raced from wingtip to wingtip, jumping, diving, rolling, fighting the demons off his dragon as much as he fought to keep his balance. Surassis screamed its song and Drinwor screamed, too.

Morigos chanted like a mad witch as he threw endless streams of violent sorcery. "Demon heads aflame! Devil eyes afire! Of killing brainless fiends, I shall never tire! *Ahahaha!!*"

Vu Verian was silent as he shot his beams.

Morning's Hope breathed fire and maneuvered wildly through the great storm of demons and dragons and palaces and sorcery.

The fighting raged on and on...

It was getting late.

The unseeable sun flirted with the lost horizon, and nighttime waited like an assassin in the shadow of the world, anxious to bloody the sky with black. By now the chaotic battle and temperamental winds of a hundred clashing sorcerous storms had swirled much of the Devil's Wind apart, and the companions fought their way into a portion of the sky that was relatively clear. They were far out over the Disintegrated Sea now, closer than ever to Nenockra Rool.

"By the light," Morning's Hope uttered in a hushed tone, "look at that. He looked huge before, but..."

Drinwor was stunned with both hate and wonder.

Viewing the Devil King at this close range, it was apparent that he was even more immense than they'd all first believed. Had his arm not still been stuck in the breach, Drinwor imagined he would have been able to reach up into space with his other arm and crush Rong and the Four Apostles with one squeeze. Tens of thousands of volcanic spirit dragons surrounded him like a swarm of fiery gnats, and a million cavorting demon slaves piled at his feet. Fires burned all over him; all around him the sky was sliced open as if he himself had ravaged it with a great cleaver. A realm darker than black lay behind the tattered fabric of Phate's sky, and within shone a galaxy of angry red eyes.

"Most impressive from this close, wouldn't you say?" Morigos noted with a chortle. "All he has to do is take a step toward us, and it's all over. Perhaps I should call to him!"

Morning's Hope flashed him such a look!

Drinwor slimmed his silver eyes, said, "It's the most horrendous, hateful, horrifying abomination of the universe I have ever seen." Then he yelled, "Closer! Closer! Take me to him!" and pointed Surassis forward.

Morning's Hope looked worriedly about. "I'll bring you closer when I can, my Lord, but I fear we've been spotted again."

She was right.

Rushing in from the far side of the sea was a great horde of beasts. They flew as one maddened mass of limbs and claws and horns and weapons, cackling as they came to annihilate the little band of companions.

"It's over," Vu Verian solemnly said, his gaze fixed on the demons. "There must be thousands of them in that swarm."

"Come for us!" Drinwor challenged.

The demons heard his cry.

They recognized the white flame of Surassis now. Recognized it for the weapon of their most dangerous opponent: the silver-black warrior who struck them like a vengeful star, the dusk elf boy who was Emperor of the Sky.

They came for him.

The companions made ready to fight, and perhaps to die.

"My Emperor..." Morning's Hope said, "I'll protect you the best I'm able."

"Have no fear!" Drinwor responded. "Fly to meet them and I'll cut them from the sky!"

"Evade them!" a cowering Vu Verian suggested.

"Kill them!" a cackling Morigos yelled. He raised his staff, ready to send a barrage of green flames into the infernal fiends.

The great flight of demons angled down to spear the companions as if upon a lance of living fire. There were so many of them! They were so close now, the companions could feel the heat they exuded, could smell their foul breath and revolting spittle. The demons' clamor elevated into roaring laughter, and the insanity of wild, fiery death reflected in the eyes of each companion.

"No," Morning's Hope whispered, "Not like this…"

And then the dragons came.

Oh, thank the Seven Glories, they arrived just in time!

Spurred by the sight of Nenockra Rool killing their kin, urged by the instinct to protect the Son and Savior of the Stars, a hundred thousand volcanic spirit dragons had massed together and dove over the Cliffs of Moaning Wishes, leaving the Wicked Plains to burn unabatedly. Now they came in with all the force of a miles-wide, fire-breathing battering ram, blasting right over the companions' heads and slamming into the diving demons!

The demons were instantly annihilated.

Molten fire burned them to cinders, and gleaming claws shredded them apart. Not a single one survived, and their remains settled down in the Disintegrated Sea.

The companions, though doused with demon parts, were saved.

They hovered in the air, quivering with relief as the great tide of dragons passed overhead. Drinwor and Morigos cheered. Vu Verian bowed his head. Morning's Hope whispered, "Thank you."

It was a last, great push to the Devil King by all those who were left. The remaining sky elf palaces, damaged and on fire, with demons clinging to their walls, came in behind the dragons. Spirit elf sorcerers could be heard, either singing sorcery or screaming in their death throes. Vren Adiri, heavily damaged and listing, flew before the rest, its sorcerers still flinging the strongest of flames. Commanded to protect their god and ruler, the legions of demons on the Wicked Plains turned around, leaped or flew over the cliffs, and came charging in behind it all.

"Drinwor!" a newly enlivened Morning's Hope roared, "we fly for the freedom of the stars, for the conquest of all that defeats hope! Ready yourself and your sword, and strike darkness in its heart!"

"One Life! One Soul! One Sword!" Drinwor cried.

"One insane dusk elf!" Morigos added.

And then they flew to join the enormous flight of dragons.

Syndreck the Brooding was gone.

Accelerating away at such an astonishing speed, he'd vanished from Soular Centurion 7's scopes. The tether of greyish magic faded, and all traces of the necromancer disappeared.

The centurion stopped.

And then the centurion calculated.

He knew Syndreck couldn't abandon Phate for too long, for the necromancer would risk losing control of the dimensional rifts that now allowed the Dark Forever access into the primary universe.

Yes, there was only one place for Syndreck to go to.

–SET COORDINATES FOR ULITH URN, WESTERN EDGE OF VOLCAR–

Soular Centurion 7 phased out of solidity...

Moments later, the galactic warrior materialized on a floor of crumbling flagstone that was suspended hundreds of feet above the ground. A tower of lightning surrounded him, and a large, disgusting pot of gurgling filth sat on the platform next to him.

–THE CAULDRON OF CARCASS CONTROL–

Good. He was back on Phate, in the precise spot where he'd been when he left.

But there was one problem.

Syndreck the Brooding wasn't there.

That was impossible—he *had* to be there...somewhere.

Soular Centurion 7 looked around, scanning. There was nothing. He turned, then leaned over the cauldron, half expecting the necromancer to jump out of it.

That wasn't quite right.

Syndreck suddenly materialized, hovering in the air behind him. With a sorcerously strengthened pair of bony arms, the necromancer grabbed the back of the centurion's head and shoved it into the boiling pot.

"Die! Die! In the name of the Dark Forever, Die!" Syndreck screamed with joyous insanity. "Imbibe the brew of the demons!"

The bubbling froth of the necromancer's cauldron was something of a scalding dimension in itself, haunted by hateful spirits who tore and slashed at the galactic warrior with spectral claws. The heat was intense, hotter than a sun's, the attacks surprisingly fierce. The circuits in the centurion's supra-steel helm sparked, and his motor control functions failed. For a moment, he was stuck in place, with fiery undead clawing at his head.

It was a strange feeling, this helplessness.

※—◖◗—◖✖◗—◖◗—※

Fighting continued raging everywhere.

Dragons burned demons, demons disintegrated dragons, and every second a thousand deaths occurred. The dying shrieks of lost souls filled the air like frightening thunder, the scent of blood and smoke weighed heavily on the winds, and the sky beyond the battle further darkened as the dying sun sat itself upon the shelf of the lost horizon.

The coming of night filled the companions with dread.

But nothing was so dreadful as Nenockra Rool.

Specter demons disguised as storms encircled him like rings around a planet, defending his flanks with lightning. Sky elf palaces orbited his torso and each of his legs, their surviving sorcerers unleashing whatever spells they could before their towers plunged down and exploded on the ragged rocks that made up the bed of the Disintegrated Sea.

The demons who fell dead from the sky got eaten by the demons lingering between the Devil King's toes and, all around, the wreckage and bones piled up into mountains themselves.

But to the companion's surprise, Nenockra Rool was ignoring the battle.

The ungodly king of evil was leaned over, his arm still buried in the breach he'd come from. Drinwor thought it looked as if he was pulling on something from the other side.

"What is he doing?" Morigos yelled over the tumult.

"I don't know," Morning's Hope said. And then she was distracted, having to blast a dozen demons from the sky. Morigos and Vu Verian flew to assist her; green fire flew from the mage's staff, blue beams from the owl's eyes.

Drinwor couldn't take his gaze from Nenockra Rool.

Every ounce of his being was begging to discharge his full strength through the sunsword. So much energy and adrenaline coursed through him, it was maddening! If his spirit had been a sun he thought it would have right then gone supernova. He pointed Surassis at the Devil King, wishing him to die.

Distracted by a disturbing sensation, the unholy ruler of darkness turned his great head, gazed through the madness of battle…and saw the small but intense white flame of Surassis.

He did not like this.

His eye twitched.

Drinwor screamed.

Morning's Hope shot her head around, just in time to see a thin veneer of flickering orange energy wrap itself around her Emperor.

Morning's Hope was confounded. "What manner of magic is this?"

Vu Verian flew up beside her. "It's the Lord of the Dark Forever, he's seen us!"

"Light us *all* on fire, he will!" Morigos bellowed.

The mystic owl called out, "Drinwor, stand down!" He pointed a wingtip toward the sunsword. "Let go of Surassis, let its light diffuse!"

"No!" Morning's Hope screamed, "he would be consumed!"

"He *is* being consumed!" Vu Verian shot back.

"Be silent!" The Greater Translucent Dragon thrust her wings out threateningly, growling, "I warned you not to interfere with the savior or his servants! Be silent or begone!"

Vu Verian shook his head and moved away from her.

Morigos somehow managed not to comment.

Morning's Hope looked back to Drinwor, pleading, "Oh, my Emperor, say something!"

All Drinwor could do was scream.

His body felt as if it had been submerged in lava, and the slightest movement compounded the pain. He was burning…burning… *"It is unbearable!"*

But just when he thought he would melt into another smear on his dragon's wound infested back, a rush of silver fire coursed down from the hilt of Surassis, streamed across his limbs, and stifled the orange energy. The scorching effects of the Devil's King glare subsided, and the agony went away.

Nenockra Rool was mystified.

How could this being not burn?

"Yes! Fight him!" Morning's Hope urged as she rose through the demonstorm, climbing closer and closer to the Devil King's head.

Drinwor was vaguely aware of her words. His attention was focused on the silver fire, which had enwrapped his entire body and was now seeping into his skin. It wasn't painful in any way, but it *was* disconcerting…

He looked up to Morning's Hope. "What is this?"

"Surassis," she uttered with reverence, "it protects you!"

"It's doing more than that!" Drinwor exclaimed as the cool fire infiltrated his organs and entwined his heart. It felt as if another spirit was taking residence next to his own. In essence, that was true. Surassis was merging the three elements together: the One Life, the One Soul, and the sword itself.

Suddenly, Sillithian Synnstrike flashed, and Drinwor flashed, too. And when both glares subsided, Drinwor appeared to have turned into a being composed entirely of the silver flames. His eyes were visible as brightly glowing ovals of white, and his demonskin's sigils, now inscribed with multicolored flames themselves, hovered a short distance in front of his chest. His hair hung from his head like sparking bristles, and his fingers seemed melded into the handle of his sunfire sword.

"The boy is exploding!" Morigos yelled.

"It is the emergence of the Son and Savior of the Stars!" Morning's Hope proclaimed. Then she slapped her wings and dared to fly yet closer to Nenockra Rool, whose head now filled all their view. "Do it, Drinwor!" she called out, "release the power of the sword!"

Drinwor heard her voice echoing as if from far faraway, and she appeared to be veiled with the same fire that immersed him. In fact, all the world seemed to be flickering with starry flames. But nothing was obscured; every outline was as sharp as could be. And everything seemed to be moving slowly—everything except Drinwor himself. It was as if time had allotted him a new space in-between its seconds, a space where he could freely roam. He strode forward and, with the energy of the sun surging through him, aimed Surassis at Nenockra Rool's leering face. The sword gushed with power…and begged him for yet *more* energy.

This was it.

The sword wanted his essence, his life force.

And now, just as that realization sunk in, Drinwor heard a strange little voice, like a whispering hiss coming from deep inside the sword. It said, *"You don't have the strength to destroy Nenockra Rool! Dare not defy him! Try and you'll die!"*

What in all the universe was this? It certainly wasn't the voice of Surassis! Or was it? No, no, it couldn't have been. This voice was chilling, ghastly, like the voice of a shadowy villain of a nightmare sprung free in his mind.

"Use the sword and die, Son of Herard! Use it and die!"

Drinwor's energy and determination dwindled. For a fleeting moment he wondered if the voice was Warloove's. But how was that possible? Whatever it was, it kept hissing at him, reminding him of his mortal fears, reminding him that underneath it all he was just a boy who was indeed afraid to die. He was confused, frightened. He shook his head, whispered, "I can't," to no one in particular, "I can't do it…"

"If you do you'll die!" the hissing voice reaffirmed.

Morning's Hope swung her head around. "Drinwor! Now!"

"Destroy him, boy!" Morigos screamed from aside, Arcynn Ahnna Jha whining with pain as claws scratched her white hide.

"Morning's Hope!" Drinwor screamed. "The sword...it isn't right!"

She couldn't hear him, for at that moment the Devil King released a bloodcurdling growl as he leaned forward and pushed his fiendish face down through the battle. Oh, what frightful thing! Sky elf palaces exploded against his cheeks. Thousands of demons and dragons perished between his tower-tall teeth. His jutting chin parted the sorcerous storm clouds and all had to beware of looking too deeply into his eyes. Yet closer and closer came his face...

"Now!" Drinwor's companions all screamed at once.

"You'll die, Son of Herard! You'll die!"

Tears of light exploded from Drinwor's silver-fire eyes. "Morning's Hope...I'm afraid!"

And then, as if she'd heard him, Morning's Hope screamed, "Drinwor, you're the savior of my soul, the savior of my kind! Release the energy of the sword and set our spirits free! Fear no fate, for I am with you for all time!" Then she looked forward and in defiance cast these words at Nenockra Rool: "Curse the Dark Forever! May the universe shine beneath the golden light of the Seven Glories for all eternity!"

And then, for but a fleeting moment, Drinwor closed his eyes and thought about the Hall of Voices. He recalled all of those galaxies shining through the back wall. He thought of those beings, of all their hopes and dreams; and he thought of his friends and father. He remembered his pledge to himself and to them—that when the time came, he would sacrifice for all.

He was Drinwor Fang, Son of Herard, Emperor of the Sky, Son and Savior of the Stars!

His courage may have faltered, but it had not failed.

He exhaled heavily, opened his eyes...

...and again heard Drekklor's voice...

"You'll die, Son of Herard! You'll die!"

Now he understood: Drakana, the One Soul, had been cursed, possessed by a demonic entity.

But it was a soul nonetheless, and the sword *still* had enough power.

"Then die I shall, fiend!" Drinwor shot back, his resolve returning, his innate strength and goodness overwhelming this hissing voice of fear. With both hands holding the sword high, he looked up to Surassis and said, "For blue skies, father."

And then he gave himself to the sword.

As his awareness drew inward, his chaotic surroundings seemed to disappear. Now his essence fled down a hallway of golden fire, and beyond that was an even greater light, a light like the one that greets dying eyes—brilliant, white, heavenly, and burning with flames that would endure beyond all time. It was the point of release, the place where the One Life and the One Soul would combine their essences with the One Sword and go blasting forth, releasing an explosion that had enough strength to annihilate all evil from the world! He flew down this hallway, going faster and faster. And then...

And then he saw the One Soul.

Drakana had all but malformed into Drekklor.

He rose up out of the golden fires right in front of the point of release, a ragged black wraith whose tendril-like limbs wavered as if they swam through some demonic sea. He spread out, blocking Drinwor's path, his very presence cursing the sanctity of the golden hallway.

"Come, boy," Drekklor screamed, *"come for me and find your death!"*

Drinwor screamed too, and accelerated, intent on smashing into this cursed thing and plunging them both into the realm of release beyond!

But then something distracted him...

His instincts warned him of a new presence, very close to him, and he felt threatened.

Right before he would have overtaken Drekklor, Drinwor withdrew his essence from the sword. The cursed soul and golden hallway fell away, and he blinked, his awareness returning to his physical surroundings. He was still on his dragon's back, and standing right before him, returned to his sky elven form, was Vu Verian.

"What...what are you doing?" Drinwor asked.

Vu Verian glanced at the darkening sky and flinched, for nighttime was nearly upon them. He looked back to Drinwor, held out a hand, and calmly said, "Give me the sword. I will do it."

Drinwor was speechless.

Morning's Hope curled her head around. "What's going on? Vu Verian! Do not interfere."

"Always a bother, this one!" Morigos sputtered as he circled above, his staff firing at any demons that approached.

Vu Verian ignored them, his stare fixed on the dusk elf Emperor.

Then the world grew darker.

The sun was slipping away...

The sky elf lurched forward, grimacing as the first strands of night pressed him toward cloudform. "Quickly, now," he said, "for soon I will not be able to aid you." A shadow passed over his features and he scowled.

Drinwor shook his head "no." He looked about, to the demons and storms and Nenockra Rool. "I can destroy all of this!" he exclaimed, his silver hair lifting in a spectral wind, his star-like eyes glowing as brightly as ever.

Vu Verian stepped yet closer to him, reaching out with a shaking hand. "Drinwor! I command you—Give me the sword!"

"No!" Drinwor yelled, "I can do this!"

"Death to you, Son of Herard!"

"No!" Drinwor screamed at both the hissing voice and Vu Verian.

Morning's Hope roared, "Leave him be!" Then she reached back and swatted at Vu Verian with an open foreclaw.

The sky elf sidestepped the strike, then strode boldly forward. "Damn you, *give it to me!*"

Drinwor recoiled.

"Morning's Hope!"

It was Morigos.

Morning's Hope looked forward...

...and right into the great eye of the Devil King. It was horrible, like gazing into the maw of a haunted black hole. The sunsword's radiance disappeared into it like the light of a swallowed star, and all that twinkled within was darkness. It was the eye of death, the eye of defeat, the promise of an infernal destiny! Beyond Phate, the cowering angels of the universe quivered with fear as the scourge of the Dark Forever stood on the edge of conquest!

Morning's Hope looked away from the eye, and in that moment, the sun finally plunged beneath the horizon.

A chorus of howls arose from the plains of Phate, the voices of the undead come to celebrate the birth of another night.

Vu Verian joined them.

He unleashed a primeval cry of anger, then stumbled closer to Drinwor, demanding, "Give me the sword!"

Nenockra Rool lifted his free arm and made to swat down and destroy all the light that blinded him.

May the Gods return, I tremble so, it is a struggle to write! Soular Centurion 7 had not survived billions of years by relying on one system. The Cauldron of Carcass Control's poisonous swill was damaging him, immobilizing him...but it did not have the power to destroy him. Now signals were transmitted all throughout the functioning cybernetic portions of his body, and his gold-flecked blood raced faster through his exterior veins. A battery of backup systems were charged up while most of his primaries were shut down, and his ghostly attributes grew in power.

He cooled.

–BYPASSING DAMAGED INTERNAL CIRCUITRY WITH CORPOREAL ESSENCE VAPOR–

His motor functions returned.

In one swift movement, his torso swiveled completely around and snapped straight up, yanking his head out of the gurgling liquid. The maneuver was so violent, Syndreck's skeletal hands were separated from his wrists, and the necromancer was thrown down right in front of the galactic warrior. With twitching bony fingers still gripping the back of his helm, Soular Centurion 7 lifted the Sword of Molecular Destruction high...

...and brought it slashing down.

"Wrecker of fate!" was all Syndreck the Brooding could manage before the sword cleaved his skull in half and sucked his soul into the black void of its blade!

–TARGET NEUTRALIZED–

Indeed, it had been done.

Syndreck the Brooding, master necromancer and wrecker of planes, had been defeated by the galactic guardian of the stars. Without a dark spirit to empower it, the remains of the necromancer's skeletal body crumbled to dust. The dust sifted through the cracks in the floor and blew away, disintegrated sometime later in the stray fires of a slain spirit sorcerer.

Syndreck's magic faded.

The vortex tower of lightning fizzled out, and all that was left of Ultih Urn exploded—the Cauldron of Carcass Control, the temples, the towers, and Syndreck's floor.

With nothing to stand on, Soular Centurion 7 fell hundreds of feet to the courtyard, and disappeared beneath tons of blasted rubble...

–ACTIVATE MOT...MOTARY...ZZRMPH...–

Syndreck's hold over the sky was gone.

All the cracks, rifts, rents, breaches, and tears let out a kind of moaning yawn, and began to seal themselves up from the ends.

The Devil's Wind was sucked back into the rifts like an atmosphere escaping into space, and everything above the Disintegrated Sea was engulfed in a hellish cyclone.

The sorcerous storms dispersed.

Demons and dragons were tossed wildly about.

Beasts smashed into the sides of the Devil King, then tumbled into the Dark Forever.

Some sky elf palaces managed to turn aside, float free of the rushing winds, while others were caught, their towers crushed as they were pulled into the closing rents, their spirit sorcerers screaming at the horrors of their fate.

Just as Nenockra Rool began to swat at the companions, his claw was stayed. The arm that had been struggling to free his weapon was yanked inward to the shoulder, and his great body toppled sideways toward the breach.

Morning's Hope was caught in a funnel of wind and struggled to keep righted. Arcynn Ahnna Jha was dragged out in front of her, Morigos cackling as he desperately hung onto the unicorn's neck.

Drinwor was unaffected by the winds.

He could hear all the chaos around him, but his attention was focused solely on Vu Verian, who was also unaffected by the whipping gusts. It was as if these two stood in a pocket of calm space that existed only atop the translucent dragon's back, while all else around them was a storming chaos.

"Stay away from me," Drinwor warned, slowly backing away, the sword held out to his side.

Vu Verian matched his steps, opened his mouth to reply, but instead grunted in pain.

Nighttime overtook him.

Having resisted the urge to go to cloudform, his slim, tall figure began to contort. His fingers curled wickedly inward and he leaned over, his knees buckling. Agonizing groans flew like grumbling shadow demons from the cavern of his throat, and he mumbled through them, "The night reaches out and torments me throughout the day! It demands the surrender of my soul and I am a slave to the fortresses of darkness!" Then he smeared a stream of black tears across his disfiguring face. Moaning with pain, he fell to all fours, a tortured servant of daylight now bereft of the life-giving sun!

"Go to cloudform!" Morning's Hope cried. She had all-the-while been craning her neck to observe Vu Verian's torment, but now had to swing her head forward just to keep herself balanced as tumbling demons and dragons bumped her sides.

"Slay him!" Morigos bellowed from afar. "Kill him before it's too late!"

And then Vu Verian stopped moaning.

His anguished cries abated.

He stood up, his silken white robes turning into swirling wisps of dark smoke. His eyes were black, flickering with yellow fires that reflected the anguish and hate that raged behind them. The deathly white flesh of his eerily child-like face pulled tight around a widening smile. And his lips parted to reveal the glint of newly sculpted fangs.

Drinwor could not believe his eyes.

He was shocked, mortified.

Vu Verian was Warloove!

WARLOOVE!

The newly awakened vampire laughed in glorious exaltation. Hands outstretched, he lunged forward with supernatural speed.

"THE SWORD IS MINE!"

Gasping, Drinwor swung Surassis wildly.

He was too slow.

Warloove stepped inside the sword's arc, grabbed the handle, and wrenched it from Drinwor's grasp. Then he struck out with the pommel, knocking the dusk elf off his feet.

Drinwor was stunned.

Warloove was ecstatic. After a thousand years of suffering, the Sunsword Surassis was his! A power like nothing he'd ever felt surged through his raving soul, and he hefted the sword as Drinwor had, with both hands thrusting it high into the air. The runes on the Gauntlets of Loathing Light blazed like storms of red fire, and Sillithian Synnstrike's golden form darkened to shadow. Then the white fire blade was snuffed from the inside, overtaken by a rising fountain of violent black flames that extended to nearly twice the original length.

Warloove screamed with unholy delight. "Victory! At last!" Now, with his dark dreams poised on the brink of realization, the voice of Darkis flew into his mind.

You've done it! Now bring it to me! Bring it to me!

Warloove pointed the sword at the cowering dusk elf and cried, "Who are you to deny *my* eternity!"

Morning's Hope looked back and growled, "No!" And again she swiped with her foreclaw, but this time with the intention to slash the abomination on her back to slivers.

She missed.

Warloove had already leaped high into the air, shouting "Freedom! Freedom in the freezing darkness of eternity! *Master, we are free!*"

Morning's Hope lashed out and snapped at him, but her head rammed into the side of a hardened black hide.

Geeter.

The Greater Demonic Dragon had snuck up beneath the companions and smacked the translucent aside. He caught Warloove on his back and shot forward.

"Damn you, demons!" Morning's Hope screamed. She tried to give chase, but the winds were too strong and she was unable to maneuver. She was helpless. Everyone was as they tumbled toward the closing breaches. Even the mighty Devil King couldn't fight the pull anymore. Nenockra Rool was leaned farther over and dragged headfirst back into the Dark Forever, a million demons falling in behind him before his colossal breach closed.

Arcynn Ahnna Jha, desperately trying to avoid a closing rent, spun over and spiraled aside, grazing the corner of the diminishing tear. She managed to elude it, but Morigos was unseated by her wild maneuver.

He yelled, "We are all slaves!" then was blasted unconscious by a bolt of energy that erupted from the breach's crackling rim. His limp body spinning wildly, the dark elf Mage of the Moom was pulled down into the Dark Forever.

Geeter sailed in after him, with a howling Warloove victoriously waving the black-flamed sunsword all the way.

Morning's Hope slammed her wings against the roaring winds, desperate to remain in the free skies of Phate. The rift that had taken Warloove and Morigos was now taking her. It jabbed her with jolts of energy, pulled her closer, closer inside. With demons and volcanic dragons continuing to bump her sides, she strained and strained, refusing to be pulled in.

She shook her head, said, "I…won't…go!"

Now the shrinking rift's space wasn't much bigger than she was. If she could just hold on for a few more seconds!

She managed to curl her head back and ask, "Is my Emperor still with me?"

Drinwor stood up. He was still unaffected by the winds, but his countenance had dimmed to normalness. The silver flames were gone. His armor was slick black, his eyes midnight blue. His appearance of increased age had left him, but he looked pale and drained. His expression was a mixture of shock, anger, and vacancy. He answered Morning's Hope rather absently, whispering, "I'm with you, my love." He felt so weak and empty. His immortally-charged energy and strength and resolve seemed to have vanished with the sword. What was left of him felt hollow and purposeless, like an old champion whose glory existed only in the memory of triumphs from years long gone.

He was the One Life, without the One Sword.

It was more than he could bear.

"Hold on!" Morning's Hope said, fighting the last great rush of winds.

"I have failed you, father," Drinwor uttered whilst grasping his sword charm.

"No!" Morning's Hope assured through her grunting, "you have succeeded! The universe is safe! We have won! Nenockra Rool has been cast back into the Dark Forever, and Phate and the galaxy are saved! There's still a chance for blue skies to blaze! Drinwor, my Emperor, my salvation, my soul, we have won, we have won!"

"But I am lost…" he whispered.

The breach was nearly sealed now; it narrowed like a shutting eye. Morning's Hope was so close to it, her snout broke through its plane. Drinwor stared down into its shadowy depths, muttering, "Surassis... My sword... My soul..."

And then he bolted.

He ran across his dragon's back, scampered up the long curve of her neck, and, with all of his strength and agility, he leaped headlong into the Dark Forever!

"**NO!**" Morning's Hope screamed before she dove in after him.

The rift sealed shut. All the rest of the cracks in the sky closed and disappeared. It was silent but for the faraway whine of demons who gathered into packs and disappeared into the less threatening night...

I sit here slouched and breathless in my chair, and I'd be lying if I said I shed no tears to write this: but for the sacrifice of our heroes, the Devil King Nenockra Rool could not ascend into the universe.

It was over.

The battered world of Phate would see another day.

Although Drinwor Fang had fallen with his dragon into the Dark Forever, and the Sunsword Surassis was lost, the universe would not on this night be enslaved. The black holes continued to pull at the stars, but the stars pulled back. For now, the oceans of echoing darkness were silenced. All across the galaxy, fathers and mothers continued to love their children, and over their heads blue skies continued to blaze. Billions of benevolent beings carried on as the Son and Savior of the Stars had, with hope, compassion, perseverance, and a little helping of humor mixed with a good measure of faith.

And when dawn's glorious glow crept over the Continent Isle of Volcar, a group of twinkling blue lights shone through the Zyrinthian Asteroid Belt.

Something long gone was returning, but was still far away...

The dying sun carried on.

Its time was coming.

But not on this day.

And from the bottom of my heart, I thank you, oh, triumphant reader, for accompanying me on this adventure, and giving me the courage and conviction to continue on to Volume II, and tell of our heroes' fate…

Perhaps we shall meet again…

EPILOGUE
ALIEN AWAITING

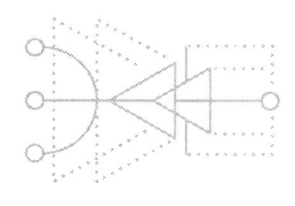

The rubble of Ulith Urn trembled as something silvery and gold lifted up through the cracked stones and destruction. Soular Centurion 7 stood, his dusty armor glinting on one shoulder, a single, lonely little gleam.

His vision was clouded. Oh, there was enough dust and fire to cause nearly anyone's eyes to blink and burn, but the galactic guardian's vision was simply malfunctioning. His head twitched, and a long-resonating 'beep' echoed across the devastated ruins and plains.

–OPTOMETRICAL REPAIR IN PROGRESS–

In moments, scintillating waves of red and blue passed before his ghostly eyes, looking like curtains unfurling to the floor. Soon he could see clearly, with only occasional flashes of lightning-like lines crossing his field of vision. No matter. For now, his sight was sufficiently repaired.

He looked about. The amount of death that lay before him was staggering. Millions of demons spread across the Wicked Plains. They were a field themselves, really, a plateau of claws and torsos and heads slit here and there with rivers of black blood that flowed through the Disintegrated Sea, dripped from falls as black and glistening as the obsidian rock they slathered. Fires raged, though not so angrily with nothing to fuel them and not much left to burn. Intertwining the myriad columns of smoke were the ghostly blue outlines of the towers of Ulith Urn, once dying now again dead. The sky was a stew of confused storms. Black winds enwrapped green gusts, grappling as if for air to breathe. And all the world seethed and quivered as if it swayed through a drunken stupor, for Phate itself was exhausted with yet another war beneath its belt.

Then a flicker came from above…

Soular Centurion 7 lifted his head.

Rong met his eye.

Ah, Rong, that moon that loomed so hugely in the Phatian sky, its four little apostle brothers encircling it faster than what the centurion had earlier perceived. Interesting, this moon. Such a cold eye it was, yet also so warm and alive, peering through the asteroids and clouds, the storms and dust. The centurion gazed at it for a moment, then noticed some bluish glints beyond it.

These weren't stars, he knew.

-OBJECTS APPROACHING FROM BEYOND THIS SOLAR SYSTEM-

Somewhat intriguing, these glints, but of little import…for now.

The centurion turned to regard the Disintegrated Sea.

Quite an impressive sight, he had to acknowledge. For any being, be it immortal or no, it was some feat to annihilate something as substantial as an ocean. He glimpsed yet more dead millions, or at least what remained of them, lining the seafloor like a fleshy bed of seaweed. He noticed some live ones, too; demons hungrily chomping on the heads of their fallen brethren, or sucking what blood they could from what bodies still held some sustenance. Some clambered into the distance, or climbed the cliffs. Some flew away. And some tried to pry open the vanished dimensional rifts.

Then something rather odd happened.

One of the centurion's recent digital transmissions flew across his partially damaged eyes.

-RESCUE OPERATION PENDING…IMPERATIVE TO PROCEED…-

Was that so? He processed what little information this transmission provided, calculated the percentage chance that his involvement would sway the fates one way or the other, and determined his proposed next course of action to be true.

He eyed the demons futilely scraping at the weary sky, and stepped to the edge of the cliff.

From perhaps, oh, some mile away from Ulith Urn, the demonlord, Champion Warrior Vorkoron, slivered his red glowing eyes at the centurion. Slick, sleek, and black as pitch was his skin, like the blood that flowed over the cliffs. He was crouched low, idly picking the bones from one of his favored kin to chew on, his burning glare steady as stone while Soular Centurion 7 fixed his own eyes upon the scene.

He watched the galactic invader leap over the cliffs; a glow of gold, a flash of silver, swallowed by some passing sentient storm that had neither the power nor the desire to tangle its windy entrails around that immortal being.

Champion Warrior Vorkoron stood, a grating growl issuing from deep behind his overlong fangs. He stretched up straight, his head rising to fifty-seven feet, his horns piercing the sky ten feet higher than that. He snapped his claws and bellowed a cry.

It was heard.

Minute by minute, one by one, demons came, slithering out of the dark. Some were as large as unholy temples, some were smaller than a speck of dirt.

All kneeled before Vorkoron.

And then, as the sun rose like a crying eye of light, Vorkoron led his gathered horde to the edge of the cliffs and mounted a giant winged beast, with combat, death, and the centurion in the forefront of his devilish mind...

THE END
OF
THE FIRST BOOK OF PHATE

"THE COSMIC FAIRYTALE"

COMES NEXT,

"THE DARK FOREVER…"

GLOSSARY

Arcynn Ahnna Jha – A rare breed of unicorn, a starlit unicorn. A large, winged beast with six legs and a hide of white spotted over with glimmering specks. One of the most magnificent of Phate's unicorns, starlit unicorns were often employed by various races to quickly deliver items or messages over long distances in times of great need. They are quiet, dignified steeds that remind those who see them of brighter times.

Areshria – The largest sky elf palace on Phate, its tallest tower stands ten miles above the high clouds. It is the pinnacle of sky elf ingenuity. Once the capital city to the sky elves, populated by millions, it is now all but empty, occupied only by Herard Avari Fang and his adopted son, Drinwor Fang. It is rumored that the legendary Sunsword Surassis is hidden there. At its peak, it was a flourishing metropolis full of artisans, musicians, and practitioners of the most wondrous magic. Now, with the exception of its two inhabitants, it is said to be occupied by nothing ghosts.

Black Claw – The only remaining, and therefore most powerful, clan of dark elf fighters in Kroon.

Castle Krypt – Warloove's spectral castle located in the bottom of a dead volcano that resides somewhere in the middle of the Mountains of Might. Surrounded by Corpsewood forest, the castle is guarded by undead dark elf sorcerers, and laden with myriad traps and diabolical spells.

Cave Port of Kroon – The bottommost level of the dark elf realm of Kroon, where great caverns lay, and a lagoon that leads to the Raging Sea resides.

Cauldron of Carcass Control – A huge, ancient pot of necromancy filled with disgusting liquid and body parts. Syndreck the Brooding uses to rile up various diabolical spells.

Cliffs of Moaning Wishes – Sheer, mile high cliffs of obsidian that rim the eastern coast of the Continent Isle of Volcar. The upper reaches of the deep elf realm of Kroon exist behind them, and Ulith Urn stands atop them.

Cloak of Winds – Vu Verian's magical shroud that renders him virtually invisible. He is able to stretch it out far around himself, and cloak those near to him.

Continent Isle of Volcar – A huge landmass that the Devil King and his legions ravaged during the first war with the Dark Forever. Ulith Urn stands on its eastern edge where the most furious fighting took place.

Cold Blooded Caves – The vast series of dark elf caverns that exist behind the Cliffs of Moaning Wishes, beneath the Wicked Plains and Mountains of Might. Kroon is the outermost region of the caves.

Corpsewood – The dead trees that dwell in Warloove's domain at the bottom of a burned out volcano located deep in the Mountains of Might. Unfortunate beings caught in the forest are likely to see moving trees, ghosts, and undead dark elf sorcerers. The forest is swamped over with mist, and can drive one mad if they should reside in it for too long. The Castle Krypt lies somewhere in the middle of it, but only shows itself when Warloove wishes.

Cygorgia – A once proud and strong nation of cyclops warriors that fell from internal political dissension between opposing factions. Unable to resolve their differences peacefully, the cyclops battles left their conglomerate of cities in ruin. Surviving bands from different families scattered across Volcar and lived mostly in isolation before they disappeared. Some cyclops were reportedly seen fighting valiantly in the war against the Dark Forever.

Dark Elves – A predominantly evil race of grey or black skinned elves who dwell in subterranean realms. Some dark elves live on Phate's surface, deep in the largest forests. There is a saying on Phate – "The deeper one goes, the darker the elves." This holds true in both physical appearance and in demeanor. Surface dwelling dark elves tend to remain neutral, and avoid dealings with other races. Their subterranean kin are far less civil, and have at times mounted campaigns to assassinate beings in any territory of Phate. In latter years, after the war, the dark elf clans, once united, divided, and now they delight in killing their own for mere sport. They eagerly await the coming of the Dark Forever, in hopes to ally themselves with Nencokra Rool himself.

Dark Forever – The lowest plane of existence in the multiverse, the hellish domain of the Devil King, an entire universe of evil in itself.

Darkis – A once powerful alien overlord from a distant galaxy, Darkis was marooned on Phate after being captured by his enemies, the Draxia Meeh. He is master of Warloove, and dwells in the bowels of the Castle Krypt, working on repairing his severely damaged starship. He commands Warloove to retrieve the Sunsword Surassis, believing the sword's incredible energy can empower his starship's engines, so that he might escape Phate before the ascension of the Dark Forever.

Dead (Dying) Towers of Ulith Urn – Spectral towers raised by ancient necromancers in anticipation of the first war with the Dark Forever. From Ulith Urn, the necromancers helped tear open the dimensional walls between the primary universal plane and the Dark Forever. The area just beyond the towers, over the Raging Sea, is the weakest point in the multiverse.

Deep elves – Mysterious beings who live in the oceans and seas of Phate, they became the most powerful race of elves after the sky elves abandoned the world. Their cities are known to be vast, but their numbers are unknown. They have necromantic powers and the ability to influence weather and tides. They are thought to be in league with the Dark Forever. Cousins of the dark elves, they deal with them when necessary, but ally themselves with no one. They are very rarely seen, and rumored to be the only race Nenocrka Rool will spare should he ascend onto Phate.

Demonkind – A general term affixed to any type of demon who hails from the Dark Forever.

Demonskin Armor – Drinwor Fang's demonskin was given to him by Vu Verian. Crated by sky elves, the leather was taken from a powerful demon's hide. The demon's spirit was exercised from the skin, and blue magical sigils of protection were placed upon the breast. Having never been tested, its full power and strength are unknown, but it is said to be able to protect the wearer from myriad attacks.

Devil King – (*See Nenockra Rool)

Devil's Wind – When enough demons are gathered densely together (at least hundreds of thousands), a great red cloud is formed, looking something like a storm of blood that screams and howls. The Devil's Wind is a horrific thing, and few who have seen one have survived to speak of it.

Disintegrated Sea – What the Raging Sea was referred to after the Devil King destroyed it.

Dragon Song of Solacing – A magical song some dragons can sing to bring temporary peace to those in pain.

Drakana, Lord of the Spirit Dragons – Drakana was the One Life in the first war with the Dark Forever. Sacrificing his life by unleashing the full power of the Sunsword Surassis, Drakana's spirit fled into the Hall of Voices, where he became the most revered of the spirit dragons. His sacrifice succeeded in defeating and banishing the Dark Forever, but it did not destroy the Devil King. Drakana offered his spirit to the Fallen Angel to become the One Soul, and again infuse the sunsword with power.

Draxiah Meeh – Vicious, powerful aliens who conquered Darkis's galaxy, captured him, and condemned him to die on Phate. Darkis and Warloove believe they are watching them from the sky.

Dreadships – Eerie looking submersible vessels of the deep elves that are impervious to the violence of the sea.

Drekklor – A particularly powerful shadow demon created by Nenockra Rool to go forth and retrieve the body of Syndreck the Brooding from the depths of a black hole. Imbued with myriad abilities, Drekklor aids in the reconstruction of Ulith Urn, and is then tasked to trail the heroes on a secret mission as they make to resurrect the Sunsword Surassis.

Drinwor Fang – A young dusk elf with smoky colored skin and silvery hair, Drinwor appeared one day in Herard's sky elf palace of Areshria. Herard cannot now remember the day he first beheld Drinwor, but he is imbued with a strong parental instinct toward him. Drinwor is a lonely young elf, innocent and somewhat naïve for his age, but possessing great dexterous skills, speed, and a penchant for swordplay. Of late, he has trouble sleeping, and believes more and more that his destiny will take him away from Areshria, which he has never left before. He is the only known dusk elf in the universe.

Ever Dying – A terrible sorcerous affliction where the victim is plagued by myriad fatal diseases, but cannot die from his maladies. The afflicted suffers the symptoms and pains of the diseases until he dies of old age or injury.

Fallen Angel – The only angel to stay behind when all the others fled the galaxy in fear of the coming war with the Dark Forever. The Fallen Angel is friend to Herard Avari Fang, and swears to do what she can to help Drinwor. She is powerful, but her magic is fading as the sun dies.

Fleeting Shadow – A rare insect dragon from Vren Adiri with swift, buzzing wings. Fleeting Shadow becomes Morigos's mount and flies him on the quest to imbue the Sunsword Surassis with a soul

Fogwall – a magical wall of vapor that holds the waters of the Raging Sea from swamping the Cave Port of Kroon.

Forest of Chanting Angels – An ancient forest whose boughs are replete with azure crystal leaves. Located on the eastern side of Volcar, the forest had for long ages been cultivated by the shadowlight elves. When the crystal blue leaves clang together in the wind, a melody is formed. The melody is different every time, every day. It is said that the trees can detect the mood of those about them, and it is reflected in the sound.

Gauntlets of Loathing Light – Black, long cuffed gloves with glowing red runes crafted by the deep elves from interdimensional matter. They were created after the war with the Dark Forever. The Devil King commanded the abyssal elves to make gloves that would allow evil beings to wield the Sunsword Surassis (which is deadly to any demons touch), so that a being of darkness could steal it, thus rendering its influence inconsequential when he next attempts to ascend into the primary universal plane.

Geeter – Warloove's mount, a colossal Greater Demonic Dragon. Born from the Dark Forever, it is a ferocious beast in combat; a huge black dragon with six legs and a scorpion's tail, who breathes acidic black fire. Geeter remained on Phate when most of the Demonkind were banished back into the Dark Forever after Drakana used the Sunsword Surassis. Geeter answers only to Warloove, the only being he encountered who could match his powers.

Glyph of Multiversal Guarding – A sorcerous ward placed over the towers of Ulith Urn by the Fallen Angel to warn her of any intruders into the spectral ruins. The ward will detect beings in any dimension.

Great White Owl – One of Vu Verian's incarnations, a white owl the size of a small dragon, occasionally spotted in Phate's high skies in the hours just before dusk.

Greater Angelic Dragon – A brilliant golden dragon that some angels are able to transform into. They are cosmic dragons, able to fly between the stars.

Hall of Voices – A heavenly, inter-dimensional place where Drinwor Fang journeys to find the One Soul. Guarded by spiteful Murdraniuss, the Lord Banshee, and inhabited by ZeerZeeOzz, the spectral seer who awaits the coming of the One Life. The Hall of Voices is filled with spirit dragons, secrets, and alleged to keep the One Soul.

Hammer of Battered Souls – The weapon and scepter of the Devil King, the hammer is comprised of billions of tightly compacted souls, taken from the Sea of Enslaved Souls in the Dark Forever. The weapon is many miles tall, and a single strike from it has been known to destroy cities, and even entire moons.

Herard Avari Fang - Thought by Phate's denizens to now be the only human in the world, a young Herard huddled in subterranean dwellings with the last tribe of his people who had survived the war with the Devil King...only to be eventually discovered and wiped out by dark elf assassins. As the lone survivor of the raid, Herard, escaped. He soon befriended the outcast cloud dragon Zraz and took to the sky, where he made his home in the sky elf capital kingdom of Areshria. As honorable a being as there ever was, he commanded both respect and virtual solitude from the dragon and elven nations. Though he has no recollection of how or exactly when, he came to be the father of Drinwor Fang, the dusk elf boy thought to be the Son and Savior of the Stars. Certain that divine intervention was involved, and feeling an intense love for his son, Herard dedicated the last decades of his life to protecting Drinwor, and securing peace in the war-torn regions of Volcar.

Invisible elves – A timid race of elves who chose avoidance over confrontation when the world went through times of strife. In the ages leading up to the war with the Dark Forever, they completely covered themselves over with cloaking magic. Known to have mostly dwelled in the great birch forest of Scimiton, they are thought to have totally disappeared right before the war. Not a single one has been detected in over a thousand years.

Iron Fortress of Forn Forlidor – A pyramidal battle fortress comprised of floating sections, Forn Forlidor hovers over the giant crater of a meteor strike that was meant to destroy it. Ruled for centuries by Lord Dark Sorciuss, the fortress was the sight of many battles, for Sorciuss constantly besieged all the lands around him. Made of magically fortified obsidian, and guarded by a legion of undead wizards, the fortress's walls have never been penetrated.

Ironskull dwarves – A race of dwarves thought destroyed during the war with the Dark Forever. A very tough breed whose skin is a deep, fiery red. They are formidable fighters and forgers of all manner of metal and crystal. Their strongholds were buried deep within Phate's largest mountain ranges, and have since remained unexplored.

Kingdom of Krykoss – The sprawling capital city of the deep elves existing on the bottom of the Raging Sea. The vastness of the population is unknown, but it is said the inhabitants of Krykoss possess great power. The Emperor of the deep elves, Volture, resides in the central palace.

Kroon – The subterranean realm of the dark elves on the eastern side of the Continent Isle of Volcar

Lion Lands of Irixx Een – A city of pillars ruled by an undead lion king. Though a small realm, it is one of the few nations still in existence. It is avoided at all costs, for the undead king is said to be especially vicious out of desperation for his starving people, as all prosperity ceased with the slow decay of the surrounding lands.

Lord Banshee - (*See Murdraniuss)

Lord Dark Sorciuss – In ages past, Sorciuss had been a ruthless tyrant, conquering all the lands around him; but after long years of warring and slaying, he found himself alone, purposeless, and empty of even hate. Surrounded only by an army of undead wizards he created, he has taken to extreme solitude. He has spent the last century locked up in the fortress of Forn Forlidor, pondering the emptiness of his evil life. Now his thoughts linger on what might have been had he embraced light.

Lord of the Spirit Dragons – (*See Drakana)

"May the Gods return" – a popular phrase adopted by Phate's inhabitants after the war with the Dark Forever, when it was believed that Phate was abandoned by the Gods.

Moom – The ruling faction of sorcerers in the dark elf realm of Kroon

Morigos – Morigos is a petulant dark elf, a once a proud, powerful mage who was held in high standing. With the continued decadence of his people, his standing fell, and he bemoans the present for memories of days long past. He begrudgingly carries out the will of Warloove, and is known by few to be his right hand. In recent years, Morigos's disdain for Warloove and his people became more obvious, and through circumstances of fate he seemingly embraced the cause of light. His true intentions are unknown.

Morning's Hope – A beautiful, powerful, and wise Greater Translucent Dragon who guides Drinwor Fang on the quest to recover and restore to power the Sunsword Surassis. She knows Herard Avari Fang and many of the remaining denizens of Phate, but her origins are as mysterious as Drinwor's. Though she fought in the first war with the Dark Forever and recalls many details of past events, there are none alive who remember her from that time period. The Fallen Angel believes her to be from a different world, sent solely for the purpose to guard the One Life the next time the Devil King attempts to ascend into the primary universal plane.

Mountain of Bones – The mountain of bones lies in the nameless sea, off the western edge of Volcar. It was formed when the Lord Banshee screamed in torment during one of the pinnacle battles in the first war with the Dark Forever. It is a piled remains of countless dragons, demons, and deep elves. The toppled battle fortress of Shirian Shirion crowns it, and its feet lies the entrance to the Hall of Voices.

Mountains of Might – The largest mountains in the galaxy, the Mountains of Might stand many miles above the surface of Phate. Once crystalline, beautiful, and teeming with both sorcerous and natural life, the mountains were burned and blasted in the war with the Dark Forever. They are now lifeless, volcanic, and surrounded by great molten pools that spread across the surrounding lands.

Multidimensional Mansion of Veeryk Vine – A large, elusive mansion that phases in and out of the sky over northeastern Volcar. The mansion is stuck between many dimensions, and occasionally appears in the primary universal plane. Its existence was unknown until well after the beginning of the construction of Phate. Its home dimension has never been located.

Murdraniuss (The Lord Banshee) – Murdraniuss was the most powerful deep elf in Phate's history. Not only was he as skilled in abyssal magic as any of his kin, but he also had a strong aptitude for the necromantic and sorcerous arts of surface sorcerers. He used his abilities to prolong his life, and over time his natural incarnation morphed him into something demonic. It was said he was then able to reach through the dimensions and make contact with Dark Forever. Soon thereafter, Murdraniuss had the current deep elf Emperor assassinated, seized control over all the abyssal armies, and led them to the surface to fight for Nenockra Rool when the Devil King ascended onto Phate. During the battle, his beloved concubine, Zyllandria, was slain and fell into his arms. Mudraniuss was so distraught, he uttered a sorcerously enhanced wail of grief that echoed so horribly, and for so long, it slew all those about him, burying him in a mountain of bones. He screamed and wailed until he destroyed even his own skin, thus ending his mortal life. But his spirit endured to ever after haunt the mountain of bones. Now in death he's become the Lord of Banshees, and scornfully guards the entrance to the Hall of Voices, denying anyone passage into the blessed realm beyond....

Mystic Trident Tower – The deep elf sorcerers' largest structure in the Kingdom of Krykoss.

Nameless Sea – The sea where the Hall of Bones resides. Many of Phate's landmarks, regions, and bodies of water lost their names when most of Phate's history and population was wiped out in the war with the Dark Forever. The nameless sea is a vast ocean whose name was lost in history.

Nenockra Rool – Purportedly as old the universe, Nenockra Rool is the grand master of Dark Forever, the seventy five mile tall king of all evil. While a sentient being, his conscience is said to be devoid of any emotion, and he single-mindedly rules with an innate desire only to squelch whatever forces or beings of light he encounters. It is said the first Gods of the universe created him and the Dark Forever to keep order in all things by way of fear. Over long eons, boredom and desire began to fester in his mind, and now he instinctively seeks to escape the confines of the Dark Forever, to topple the balance of light, and to entertain his longing of destroying righteous beings. As one philosopher put it – He is as a malevolent dragon who has too long slumbered in his cavern….

One Life, One Soul, One Sword – This legendary mantra simply describes the three components that comprise the fully activated Sunsword Surassis. The One life is the wielder; the One Soul is a purely good soul that exists within Sillithian Synstrike, the tiny solar dragon in the sunsword's pommel; and the One Sword is the sword itself. If the One Life and the One Soul conjoin their essences to utilize the sword's full power, its effects can be devastating for evil opponents. The mantra is often spoken with respect and reverence.

Phantom Falls – Gigantic falls of liquid sorcery that flow over the nation of Syrox that's embedded in the cliffs on the eastern edge of Volcar.

Phate – A once wondrous planet immortals from a distant galaxy long ago created with sorcery. It is a huge world that housed the universe's most powerful magic and greatest dragons. Its long and rich history were all but lost in the war with the war with the Dark Forever, and many of its races destroyed. Now much of the planet is empty and haunted, its fields and mountains burned and black, its skies filled with empty kingdoms. The galaxy in which it exists floats alone through the cosmos, as all other galaxies race away from it in fear of the Devil King's inevitable ascension into the primary universal plane. Phate exists in the weakest point of the multiverse, a place where the walls between the dimensions are most easily torn: a product of its glorious construction.

Pyrlovos – A massive prison compound on the eastern edge of Volcar. Constructed by sky elf wizards, Pyrlovos was a prison for demons and criminals captured in and around the time of the war with the Dark Forever. After the sky elves left it unattended, its airborne islands broke apart, went volcanic, and its prisoners mostly escaped. Now it is a wild dangerous place that is avoided.

Raging Sea – A violent sea on the western side of the Continent Isle of Volcar. The Raging Sea is controlled by the deep elves, and its waters are purposefully kept rough to ward off enemies or intruders. Its waves are known to reach a thousand feet high. Sorcerous storms endlessly hover over the sea, and ghostly dragons and other unknown entities exist both in and above its waters.

Ring of Floating – A magical ring that slows the descent of the wearer when freefalling through the sky.

Rong and the Four Apostles – Commonly referred to as the Five Moons of Phate, Rong is the largest of the moons. It is orbited by the second largest (the first Apostle); and the second largest is orbited by the third largest, and so on. Each moon is a gaseous giant, believed to be uninhabited. Many legends of the moons have been passed down over the ages. Some such legends claim that each moon is actually the spiritual embodiment of an immortal creator of Phate, and ever do they watch over their child world. Some say the moons were what was left over of the tangible sorcery that formed Phate, great flowing clouds that in time gathered to form the moons. The sky elves were believed to have attempted a number of expeditions to the moons over the years, but no reports of their findings have ever been imparted.

Scimiton – A gorgeous city of mile high, white birch trees, home of the invisible elves. As the once beautiful and relatively peaceful world of Phate became more chaotic in the times leading up to the war with the Dark Forever, the elves concealed their trees as they did themselves: they went invisible. The forest still exists, but its inhabitants are thought long gone.

Seven Glories – Heaven for those good beings who have died and passed on. But when the threat of darkness returned to Phate, all the angels and Gods of the galaxy fled in fear of impending doom, and the heavens were abandoned. The gates to the Seven Glories have been closed for centuries, and those who die either flounder between the dimensions, find refuge in the Hall of Voices, or fade into nothingness. Of all of Phate's truly heavenly beings, only the Fallen Angel remains on Phate.

Shadow Demons – Virtually undetectable demons able to travel at great speeds through any environment. They are a constant bane for the forces of light as the most powerful of them can surpass the boundaries of the Dark Forever.

Shards of Zyrinthia – The shattered remains of Phate's sister world that accompany it in orbit around the sun as an asteroid belt. Every few hundred years Phate's orbital path crosses into the cosmic ruin and endures Zyrhinthia's severe meteor shower. Legend says that the next meteor shower will coincide with the Devil King's latest attempt to ascend into the primary universal plane.

Shirian Shirion – A sky elven battle fortress of warrior wizards that was attacked by the succubus Zyllandria during the war with the Dark Forever. Its inhabitants were all slain when the Lord Banshee cried out, and the fortress toppled over, fell down throught the sky, and crashed into the mountain of bones.

Sillithian Synnstrike – The tiny solar dragon who dwells in the hilt of the Sunsword Surassis. This dragon lies lifeless until infused with the One Soul. When resurrected, the sword's fiery blade is able to spew from the hilt, and Sillithian Synstrike flies about within the crystal.

Sky elf graveyard – When sky elves die, they turn into flat grey rain clouds that hover as misty tombs in the high sky. A sky elf graveyard consists of anywhere from dozens to hundreds of perfectly even-spaced clouds.

Sky elves – Once the rulers of Phate, millions of sky elves lived in great cities and palaces they had sorcerously suspended in the world's massive cloudbanks. They were the most cultured race on Phate; their numbers included the best artisans and sorcerers, and they were the direct descendants of the immortals who crafted the world. Their devotion and dependence to the sun over time led them to only be able to appear during the daylight hours. At night they either lock themselves in their palaces or transform into clouds. They suffered much and sacrificed many of their race during the first war with the Dark Forever. Fearing the death of the sun, reprisal from the Devil King, and the abandonment of the Gods, the fled Phate for the stars. Their whereabouts are unknown. How many are still alive is unknown. The sky elves were lambasted by the rest of the world for leaving, and for damaging the sun with the creation of the Sunsword Surassis. Vu Verian is the only sky elf to remain on Phate.

Son and Savior of the Stars – The title given to the one who is believed destined to defeat Nenockra Rool with the Sunsword Surassis.

Son of Herard – Most notably, the name Warloove uses to taunt Drinwor Fang.

Soular Centurion 7 – The last known surviving galactic guardian, the centurion possesses immortal power. He is composed of fleshy, metallic, and apparitional appendages that are preserved by allegedly godly means. Millions, perhaps billions of years old, the centurion has guarded the universe as long as galactic history has been recorded. Unconcerned with planetary sized conflicts, the guardian's primary concern is of the continuance of the universe as a whole, and to guard against Total Universal Annihilation. Though sentient by means of a living brain enhanced by cybernetic implants, no being has ever heard the centurion utter a word, and it is not known whether he possesses a soul.

Specter demons – Demonic spies of the Dark Forever. Similar to shadow demons but not quite as strong. They are capable of wilting and rotting living things, and their vision sees far and wide. Usually used as spies.

Spirit elves – Unable to ascend into the Seven Glories, these elves remain on Phate even after their mortal shells decay. With many of the elf races born of Phate, something of their spirits are intrinsically tied to it, so much so that their corporeal selves can move about and perform actions as they did when they were alive. They tend to gravitate to sky elf palaces, and to what dragon clans will accept them.

Sun – Phate's sun was irrevocably damaged when sky elven sorcerers took too much of its power to craft the Sunsword Surassis. Its rays turned red and its fires burned wilder. The sun is not expected to last long; it is strongly believed by many that it is soon go supernova.

Sunbeam Swallow – A rare breed of bird adorned with colorful, crystalline feathers. Once a teeming species who migrated together in large flocks, these beautiful birds, now nearly extinct, live solitary lives. They are almost never seen, and take flight upon the first hint of approaching life. To see one is considered good luck.

Sun's Remembrance – A gigantic jewel fixed in the ceiling at the top of Vren Adiri's main chamber. The jewel catches the light of the dying sun outside, turns it bright and healthy, and casts it down into the chamber. With the walls painted blue and dragons and clouds floating about, the chamber beneath the Sun's Remembrance mimics the skies of old, before the sun was red and dying.

Sunsword Surassis / The One Sword – The legendary sword crafted by sky elven sorcerers to destroy the Devil King, Nenockra Rool, before he could ascend into the universe. Crafted with gold and laden with jewels, its dragonclaw pommel holds a crystal that houses Sillithian Synnstrike, the miniature solar dragon whose life embodies the life of the sword. Harnessing the power of the sun, its huge blade is made from pure sunfire. The sword needs the One Soul to empower it, and the One Life to wield it. When empowered, it has ability to unleash a supernova-like explosion of light that destroys all evil beings for thousands of miles around. This unleashing of power costs the wielder his life, and the soul diminishes into nothingness.

Sword of Molecular Destruction – Primary weapon of Soular Centurion 7, this sword's blade is made from matter taken from a black hole. It has many extraordinary powers. Its blade contains a plane of space, filled with many little stars, and is surrounded by a purplish supernova-like swirl of light. Its crafter is unknown, its age unknown; though it is believed to have been with the centurion since his creation.

Syndreck the Brooding – A necromancer who has a penchant for tearing dimensional walls apart, Syndreck was the head sorcerer of Ulith Urn in the first war with the Dark Forever. When the Dark Forever was defeated, agents of the Devil King hid Syndreck in the bowels of a black hole. Syndreck's soul is vital to the Devil King's next attempt at ascension, for he is the only being known capable of reopening the dimensional tears and again setting the Dark Forever free.

Syrox – A nation of weakling wizards who attempted to mine magic right from the ground. They found a sort of vaporous, gelatinous liquid, and attempted to use it to further their arcane strength. They failed, and disappeared during the war with the Dark Forever.

Syroxian Sea – A perfectly smooth reservoir of magical liquid ore at the bottom of the Phantom Falls.

Tatoc – Dark elf nephew of Morigos. Part of the Black Claw, the ruling clan of dark elf fighters in Kroon. Tatoc is a vicious young warrior who often kills his own kin for sport. He delights in disagreeing with his uncle, Morigos, and to this end he infuriates him endlessly.

Titan crabs – Fortress sized crabs that guard the outskirts of the deep elf Kingdom of Krykoss.

Total Universal Annihilation – Any event that is catastrophic enough to bring about the destruction of all the galaxies in the primary universe. Nenockra Rool's ascension onto Phate is potentially one of those events.

Tyranticuss – Darkis's home world. A large planet located near the center of the galaxy, Tyranticuss is completely covered over with artificial oceans and multiple levels of highly technologized cities, and surrounded by numerous constructed rings and starships. It was considered the capital planet of the universe before being taken over by the Draxiah Meeh. It is rumored that the Draxiah Meeh have bartered with Devil King, and Tyranticuss will be the last planet enslaved when the Devil King ascends into the primary universe.

Vorkoron – A champion demon warlord of the Dark Forever; a fearsome fighter and devastatingly strong opponent.

Vorz Abyzz – A region in the northwest waters of the Raging Sea where a great oceanic war took place. The sorcery that was employed during the war was so wild, its effects created sentient storms, fiery waves, and even raised undead sailors from the sea. Giant beasts swim beneath the surface and the realm is mostly avoided, traversed only if there is great need.

Vren Adiri – The second largest sky elf palace on Phate, where the Fallen Angel resides with hosts of dragons and spirit elves. Vren Adiri floats through the sky, and is often disguised behind a massive bank of storm clouds. It is smaller than its sister palace Areshria, but no less magnificent.

Vu Verian – Last of the sky elves, and longtime caretaker of Areshria. Depressed, lonely, and saddened by the disappearance of his people, Vu Verian ceded control of Areshria to young Herard Avari Fang, who had successfully bartered for peace between the world's remaining surface dwelling elves and the dragons. Vu Verian also gave Herard his emperorship. He spends most of his time floating in the sky in cloudform, even during the day, but will occasionally visit Herard and Drinwor, his only friends, back in Areshria. Vu Verian promised Herard he would watch over Drinwor should it be necessary. Vu Verian's isolation is also spurred from being blamed for all the failings of his kin. In recent years he has been known to appear as the Great White Owl, drifting by himself through the upper skies.

War with the Dark Forever – The first war took place a thousand years ago, when Ulith Urn was mighty and Syndreck was young. The armies of the Dark Forever, a billion demons strong, nearly overwhelmed Phate before the sky elves delivered the Sunsword Surassis to the solar dragon, Drakana, the One Life. Many battles took place all over the world, and Phate was all but destroyed. Most of its historians and scribes were slain, and many of its races were lost or destroyed before Drakana ignited the fires of the sunsword. Millions of demons were killed, but the Devil King and many of his horde managed to elude destruction and escaped back into the Dark Forever.

Warloove – The white-faced, smoke shrouded vampiric dark elf servant of the alien Darkis, Warloove is obsessed with escaping Phate with his master before the Devil King ascends or the dying sun goes supernova. As the ascension of the Dark Forever looms, he relentlessly seeks out Drinwor Fang and the Sunsword Surassis. He is the Ruler of the Dark Elves, but seldom has dealings with them beyond using them as henchmen when he sees fit. He spends his daytime slumbering deep in the dungeons of the Castle Krypt, his home in the Forest of Corspewood at the bottom of a dead volcano.

White universe – Drinwor's dreams of late have been inhabited by visions of a white universe filled with colorful stars. He believes it has something to do with his destiny. He is at once strangely terrified of this, and also desires to see it with his waking eyes.

Wicked Plains – Huge fields that reach back from the edges of the Cliffs of Moaning Wishes behind Ulith Urn. Once lush with grasses and life, the fields became a battlefield in the war. Now they are barren, rocky, and filled with a million corpses. Rivers of lava course through them, and they are a reminder to many of the terrible losses sustained against the demonkind of the Dark Forever.

Winds of Hurricane Force – One of the most diabolical spells every contrived, Warloove is the only known being able to employ it. The spell creates a storm of ferociously powerful winds that are laden with millions of fangs, skewering enemies into pieces in mere seconds. The spell's utilization was banned by every conclave of sorcerers and wizards on Phate before the war.

Zraz – A swift and fast cloud dragon, loyal and faithful mount of Herard Avari Fang. When called upon, she has the ability to slip beneath the dimensions and turn into a cloud. Treated as a cast out for being smaller and weaker than most of her kin, Zraz left her clan and bonded with Herard Avari Fang right after he negotiated peace between the elves and dragons. Standing by his side for decades, she has sworn to die for him.

ZeerZeeOzz – A ghostly seer who oversees the Hall of Voices where the One Soul is said to reside. ZeerZeeOzz has been harboring dragon spirits who have been secretly waiting to combat the Dark Forever should the demonkind return to Phate.

Zyllandria – Purposefully named similarly to her homeworld of Zyrinthia, she was said to be the most beautiful woman to have ever lived on that world. Her father was king of a sprawling, prosperous nation, and loved his daughter dearly. But in her youth Zyllandria grew restless, and snuck with an immortal off world onto nearby Phate as its creation was nearing completion. Years later, by happenstance, she encountered Murdraniuss on one of his few forays onto the surface world, where he was immediately stricken with passion for her. At first hesitant to respond to his advances, she eventually gave in to his temptations as he promised her immortality, Using his vast abilities, he made Zyllandria more like him, and she quickly darkened, both of heart and body. She became demonic, a succubus, and stood loyal by Murdraniuss's side for many, many ages. She fought with him in the war with the Dark Forever, where their destinies would forever be tied.

Zyrinthia – Phate's more ordinary sister world, where the immortals who constructed Phate resided whilst creating it. It is believed that the Draxiah Meeh, fearing the construction of Phate would sway power from their galaxy, attacked Zyrinthia's solar system, for a tremendous energy blast destroyed Zyrinthia from afar. It is believed that Phate was its intended target, but no one was ever certain, nor could the Draxiah Meeh ever be positively identified as the ones who fired the shot.

ABOUT THE AUTHOR

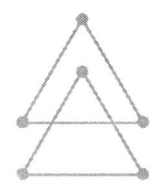

Jason Alan was born and raised on Long Island, New York, where his childhood was immersed in developing his vast imagination. He grew up reading as many books as he could get his hands on, enjoying 1980's science fiction movies, and commandeering his parents' butcher block kitchen table for countless nights of Dungeons & Dragons role-playing. All of this played a huge part in influencing his creative writing skills.

Jason currently resides in Cape Coral, Florida, where he works as a graphic designer for a local publication. He is a co-founder and writer for the StarWarsReporter.com fan website, and writes an ongoing fantasy fiction article for OlorisPublishing.com. Jason's passion for writing is nearly equaled by his passion for music. He plays and records lead guitar with a variety of local bands, including the progressive instrumental project *Mourning's Hope*.

Every so often, his friends try to remind him that there's more to life than his work and creative pursuits, and his family prays that someday, maybe, he'll find a wife. Nevertheless, he continues to make music and focus on completing the Five Books of *Phate*.

www.JasonAlan.net
Follow Jason on Facebook & Twitter **@JasonAlanPhate**